Swimming
to
Lundy

ALSO BY AMANDA PROWSE
Novels

Poppy Day

What Have I Done?

Clover's Child

A Little Love

Will You Remember Me?

Christmas for One

A Mother's Story

Perfect Daughter

The Second Chance Café

Three and a Half Heartbeats

Another Love

My Husband's Wife

I Won't be Home for Christmas

The Food of Love

The Idea of You

The Art of Hiding

Anna

Theo

How to Fall in Love Again (Kitty's Story)

The Coordinates of Loss

The Girl in the Corner

The Things I Know

The Light in the Hallway

The Day She Came Back

An Ordinary Life

Waiting to Begin

To Love and Be Loved

Picking up the Pieces
All Good Things
Very Very Lucky

Novellas

The Game
Something Quite Beautiful (collection)
A Christmas Wish
Ten Pound Ticket
Imogen's Baby
Miss Potterton's Birthday Tea
Mr Portobello's Morning Paper
I Wish . . .
A Whole Heap of Wishes

Children's books

The Smile That Went a Mile (with Paul Ward Smith)
Today I'm In Charge! (with Paul Ward Smith)

Memoirs

The Boy Between: A Mother and Son's Journey From a World Gone Grey
(with Josiah Hartley)
Women Like Us

Swimming

to

Lundy

Amanda Prowse

LAKE UNION

PUBLISHING

Text copyright © 2024 by Lionhead Media Ltd.
All rights reserved.

Published by Lake Union Publishing, Seattle

www.apub.com

Amazon, the Amazon logo, and Lake Union Publishing are trademarks of Amazon.com, Inc., or its affiliates.

ISBN-13: 9781542023023
eISBN: 9781542023030

Cover design by Emma Rogers
Cover image: © barkas, Butter Bites / Shutterstock; © artvea / Getty Images; © fStop Images GmbH/ Alamy Stock Photo

Printed in the United States of America

*This book is dedicated to the memory of Suzanne Smith
who was taken from her loving family too soon.
She lived her life to the full and leaves behind a
daughter, Danielle.
She loved and was so loved in return. As her mummy says:
'I spent forty-nine years loving you, and will spend
the rest of my life missing you . . . always.'*

CHAPTER ONE

TAWRIE GUNN

MARCH 2023

Tawrie Gunn wanted her situation to change and understood that it was she who needed to change it. With an itch to her spirit and a restlessness to her bones, it was time she faced up to the inaction that had led to this feeling of stagnation. It was born, no doubt, of living in the same town, in the same house and doing the same job since school.

It wasn't so much that she was bored, rather she was curious about the world that everyone else returned to when they left her seaside haven. This curiosity was a fairly recent thing for her; she'd always assumed that because visitors were so keen to return to this little slice of North Devon, even shedding tears when they left, she must surely already be in the best place.

Standing at the foot of her bed, Tawrie rolled her shoulders and took deep breaths. She had seen athletes performing similar rituals prior to a big event so it felt awkwardly appropriate. In that moment she was rather glad of her single status, which left her free to act a little oddly, chattering to herself and bending this way and that, safe in the knowledge that no one would barge in on her.

Today was the day. March the fourteenth to be precise. The day she had chosen to take the plunge.

'You're going to do *what*?' her nan, Freda, had exclaimed when Tawrie had told her about her plan, pausing mid custard cream and screwing up her eyes, as she did when she wanted to hear better – as if her eyesight and less-than-perfect hearing were in some way connected.

'Well, the simple answer is I'm going to swim! I'm going to swim and get better at swimming! That's it!' Tawrie flapped her arms and let them fall to her sides like a penguin.

'Every day for *how* long?' Freda needed this confirmed.

'Every day between March and September. Or at least, that's the idea.' She pulled a face and tried not to think of all the reasons she might fail.

'It'll be a bit dark some mornings. Might even be raining.' Her nan, as ever, sipped from the negative side of the cup.

'Yes, and it's not only the early start or the thought of rain that puts me off, or disrobing in public – not that there'll be many people around at that hour – but also I know the water is going to be cold! So cold!' She mock shivered inside her hoodie.

'I'm not saying it's a *bad* idea . . .' Her nan paused in the way she did when she was about to do exactly that. '. . . but let's face it, you're not that keen on jumping in when the sun's out, let alone at daybreak when even the spadgers are looking for a hat and scarf to ward off the chill! I mean, the summer will be all right, but March and September? No, thank you!'

'Well, no disrespect, Nan, but I already figured you wouldn't be joining me. And you're right it might be a little—'

'Seriously, Taw.' Her mother, sitting at the kitchen table, abandoned her eyeliner, put down her magnifying mirror, took a drag on her cigarette and joined the conversation. 'What do you know about "winter swimming", "wild swimming" or whatever else it is they want to call it? Makes me laugh.' It was her mother's turn to pause in the way *she* did before going on to trash an idea or topic that clearly didn't make her laugh at all. 'We've always just known it as taking a dip! Having a swim! I mean, seriously, when did it become a thing? Why do people have to hijack everything and try to make out they invented it? Why can't people just swim quietly, privately, without announcing to all and sundry that they're "wild swimmers" as if it's a superpower? I mean, anyone can shove on a cossie and get in the bloody sea, it's not that difficult. It's the same with vegans and dyslexics; just get on with it! Don't eat meat, don't spell things right, but for the love of God, stop going on about it!'

Tawrie was trying to think how best to respond to her noxious diatribe when her nan cut in.

'You're not wrong about vegans. Everyone's a vegan nowadays. Mrs Frinton was only telling me the other day when I saw her in Lidl that her daughter has just turned. The poor woman was all of a dither over what to put in her sandwiches. Although she's still eating bacon at weekends, so it's a bit easier.'

Tawrie opened her mouth to explain that anyone who ate pig at weekends was not vegan. Her mother, however, wasn't finished.

'And what does "wild swimmer" even mean? Are there tame swimmers too? What are they? Swimmers that don't bite you or ransack your picnic basket before shitting on the shoreline?' Annalee Gunn wheezed with laughter at her own joke. 'Once upon a time we'd think folks needed their noggin looking at if they stripped off in winter, but now? It's all the rage, apparently. I'm not trying to talk you out of it, but what in the name of Larry is it all about?' Her mother's response was no surprise: disparaging with a heavy peppering of sarcasm.

Tawrie stood her ground. 'I read about it a while ago and I've seen a few people taking a dip, even in the rain. Apparently there are loads of benefits to getting into colder water: it raises your endorphins, improves circulation and can help ward off the winter blues, plus it's a good way to burn calories. And I'd be happy with any of those right now.'

'You feeling a bit low, little love?' Her nan's voice echoed with genuine concern.

Her mother had gone back to her eyeliner, while blowing cigarette smoke from the corner of her mouth. This was typical behaviour: spouting her piece before disengaging completely. The verbal equivalent of throwing a rock into a quiet pond and then legging it to avoid looking at the ripples as all the little fish and frogs ran for their lives. Or swam – swam for their lives.

A bit low . . . How could she best explain it without giving her beloved nan any cause for concern? The truth was she wasn't low exactly, certainly not depressed, but neither was she happy, nor excited, nor hopeful. No, low wasn't accurate, she just wanted . . . more.

Tawrie found herself stuck in the middling lane of mediocrity, plodding, looking left and right without the first clue where or how to turn. Life at this stage was, for her, a little disappointing. Stuck in a familiar groove and aware that she'd left school, blinked, and suddenly she'd be turning twenty-eight next birthday.

She carried the nagging feeling that she was missing out. She had loved to study and never found her school work a chore. With good grades and a love of biology, she'd dreamed of becoming a midwife. But responsibilities and circumstances had conspired against her. Her cousin Connie had offered her a job in her café, only ever as a temporary measure, so she could be close to home. Now here she was, about to clock up a decade of service at the Café on the Corner. Life had sidetracked her, and the fact that it was easy, familiar, meant she had seen no real reason to change. Until recently, when the walls that had kept her confined, safe, suddenly seemed a little oppressive and she was finally plucking up the courage to peer over them.

She'd watched enough clips of people in dry robes or with towels around their shoulders extolling the virtues of wild swimming to want to give it a go. She was envious of their rosy complexions and the smiles on their faces as their eyes danced lovingly over the water. Could it be that jumping in the Atlantic, which was right on her doorstep, was the solution? And how crackers would it be if it turned out that the answer to feeling like she was caught in the nets had been right there all along? She was at least willing to give it a go.

'I just think it might be good for me.'

'I don't like the idea of you getting in the sea on your own, I really don't. Can't our Connie go down with you?'

Tawrie snorted her laughter at the very thought of her cousin agreeing to jump into the sea and ruin her make-up, or even give up sleep to watch Tawrie paddle. It wasn't going to happen. Plus, and she wasn't sure how to explain it without sounding a little mean, she liked the idea of making new friends, doing something that was only hers.

'I'm not going on my own, Nan. You can't go into the sea alone in all weathers, it's rule 101 of wild swimming: don't go alone.'

'Who's going with you then?' The old lady stared at her.

'I've . . . I've joined a club, actually.' She hated the embarrassment that surrounded her admission. The Gunns weren't 'club' people. They mocked clubs, teams and anything that required group participation. The unwritten rule was that it was better to run your own race, rely on yourself and crack on.

'What kind of club?' her nan barked, with an edge that made the whole affair sound slightly nefarious.

A chess club! What do you think? Tawrie's mouth twitched into a smile at the prospect of sharing this thought with Connie later in the café.

'They're called the Peacock Swimmers and they meet at Hele Bay Beach every morning and look out for each other, and then they just . . . swim!' She raised her arms and let them fall by her sides, aware of sounding vague and ill-informed. When it came to the actual activities of the Peacock Swimmers, she was both.

Messages had been exchanged via Facebook, where the photographs of the gang's activities were shoddy and not that helpful: arty-farty close-ups of foaming seas and an image of a lost flip-flop found on the beach wall, along with a list of dos and don'ts when it came to wild swimming. The list was surrounded by a purple floral frame that to her untrained eye looked to be Easter-themed and seemed a little incongruous to the safety message. Their exchanges had been sparse and to the point: time, place and suggested swimwear.

'The Peacock Swimmers, eh? Well I never did!' Her nan shook her head, whether in admiration or horror it was hard to tell.

And here Tawrie was. Day one.

Her bed looked soft and welcoming. She felt drawn to the space lurking beneath her carelessly flung duvet, the spot where her mattress carried the almost imperceptible sag, the springs that had supported her in gentle slumber for the last fourteen years or so now a little worn. The temptation to fall back on to it was strong. She walked to the window where the sea sat bleakly and in shadow in the distance. Another few shoulder rolls and deep breaths helped her focus and find the resolve to commit to her plan.

Hers was a room with an enviable vantage point: a perfect view of the quayside and the Hillsborough Nature Reserve, known locally as Elephant's Head, to the right. A curious name, inharmonious even, for this peninsula on the North Devon coast, until you stood at a precise point further up the hill and saw the sleeping elephant in all its glory as the dramatic rockscape wound its way around the coast. Her family home, Signal House, was perched on a terrace behind Fore Street, which ran all the way from Ilfracombe High Street to the harbour, and was home to three generations of Gunn women. Tawrie, who would be twenty-eight next birthday, her mother Annalee, who would also, at her own insistence, be twenty-eight next birthday, and her nan, Freda, who unlike her daughter-in-law, found her age to be a source of pride and was about to turn seventy-three.

It was a strange thing, a unique thing, and a much celebrated thing that the three Gunn women were all born on September the fourteenth. Freda delighted in the fact that she'd been sent a granddaughter on her birthday! Tawrie was the only child of Freda's eldest son, Daniel, who had been married to Annalee. This special day, for as long as Tawrie could remember, was one of celebration, culminating in a bonfire and a gathering at Rapparee Cove, an event that was known by all and sundry as 'the Gunn Fire'. No one was invited, no one turned away, yet each year they gathered: friends, family, the odd tourist, and neighbours, all looking for one last burst of summer, one last dance under the stars, one last night of carefree laughter before the sharp winter winds took the heat, laissez-faire days of plenty and the tourist pound, spiriting them out of reach for another season.

From a distance, their house on the hill smacked of opulence, boasting turreted attic rooms, floor-to-ceiling gothic framed windows and a wraparound porch. Close up, it was easy to see that its best years were probably a century or so behind it and what was left – a rather weathered building full of holes with wobbly windows and ill-fitting doors – clung to its former grandeur with as much vigour as it clung to the cliff into which it was hewn. But it was home. It had always been home and probably always would be. That was how things worked in this harbourside town.

In truth, Tawrie Gunn wasn't a woman who had desired travel or to gather mementos from the far corners of the globe; she had never longed to sample food made from unfamiliar ingredients and didn't feel the need to regale strangers with tales of her wanderings. She was a home bird, a proud Devonian, who might best be described as contained. Her tone was measured, her back straight, hair dark and wild, eye contact level, and her inner circle small. Minute, in fact. She served hearty breakfasts to fishermen and lifeboat crews in Connie's café down on the quay year round, and to tourists and day trippers throughout the season. Connie's dad, Tawrie's Uncle Stanley, known to all and sundry as 'Sten' on account of their surname, summed up life with his favourite phrase: 'It's the four Ps, Taw! That's what counts. It's all the Gunns need to be happy! Pasty, pint, paddle and a piddle – it's the secret to a contented life!'

And yet she wasn't content, not really. Hence the itch to her spirit and the restlessness in her bones. Maybe Sten was wrong, it might actually require five Ps to make her happy: pasty, pint, paddle, piddle and *peace* . . .

As she looked out of the wide window she again hoped she might find answers in the ocean. If nothing else it felt like a fine place to start, and that began with finding the confidence to get into the water. Stuffing a towel, wetsuit, swimming hat and goggles into her duffel bag, Tawrie rattled down the stairs.

'Where you off to at this hour, little one?' Her nan, always an early riser, was sitting in her armchair wrapped in her tartan wool dressing gown watching the news. She still addressed Tawrie as if she were a child, not that Tawrie minded, knowing it was a hard habit to break.

'I told you, Nan, I'm going swimming.'

8

'You really meant it?' Her nan twisted in the chair to stare at her, open-mouthed.

'Yep, of course I meant it! Every day, in all weathers, from March to September. Starting today.' She tried not to look at the bruised sky beyond the wide sash window.

'Oh my goodness, Tawrie. I'm not sure I like the sound of it now I know you actually mean it. There's other ways to lose weight! Who said you're fat?'

'No one!' She balked at the assumption and how quickly they'd got there.

'Good, cos you're not. You're really not. Just ignore them. And if anyone is picking on you, then you tell me!'

Her nan's words were formed in a mouth that recited only love, no matter how wide of the mark.

'First, Nan, I'm twenty-seven; if anyone picks on me then I can deal with it myself. And second, I don't think I'm fat; I mean, a bit wobbly in places, but . . .' She reached back and grabbed her bum cheek, feeling it squish generously in her palm, and was forced to admit, to herself at least, that anything that helped her feel happier with her body would only be a good thing.

'That's right, you're not fat, and don't let anyone tell you different. Big across the shoulders like your great-aunt Heidi and robust of leg, yes, but there's no shame in that, Tawrie Gunn. We're working stock and proud of it! Not for the Gunn women a pretty seat and needlepoint. We're log-shifters, hole-diggers, net-menders, barrel-hefters, fish-gutters.'

'Yes, thank you, Nan, I get the message. But I'm not doing this to lose weight. It's about challenging myself, changing my routine, committing to something.' She felt any previous confidence flutter out beneath the whistling gap at the bottom of the front door.

'That's the spirit, you keep telling yourself that! And where are you going to swim to, anyway?'

Tawrie exhaled and looked out over the sea, her eyes coming to rest on the spot where, in daylight, a shadowy land mass sat on the horizon. An island no more than one point four square kilometres and a place of fascination for Tawrie for the last twenty years. A mound upon which her gaze liked to fall as she walked. An island landscape that filled her dreams with imagery so strong, it roused her from sleep in the early hours. A marker in the expanse of ocean, a place of great significance, in her mind at least: the island where she dared to dream she might find her dad.

'Lundy. I'm going to swim all the way out to Lundy Island.'

'Lundy? Good Lord! How many miles is that?' Her nan sat back, her hand at her throat, gathering the braid-edged collar of her dressing gown to her chest.

'Twenty-three, twenty-four miles,' she guesstimated.

'Well, make sure you're back in time for your shift. Don't want our Connie on the phone, you know what she gets like.'

'Yep.'

Tawrie made her way out into the early morning, thankful for the Victorian cast-iron street lamps that helped light the way. Her nan's casual observation had made her laugh; the very thought of her swimming all that way, even if it were possible to navigate the rocks, wrecks and shipping lanes that lay between the mainland and the island was ludicrous. It was a feat only achieved by one or two people at most, ever, and they had started their swim further around the coast from Hartland Point. As she'd be swimming from Hele Bay Beach, not only would she be on the wrong side of the peninsula, but it was an almost impossible distance to swim, novice or not.

On her sturdy bike, she navigated the back roads, lanes and snickets of the town. There was something thrilling about being out and about at this hour, as the town was still waking; it changed the way the place felt. The streets were quiet yet familiar, curiously intimate and with a peach glow not dissimilar to the wintry evenings of her childhood. It reminded her of walking home from school in all weathers, running to keep up with Connie and her lipstick-wearing, boy-chasing friends who ignored her. It also evoked memories of her dad, and with this thought came the curious smell of nail polish.

'Time heals all wounds . . .' It was a familiar phrase, and countless were the times she'd heard it mouthed by good-hearted acquaintances. It had been hard to understand the meaning of it when her dad died when she was only seven. And when finally she reached an age when she did understand it, she also knew it to be utter crap. Time did *not* heal her longing to be back in his arms, to hear him laugh, to ask him all the questions that she didn't know she had to ask, to dance with him in the kitchen, to ask his advice, to have his presence on birthday and Christmas mornings, smiling, proud . . . Healing didn't come into it; it was more a case of muddling through and hoping things might get easier, that she might ache for him a little less.

Kitchen lights popped on as she cycled by, no doubt followed by the click of a kettle for that first cuppa and the rubbing of eyes as Ilfracombians got ready for the day ahead. Georgie, who delivered the milk, lifted his hand in a wave. It was nice to see him; usually the only sign of his presence was the crate of semi-skimmed and full-fat left at the back door of the café – an order that quadrupled in the summer months. Georgie was one of the happiest people she knew, having arrived in the town only a year ago. He and his wife Cleo lived in a bungalow on the outskirts of town. He was always smiling and never more so than when he got the opportunity to show her a picture of his little boy – a beaming toddler called Tommy who looked just like his milkman dad. His paternal pride cut her with a knife made of longing.

Making good use of her robust legs it felt like no time before she pulled out on to the top of the slipway that took her down to

Hele Bay Beach. Leaving her bike on its side, she tiptoed across the wet sand and shingle, feeling the crunch underfoot as she listened to the ocean jump against the rocks. Its roar and the fine spray of water it threw into the air seemed to her to be, if not a statement meant to challenge her, then certainly a question. Despite the fact her eyes had become accustomed to the shadowy morning, it was hard to see too far out into the bay. She was, however, acutely aware of the vast body of water that both called to and repelled her. This body of water that had swallowed her dad whole and failed to spit him back out. Who in their right mind would want to get into it?

'You don't have to do this, Tawrie. You can chicken out. No one cares,' she whispered.

But that wasn't strictly true.

She cared.

Looking around, she was slightly surprised to realise she was the first to arrive. Surely the seasoned Peacock gang had not cried off today of all days. Although she had to admit it was a sound excuse for abandoning her mission, and she decided there and then that if no one else arrived, she would take it as a sign from the universe that she'd be better off in bed, and trudge home, showing mock disappointment.

'Hello, dear!' She heard the voice before she saw the wiry form of an old woman walking slowly up from the shore.

'Oh, hello!' She waved. With at least one other Peacock here, this was happening! Her gut bunched with nerves.

It was only as the woman drew closer that Tawrie noticed she was not just old, but really old. At least a generation older than her gran. She was also not alone, as an elderly man followed a few paces behind. Of similar stature, both were wearing thick vintage-style wetsuits that came over their heads and zipped up under their chins, allowing their faces to peep through. She did her best not to reveal the mixture of surprise and admiration she felt at their age. They looked like bowlegged Jacques Cousteau impersonators, with inflated pink floats dangling from their waists to their ankles.

'Are you Tawrie Gunn?'

'I am.' She gripped her duffel bag to her chest as if it were a shield.

'You must be related to Freda then?' The woman smiled as much as her tight hood allowed.

'Yes, my nan.'

'I know her from the doctors'; we've chatted there in the waiting room a couple of times. She's friends with Mrs Tattersall over in Combe Martin, isn't she?'

'That's right.' This wasn't uncommon in a small town, everyone keen to join the dots, find a connection.

'Well, we live next door to Mrs Tattersall's son Henry.' The woman pointed up towards a row of cottages a stone's throw from the beach. Tawrie envied their front-row seat and view of the water.

'Ah yes, I know Henry.' The man sported a fierce moustache, which must take a lot of work to maintain.

'And Henry went to school with our daughter Alisha, who now lives in London. She's a physiotherapist.'

'Oh great!' This passing of information, too, all quite standard. It was the showing of credentials, proof that you belonged. It also left her with the tang of envy on her tongue: lucky Alisha to have upped and left, followed her dream . . .

'She's divorced.' The woman's mouth narrowed in disapproval and Tawrie felt a flicker of pity for Alisha, the London-living physiotherapist, who she suspected might be on the receiving end of that tight, disapproving expression more often than was fun when it came to the subject of her marital status.

Her body gave an involuntary shiver.

'Anyway, welcome to the Peacock Swimmers!' the woman yelled with her arms held out, full of energy despite the early hour. Tawrie wanted to laugh at the absurdity of it all.

13

'Thank you.' Looking over the woman's shoulder as the old man came closer, she wondered where everyone else was.

'I'm Maudie and this is my husband Jago.'

'Hi there.' She smiled at the diminutive man who bobbed his head in greeting in return.

'I'm Jago!'

'Yes, hi.' It felt rude to say that Maudie had already given this information.

'He's as deaf as arseholes!' Maudie pointed at him.

'Oh!' She didn't know if it was rude to laugh at Jago's expense or rude not to laugh at Maudie's humour.

'How are you feeling? Excited?' The twinkle in Jago's eyes suggested he might be speaking for himself and had clearly not heard Maudie, more than proving her point.

'Nervously cautious, I guess, and excited, yes.' She over-enunciated. Loudly.

'Good.' He nodded and exchanged a look with Maudie, suggesting Tawrie had inadvertently passed a test.

She was actually a tad more than nervously cautious. She was afraid. Not that she was about to share this with the primary members of the Peacocks. It was ridiculous really, considering she had always lived in Ilfracombe, woken each morning of her life and looked out over the sea. Some, she knew, opened their eyes to stare at a wall or a building, a park or a forest, a busy road or a lane, a shop, a hill or mountain, but it was the big, big sea that was her next-door neighbour. Her constant companion.

Sometimes in the café, she'd hear those that didn't know the ocean talking about it as if it were nothing more than salty water where their cod lived before it got slapped into a box with chips and smothered in salt and vinegar. Tawrie knew it was so much more than that. She had long held it in fascination, the shifting landscape a moving picture. She captured it each morning in her mind:

sometimes brown, often green, occasionally blue with white crests and foaming arcs, or flat ripples and wide waves; floating weed and brown sticks, softened glass and stripped wood, and the redundant shells it spat on to the shore. It was a changing thing that called to her in soft murmurs as it kissed the wet sand. She heard it roar in fierce winds, dousing her in winter and calming her in summer. It was a barometer of life. As well as being a powerful force that could just as easily take life. This much she knew.

She had, contrary to her mother's observation, always paddled, idled in its embrace. The earliest photograph of her was taken right there on Hele Bay Beach, sporting a fat nappy, hanging low on those barrel-hefting legs, a smiling face and a handful of sand held up to the camera. She wondered now who had taken it. Her dad possibly? She liked to think so. Liked to think that he carried the image of her looking up at him in her happy place, right there on the sand.

'Right then, dear, you get yourself changed and we'll meet you on the shoreline. And don't be nervous, this is a magical day! It'll change your life!' Maudie spoke with authority and Tawrie felt the stab of hope that it might just be true.

'Okay.' She let her duffel bag drop at her feet. 'What time will everyone else arrive? Do we have to wait for them or do you just turn up and plop in one by one? Like those penguins who tramp for days looking for food and then jump the moment they get to the water's edge.'

Maudie stared at her, looked towards Jago, then back again. 'What do you mean everyone else?'

Tawrie's heart sank and her stomach dropped to her feet as she realised that Maudie and Jago *were* the Peacock Swimmers. All thoughts of making new friends and enriching her pretty non-existent social life carried away into the sea spray.

15

'Oh, I just thought that . . .' She paused, wary of causing offence. 'I figured that maybe . . .'

'Come on! Time and tide and all that!' Jago clapped, seemingly keen to hurry her along, like she was a dog that needed geeing up a bit.

As she struggled into her wetsuit, she watched Maudie and Jago plod along side by side, exactly like two little penguins returning to the water. Her gut stirred with doubt, questioning why she was getting involved at all. But also with something that felt a lot like envy at the sight of the couple, living their best peacock life.

Hesitantly, she kicked off her trainers and peeled off her thick socks. The cold hit her feet and she shivered, feeling every bit of her skin goosebump as her muscles bunched and her jaw tensed. Next, she stepped out of her tracksuit bottoms and shrugged her arms free from her hoodie, revealing her racing-back swimming costume, which she'd had the wisdom to put on in the comfort of her bedroom. With her wetsuit now clinging to her skin, goggles in place over her swimming cap, she trod with caution to the water's edge, feeling the bite of sharp stones on the tender soles of her feet. The second the white foam tickled her toes, she jumped back.

'Shit!'

The cold was on another level. It wasn't the best start. She was, however, thankful that no one other than Maudie and Jago were around to witness her rather embarrassing debut.

'Don't overthink it, dear! Just wade on in!' Maudie called from the water where she and Jago bobbed, shoulders submerged, like two bright-eyed seals. They made it look so easy.

She knew she could simply turn and run back up the beach and shove on her fleece-lined dry robe; no one would ever know. Apart from maybe in the weeks to come when her nan encountered Maudie in the doctors' waiting room. She could even say she'd done it! Make out she'd dived in, given it a go. Trouble was, Tawrie Gunn was many things but she was not and never had been a liar.

But it all seemed like too much too soon. Swimming felt risky – too risky – and her heart thundered with fearful anticipation as she wondered what it might have felt like for her dad. Had he been cold, afraid . . . and all alone? Did he know he was about to take his last breath or was he dead before the sea claimed him? She shook her head to clear her mind, deciding there was no reason she couldn't step in and let the salt water lap over her shoulders, count to three and run out again.

'That's it, Tawrie! You're already up to your knees, that's a quarter peacock!'

This crazy commentary was enough to make her laugh hard, and that alone was something that had been missing of late, as the years marched on and the fear of life passing her by had intensified. With her numb feet pushing onwards and her spirits lifted by her laughter, she realised that this was exactly what she had wished for, even if it wasn't quite the club she had envisaged.

'Your waist, Tawrie! It's up to your waist! Once you've got your bits and pieces in that's the worst of it over!' Jago called, and she laughed even harder. It might be bloody freezing, but she was, by her reckoning, now at least half peacock. And that was a start.

CHAPTER TWO

Harriet Stratton

July 2002

Harriet Stratton sat in the soft, low leather chair that had been in her family forever. The cottage might have been new to her, the surroundings strange, but to sit in the familiar confines of the chair made her feel a little more at home. With her long legs curled beneath her, the green cloth notebook rested on her knees as she tapped her favourite ink pen on her teeth – a terrible habit that she knew would cause minute fissures, dents and damage to the enamel, almost imperceptible and yet enough to lead to nothing good in old age. Not that she was remotely fussed about aesthetics or even function as she carried on tapping, quite liking the distracting rhythm in her head. She didn't care about much right now. It was more a case of trying to stay upright and she had few reserves for anything else. She needed all her energy to try to figure out how to go forward, how to reclaim all that was once hers.

Opening the stiff front cover, she stared at the blank page and felt ridiculously self-conscious. It wasn't the kind of thing she did, keep a diary. It felt indulgent, vain, silly even. I mean, who had time to write a diary? If she wasn't travelling to and from work, she was whipping up supper for the kids, washing their clothes, tidying the house, chasing the hamster around the bathroom floor, constantly dashing to collect a prescription, a package, dry cleaning, groceries, a child from a friend's house or an after-school event, and when the sun came out she mowed grass and did her best to keep the weeds at bay in the flower beds, wishing she had more time to tend to the garden she loved. Always something to do . . .

Her conversation with her sister Ellis came to mind.

'It's good for your soul, cathartic! Write it all down! Get it out! And do let me know that you're doing it; at least then I'll be able to look beyond that sanguine smile and know that there is rage being expelled on to the page! I'll sleep better.'

'Oh, well, if it'll make you sleep better . . .' she'd laughed, wondering if there was any truth in it. Could capturing her thoughts and secrets in a journal be of benefit? And for whom? Herself? What a preposterous idea. She was a scientist, not a writer. Happier with data sets, chemicals, droppers, test tubes, and a question to be answered. She preferred to have a Petri dish in her hand rather than a pen. It had always been the clear demarcation between her and her sister. Harriet was bookish, bespectacled and busy, while Ellis was creative, careless and calm. Their mother used to say that if she had had one child with all their attributes they would surely be the most rounded human being on the planet. Instead she'd given birth to two halves of the apple.

She felt the inevitable squeeze to her heart at the thought of her late mother.

'Right,' she spoke aloud, as she removed the pen's cap and placed the long nib on the paper, 'here goes nothing.'

July 2nd 2002

A diarist!

Who even am I?

I jest but there's truth in it. I hardly recognise the person sitting here in this pretty sitting room. The French doors are thrown open and sunlight streaks the honey-coloured dusty wooden floor. Another job to add to the list! The hallways are still cluttered with boxes. In my distracted state, I neglected to label them properly, despite Hugo handing me a clutch of fat black markers for just that purpose. So rather than put obvious notes like DINING ROOM, ATTIC or CHARITY – I have instead created merry mayhem. I'm staring at a box through the open door right now, one of several stacked against the wall, and it says quite simply WOOL. For goodness' sake, Harriet! Does that mean jerseys for the closet? Socks for a drawer? Blankets for the ends of beds? You can see my quandary. So with no one to blame but myself, each box requires opening and sorting through before the contents can be allocated a final home. Hence the clutter, confusion and the need to navigate the obstacle course every time we leave or enter the house. I think the kids would love it, having to boulder their way into the sitting room or kitchen.

And trust me, clutter and confusion are two bedfellows I can't wait to kick out. Which is, in part, the reason we have moved here, away from Berkshire, away from our home in Ledwick Green. It's the prettiest village with all the usual attributes: a little school with flint walls and a matching church. A pub, post office and shop. An Easter egg hunt, Christmas carol service, summer fete. And enough well-off busybodies to ensure each event runs like clockwork and with lashings of cake.

It was a decision made in haste. When the shouting had almost stopped, the tears slowed, and my body lost some of its tremble, we made the decision to rent the place out one night before bedtime, on the landing as we passed each other in our pyjamas.

'Should we go? Get away? Start over?' I think it was him who said it and I nodded. It seemed obvious.

'Yes.'

That really was the extent of our exchange, as if he'd asked if I fancied porridge for breakfast or had I finished in the bathroom. It set a course for us for which I was thankful, am thankful, as it means I don't have to think. I have, for the last eight weeks, let the current of events carry me along: tending to the children, packing boxes, cleaning corners, folding clothes and bedding, and soaking in the tub at the end of every day wondering when the world might stop spinning.

We put the word out, abandoned half our furniture, and here we are in a new county, in a new house, hoping the incoming tenants of Ledwick Green – a family returning to the UK – treat our furniture kindly. They don't arrive for a month or so. We met them briefly, the Latteridges.

They're a fashion-conscious, neat couple who are rent-ing it for a year; a couple who seemed far too pleased with themselves to be my cup of tea. The kind my mother would horrendously describe as nouveau riche. Her snob-bery was legendary and so overt it was quite humorous. I'm certain she over-egged it just for us.

'Oh, please, Harriet, packet bacon? Did I not raise a daughter who understands the value of befriending and supporting a local butcher? What next, paper napkins? Those ghastly gluey blobs that sit in one's loo? Over-tipping staff? It's enough to make your poor mother shudder!'

I wonder what she'd make of all this. It's not like she didn't have practice dealing with disaster after disaster. I refer, of course, to my darling little sister Ellis and the lost dog, the flooded basement, the drunken New Year's Eve, the arrival of Maisie . . .

Poor Mum. I can picture her now, rolling up her sleeves, jutting her chin and saying, 'Right . . .' before launch-ing into a detailed strategy of how things were going to get resolved. Not sure even she could resolve this knotty mess. But I know she'd have given it a good try. How I miss her. Selfishly, I think what I miss most is the safety net she provided when things went belly up. Knowing I could always call on her for any emergency, big or small, it made me feel . . . safe. Now I'm a little adrift. Thank God for Ellis, and Maisie too, who might have her head in the clouds like her Mumma but is a beautiful soul. She wrote to me. I hid the letter from Hugo – he has always adored her and let's just say her commentary on her uncle was not that favourable.

Don't think he has ever been called a bloody idiot – and yet these were her words of choice. Can't decide if she's being disrespectful or heroic. One thing's for sure, she's made her allegiance clear and I take comfort from that. Not that we are or will ever be at that 'pick a side' stage. Of course not. But I'd be lying if I didn't admit that to know this is how our niece feels is nice for me.

I can hear Hugo in the kitchen. He's clattering around, making an unholy racket. I expect he's filling cupboards, putting the kids' nursery handprints up on the fridge door, unwrapping crockery, placing utensils into the earthenware pots in which they live and pressing buttons on the cooker to try and set the time.

And he's singing.

Singing.

And why not, I suppose? It's not something that's possible for me right now, not yet. I have a small pebble of hurt that sits at the base of my throat and try as I might, I can't shift it. Talking and swallowing are tricky enough, let alone belting out a melody as Hugo is right now . . . I think it's Toto's 'Africa'. Yes, yes it is. He's just got to the chorus.

To think only three months ago I would have jumped up, run to him, grabbed a spoon, and made it a duet.

He always brought out my sillier side. I guess he gave me the confidence to be silly. He gave me confidence full stop.

But now? I'm cloaked in self-consciousness. My confidence is water thin and my heart . . . my heart is in tatters. But I'm determined. There are even moments of optimism. Glimpses of the before life – small things like the mindless retelling of something seen, a book recommendation, a fact heard on the radio, a chat about supper – and when they occur, we cling to them, elevate them, and over-celebrate; so much so that it only serves to highlight that for the rest of the time we are pretending.

Yet still I cling to those moments. Like now, as I sit here, a little broken, listening as he sings . . .

'There you are!' Hugo walked into the sitting room and as unhurriedly as she could manage, Harriet closed the diary.

'Here I am.'

He walked straight to the French doors, standing in the dying light as if disinterested in her scribbling – or unnoticing. Either way she felt a flush of relief. Her writing was not something she intended to share.

Ever.

'It's a beautiful evening, the sky is on fire.'

'Do you think we'll ever get sick of it, take the view for granted?' She stood, placed the book on the lamp table and came to rest behind him, standing so close she could smell the end-of-day sweat mixed with his cologne. He reached back and pulled her arm over his shoulder, kissing her fingers and holding her hand inside his, knitted over his heart as they stared at the sunset.

'How could we ever take it for granted? It's beautiful and different every time. What could possibly spoil such a majestic moment?'

'Mmm.'

She made the noise, not wanting to risk talking or giving free rein to the tears that threatened. How could he possibly know that in that second, as she stared at the pale stripe of his cotton shirt and wondered if this was one he'd worn when he was with *her* – the woman who had taken a scythe to all Harriet had thought was secure – the moment was entirely spoiled for her?

Her thoughts returned as they often did to that sunny May evening as blossom lay on the ground.

'Are you . . .' She had swallowed, feeling ridiculously awkward, foolish even in having to ask. 'Are you having an affair?'

His reply had been instant, insistent, strong in the denial. 'What a bloody ridiculous thing to say to me! No!'

'I need to know who you were on the phone to.' Her voice quieter this time, not so confident in the face of his absolute denial.

'I . . .' His lips had turned bloodless and nerves instantly made his face shiny.

Her thoughts returned to this point often, that moment when her marriage, her life, had begun to unravel.

CHAPTER THREE

Tawrie Gunn

August 2024

It was just over seventeen months since Tawrie Gunn had become a fully fledged member of the Peacock Swimmers, and it would be accurate to say she was at one with the sea. It felt like a secret, this relationship she shared with the ocean. The pure exhilaration, the joy felt like a gift from mother nature to her. Time lost meaning with every moment she spent as a guest in its watery embrace. Worries evaporated in a floating pool of endless possibilities. It was a carefree world where the many constrictions of daily life did not apply. Another dimension, where those within it wore different clothes, made different movements, existed in a different temperature, and felt unique sensations. A soft, fluid environment that held her fast while setting her free. A topsy-turvy place where sounds echoed, the world's noise softened and instead of big slabs of sky above there were deep, invisible depths below.

'Here I am, Dad,' she would whisper into the fathoms and smile at the feel of the water's response, knocking her shoulders and tickling her neck. 'Here I am. So what's my news? Not much to tell today really. I slept well. The busier we are in the café the better I sleep. There's something about slipping between the sheets with aching limbs and weary bones that makes the sleep even sweeter. As if I've earned it. And other than that? As I say, not much to tell . . .'

It felt easy to talk to him out here in the sea. No threat of being overheard by her relatives, no other chore calling for her attention. And it was no surprise that here in the water where he'd lost his life, she felt closest to him. Even on the coldest of days, the shiver in her bones shook off any malaise, dispersed her thought-fog and left her with a singular clarity of mind that was as good as a mental reset. And on the warmer days, there was nowhere else on earth she would rather be. She knew that nearly three-quarters of the world was covered in water and yet as she took a deep breath and immersed her body in the salty blue, this tiny bit of it felt like hers alone. This cool sea coaxed her thoughts, caressed her limbs and urged her on silently from its depths . . . the message always:

'*You've got this, Tawrie Gunn, everything is going to be okay.*'

They were a curious trio, Maudie, Jago and her. On some days they were silent, as if bowed by the majesty of the rising sun and the water before them. Silently swimming, close enough and yet in their own worlds, almost in reverence to the act that bound them.

When they left the water, however, that was when the gang came together, chattering through the shivering after-drop as their bodies cooled, comparing notes, sharing any glorious experiences that ranged from the interest of a nosey seal to the sighting of a cumbersome piece of driftwood that for a split second, out of the corner of Jago's eye, took on all the characteristics of a crocodile. She liked to sit with them on the rocks that edged the bay, enjoyed their ribbing, their comedy and the snippets of their everyday life. Married for an unfathomable sixty-eight years, it fascinated her how they had morphed into one entity: walking in unison, pausing

27

to allow the other to catch up and donning their wetsuits every morning to climb into the sea. Time spent in their company both gladdened and saddened her. It made her see that it was possible to find someone and live a happy life and yet it felt as out of reach for her as it always had. She knew practically everyone there was to know in the town but without a wider social network it was hard to meet new people. This, in no small part, was behind her motivation to start swimming, and not that she didn't adore Maudie and Jago, but it wasn't quite the gang she'd imagined.

'That was a tad chilly!' Maudie reached for her towel, while with the other hand she rubbed her stomach.

'Are you okay, Maudie?' She felt the familiar flicker of concern, aware of the age of her fellow swimmers, although their fitness was astounding.

'Yes, it'll pass. Period pain.' Maudie pulled a face.

'Period pain?' She must have misheard.

'Of course not, you daft thing! I'm eighty-bloody-six! I hurt because I'm eighty-bloody-six!'

Tawrie laughed loud and hard as she dried her hair and pulled on her thick socks.

'What's she on about?' Jago sat down hard on a flat rock and caught his breath.

'Women's talk,' Maudie yelled at him and he nodded. Knowing better, it seemed, than to enquire further.

Tawrie felt invigorated as ever by the feel of the cold morning on her damp hair and wet face as she cycled home. It was her happiest time of the day. Buoyed up and refreshed, she felt ready for anything. Her mood slid accordingly as the hours since her body had been held by the water ticked on. The connection with the ocean weakened as the day passed and when finally she climbed into bed, just as darkness stole the day, she was already dreaming of her dip in the big briny when she awoke.

Her swim was also the only time in the day she didn't have to pretend. Didn't have to find a smile for her heartbroken grandma, didn't have to avoid contact with her mother – the prospect of hearing about her drunken exploits always enough to crush Tawrie's soul and spirit.

With her bike stowed and the front door closed behind her, she kicked off her trainers, abandoning them on the stripped wooden floor, and raced up the wide creaking stairs to her bedroom.

'Is that you, Taw?' The voice came from the kitchen at the back of the house.

'Yep. It's me, Nan.' She paused on the half landing, calling down through the bannisters, while resisting the temptation to be sarcastic, swallowing the suggestion of irritation at the fact that her nan called this out every morning when she climbed the stairs at precisely seven fifteen.

'Where've you been?'

She bit her lip and dismissed more ludicrous and fanciful scenarios: *It's been quite a night, just got dropped off, been wined and dined by the man of my dreams. We had a picnic and sat on the beach watching the sun go down and got on so well, we stayed there until the sun came up* . . .

'Just the usual, been for my swim!'

One, two, three . . .

'Swimming again?'

Theeeeere it was.

'At this time of the morning, must be freezing!'

'Yup.' *No colder than it was yesterday and probably as cold as it'll be tomorrow* . . . 'Just going to get changed and head off to work.'

She plopped her towel and swimming costume over the metal rail that was attached to the radiator in her bedroom and abandoned her duffel bag on the chair behind the old pitch pine desk. It was the place she loved to sit, in the bay window of her bedroom on the top floor of Signal House. The desk was busy but ordered: the drawers neatly packed with stationery, correspondence and the general administration of life. To the casual observer the set-up might have seemed cluttered, but not to Tawrie, who liked the tumble of books on which her tasselled bedside lamp teetered. She was happy to have an array of pens, pencils and paintbrushes in an old jam jar, which, when the sun caught it, sent tiny prisms over the wall. And she appreciated the cool touch of the old hand-painted floral tile, dug up from the shoreline over at Barricane Beach, on which she rested her morning cup of tea.

Also on her desk sat a framed black-and-white photograph of her dad, Dan, and his brother, her Uncle Sten, when they were no more than teens. Everyone knew Sten, and everyone loved him. Never without his grotty beret, a new joke or advice on anything from how to reverse out of a tight space to world politics, he liked to stick his oar in. She happened to know that there was a little more to his happy life than the 'four Ps' – namely his investments in construction that meant he owned large chunks of real estate all along the North Devon coast. Her nan often hinted at a king's ransom stashed away, yet to look at Sten, you'd think he slept in a skip. And in truth this would not have been a surprise.

She felt warmed now at the thought of her beloved uncle, glad that he and her dad had shared so many happy days and beyond grateful that Daniel Gunn had had a good life, as the alternative – that his shortened time on the planet had been miserable – was more than she could contemplate. She tousled her damp hair and reached for her jeans and long-sleeved t-shirt, over which she'd shove an apron when she arrived at work.

August was the busiest time of year. With the café full of holidaymakers day in and day out, she had to run for her entire shift, grabbing glugs of water and bathroom breaks where she could, and falling into bed each night with muscles that throbbed on her bones with fatigue. With more dry days than not and the sun showing its face for longer periods, tourists and day trippers were filling up the car parks and wandering the harbour in search of cups of tea, ice creams and snacks.

She loved the business and excitement of this time of year, but June was her favourite month, when the town slipped into summer. The changes were subtle at first: noise levels grew, tables that had been stacked neatly for the off-season began to pepper the pavements, and the winter moss and slime that sat on rocks and walls dried up and disappeared. Any journey took longer, whether on foot, by bike or car, as she moved en masse with people who didn't share her sense of urgency.

Restaurants, bars and shops that had slumbered through the cold months had their doors thrown open and their frontages scrubbed with buckets of hot, soapy water until the windows sparkled. Deliveries arrived, floors were swept, fresh paint licked the walls and festoon lights were strung up around awnings.

It was impossible not to feel the buzz of excitement, the hum of activity, and for her spirits not to become infected by the laughter of those who were in holiday mode and could, just for a few days, forget all that ailed them in the real world. By August, however, her energy was starting to flag.

'How d'you get on?' Her mother's voice from the bedroom doorway startled her.

Tawrie glanced at her as she slipped into her jeans and scraped her thick hair back into an imperfect ponytail. Her mother looked awful. And while this was not a surprise, it was no less jarring to see. Her skin looked almost grey in the morning light, her eyes bloodshot, her thin shoulders as ever hunched inside her silky kimono, and her fingers shook as she lit the cigarette that clung to her bottom lip like sticky seaweed to a rounded stone. The sight of her smoking at this hour, at any hour, made Tawrie's stomach roll. She detested the habit but had long since given up trying to get her mum to stop. Like everything that bothered her about Annalee's life, any comment or criticism would only fall on deaf ears. Her mother was wrapped in an impenetrable shell, hardened by her years of widowhood. Tawrie carried a vague memory of Annalee holding her hand and laughing as they skipped along the quay. At least, she thought she remembered this, but could have spun her desire for such a memory into life, tricking herself with this sliver of happiness that in times of need punctured her loneliness.

'All right.'

Her mother drew on the cigarette like it was fresh air and Tawrie watched as the end lit up and crackled like a tiny firework. A firework held between fingers with long nails, where red, red polish clung on despite being chipped in places.

She saw a flash in her mind of purple nails, purple with flecks of glitter . . .

'Well, you've stuck to it, that's for sure.' Her mother sounded neither impressed nor judgemental, not that Tawrie cared either way.

'Yep.'

'You said you'd swim every day of the season, and you have. So far.'

'Yep.'

She found this stilted monosyllabic communication easier. It got the interaction over quicker and didn't invite any of her mother's bullshit, which had the habit of living in her mind for days.

Tawrie sat on the side of her bed and pulled on fresh cotton socks and her work sneakers, comfy enough to see her through the day.

'I'll let you get on then.' Her mother turned and walked slowly back down the stairs, heading no doubt to her bedroom on the half landing next to the bathroom. Handy for when she needed to vomit, which she did frequently. Or if one of her 'guests' needed to pee, which also happened a lot.

Tawrie stared at her mother's back. Her buzzcut made her head look small, her neck frail, and Tawrie was reminded of an image: her mother with a little meat on her bones, hair in a thick, tousled mess piled up on top of her head, and eyes that had life behind them.

Her phone pinged and she read the text. It was from Connie.

YOU ON YOUR WAY OR WHAT?

Her cousin was, as ever, succinct.

A quick glance at the clock and she realised with a quickening to her pulse that she was running a little behind schedule. And just like that the serenity and joy that had filled her after her morning dip were elbowed out of the way by the demands of life.

COMING RIGHT NOW, she replied, then shoved her phone in her jeans pocket, grabbed her hoodie, and slammed the bedroom door behind her.

'See you later, Nan.'

'Where you going?'

She did her best to control the twitch of irritation under her left eye. 'I'm going to work. Where I go every morning.'

'Course you are!' Freda chuckled. 'Give Con a big kiss from her nanny!'

'Yep.' It felt easier to agree than explain how planting a smacker on her cousin's face during a busy service would not really cut it.

Having negotiated the twisting steps that led from the front terrace to the lower street level, she did her best to run down Fore Street, which was already filling up with meandering early-bird visitors who cluttered up the pavements and snapped shots on their phones as the sun peeked over the harbour wall, littering the surface of the sea with diamonds. It seemed they had all the time in the world as she dodged them, sidestepping couples as they pottered arm in arm. She had to get to the café! The fact that Connie had texted meant she was already feeling a little snowed under. Gaynor would be in by now, but, much as they loved her, although she arrived at seven sharp, she didn't actually get going until at least eleven. And to put it politely, even then her pace wasn't exactly lightning.

'Cheer up, Taw, might never happen!'

Distracted, she looked up to see Needle sweeping the pavement in front of the King William pub. Needle had been in Connie's year at school and was one of those characters who had always been around. In the winter he laid carpet for a bloke with a van out Barnstaple way, but in the summer he worked shifts at the pub, holding court at the sticky bar, serving warm pints that got slopped over the ancient flagstones, sneaking gravy-flavoured treats to any four-legged visitors, intervening if things got a little heated on quiz night, and making snide comments about cocktails to anyone who dared ask for a slice of lemon, as if that was too fancy.

'All right, Needle.'

Pushing her hands into the kangaroo pocket of her hoodie, she slowed but kept moving; there was no time to stop and chat and his greeting was familiar. She had long ago accepted that her resting face was not exactly perky.

'You missed a cracking night last night; your mother was hilarious!' he wheezed.

'I bet.'

She felt the bloom of embarrassment spread over her chest and throat and her gut jumped with all the dire possibilities of what this comment might mean. Too often had she witnessed her mother's *hilarious* antics: singing loudly out of key to the packed pub,

34

backing music optional. Flashing her breasts at a passing coach full of OAPs on a jolly to the seaside. Picking a fight with a large seagull who'd had the audacity to try to steal one of her chips. Urinating over the drain, not five minutes from home. Snogging the face off any number of men as they slid down the wall . . .

'Give that cousin of yours my love.' He leaned on his broom.

She ignored him.

His words gave some explanation for her mother's look and demeanour earlier. Not that any of this was a shock. The bar at the King William – or the King Billy, as it was known – was one of the many establishments her mother graced with her presence. Sitting on a stool with her handbag on the bar, Annalee no longer had to ask for a drink; a mere raise of her eyebrow and point of her finger was all the instruction needed. While she tottered outside to smoke, Needle and other willing hosts would top up her glass, which would be waiting for her when she retook her seat. Annalee Gunn, 'such a laugh', 'a right old giggle', 'up for anything', 'fun'.

A drunk.

Nine-year-0ld Tawrie and her nan were sitting on the bench on the wraparound porch of their house. It was without a doubt her favourite time of the day, when the fire-red sun set over the harbour. She had nestled back on the floral cushion and placed her feet in her nan's plump lap and run her fingers over the crêpey skin on her arm, liking the way it wrinkled and moved under the pressure.

'What's the best place you have ever lived, Nan?'

The woman's laugh was hearty and Tawrie felt her shake and jiggle beneath her. This is what they had always done: shared easy chatter, talking about nothing much, passing the time, happy.

'Well, that's easy peasy. This place, this house.'

'Because we get to watch the sunset from here on the terrace?' Even at that young age, she was aware of the privileged view that was theirs alone.

'Oh, most definitely, but also it's a bit of a trick question!'

'What d'you mean?' She had turned to face the woman who had looked after her faithfully, watching her every move, fingers twitching, as if waiting to catch her if and when she fell. 'Why, Nan?' She was unsure if she was comfortable with the accusation of trickery. It felt a bit like being called a liar and lying was the worst thing.

'Because it's where all my memories live. It's the only house I've ever lived in, the only house your daddy lived in too, and the only place I've ever called home. The Gunns have lived in Ilfracombe forever, we're part of the landscape. In fact, little one, I reckon if you cut me open I'd leak seawater scooped up from the harbour down there on the quayside.' She pointed the hundred yards down the hill where the view opened up like a fairy tale: flapping bunting, sparkling festoon lights, the waving masts of boats, chattering loved ones walking hand in hand, families eating al fresco, kids running in sandals still with sand between their toes, and the call of the gulls circling overhead relaying messages as they swirled and rose en masse, following the trawlers out into the water and hoping for a fish supper.

'And the only place *I've* ever lived,' Tawrie had noted with a slight lament to her tone, as if she might, on occasion, want to be somewhere without memories that cut her like a knife lurking behind every corner, somewhere without people nudging, pointing, and whispering as she walked past.

'*That's his daughter . . .*'

A year might have passed since her father had been lost, but the attention hadn't lessened.

'Yes, but you have many more years ahead of you, little Taw, who knows where you'll end up? I'll say to you like I always said to my boys, go wherever the wind takes you. I will never clip your wings, but my God I hope it blows you back to this little town.' Her nan had reached for a tissue and wiped under her eyes.

The topic of her boys, one now gone forever, was still painful. Tawrie more than understood; her own life was framed by the raw edges of loss, a feeling of being different, as if living cloaked in sadness was unique to her family. It certainly felt that way growing up. Age and perspective had helped shatter this illusion, but in her mind, everyone else in her class went home to a happy household where two parents helped with homework and cooked supper. It was a fantasy she liked to envisage, like probing a bad tooth with her tongue, inviting and dreading the pain in equal measure. She might have been young, but she understood enough to know that her self-appointed role was as chief distractor, to help provide her nan with moments of happiness that she knew offered brief respite from her grief. It was as exhausting as it was limiting. Tawrie couldn't imagine what her nan's life would be like if she wasn't around and felt the weight of the responsibility. She did her best to rally the mood.

'I'd like to travel a bit, I think, but still end up right here in Signal House.' She couldn't imagine being away for too long, couldn't imagine not having her nan within reach.

'You might say that now, but no one knows what the tide'll bring in, love. That's the beautiful and terrible thing about life. You just never know.'

A raucous scream had echoed around the garden, a noise that came from out of sight at the bottom of the steep steps that led from Fore Street up to the front garden of their home. She felt her nan shift beneath her, sitting upright, as if on high alert. The sudden noise and shared anticipation was jarring and they both stared at the path, waiting. It wasn't the first time Tawrie had heard the familiar wail, it happened often of an evening, but it was still a kind of relief when two lolling heads appeared at the top of the steps.

'Ahoy there!' her mother had shouted. 'This is Rod. He's very kindly walked me home from the pub.'

'Rob!' the man giggled and corrected. 'Not Rod.'

'Rob! That's what I said.' She batted at him, catching the side of his head with her cupped palm.

'Hello, Rob!' Tawrie waved and almost instantly her nan reached for her hand and tucked it down by her side. It changed everything, these two people coming up the stairs, screaming, laughing, falling, touching each other's backs, and leaning their heads close together. It was as though they'd taken a rock and lobbed it hard at the happy moment she'd shared with her nan, leaving them staring at fragments of the lovely time just passed. This was the first time her mother had brought a guest. Tawrie, too young to fully understand the implication of it, still felt her tummy flip, as if instinctively she knew this was no good thing.

'Rob's going to have a look at the damp patch in my bedroom.'

'With any luck!' The man wheezed and almost toppled backwards before steadying himself on the wall lined with ancient shells that had been pushed by patient fingers into the drying concrete long ago, then painted white.

Annalee had roared as the two stumbled forward and made it through the grand front door. This time her nan pulled her close to her.

'Don't wait up, night night, Gunns!'

'Night night, Mummy!' Tawrie was about to wave again but remembered her nan's unspoken instruction, and so sat very still. It was conflicting, wanting to make her mum happy like she did her nan, but aware, by the weighted atmosphere and her nan's reaction, that to wave might not make *her* happy.

'Bloody disgrace,' Freda had muttered and settled back into the chair, but the magic had gone entirely. Their chat was spoiled. The air had turned chilly, and the fire-red sun had sunk behind the wall of night, leaving them once again in shadow.

◆ ◆ ◆

'I mean it, tell Connie that if she fancies a trip out on my yacht . . .' Needle's shout pulled her from the memory, his words left trailing.

His yacht was in fact an inflatable rib but was no less loved by him for that. Ilfracombe and all its surrounds might be in Tawrie's blood, but she didn't go on boats, big or small. The idea made her skin jump. Her swimming was proof that she had no aversion to the sea per se but was far more comfortable walking into and swimming in the water rather than being on it. She understood more than most the danger of getting it wrong while out boating . . .

'I'll tell her. Can she bring a friend?'

'No, only room for two, I'm afraid!' Needle laughed.

Tawrie waved over her shoulder and sped up.

'Afternoon!' Connie called from the grill, her way of letting Tawrie know she was late. Not that she needed the jibe – she was as bothered about her tardiness as anyone.

Without waiting to exchange pleasantries or offer an explanation, she grabbed her apron from the hook on the wall. The grill and kitchen were open to the café, diner style.

'Give it to me one more time, Gay.' Connie's mouth was set in a thin line, an expression of frustration she recognised, as her cousin faced the older woman whose grey hair was fastened in a plait down her back, her glasses perched on the end of her nose, a confused crease in the middle of her forehead. Gaynor might have been the wrong side of sixty-five but was still beautiful. Her hands were elegant, her manner particular, but her ability to waitress? She and Connie had often remarked that no one got all the gifts!

'Don't rush me!' Gaynor studied the paper docket in her hand, pulling it further away and then drawing it close.

'Here's the thing, I need to rush you because orders will start backing up and that leads to unhappy customers. If you can't read your own handwriting, what chance do the rest of us have?' Connie exhaled, tucked a stray blonde curl behind her ear, and turned her attention to the row of bacon crisping on the griddle.

Gaynor held the slip of paper up to the light. 'Right, let's have a look. It could be four toast or no toms, meaning tomatoes, I'm not sure. I'd better go ask again. Morning, Taw.'

'Morning.' She smiled at the kindly woman who was good friends with her Uncle Sten. Rumour had it they were more than good friends and that she had stepped in to plug the gap left when Sten's wife Wanda had upped sticks and set sail with a Danish skipper nearly two decades ago, but she was not one to overthink rumours. In a small town like this, where information was collateral and gossip currency, pondering on such tittle-tattle could occupy her whole day if she had a fancy for such things. There had been many theories swirling in the bottom of pint glasses when it came to her dad.

Probably did a runner . . .
I heard it was something shady . . .
My mate reckons he led a double life and faked it all . . .
He's been seen, ain't he? I'm sure he has . . .

Yes, rumours were not to be given much heed in a small town.

'Your mum was a hoot last night.' Gay shook her head. 'Had us all howling!'

'Yep, so I heard.' Tawrie put her hand up to stop the woman saying anything further on the topic. 'Which reminds me, Con,

Needle says he wants to take you out on his boat. And there's only room for two.'

'Yeah, and I want to wake up next to Zac Efron, but both are very unlikely to happen.'

Connie addressed the wall as she cooked. Tawrie smiled at her cousin's back. Connie was pretty, sexy, buoyant, shapely, with a narrow waist and an ample bosom that strained against the bib of her apron. In the summer months, when shorts and vests were the order of the day, walking alongside her cousin only made Tawrie more aware of her broad shoulders and robust legs – the swimming had done nothing to change that; in fact, it had only made the situation worse. Not that she'd give up her morning rendezvous with Maudie and Jago for anything.

With her shoulders back and ready for the day ahead, she walked briskly to the rear of the café with its whitewashed walls, wooden nautical bunting and pale-blue, wipe-down tablecloths dotted with anchors. All eight tables were full. At least three with locals, keen to get their working day started and even keener for the fried fare that would provide sustenance. The couple she now approached held hands tightly across the table, holding on for dear life as if to be separated might be painful. She had never held hands with anyone like that and was fascinated by the act, wondering what it might feel like.

'What can I get you?' She found a smile.

'Nick will have the full English, eggs scrambled, please.' The upbeat woman, whose silk neck scarf was tied at a jaunty angle, spoke on her boyfriend's behalf while he stared at her, as if she were an angel fallen to earth with the sole purpose of relieving him of the responsibility of having to voice his own breakfast choice.

'Certainly.' She jotted on the little notepad. 'Is that with tea, coffee or juice?'

'What drink would you like, Nicky?' jaunty-scarved woman asked him directly, as if he were a dumdum and needed her intervention.

'Sorry, I wasn't listening. What are my options?' He addressed his love directly as if Tawrie wasn't there at all.

'That's okay, darling.' The woman's tone suggested he actually was a dumdum. 'You have the choice of tea, coffee or orange juice.'

'Oh, erm . . . can you come back to me?'

'Of course we can!' The woman made it sound like she, too, was working there. 'While Nick decides on his drink, can I order the poached egg on toast, but I like the egg well done and I don't want salt on it, some places do that, don't they, large flakes of the stuff, but I don't want salt.'

'Got it, well-done poached, no salt.' She wrote slowly. 'And for your drink, sir?' She smiled at the dumdum, hoping to hurry him along.

'He'll have the orange juice!' The woman spoke up. 'Oh, and with the full English, can you please leave off the black pudding, he's not a fan, are you, darling?'

'No.' He shook his head. 'Liked it until I found out what it was and then . . .' He made out to vomit under the table.

'Of course.' She made a note. Jaunty-scarved woman wasn't done.

'And can you make sure that on Nick's plate the beans are not in any way touching the scrambled egg as that turns his tummy.'

The man shuddered, on cue. 'Always been that way, the thought of beans and egg mixing . . .' Again he lowered his head and made a spitting motion.

'Do me a favour, Tawrie, can you tell Con that it was four slices of toast, and table six are waiting.' Gaynor spoke as she passed with a single dirty plate in her hand.

'Sure.' She smiled back at the couple.

'That's a very unusual name.' The woman smiled too. 'Tory? As in Boris Johnson and his cronies?'

'No, definitely not. Tawrie as in Taw, the river Taw, T-A-W, runs right through Devon.'

'Well, how lovely!'

'Yep, my dad named me after the local river, which could be worse, we might have lived by the Amazon and I'd now share my name with the online shopping giant!' She forced a smile; it was still painful to recall her dad. It was that tooth jab again. She whisked the order to Connie who grabbed the docket and placed it on a little metal shelf with a magnet.

'No beans touching scrambled egg?' Her cousin turned to face her, narrowing her heavily mascaraed lashes.

'Yep.' They exchanged a lingering look. Connie, she suspected, like her, was wondering how the day might unfold if this was how it started.

The morning passed quickly as it always did. Waiting tables, washing dishes, fetching supplies from the store room, interspersed as ever with laughter when the pace dropped.

'How long has Needle been asking you out?' Tawrie was curious.

Connie took a sip from her mug of tea and rested on the sink as she considered this.

'I reckon since I was twelve.'

'And you're now . . . thirty-five?'

'Yes, thank you, Taw, for that timely reminder.'

'Well, I'm twenty-nine this September! Not that far behind you.' She hoped this helped a little.

'What are we going to do for the Gunn Fire? I was thinking a hog roast?'

Connie liked to plan a theme or think up something to make the event special.

'I'd like a glitter ball – a big old disco orb that we can dance under!' She smiled.

'On a beach? And how do you suggest we manage that?' Connie tutted.

'I'm allowed to have an idea!' she protested.

'Oh, I should have said' – Connie tapped her own forehead – 'only good ideas! And that's a shite one.'

'You're no more than little Tom Toddys the lot of you!' Gaynor, who had the age advantage, laughed. 'But be warned, Con, after two decades or so, Needle might stop asking.'

'Two decades. Bless him.' Tawrie felt a flicker of sympathy for the man who if nothing else had proved to be steadfast.

'It'll be a bit longer an' all before I say yes!' Connie rolled her eyes.

'He deserves marks for persistence, if nothing else.' Gaynor voiced Tawrie's own thoughts.

'Yep, well, his persistence might have paid off once or twice.'

'In what way?' This was news!

'Well, we might have had a little snog at the Gunn Fire last year.' Connie put her mug in the sink and cracked an egg on to the griddle, standing back as it spat.

'You sly old dog! You kept that quiet.' Secretly she was delighted that Connie not only felt she could confide in her, but also that at least one of them was having some fun.

'I kept it quiet because it's Needle! *Needle!*'

'Well, for what it's worth, I think he's all right.' She spoke in defence of the man.

'Yep, and that's all we can ever ask for, isn't it? To spend the rest of our lives with someone who is "all right"! I mean, Jesus, I tried that with Gary and look where that's landed me? Divorced, skint, and me and my son living back in my dad's house! I sometimes wonder if I should take a leaf out of my mother's book and bugger off with a tall Dane!' Connie made light of the event that Tawrie knew had broken her cousin's heart.

'We don't get many tall Danes in here.' Gaynor pointed out the obvious.

'You could always both move to Nan's, you know that.' She rather liked the idea; the thought of having eight-year-old Sonny around was a lovely one. She was certain that part of her cousin's decision not to do so was to shield her son from the grubby life of Annalee.

'I know, but I think Dad likes having me around.'

'Oh, he does, love.' Gaynor spoke with conviction, suggesting if nothing else that she and Sten Gunn were more than friends.

'He drives me mad, but I think that's what families are supposed to do; that way it makes it easier to leave when the time comes.' Connie flipped the egg and reached for another.

Tawrie nodded, having little to add as she had never left. Right now, as it sometimes did, this felt like a failure on her part, and not for the first time her thoughts strayed beyond the harbour wall.

'But I mean it, I'm holding out for Zac or at least a Zac lookalike. Needle doesn't exactly fit the bill.'

Her cousin's tone made them all laugh. Tawrie knew she was right: settling was not an option.

'Didn't realise we were talking about the rest of your life, thought he was just asking you out on his yacht.' She laughed, as Connie lobbed a tea towel at her that thwacked her on the head.

'May as well take your break, Taw. 'S'quiet now.'

She stepped outside and looked up at the big blue sky. The café backed on to the cobbled quayside where there was a row of wooden benches with views out over the busy harbour. Each had at least one little brass plaque on it, commemorating the life of someone who had enjoyed the view as much as the person staring at it. Tawrie loved these seats; not only were they the perfect place to sit and rest, to take in life, but they were also a salient reminder that their time here was temporary. This she understood more than most.

Inevitably her thoughts returned to her dad. Not that she'd ever admit it but her memories of him were sparse. The day he died, however, was vivid. Not the events themselves, but the feeling of panic all around her: the fear, the sound of screaming, crying and the constant stream of visitors had been enough for her to learn not to speak about it, not to ask too many questions, as the thought of invoking that uproar again, sending the adults into freefall – it was more than she could contemplate. But those first seven years with him reading her bedtime stories, tucking her in at night, taking her out on his boat, teaching her how to skim stones, kick a ball, lifting her up so she could see over the heads of the crowds at carnival or over the harbour wall . . . It was all learned second-hand from the tales Nana Freda told her. Nana Freda who, upon hearing that her son's boat had washed up on Lundy, had grabbed Tawrie and held her close, folding her into her lap where she did her best to use her granddaughter's soft form to plug the hole left by her son.

Tawrie had held her breath, sitting as still as possible, wanting her nan to stop crying, to stop rocking, although she had sensed in that moment that *she* was the thing of comfort for which her nan would reach. And she was still reaching for her nearly three decades later. And in some ways, Tawrie was still keeping still, holding her breath.

Maybe that was unfair. They shared a special bond, she and her nan, which was lucky when she considered the state of her mother. Tawrie wished she'd had the chance to get to know her dad better, wished she'd had the chance to ask him questions. In particular she wanted to know why, when according to Uncle Sten and others who had known and loved him, he had been a smart man, an engineer, clever, he'd chosen an old soak like Annalee to be his wife. It made no sense. None at all.

With her head tipped back and eyes closed she let the August sunshine kiss her face and felt the tingle of warmth on her skin. She knew her cheeks would flush red, but it felt good, healing, like drinking in the rays. Time was skewed as she daydreamed away the minutes, lost to the sounds around her, the clank of metal against the masts and the clement weather that wrapped her in its soft embrace.

'Taw!' Connie bellowed from the side door of the café.

Her cue to get back. Her break cut short as customers gathered. Not that she minded, she was slightly restored by her brief sit in the mid-morning warmth.

She opened her eyes, letting her vision settle. As she stood to let a large family pass by, something made her heart take a double beat. She was aware of him before she actually saw him – or maybe that was only how she would remember it. She looked to the right and held her hand over her eyes to block the sunlight and see better.

He came into view and she held her breath as she took in his floppy hair, shot through with auburn, green eyes and the less than taut bod that nestled inside his pink shirt. He was a little doughy, real. She had never found the muscle-bound, gym-honed, Speedo-wearing type attractive. This guy looked like someone who would be good to hold and be held by. He looked . . . kind, and Tawrie felt all kinds of fireworks leap in her gut as she followed his advance along the quayside.

A group of day trippers shuffled along, stopping to ooh and ahh at the boats bobbing on the sea, masts swaying in the gentle breeze. Some were holding ice creams, others cameras, most were in hats of one form or another. He seemed taller than most, sur-rounded by the group, his face clearly visible, looking right at her, or so she thought. And he was smiling. Smiling at her? She waited, as if they were meeting by appointment. The breath stuttered in her throat and her pulse raced.

There you are . . .

This her overriding thought, as if she'd been waiting for him, waiting for him without even knowing it. And now the wait was over because he was walking towards her.

Self-consciousness kicked her in the shins, and she took a step forward and then one back, the dance of the overly aware, not sure where to look, where to stand, folding then unfolding her arms, and by the time she took up the exact position she'd only just left, he waltzed past her.

Transfixed, she stared at the way his heavy fringe lifted and settled on his forehead, the sleeves of his shirt rolled to just below his elbow, the front misbuttoned with the shirt tails hanging down unevenly. His freckled forearms hairy and a little sun-kissed; his orange digital wristwatch; his purposeful stride, the soles of his deck shoes worn flat on the outer edge, the leather stained by salt water and the laces thin. All this detail was taken in quickly and filed away for further dissection later. It felt important. It was important. Then just like that he was gone and she dared not turn to look at his back, couldn't be that obvious. She needed to take a deep breath, recalibrate, calm down.

Love at first sight.

That was rubbish, complete and utter bunkum. There was no such thing, of this she was certain. Anyone who expressed such a sentiment was a little soft in the brain department, overly romantic, gullible. Possibly all of the above. Tawrie was convinced that the truth was no more than the desperate elaboration of someone who was quickly smitten and needed to add seasoning to the mundane tale of how they'd started. She was entirely committed to this belief, and yet, and yet . . . She felt the rise in her stomach of something close to happiness, of pure joy, excitement. This man, who'd done no more than walk past her in a crowd, had captured her attention. And yet she knew nothing about him: not his name, sexuality, nationality, job. Was he creative? Local? Smart? Deviant? Dangerous? Dull? Funny? Married? These and many other questions pinged inside her mind.

She glanced to her left but he had disappeared.

'For the love of God have a word with yourself, Tawrie Gunn!' she snapped to herself, as she navigated her way through the ice-cream lickers and the pasty nibblers who sauntered on the cobbled quayside back towards the café on the corner.

CHAPTER FOUR

HARRIET STRATTON

JULY 2002

Harriet paused from folding the clean laundry into a pile and stared at Hugo. It was a hot, sticky, airless day and her energy levels were low, her actions a little sluggish. It happened like this sometimes, when one other factor, in this case heat, conspired to jump on her sadness and pull at her bones, filling her with a need to lie down somewhere cool and nap, just for a while.

'So what do we need, apart from a decent bottle of red and toothpaste?' Her husband stood with her shopping basket perched comically on his arm.

'Milk, olives and anchovies, please. I've got everything else. Thought I'd make spaghetti puttanesca tonight?'

'Smashing, I'll make it two bottles.'

'Fab.'

'And shall I get garlic bread?'

'Sure.' She smiled at the handsome man whose slight paunch sat over the waistband of his cargo shorts. He never missed an opportunity to go extra where carbs were concerned.

'I could make tiramisu?' he offered casually.

'Hugo, we'd never get off the sofa! Pasta, bread, pudding . . . why don't we go the whole hog and grab cheese as well?'

'Really?' She noted the excited glint in his gluttonous eye, and was quite taken with this moment of refreshing normality.

'No! Not really, I'm joking!'

Grappling with the basket so he could get close to her, he leaned in and kissed her cheek, then stayed still, his face close to hers, both inviting and expecting more. This was how he usually initiated sex. A kiss, a hug and then this anticipatory hovering, waiting to see what her hands did next, where her mouth landed, what words leapt from her tongue. It was an established ritual.

They had, over the years, become adept at grabbing opportunities for intimacy when they arose. When both kids were at a sports match, when Hugo's mother took them for a movie and pizza on the odd Saturday night, if ever their schedules coincided and they found themselves both at home during a school day, if the kids were engrossed in an activity, or even if they simply found themselves in the bathroom with its functioning lock. In truth, the snatched liaisons were made more fun by their unpredictability. Sex had never been an issue for them.

Until now. Moving her head away from his, alarmed at how quickly the joviality had stalled, she twisted her body and grabbed the pillowslip, which was still warm from drying in the sun, folding it in half and half again, the edge tucked under her chin as she concentrated on anything other than the fact that he was still standing uncomfortably close to her.

His proximity, his expression, his almost imperceptible wrinkle of the nose . . .

She felt they were sliding towards if not a row, then certainly a frank discussion about what happened next. The truth was she didn't know the answer, didn't know how to rewind to that time when she wanted his skin next to hers, loved him to kiss her neck, tell her she was beautiful, their breathing in unison as a delightful crescendo built beneath the Egyptian cotton sheets which had been a wedding present. It was as heart-rending as it was uncomfortable that at the merest suggestion of intimacy, she wondered what rituals he and his lover had established. A wink, a nod, a text, a gesture? What were the stepping stones they trod before engaging in sex? The path they walked that led to the most intimate of connections? The fact that they would have danced towards the point of contact in this way was just as galling, if not more, than the act of sex itself. There was a particular closeness in the build-up, the anticipation, the planning, that was, for Harriet at least, harder to see past, to forgive. The physical act was one thing, but the thought of those snatched moments tortured her sleep and were far more damaging to her marriage. Far harder to ignore.

'I'd better get this put away!' She spoke with more enthusiasm than was necessary for the mundane task.

Pretending . . .

Harriet had just placed the linen in the old housekeeper's cupboard on the landing when she heard the front door close. With a need that she knew would have impressed her sister, she made her way down the stairs and pulled her diary from the shelf on the dresser, before settling into the old leather chair where she liked to write.

> *Hello – never know how to start writing or what to say or whether I need to have a particular format, still feels a bit, awkward . . . but what I do know is that Hugo has gone to pick up a few bits and pieces from town and*

I'm taking the chance to put pen to paper. Ellis was right, this is cathartic, helps me order my thoughts, work things through and, ye gods, is there a lot to work through . . .

It still feels like we are both tiptoeing around all that needs to be said. I have so many questions! Truth is, most of them I'm afraid to ask. I don't want the detail and yet I do. Am I nuts?

I want to know what he's thinking. I want to know if he's happy now, or does he miss her?

She paused from writing; did he miss her? The thought alone enough to make her body shudder involuntarily. A memory came to her now: Wendy at their Christmas party. Her long, dark hair was bouncy, shiny and it made Harriet think she should probably get her own ratty tails trimmed.

'You look absolutely gorgeous!'

That's what she'd said to the woman who stood in her kitchen, leaning on the island she and Hugo had chosen together, the place where Harriet had cooked a thousand suppers for her family. The woman had a glass of champagne in her hand, *absolutely gorgeous . . .* Harriet had meant it, noting the sparkle in her eye, the weight she'd lost, her neutral manicure, nice make-up; the kind of look that was expensive and well applied, fancy autumnal shades daubed to highlight her eyes, her cheekbones and accentuate her mouth. And all the while, there was an undercurrent to her behaviour that was almost impossible to identify. She carried the magical glittery aura of someone high on life, someone who had a secret.

The secret was that when Harriet was away from home, Hugo took her to their bed. The secret was that Hugo met her in country hotels when he was supposed to be at a conference. The secret was that Wendy Peterson held scissors in her manicured hands and she used them to cut up the life Harriet knew. The life her kids knew. The life they, as a family, had built.

'You look gorgeous!'

That's what she'd said and Wendy's reply?

'Thank you, doll, I feel gorgeous!'

There were two things about the exchange that replayed in Harriet's head and bothered her still. One: how Harriet had complimented her husband's mistress, was outdone by her, as she shone brighter than his dull, exhausted wife who hadn't had time to change her blouse or shower and had settled for a quick spritz under the arm with deodorant and a liberal squirt of perfume. And the second, that Wendy called her 'doll'. *Doll!* Something to be played with. Not for the first time she felt the punch of deceit in her gut and it lit the flame of fury. She was hurt by Hugo, of course, but also found the actions of Wendy Peterson unfathomable, knowing that no matter how strong the temptation, she could never do similar to another woman. She gripped her pen.

> *I want to ask him if he misses her and yet am fearful of his reply. He can't win, really. If he says he doesn't miss her then I will doubt his answer, and this will stab at my heart and I'll stew over it that's for sure. But if he tells me he does miss her, then what do I do with that information? That'd be it, wouldn't it? I mean how would we recover from an admission like that? I'd forever feel like his jailer, keeping him here away from Miss Luscious Locks against his will.*
>
> *I'm thoughtful for much of the day, quiet even. I'm ashamed to say I feel joy when Hugo is distressed. It feels*

like penance and in that moment when he is crying and I'm not, it gives me the strongest hope that we might come out the other side, because that's what we both want. That is, after all, the sole purpose of uprooting our lives and coming here. Ordinarily it's at the end of the day when red wine seeps in his veins and his guard is down that his smile slips, and with his hair mussed, shirt open, his tears flow freely and he begs for forgiveness . . . Yes, that's when I feel the prickle of happiness on my skin. His remorse is raw and so simply expressed it reminds me that we have something worth fighting for and that I have something worth staying for. It's a power shift. In that moment I don't feel like the wronged wife, I feel like the one who holds the sceptre while he sobs and asks me to let him stay.

There are also these minutes in the cold light of day when I get to reflect on how I've moved away from the house and village I loved. Given up the job I liked very much, the job where I was held in high regard, hopeful of advancing my career, said goodbye to those neighbours who had smudged the line and become friends – and all through no fault of my own I find myself here. It feels a bit like punishment.

She drew lines through her words with vigour.

No, that's not fair. It's a beautiful place and I wasn't frogmarched here. How to phrase it? It feels like hiding. Yes, that's it, and it doesn't feel good. As if I am tarnished with the guilt that covers him. And her. I don't deserve it. I don't deserve any of it!

I think about her, of course, and I wonder if she feels relief at my leaving, no longer worried about bumping into me in the post office or standing next to me in the pub. And I don't like the idea of having given her such a gift. Or maybe she feels only sadness at the loss of him. I wonder if she is sitting somewhere right now, thinking about what she's done, the part she played in creating the tornado in which we now spin. Her actions that have left the thick rind of scar across what I thought was a happy marriage. At least it was for me.

For my husband, I'm guessing not so much, otherwise he wouldn't have reached out to her, taken her hand, and embarked on an affair that has cost me so much.

My insides feel hollow, scooped out. I'm in freefall. I'm trembling head to toe, inside and out. I want it to stop. I want to rewind the clock. It's my dream to recapture the solidity of that old life. To know beyond a doubt that I can trust him. Is it even possible?

This is a new beginning in this new place.

The house is solid, a three-storey, higgledy-piggledy cottage, with an open-plan sitting/dining room, square kitchen, sash windows, pretty carved portico above the front door and all the window frames painted white, making them stand out against the pale external walls. A solid house . . . and yet I feel that as a person, and we as a family, are on very shaky ground.

She hadn't heard the front door and was a little startled to look up and see Hugo standing in the doorway.

'That was quick!' There it was again, that sing-song voice of pretence.

'I only got halfway.' His expression was pensive as he walked forward and took a seat on the wide William Morris covered footstool that had lived at the foot of their bed in their former home.

'What's the matter?' She folded the book down into the seat cushion and sat forward.

'I just wanted to say . . .' He paused.

'What, Hugo?' Her heart fluttered at the thought that he had read her mind, or worse, her diary.

'You can ask me anything, you know. The idea makes me uncomfortable but I'm aware I have created this God-awful mess and I will do whatever I can to help put it right.' He spoke softly, earnestly, as he put the empty shopping basket on the floor. 'That was it, just wanted to say that you can ask me anything and I will answer truthfully. Do you think that might help?'

'It . . . it might,' she whispered.

Since the day he had confirmed her suspicions, breaking down in tears, curling into a ball on the floor and begging her to forgive him, her whole existence could be likened to feeling her way in the dark. It was, in her view, a miracle she had not plummeted off the edge of a ravine. She had told him sternly to get up off the floor; she didn't have the time or patience for his self-indulgence, as if it were he who had been so wronged. And he'd stood, dusted off his trousers and sat quietly on the sofa, like a child awaiting instruction. It had nearly killed her, the terrible conflict of missing and loving the man she had thought Hugo was, her forever . . . The pain raw and all-consuming, seeing him in this new light, unmasked, revealed, while trying so hard to reconcile with him, to plot a future, and all the while pretending everything was going to be okay for her little family.

'We won't tell the kids, no point.' She'd spoken while looking out over the garden.

'I agree.' There was no mistaking the relief in his words. She decided against pressing the point that this was a decision made to shield them, not protect him.

'And our decision to move is the right one, isn't it?' She'd turned to face him then. 'To go somewhere I'm not going to be sitting next to her in a traffic queue or bumping into her at the school gates. The thought of seeing her . . .' She shook her head, knowing it required no further explanation. 'That's the plan, isn't it, Hugo? It'll make things easier, won't it? If we go somewhere I'm not going to have to smile and make small talk with the woman you have been shagging?'

As if on cue, he'd cried again.

And now he was offering her the chance to ask more questions. It was a prospect as exciting as it was terrifying, but an opportunity nonetheless and one she would not let slip through her fingers.

CHAPTER FIVE

Tawrie Gunn

August 2024

Tawrie had found it hard to sleep. And not for the usual reasons of sleeping with one ear cocked, waiting for the reassuring sound of her mum safely home. Or listening out for the tell-tale creak of the stairs that meant her nan couldn't settle and was on the move, no doubt heading to the kitchen in search of biscuits and a cup of tea. This she had done routinely since the day her son had failed to come home.

Last night was different. Tawrie hadn't been able to sleep because the image of a floppy-haired man in a pink shirt had filled her thoughts. How could she explain it? Not that she'd ever try, knowing if she heard the same from anyone else she'd think they'd lost all reason. And in a way, she had.

It was early, earlier than usual – a full fifteen minutes before her alarm – and yet she was wide awake. With her bag packed ready for her swim, she trod the stairs and paused before she left, stopping at the sofa that faced the television to kiss her nan on the back of her head. The old woman reached up and patted her hand.

'Off on your swim, love?' The old woman's voice carried the croak of one who had been silent for many hours.

'Yep.' Tawrie spoke softly, as she pulled the blanket up over Freda's shoulders and left her to doze. The shopping channel was on with the sound muted. A girl with bouncy blonde hair was holding up a curling wand, eyes wide, like it was a gold bar she'd found, running her fingers over it as if it were a very precious thing.

As with any chore when her mood was joyous, her bike felt light as she lifted it down the steps and clambered on. Her trusty duffel bag she slung across her body. The town had a life of its own at this time of the morning: fishermen and day-boat skippers alike trundled towards the harbour with bags, boots and packed lunches in their hands. Council gardeners drove slowly in their vans, stopping at the various hanging baskets, tubs of flowers and planted verges to water the blooms and ensure another bright and beautiful day for all who intended to spend time in the seaside town. It felt like a privilege to be in the streets as they came alive, to see traders unlock doors, turn signs from 'closed' to 'open', and shake off the previous day's fatigue, preparing to do it all again.

Her ride was easy, not a bump in the road or slow-moving tractor hampered her journey to Hele Bay Beach. She arrived just as the sun broke free of the horizon. It seemed particularly beautiful today. Her spirit was light, her hopes high and her routine now slick. She had a spot to leave her belongings and a preferred path down to the water's edge; both made for a speedy entry into the green-blue sea. Quickly she stowed her bike on its side, impatiently yanked off her trackie bottoms and dry robe and slipped into her half wetsuit, perfect for the warmer water at this time of year.

Raising her hand in a wave, she greeted two-thirds of the Peacock Swimmers, who were already in the sea. Jago and Maudie pulled through the water like a couple of selkies with their pink inflatable floats tied to their backs. She liked to tease Jago about his pace, pointing out how she could go twice as fast when they swam alongside each other. He liked to remind her that at eighty-six, that was his prerogative. There was something comforting about the sight of them each morning, nice to know they were expecting her, looking out for her, this couple who had welcomed her into their routine, and into their lives, with open arms.

With her clothes and bag in a neat bundle, dry robe ready to put on the moment she needed it, and positioned just so, she almost ran to the shoreline. Gone was the hesitation of those early days, as she waded purposefully into the foam-edged waves, and breathed deeply as her shoulders dipped beneath the surface. It would have been a hard thing to fully explain, but that first second of immersion was like a note of heavenly music, a beam of perfect light, a singular feeling of contentment, leaving her feeling happy, clean, clear and energised for whatever the day might hold!

For those unfamiliar with the bay, it might have seemed daunting, compared to the neat, tight boundaries of a public swimming pool or lido, which not only hemmed you in, but kept you from venturing beyond its tiled walls. But so accustomed was she to the placement of the rocks, the cut of the cliffs, the slope of the sand and the dips and troughs of the seabed that it fuelled her confidence. The idea that she could, in theory, swim and swim until she hit land, was exhilarating. Or even better, the thought of swimming and swimming, and changing course until she hit Lundy . . . now that really would be something. If only she weren't so fearful of making the trip.

She chose a familiar route and pulled her arms through the water, always starting with the breaststroke while she let her body acclimatise before switching to front crawl.

'Here I am and what a morning it is! What to tell you, how to tell you!' She smiled, softly whispering the words to her dad that felt too personal to voice out loud. 'It's a weird thing that even I'm finding hard to fully fathom. It feels like a big thing but is actually nothing. And so if it's nothing, how come it feels so strongly like something? I'm waffling, I know. So here it is: yesterday, I saw a man. That's it! I wish I had more! No interaction, no conversation, just plenty of attraction – from my perspective anyway. I don't even know if he saw me. There was something about him . . . I can't shake the image of him in my head. He's stuck there, not that I'm complaining. So that's it! As I said, a big something that's actually nothing, but everything has to start somewhere, right?'

Moving now with purpose, her breathing and movement were in sync as the sounds of the ocean calmed her and she crawled against the motion of the tide. Having swum for no more than twenty minutes, slowing as her session came to an end, taking her time to tread water, to lie on her back and stare up at the big sky, she bobbed on the salty waves and let the sun glance her face with its morning kiss. With her mood buoyant and excitement fizzing in her stomach, she enjoyed the feeling of strength from another swim completed as she made her way to the shallows.

'Oh, I see, another half session for our youngest peacock!' Maudie yelled.

'Some of us have to get to work!' She laughed her reply.

'My heart breaks for you.' Maudie flipped on to her back. 'I don't miss it, living to the beat of the ticking clock. I can highly recommend retirement.'

'Doubt I'll ever retire, not with the state of my finances.' Her humour cloaked this dire truth and not for the first time she pictured herself on a ward, in a uniform, just as she had when she was young, and had felt like anything was possible. If life had taught her one thing, it was that it never turned out quite how you might think. She could never have foreseen, at that young age, events so catastrophic that she would find herself acting as human glue to keep the Gunn family from falling apart. She wondered what plans her dad might have had.

'She's fibbing, Tawrie, just ignore her,' Jago piped up. 'She'd go back to her job in a second! Wouldn't you, love?'

'Maybe.' Maudie stared up towards the sky as if in thought and Tawrie wondered if 'maybe' meant she might like to return to those younger days if not the job itself. She knew she'd worked as an administrator for a family optician for decades.

'We'll be out in a bit.' Jago surged forward and continued with his swim, leaving his wife to bob like a seal on a rock as the day grew livelier around them.

Tawrie left the water and trod the slight incline towards the spot where her bike and dry robe awaited. She unzipped her wetsuit and let the top half fall down to her hips, to reveal her swimsuit; she tousled her thick hair with her fingertips, rather liking the way the slightly damp ends curled up under their spritz of salt water. Tipping her head to the left and then right, she did her best to rid her ears of water. Facing the sea, she revelled in the feeling of achievement, enjoying the shiver on her skin as she looked at the vast body of water that from this point looked quite foreboding. She thought of the conversation she'd had with her nan when she first started, and it made her smile.

'*Where are you going to swim to, anyway?*'

'*Lundy. I'm going to go all the way out to Lundy.*'

That her nan hadn't questioned it was endearing, but it was typical; Freda adored her, never underestimated her and had always done her best to increase her granddaughter's self-belief. It also wasn't lost on Tawrie that she kept her close, as if believing she could prevent further heartache by keeping her within sight.

Ensconced now in her dry robe, she slipped her wetsuit out from beneath her and pulled down her costume, kicking it into the cosy nest on which she now stood, and with her knickers and sweatpants in her hand, she took another few seconds to stare at the ocean.

'I still wonder where you are . . .' she whispered, letting her words drift out across the big blue on the gentle breeze.

'Have you been in?'

She jumped. The voice was unexpected, loud, energised, excited, and took her entirely by surprise, but it wasn't even close to the shock she got when she turned her head and there he was. P-p-pink shirt man, standing near her bike and fixing her with a grin.

The words caught in her throat, as her brain scrabbled to find a response. Her face and chest flushed hot; she had, after all, been talking about him mere minutes ago. The possibility of him over-hearing was non-existent, but no less mortifying in the imagining. He was wearing a t-shirt, shorts and flip-flops and his hair stood up as if he'd gone out without washing it or looking in a mirror. Not that she cared. To be this close to him, to see him again, to have the opportunity to stand face to face with the man who had kept her from sleep; it felt like fate, it felt like an opportunity, it felt bloody marvellous!

Tawrie had never been vain, but in that second she was aware that her hair was a mess, she was doused in salt water and swamped in a dry robe that could do with a wash. She wished her cossie and wetsuit weren't bunched beneath her wrinkled feet and that she wasn't holding her knickers and sweatpants in her hand.

'Been in, yes, yes I've been in,' she babbled, pointing at the sea, wishing she were calmer, and that she had her underwear on.

'Is it cold?'

'Everyone asks me that.' She took in his freckled skin, his clear eyes.

'Of course they do! Because no one other than a fruit loop would consider jumping into the Bristol Channel, it looks bloody freezing!'

She liked his voice. His accent neutral, his tone pleasant, the pace not too fast or too slow, not boorish or sarcastic. He sounded as nice as he looked.

'Well, I guess I'm a fruit loop because I do it every day from March to September.'

He lifted his arms above his head and exhaled slowly, resting them flat-palmed on the top of his head. Her eyes were drawn to the gap where his t-shirt lifted and she saw the slight roll of a tum over the waistband of his shorts, the dark hair sprouting, his sun-kissed skin. She found it hard to explain her desire to touch him. She gripped her clothes bundle – something, anything to occupy her twitchy, nervous hands.

'You do it every day without fail? You're not being serious? You don't mean like when it's raining too?'

'I do mean every day. I am being serious and yes, in the rain too.' She was, in that moment, proud of her efforts, glad to have this one thing that set her apart, and even happier to be sharing it with him.

'You're right, you are a fruit loop.' He hugged himself and laughed. 'I'm joking! It's awesome!'

'Is it? Why?' Delight flooded her being at the prospect of him finding her or any aspect of her 'awesome'.

'Because how many people can say they do that? Not many, I bet. I mean, I know people who take a dip in the local pool or jump into lakes when they get the chance and, of course, a swim on holiday, but to come here every day and get in the sea . . . that's awesome!'

His words felt like praise, like approval, and she felt her heart race, struck by how easily they chattered and how delighted she was by his presence.

'I suppose.' She stood up straight and sucked in her tummy.

'So I guess the question is, why do you do it?' He sure was full of questions and she was flattered by his interest.

'Why?' she stalled.

'Yes, why do you get out of, what I am assuming is a warm bed, and put yourself through it?'

'Erm, it makes me feel good, it makes me feel . . . better.' She wasn't about to give him every detail, not when he felt she was already, apparently, in fruit loop territory.

'Brilliant.'

'What is?' She looked up at him, this time a chance to study the shape of his jaw, his neat top teeth, uneven bottom row, his Adam's apple. Her eyes settled on his hand. No wedding ring. Not that everyone wore one, of course, and she knew you didn't have to have taken vows to be in a committed relationship.

'The fact you've found something that makes you feel good, feel better. That's the key, isn't it? Discovering the things that get you through the day and going for it!'

'I guess so.'

'And you swim alone? You don't *drag* your partner down here on dark, rainy mornings?'

'No partner to drag . . .' Was he fishing? She felt her stomach jump with excitement at the possibility, and wished Connie were here to ask – she was so good at decoding flirt-speak and picking up on those subtle signals that might mean attraction. Actually, that was a bad idea. One look at Connie with her fabulous boobs, big mouth, doe eyes and tiny waist and Tawrie's own broad, barrel-hefting shoulders and robust, log-shifting legs could only fare unfavourably in comparison. She'd do her best to keep him away from Connie for a while. This she thought only half in jest.

'But I don't swim alone, that's a big rule of wild swimming: safety first, obviously. We're in a club, the Peacock Swimmers.'

'Oh right.' He looked around. 'Where's the rest of the ostentation?'

'The what?'

He laughed again, but in a manner that was friendly and not mocking. 'That's what you call a group of peacocks – an ostentation. Isn't it great?' Enthusiasm spilled from him. 'Those glorious feathers, the display, the theatre, is there anything more ostentatious?'

'Not that I can think of. You're right, it's great!' And it was. 'There are only three of us, actually, and the other two are still swimming.' She pointed to the dark, bobbing heads of Maudie and Jago, trailing their inflatable, pink floats.

'Ah yes, I see them.'

'But even though we're a little gang, I like to swim alone, secure that they're close by, but it's all about the solitude. Time to think, getting lost in the moment.'

'I see. And here I am spoiling your morning, interrupting your thing!' He slapped his forehead. 'I should go, let you stay in the moment or whatever.' He rolled his hand.

'No!' She spoke with a little more force than she'd intended, not wanting to sound super-keen while feeling super-super-keen. 'I mean, you're not spoiling my morning, interrupting my thing, not at all.'

'I'm Edgar. Ed.' He touched his fingers to his chest as if English might not be her first language. It made her want to laugh. In fact she wanted to laugh anyway, she felt a little giddy.

'I'm Tawrie, Taw.'

'Tory? As in Thatcher? Old Etonians and privilege?'

Resisting the temptation to scoff, and not for the first time, she explained, 'No, Tawrie as in the river Taw, T-A-W. The river.'

'I've never heard it as a name. It's . . . different! And different is good. There were three Rebeccas in my class at school.'

'There were three Tawries in mine.'

'Were there?'

'No.' She smiled, happy that he'd taken the bait. 'Actually, my dad chose it. Could be worse, we might have lived by the Mississippi and then everyone would sing at me wouldn't they. "*Mrs M, Mrs I, Mrs SSI Mrs SSI Mrs PPI!*"' Edgar stared at her and she felt her face colour. 'Did you not learn that rhyme at school?'

'No.' He shook his head. 'We did maths and English, art, that kind of thing. No river poem songs.'

He was funny too. *He was funny!*

'Where are you staying?' It was her turn for questions.

'Fore Street.'

'Oh okay, well we're neighbours. How long are you staying?' *Forever? Say forever!*

'Not sure.' He shrugged and she caught the double blink that gave away more than his vague response, wondering what was behind it. Was he nervous, hiding away? She understood the desire to do both.

'Well, I have to get to work.' She hated the thought and could have quite happily stayed there all day, getting to know ~~pink shirt man~~, Edgar. *Ed.*

'Where do you work?'

'The Café on the Corner, it's my cousin's place.'

'Maybe I'll pop in?'

'Sure, it's by the quay, on the, erm, on the corner.'

'I guess the clue is in the name.' He stared at her.

'Yep.' She swallowed, nerves filled her up and it took all of her energy not to give him her number, arrange a time and place to meet, pin down the detail. Luckily this was Ilfracombe and it was pretty hard not to bump into people.

'Taw . . . Tawrie.' He spoke her name and seemed hesitant, shy even. She felt her gut bunch with desire, the sound of her name on his lips was something quite fabulous. 'Tawrie,' he began again and she stared at the man who displayed similar nerves. Could it be that he was feeling the same?

'Yes, Ed?' She took a step towards him and looked up at his face, speaking his name as deliberately as he had hers.

'I-I'm not sure how to say this.' He licked his dry lips and her heart jumped.

'Just say it!' She giggled like the swishy-haired girls who had always felt alien to her, like the blonde who had held a curling wand as if it were gold.

'Tawrie . . .' He took a breath.

'Yes, Ed?'

'You've dropped your knickers.' He pointed at the grey blob that sat by her foot and as she stooped to gather them into her hand, she made a wish that when she righted herself he had disappeared, but no, there he was and he was laughing.

'You've been a right dizzy tits this morning, what's the matter with you?' Connie as ever cut to the chase as Tawrie concentrated on using a fresh cloth to wipe the drips from the bottles of ketchup that got sticky after a day on the job.

'Don't know what you mean.' She felt the twitch of a smile around her mouth.

'You're being odd. Smiling and humming as if you're actually enjoying yourself! And let's be honest, most of the time you look . . .'

'I look what?' She laughed despite the accusation that she knew was coming.

'Not so smiley.' Connie opted for tact. 'And when Gordy and Nora came in with Amber the dog and asked for bacon sandwiches with brown sauce, followed by carrot cake with the usual two forks, you took them a couple of flapjacks and waltzed off as if nothing was amiss! Gaynor had to whip the plates off the table and get the order right. Luckily Nora doesn't mind much, being the girl's girl that she is, but Gordy looked like he'd dropped a quid and found a feather!'

'I didn't realise!' She giggled.

'That's exactly my point!' Connie stared at her, her face screwed up. 'Oh my God!' Her cousin put down the loaf she was wrapping in clingfilm. 'You *like* someone!'

'What?' She felt a flutter of panic at her accurate summation.

'You heard me.' Connie continued to study her. 'You've got that look, as if you're daydreaming about something, or more specifically someone.'

'Ah, is it the same look Needle has when he asks you to go out on his boat?' Deflection was, she figured, her best form of defence. How could she begin to explain the ridiculous, fanciful and unfounded feelings she had for a man she'd only seen twice? She was not that person!

'Oh my God!' Connie repeated as she stepped out from behind the grill and called out, 'Gay, can you keep an eye for a minute, Tawrie and I are just going to the benches.'

'Sure, love!' Gaynor gathered up the dirty cups that littered a tabletop and in this moment of quiet, Tawrie let her cousin grab her by the arm and drag her out to the seats by the quayside.

'Sit!' Connie pointed and she did as instructed. Her cousin sat by her side. 'From the top. Go! And I want it all, every detail, every second, all of it.'

'You're so bossy! Always have been.'

'Stop stalling, come on, spill!' Connie clicked her fingers.

The truth was she kind of welcomed the chance to talk about him, wanting her cousin's feedback or at least validation of the complex feelings that filled her up.

'It's weird, Con, I only saw him for the first time yesterday.'

'Where?'

'Right here, actually.' She jerked her head to the cobbles behind them.

'Who is he?'

'His name's Edgar, Ed.'

'Wanker name.' Connie pulled a face.

'I don't think so, I think it's lovely.' She smiled at the thought of their chat at Hele Bay Beach earlier.

'*Lovely?* Who are you?'

'I know!' She closed her eyes briefly, acknowledging that this dizziness was most out of character. 'And then I saw him again this morning; he was on the beach when I came back from my swim.'

'A stalker?' her cousin gasped, the glint in her eye suggesting this was just as juicy.

'No! Nothing like that. He was just out and about and we chatted . . .'

'Okay, well I'm going to have to stop you right there. You know the rules: no tourists, no holidaymakers, no day trippers, they're never worth it. Never! Nine times out of ten they're tethered to a missus back home and are looking for either a shag or a free stay for their next holiday. Sometimes both. And if you let yourself get involved, it's only you that's going to get hurt.'

'Do you think I just arrived here yesterday? I know all that, of course I do, but have you ever seen someone and it's like *bam*!' She punched her palm. 'You just . . . I don't know, like . . .'

'No, Taw. I never have.'

'Not even with Gary?'

Connie shook her head and looked out over the water, clearly thinking about the man she'd been at school with, his family local like hers. They were married and divorced within ten years of leaving school. And shared the care of their eight-year-old boy Sonny, whom they adored equally.

'Not really. I mean I loved him, still do in a way, probably always will, but what you're describing? Nope. For us there was no *bam*, more like we drifted into our relationship. There was no moment of impact, but then neither was there a sharp fall when it ended. It was tame, easy, nice, just not enough. Not enough for either of us. And I'm happy he's with Lena, she's good for him and is great with Sonny.'

There was a beat of silence while this settled.

'It can't be real, though, can it, Con, this crazy storm that's raging inside me? It has to just be a silly thing that will come to nothing. I'll get to know him, find out he's a psycho or a moron or boring and that'll be that, right?'

'Yes, probably.'

'Thank you for helping set my expectations.' She nudged her cousin.

'You did ask! And for the record, I'd like nothing more than for you to find someone who makes you feel this way. I want it all for you, Taw: the bells, the whistles, all of it.'

Tawrie felt a surge of emotion in her throat, thinking two things: first, how comforting to hear this was how her cousin felt; and second, if and when she did find someone, how sad it was that her dad wouldn't be here to witness it.

'But a tourist whose life is elsewhere? That's also not enough, not for you. I mean, I'm not saying don't have fun – do! Have lots of it! But don't let him in.' Connie placed her hand over her heart. 'Don't let him get to your heart.'

'I won't.' She hoped it was a promise she could keep as she tried to ignore the flame of joy that roared in her chest whenever she thought of him.

A car beeped its low, loud horn behind them and they both jumped. She turned to see her Uncle Sten pull up in his shiny double cab pick-up with the windows rolled down.

''Ark at you two lazy wenches! Sunbathing instead of runnin' that café! Place could go up in smoke, but as you two've got a decent suntan, s'pose that's all that matters!'

'Give it a rest, Dad, we've only been out here five minutes!' Connie yelled their defence.

'That's what I always say when I get caught napping on the job!' He laughed. 'Anyways, I've just seen Needle, he says do you want to—'

'No, I bloody don't!' Connie shot him down. Sten laughed heartily.

As they stood, Connie took her arm and held her eyeline. 'I want you to have a great summer, Taw, but be warned, if any wanker-named blow-in causes you a moment of grief, I'll bash his face in, got it?'

'Got it.' She laughed, peering along the quayside in case Edgar should pop up. 'But I don't think I need to be worried; he seems . . .'

'Oh Taw, give it a rest, they all seem . . . until they're not!'

'I dropped my knickers.' She stared into the middle distance as she recounted the event.

'Jesus, love! Fast work! I don't know whether to be horrified or impressed!' Connie's mouth was open.

'No, not like that! I mean literally, they fell out of my hand and he just . . . he made it okay.'

'Oh my God! Are *you* the stalker?' Connie gasped.

Tawrie fell into her as they laughed. It was a moment of welcome silliness as they made their way back to the café while her Uncle Sten checked his teeth in the rear-view mirror of his cab, no doubt wanting to look his best for Gaynor. His *friend*.

CHAPTER SIX

Harriet Stratton

July 2002

Harriet did her best to control her anxiety as she made a pot of tea, letting the bags steep in the hot water, stirring gently and slowly inside her dotty Emma Bridgewater teapot until she was satisfied by the colour. Her pace was deliberate, not only putting off the conversation that awaited, but also a task she took pleasure in, a ritual that she hoped might abate the flurry of nerves in her gut. Next, she poured the tea into two generous mugs and handed one to Hugo, who had taken a seat at the scrubbed farmhouse kitchen table.

'Thanks. I feel' – he drew breath – 'a bit nervous.' His tone confirming this feeling was as alien to him as it was for her.

'Me too.'

They both gave an awkward laugh as she sat opposite. The tea was too hot but she sipped anyway, grateful for the prop.

'It's not often I wish the kids would run in and disturb our peace, but I do right now.'

She liked his honesty. Liked, too, the reminder of their normal lives and their two beautiful kids. He tapped his fingers on the wood and she felt his knee jumping under the table as his foot danced.

'I don't really know where to start.' She took the lead. 'But I do have questions that are whizzing around my head, things I've avoided asking, partly, I think, because I don't *want* to hear the answers, yet I know I won't settle until I do, if that makes any sense. And partly because I figured that the less I knew, the vaguer things were, the less I'd have to visualise the reality, and it might help us move forward.'

'Trouble is we're not really moving forward, are we?'

Harriet shook her head. Equally fearful and excited at the prospect of their discussion.

'And I want us to move forward, H, more than I can say.'

'Me too.' She coughed to clear her throat. 'I guess one thing that bothers me, that I'm curious about is . . .' It felt weird asking this of the man she loved, her husband. '. . . do you . . . do you love her or did . . . did you love her?' And just like that they were off. She only realised she was shaking when she raised the mug to her mouth and saw the tremor on the meniscus of her tea.

Hugo shook his head, his tone definitive. 'No. I don't and I never did. Not that.'

Her relief was a physical thing as her back muscles softened.

'Did she love you?' This she wanted to know as it would help shape the way she looked at her husband. Was their affair on an equal footing? Did he string her along?

'We didn't have that exact conversation, but I think she was certainly heading that way, but I made it clear that it wasn't a road, erm . . .' He swallowed. 'I made it clear I was fond of her but nothing more and so I think she held back in being open about it.'

Fond . . . such a shitty word. Inadequate at best and in this context quite condescending.

'I love you, Harriet. I love you, always you. Only you. I love you so much this is killing me!'

She chose to ignore the words, which in the face of his actions felt a little thin.

'Did you have sex in our bed?'

Hugo nodded. 'Yes.'

His response a needle of distress that lanced all progress.

'How many times?' She pushed her teeth together, tensing her jaw, liking the distraction of the discomfort.

'Three times.' His reply sticky from a dry mouth.

'Shit!' She closed her eyes and pictured the nights she must have climbed between the sheets when only hours before . . . her whole body shuddered. She controlled her desire to pull a face, to exclaim her revulsion. She was happy they'd left the bed in the old house, but not happy that there must have been at least one hundred nights she'd slept in it unaware of what that creaky old walnut base had withstood. The false promises and whispers that had floated into the headboard, padded and covered in her beloved, carefully chosen Osborne and Little fabric. The bed where she had given birth to both of their children, in which she would never spend another night.

'Did you . . .' He took his time. 'Did you never have an inkling, nothing?'

'Nope.' She stared at him. 'Not really. I mean not until the day I found out. Does that make me stupid?'

'No, no. It makes you trusting. It makes you, you.' His eyes were wide in the way they were when he complimented her or told her he loved her. She looked away. The news that he had slept with his mistress in their marital bed still hadn't fully landed.

'I guess that's the thing when you believe what someone is telling you; you *believe* what someone is telling you! And that's that. For me there's no degrees of trust, there's only trust or no trust. I've never questioned it. Never. It was you, Hugo, my *husband*, and so I never knew I had to question anything. That level of mistrust, marriages with a shaky foundation, that was for other people. That's what I thought.' She felt her throat tighten at this truth; the facts still carried the power to shock her even though she knew them to be true. And even after all these weeks, it didn't hurt any less. 'Do we have enough cereal? *Yes.* Shall we go visit your mother on Sunday? *No.* Does this dress make my bum look big? *No.* Do you promise to love, honour and cherish this woman for the rest of her life? *I do.* That kind of thing.'

Hugo sipped his tea. She noted the beads of sweat peppering his top lip and understood that he now used the mug as a prop too. His silence another opportunity for her to expel all that rattled in her brain.

'When we first met, Hugo, you told me that nothing less than forever would do for you. You said that you hated the fact that we'd met when we were in our twenties and that there had been two whole decades with us both on the planet, unaware of the other. You said it was a waste. And I believed you. I thought nothing less than forever would do, too. I never doubted it. Never looked at another man. I was always off the market. Yours.' It was painful to recall and yet necessary; she wanted him to acknowledge the phrases that raced around her head in the early hours.

'I love you. I do, I love you. I love you so much!' He kept his voice low as if still wary of this phrase, once a cure-all for each minor upset, but understanding the inadequacy of it now.

'And I love you.' Her sigh was almost involuntary. 'I guess that's the problem. If I didn't care it'd be easier . . .'

'Not for me.' He spoke firmly.

There was a beat of silence as her mind played tricks on her, allowing her to feel joy at his lamentation of love so sincerely spoken, before she mentally pulled up; it wasn't enough to restore harmony, not any more.

'I've loved you from that first date.' She still pictured the night fondly, one of the best of her life, as if she knew that it was important, more than just a fling, a snog. He'd made her feel special, and she had wanted more and more of that feeling, more and more of him. 'That night at uni when you turned up with a bottle of rum and you'd put eyeliner on.'

'Guyliner.' He corrected and smiled, but not even his quip could cut the tension.

'And it was like every milestone we reached – sleeping together, meeting parents, our first holiday, getting engaged, marrying, buying the house, the kids – every single thing felt like a tightening of our commitment, stronger glue, locking us in. I had no doubt. Have never had any doubt, didn't question whether we were right for each other or whether there might be someone more suitable. It was a fait accompli. I fell for you. I committed to you and that was that. And crazy as it sounds, I'm still in shock. I don't think I'll ever be able to fully accept the choices you made.' *Or how you hoodwinked me.* This she kept to herself.

'It's not crazy,' he whispered, shaking his head. 'I'd feel the same. I can't imagine it. I don't know how I'd survive if it was you who'd strayed.'

She supposed there was a compliment buried in his trite phrasing.

'I'm glad you can't, Hugo, because it's utter shit. The worst.' Her hands flew to her throat and she rubbed where the hurt gathered in lieu of tears. She swallowed. 'I still wake each morning and there is this split second where I don't remember what's happened and I feel how I used to feel: excited to face the day, happy. Then I open my eyes, look up at the strange ceiling in the room that's now ours and I feel—'

He cut her short. 'I'm sorry, H. I'm so, so sorry. And if I could turn back time . . .'

'Oh yes, the old time-travelling wish. Wouldn't that be something?' Her sarcastic tone leaked from her. 'I used to wish we could go back too, but then sometimes I wonder if it's maybe better that I know the real you. Good that I've had the scales removed from my eyes.' She wanted to wound him a little, wanted him to feel how she felt every waking second, stumbling in disbelief and distress, doing her best to get through the day.

'You do know the real me! You do! We've been together since we were twenty!' he pressed.

'You're right, Hugo, I do know the real you – *now*.' She couldn't help it, knowing these verbal daggers came from a place of hurt. He sat back and let them pierce his skin. 'I don't see how we stop the kids finding out.' This was one of her fears: how to manage the fallout and protect their children. Their son and younger daughter, just the thought of their distress, brought to their door by the very people who were supposed to make things better, the people they trusted to keep the ship afloat caused her stomach to roll with nerves. She would do all she could to keep it from them, but she hoped that if they did ever find out, enough time would have passed so she and Hugo would be in a better position, unified, stable, and able to keep them all steady.

Hugo buried his face in his hands.

'I can't stand the thought of it.' He rubbed his face and shifted in his seat. 'I worry about the rumour mill, you know how people love to talk, and so I guess that if there came a time when we couldn't keep the information from them, we'd need to concentrate on keeping the worry from them; show a united front. And no matter what they hear or when they hear it, we answer their questions fully and we don't give them any reason to fret, because all they would worry about is that we are okay as a couple, that we are solid, as a family. Right?'

It was Harriet's turn to nod and sip her tea. She prayed silently that it wouldn't come to that.

'Can I ask *you* something now?' He spoke slowly, sitting up straight in the spindle-backed chair.

'Sure.' She put down her mug.

'Are you ever going to be able to get over this enough so it doesn't sit between us like a spikey thing that we have to navigate? And I don't mean to sound flippant, I genuinely want to know.' He licked his lower lip. 'I wonder if you are ever going to get over it enough so that we can have sex again?'

The wry laugh that escaped her mouth was born of nerves. 'Is that your biggest concern? When you can get your leg over again?' It was coarse and she knew it but couldn't care less. A low blow.

'No!' His whole demeanour slumped as he pushed his fingers into his hair, looking close to tears. 'No, it's not that. I ask because physical intimacy for us was always a marker. If we were having a great time, when we were laughing, the kids were happy, sex was a priority, just another lovely aspect to our lives. But when we've been stressed or tired, whatever, there's been a bit of a drought and so I guess what I'm asking is, will you ever forgive me, Harriet? Do you think we will ever get back to a point close to where we were before?'

She took her time in forming a response, his words a reminder of how their marriage lay in fragments all around them, shattered. It filled her with a sadness tinged with anger. Why had he done this to them, to her? What an idiot! Maisie's words of support came to her now. Her niece was right, he was a bloody idiot.

'I-I know I miss you. I know I miss us.' This was her truth.

In that moment she could only hope it was enough.

'I miss us too, but that's why we're here, right?' He sounded desperate as his eyes misted. 'Starting over, a fresh beginning, new place, new house, new everything!'

Hugo's phone rang. Its ring was invasive. Her jaw tensed as he reached for it with a certain reluctance.

'Hey, buddy!' His face broke into a smile and he pinched the bridge of his nose. The sound of their son's voice floated from the mouthpiece. She could pick up the odd word, something about a bike chain and a can of oil on Aunty Ellis's garage floor.

Leaving them to their conversation, and with hurt and pain swirling inside her, she took the remainder of her tea and sought refuge in the warm embrace of the leather library chair.

Dear Diary . . .

Still don't know how I'm supposed to start?

Dear Me . . .

How about 'Dear Future Me' – as I hope to impart wisdom that might someday be good to read. Who am I kidding? Writing this is for me an exercise in mental water-treading, which I need right now, a moment of escape. Conversations with Hugo can feel like a weight that pushes me down, crushing me, and sometimes I need to wriggle free and write alone, quietly.

It's quite nice, retiring to the chair, flipping open this book with so many blank pages and filling them gradually with whatever is in my head. I doubt anyone will ever read this. And would I really want them to? Probably not. I shall decide what to do with it when it's full or finished or I get lazy or bored with the exercise, or maybe when I'm fixed, when we're fixed – how about that?

The idea that I won't want to write it any more because Hugo and I will be back to living in clover, holding hands over the duvet cover at night, eating bowls of garlicky pasta at the countertop and laughing at everything from the antics of the neighbours, something funny we've read, or something stupid his colleagues have done . . . waking each day with a smile at the thought that he's sleeping next to me . . . and just like that, the word 'neighbour' is enough to conjure a picture of her – the woman who had sex in the bed where I gave birth.

Three times.

I still think of her as Mrs Peterson, crazy, isn't it? I used to shout out, 'Morning, Mrs Peterson!' 'Happy Christmas, Mrs Peterson!' We were never friends. And all the while she slept with my husband. A fact that still feels like a lie no matter how often I think, say, or write it. I can't bring myself to call her Wendy in my mind. Wendy . . . I don't hate her. I hate what she did but I don't hate her. She's not married to me, he is.

Wendy and Hugo . . .

Hugo and Wendy . . .

Nope that is not a rabbit hole down which I am going to dive. It can only lead to no place good.

Urgh, not writing any more today, might even rip this page out.

It's horrible.

It's exhausting.

This was supposed to be my moment of peace. Ha! Fat chance. I'm now more tightly wound than I was before I started . . .

'Hey?' Hugo came towards her with the phone outstretched. Hurriedly she closed the book and reached out. 'It's Dilly.'

'Dilly Dally Donks!' She held the phone close, feeling her spirit soar knowing she was connected to her little girl.

Her daughter launched into a fast-paced diatribe. 'Mummy, Aunty Ellis bought us popcorn and Bear said we'd have it when we watched a movie tonight and I just found the packet in the sink, he ate it all!' she wailed.

'Okay, well, that was naughty, I'm sure Aunty Ellis will—'

'And I couldn't find Paw-Paw.' Dilly rarely went anywhere without her teddy bear. 'And Bear said I was a baby because I cried and then Aunty Ellis said he was a baby because he didn't know how to share popcorn and then he took my bike and—'

'Dilly.' Harriet cut her short. 'You're supposed to be having an adventure and you guys promised me that you'd try and get on while you're at Aunty Ellis's house.'

'I'm getting on with Bear, it's him that's not getting on with me!' she protested.

Harriet closed her eyes and took a deep breath. 'You're coming home soon. Only another week and you'll be home and I can't wait to see you, pumpkin. I've missed you both so much.' She cursed the crack to her voice. Hugo dropped down on to the footstool and rubbed her leg as she spoke. 'We both have,' she added. This was how it had to be, a united front for the kids.

'Home to Ledwick Green?'

To hear the excitement in her daughter's voice at the mention of their old house, which would never again be home, was jarring. Almost instinctively she brushed Hugo's hand from her leg.

'No, darling. To our new house. It's lovely. You have a beautiful bedroom waiting for you with all your toys and bits and pieces' – well, she would when she finally located them among the stacked boxes in the hallway – 'and you will be right across the hall from Bear and there's so much to do here!'

'Where is it again?'

It tore at Harriet's heart that her little girl couldn't remember the name of the place they were now going to call home.

'It's Ilfracombe. And there's a beach and a harbour and places to swim, and ice cream!'

'I miss you, Mummy.' Dilly's voice was small and Harriet's throat narrowed with distress for all the changes they were going through and with the desire to hold her baby girl.

'I miss you too.'

'Just one more week.' Her daughter, she could tell, was trying to sound brave and it tore at her heart.

'That's it my little love, just one more week.'

As the call ended, Hugo stared at her and once again put his hand on her shin.

'I wish things were easier, I wish things were different, but never doubt that I love you.'

She stared at her husband and smiled faintly, still wondering, despite his denial, if he'd ever said this to Mrs Peterson.

CHAPTER SEVEN

Tawrie Gunn

August 2024

The Ilfracombe weather was a great dictator of mood. There were bright days with a wide Devon-blue sky that could lift the lowest of thoughts. Days when the kiss of sunshine on winter skin gave Tawrie faith that all was going to be right with the world, that somehow she'd make it through. And sometimes the little town laboured under the bruise of a storm. This dark veil was, in its own way, equally stirring, as the flash of lightning bounced on the water, thunder cracked across the quay and rain lashed the paths and windows, forcing under-dressed tourists to put newspapers, bags or hands over their heads as they headed for cover. And then there were days like this – in between days when the world looked grey, dull and quieter than was comfortable. Days when the water was calm, gulls perched silently and the atmosphere was a little sluggish.

Tawrie would be lying if she didn't admit that she'd half expected Edgar to turn up at the café after their beach encounter, but he hadn't. Worse still was that Connie had looked up every time a man walked in as if she too was on tenterhooks. It made them both jumpy. It was now three days since Tawrie had seen him and she was riven with fear that he might have gone back to wherever he lived. The thought left her a little out of sorts. How on earth could she explain it? A man she'd seen twice and spoken to briefly only once – how could she possibly justify the amount of space he took up in her thoughts or the level of distress she felt at the prospect of never seeing him again?

And as if that wasn't bad enough, she knew nothing about him: not his surname, telephone number or even the city he called home. There were many holiday rentals on Fore Street, and with no clue where he'd stayed, it wasn't as if she could make enquiries. And even if she knew who he was and where he hailed from, she wasn't sure how it might help. The thought of tracking him down like a sad loner, only for him to tell her she'd got the wrong end of the stick entirely, was more than she could contemplate. This thought took her back to square one: the reality that she was preoccupied with this stranger. It was ridiculous. And yet the thought of him and all the romantic associations that followed thrilled her! She craved the image in her head: love, friendship and a future that was more than her biscuit-eating nan and her vodka-guzzling mother.

She threw herself into her morning swim.

'So that's it, Dad,' she whispered, putting her words out into the surf. 'As I said before, it was nothing; I didn't even know him. So why am I so sad at the prospect of not seeing him again? What's going on? What do you think I should do?'

The silence of the waves bothered her.

With her heart pounding and her limbs aching from a strong session, she made her way to the middle of the bay and lay on her back, part of her morning ritual, letting her eyes take in the majesty of the big sky and feeling the water embrace her. As ever, a little overwhelmed and in awe of the vastness of the sky and the ocean below her.

'I'll be back tomorrow,' she whispered. As she turned to swim back, she became aware of a figure on the beach. Instantly she trod water and stared at his outline. Her heart leapt at the sight of him and the happy realisation that all was not lost.

'Your friend's back!' Maudie yelled playfully, pointing in his direction.

'So he is.' She turned and beamed at the woman whose eyes glinted with delight.

Edgar lifted his hand in a wave. She waved back, wishing again that she was half-decently dressed and not in this wetsuit that showed all her lumps and bumps. Jago continued to pull through the water, seemingly oblivious, and Maudie did her best to catch him up.

Making every effort to look calm and collected, she tried as elegantly as possible to tread the shoreline and make her way up the beach. Overly conscious of her walk, she faltered and tripped, something she never did! It was typical, and she decided there and then not to attempt to remove her suit, but instead to put her dry robe over her wet stuff, therefore avoiding the mortification and possible repeat of the knicker-dropping incident of a couple of days ago.

'Hey!' he called as she approached, his manner and tone suggesting they were meeting by arrangement, which suited her just fine.

'Hi!' She felt her pulse race as she got closer to him. Connie was right, who *was* she?

'So, was it cold?'

She laughed as she reached for her towel and rubbed it over her hair and face, trying not to let her eagerness at the sight of him burst from her, swallowing all the glittery rainbows and hearts of joy that she was sure would rush from her throat if she were to sing.

'As I've said to my nan on more than one occasion, about as cold as yesterday and probably the same as it'll be tomorrow. No matter how I dress it up, this ain't the Caribbean!'

'True.' He sat on the sand and it felt like the most natural thing in the world to sit next to him. Aware that time was marching on, she hoped Connie would understand that this was an emergency – or at least an opportunity. Either way, she was staying put. Gordy and Nora could wait for their bacon sandwich or carrot cake with two forks, and Gaynor would simply have to step up her game.

'So what brings you up to Hele Bay at this time of the morning?' She hoped he might say 'you' and braced herself accordingly.

'I like to walk and I like it when it's quiet before the whole town wakes up and the streets and paths become crowded.'

'Yep, that's the downside. When you live somewhere like this, you can't mind sharing it with crowds when the sun comes out. I'm not complaining; I'm always ready for the summer when it arrives, but I do like the winter months, and the quieter times in the day. It feels like an entirely different place.'

'I've only ever been here in the summer.'

'You should come back in the winter.' Her words filled her with instant regret. Why had she said that? The last thing she wanted him to think was that she was making a plan, asking him to come back, assuming something!

'I will.' And just like that her nerves dissolved and she was again filled with something light that felt a lot like happiness.

'So where do you live?'

'London.'

She nodded. It figured, most people came here from cities like London, Bristol, Birmingham, looking for an escape.

'And what do you do in London?'

'Well, until recently I worked in a bank.' He pulled a downward mouth. 'Very, very boring. Do you like working in the café?'

'I do.' She was aware her tone was a little lukewarm. 'I thought about studying midwifery.' It was a rare admission, especially to this stranger. 'Can't think of any job more rewarding than being there at those first moments of life.'

'So why didn't you?' he asked, unaware of all the stumbling blocks she'd have to clamber over for this to be possible. She was unsure how to answer, without giving him an accurate picture of life with Annalee; her role as chief comforter and distractor for her nan and the fact that she was wary of leaving in case . . . in case her dad returned and she wasn't here. Yes, this was at the heart of it. Even though she knew it to be madness, it didn't make it any less of a preoccupation for her.

'I guess I kind of drifted into working for my cousin, Connie, and it's not too bad, it's okay, and so I stayed.' There it was again, that pithy response. 'So, you're no longer at the bank?'

'Nope!' He grinned, like this was an achievement. 'Pretty much like you said before, I woke up one morning and decided I needed to find something that makes me feel good, makes me feel better, and so I've taken a mini sabbatical and am trying to figure out what that might be. I'm having a life rethink. Do you know Corner Cottage on Fore Street?'

'Yes.' Of course she did, having walked past it nearly every day of her life. She'd had to pass it to get to the High Street, to school, the shops . . . It seemed to be a popular holiday rental, right in the thick of things.

'Well, I've covered the kitchen table with a huge sheet of wallpaper and I'm kind of doodling the future, trying to figure out my next move. At the moment I'm thinking of retraining as a teacher or maybe learning to paint properly!'

'You should talk to Nora, one of our customers – she and her husband have a house on the harbourside and her father was a famous artist. She has one of his pieces in her hallway. It's very clever, especially to people like me who can't draw or paint well at all. I dabble but my work is like a child's!'

'Maybe I will. And I'm certainly no great talent, but I enjoy it.' He kicked at the sand.

'So which is standing out, artist or teacher?'

He took his time formulating a response and she took the opportunity to study his face: the long eyelashes, the laughter wrinkles at the outer edge of his kind eyes, his easy manner. Her stomach bunched with a longing to touch him.

'I think the teaching. I don't know the first thing about it other than remembering some of my teachers who had an impact, good and bad, but that feels like a good place to start.'

'I think it's great you're not afraid to make changes that you know will bring you happiness.' She wished she had his strength of conviction.

'Well, that's the plan, but we'll see. I've never had this kind of freedom before. I went straight from school to uni to work and only changed jobs once, hopping from one bank to another, and here I am.'

'Here you are.' She roughed her hair with her fingertips, wanting it to dry and stop sticking to her face. 'I'm not exactly the great adventurer myself. Born here. Stayed here.' Her tone carried the almost subconscious whiff of embarrassment that she'd never left.

'It's all about finding happiness, right?' She nodded in response. 'And I have to admit you've inspired me, Tawrie.'

Her name on his lips was . . . intoxicating!

'I have?' She thought he might actually be able to see her heart as it leapt in her chest.

'Yeah. I think seeing you swim and knowing you do that come rain or shine, it's cemented the fact that I want to find something I love doing. But it feels scary, I suppose.'

'Well, that's what your wallpaper on the table is for, right? To come up with your next big thing?'

'Yes.' He closed his eyes and drank in the morning air. 'I feel different here.'

'In what way?' It was astonishing to her how easily she could chat to this man, as if they'd known each other for a lifetime.

'I don't know, really, but in Balham I'm always on the go and it feels like I run from appointment to event to dinner to seeing a friend, to catching a bus, jumping on a train, hailing a cab, riding a lift, seeing a movie. Always something I need to do and somewhere I need to be, but here . . .' He exhaled slowly. 'I can just be.'

'I sometimes worry I might be missing out on life not being somewhere busy but, you know, life could be worse and I wonder if maybe I'm actually where I should be and that's that.' She trotted out the standard cliché that was becoming less sweet in her mouth the more she voiced it.

'How old are you?' he interjected, as if unaware that it wasn't a standard question past the age of seventeen.

'Twenty-nine next birthday.'

'Same.' He nodded and she smiled at this, another connection.

'Yeah.' Tawrie drew breath. 'Sometimes I regret not becoming a midwife, wonder what my life might have been like, but then I remind myself to look up and appreciate all I have around me.'

'Like the sea and your daily rendezvous with your Peacocks.'

'Exactly. I was cautious at first about swimming. Actually, more than cautious, I was really scared.' *Swimming in the sea that took my dad . . .*

'I get that.' He pulled a face and they listened to the waves crash against the rocks. 'Starting something new, leaping into the unknown.'

'Bonkers, really, as I've always lived here on the coast, woken each morning of my life and looked out over the sea with gulls squawking their hello. Those that don't know the sea think it's just a vast body of water. But it's so much more than that. It changes every day, a shifting landscape, a moving picture. A home itself, teeming with life: fish, seals, dolphins, even the odd whale – I've seen them all. It's a changing thing that calls to me. It whispers in soft murmurs as it kisses the wet sand. It roars in fierce winds, douses me in winter and calms me in summer.'

'Wow!' He stared at her as if her words were prophetic, meaningful, and the fact that he was impressed felt like a huge reward. 'You've really got the bug!'

'I have. My dad and I used to paddle, but nothing like this, nothing like this feeling of being part of the water.' The mention of her dad was enough to cause her throat to tighten. She didn't want to feel this way, not here, not now and not in front of Edgar. Not when it felt like they were getting on, making progress. And yet it happened like this – unpredictable moments when her grief rose up, reached for her and held her fast. Even now.

'So your dad . . .'

'My dad what?' She didn't mean to sound so defensive; it was more a reflex when the subject that sat like a tear across her heart was raised. It made her uneasy to see the red bloom of embarrassment rise on his neck. It wasn't his fault. He was merely entering stage left at this point in the drama, unaware of the tension, the sorrow, the event that had shaped her life.

Shaped all of their lives.

'Do you . . . do you see him?' He swallowed, picking up on her verbal shift in tone.

'No.' She bit her lip, looking at her wet feet.

'I'm sensing this conversation is leading me down an alleyway that you don't want to walk, so how about we change the subject?'

He was insightful and she was grateful.

She took a deep breath. 'It's not that I don't *want* to talk about it, it's that I *don't* talk about it. And so, like anything you don't do, whether it's climbing a hill or tackling a tricky subject, it makes it harder when you do try.'

'I get that. So I guess the obvious thing to say is that maybe if you *try* to talk about a difficult subject then it will stop being tricky?'

'Now why didn't I think of that?' She threw a limpet shell at him.

He caught it in his hand. 'Good skills.'

'Thank you.'

He smiled and it felt like a moment, playful and comfortable. 'So, I don't want to push, but I do know a thing or two about broken families. Is it that you don't see your dad at all?'

Oh I see him . . . every time I let the water slip over my shoulders, every time I catch my breath in a wave, every time I see my mum draped over the arm of someone who isn't him. I see him, I think about him, and I imagine, even if it's only briefly, a life where I don't have to have this conversation because he is here.

'I don't see him, no.' She paused and rolled the words around in her mind, hoping they might make their way out of her mouth without too much consideration, no high drama or emotion. It was how she kept the subject in check, how she kept everything in check.

'That sucks.' He held her eyeline.

'It really does.'

She shivered as her body cried out for sustenance or a warm drink. Not that she had any intention of going anywhere in that moment.

'Do you want to do something later?'

'Like what?'

Like what! Why did you say that, you moron? His question and timing had caught her off guard to say the least. Having blurted her ill-considered response, she wished for a rewind button so she could answer more appropriately, deciding that if a do-over was possible, she'd say, 'Yes, that'd be great!' Or 'Oh, I was thinking the same thing!' Or 'Yes, I think I might love you! Why don't we just cut to the chase and go get married, right now, today?' Having mentally run through these permutations, she decided, on balance, that 'Like what?' maybe wasn't so bad after all.

'I don't know, erm . . .' He rubbed his chin as he thought. 'We could go for a walk around the harbour or go down to Rapparee Cove or up around Capstone Hill, whatever you want to do.'

'Okay, great. Shall I come and knock for you at seven?'

Again she cringed, aware she sounded like a teen looking for a mate who fancied a kick about.

'That'd be great.' He laughed. 'Come knock for me. I'm at Corner Cottage.'

'Yes, you said and I know where it is.'

'It's on the corner of Fore Street and Mill Head,' he explained and she saw his own anguished expression, as if he too were cringing, aware that she would know every house in the street far better than he. The idea that he might be a little nervous too, a little kerflummoxed with nerves, thrilled her.

'So that's a date.' He wiped sand from his hands on to his shorts. 'I mean, not a date . . . I mean . . .'

Tawrie stared at the man. 'I know what you mean.'

◆　◆　◆

'Well, it's nice to see you, Taw, thanks so much for coming in!' Connie turned from the grill with a look of thunder.

'I'm sorry, Con, I got held up.'

Grabbing her apron and fastening it around her waist as quick as she was able, she was aware of the grin that split her face, making a mockery of her apology, and which she would have controlled better if she were talking to anyone other than her cousin. Having never been habitually late – she was a stickler for timekeeping, in fact, unable to stand the thought of keeping anyone waiting – she tried whenever possible to extend the same courtesy to others. She figured, however, that one rare slip-up was allowed. Especially when the cause was an important one.

'Oh my God, look at your face! You were with wanker-name lover boy, weren't you!'

'I might've been.' She screwed up her face and raised her shoulders.

'I want to give you seven kinds of warning about him, Taw, but I can tell it's too late for all that. You're proper smitten, aren't you?' A twist of a smile appeared on Connie's carmine lips.

'I think I could be, depends how tonight goes.'

'What's happening tonight?' Gaynor popped up at her shoulder. 'Three crispy rashers for table two with extra toast and one more tea, please, Con.' She rattled off the additions to the order and stuck her biro into the back of her hair for safekeeping.

'Righto.' Connie nodded and peeled rashers of bacon from the waxed paper to throw on to the grill.

'What's happening tonight?' Gaynor repeated. 'What have I missed?'

Tawrie hesitated, aware that telling Gaynor, who would pass it on to Sten, was the verbal equivalent of taking out an advert in the *North Devon Gazette*.

'Taw's got a date!' Connie let her mouth fall open comically.

'I wouldn't call it that.' She tried to play it down despite the sparks of joy that crackled in her stomach. 'It's not really a date, it's more of a get-together.' She felt the bloom of embarrassment on her cheeks and chest. It was almost impossible to stop grinning!

'I see, and who are you getting together with exactly for this not-really-a-date?'

Tawrie saw the excitement in Gaynor's eye, the ribbing that came from a place of affection.

'He's called Sebastian Farquhar,' Connie interrupted.

'He's not, Gay, ignore her. He's called Edgar, Ed, and I don't know his surname.'

'Don't know his surname? A man of mystery! That's exciting!' Gaynor winked at her.

'I wish I'd never told you, Con.'

'Yeah, and I wish you weren't still standing here dilly-dallying and all of a dither, instead of taking bloody orders!'

She took the hint and made her way to the tables where impatient customers waved and tapped menus, as if this might make her hurry up. Not that their impatience could dull her mood – nothing could, not with the prospect of an evening spent with Sebastian Farquhar looming large in her thoughts.

The day passed quickly and her feet barely touched the ground, not only due to the fact the café was busy, but also because her excitement meant that, instead of her usual thudding gait, she felt as if she were hovering on bubbles of possibility. They carried her, lightening her load, so that instead of being dogged by weariness when Connie turned the sign to 'Closed' and another day came to an end at the Café on the Corner, she was still raring to go. It was only as she hung up her apron that nerves edged ahead of excitement.

'Bit scared.' She pulled a face at her cousin.

'Course you are. Because it's scary.'

'You're not helping!' She had hoped for more encouragement.

'It is though, isn't it? Putting yourself in the emotional firing line, making yourself vulnerable. Especially someone like you,' Connie added, as she leaned over, using her biro and notepad to tot up the figures for the day, and counted cash into bundles before shoving it into tiny plastic bags ready to deposit at the bank tomorrow.

'What do you mean someone like me?' She blinked at the implication that she was in some way peculiar.

Connie paused from her task and chewed her bottom lip with her large teeth, as if keen to get the phrasing right.

'I guess what I mean is that you're lovely, Taw. You're that person, the one everyone loves: kind, bit quiet, caring, just . . . lovely! That's the best word. You're not cynical or jaded when it comes to men. You believe the best about people. You're trusting. You're the one who hands in lost mittens and feeds injured birds. You do the right thing and this is a leap into the unknown.'

It was a nice way of summarising her lack of experience but did little to calm her. But Connie wasn't done.

'This Farquhar bloke . . .'

Tawrie knew there was little point in objecting to his nickname, it had already taken hold.

'. . . you've only met him a couple of times, barely spoken to him, and it feels risky. If you were the kind of woman who hooked up with a different bloke whenever the fancy took you' – Connie looked at the floor and she knew that, like her, her cousin was thinking of Annalee – 'then whatever happens next would be water off a duck's arse, but you're not. You're our sweet, slightly grumpy, serious-faced Tawrie Gunn and I don't want you to get hurt.'

'I just want to have a nice time. I like feeling like this – a bit excited!' She did her best to explain it.

Connie reached out and cupped the side of her face in her palm. Her cousin might only have been a few years older but she had always loved and mothered her in this way.

'You're right, Taw, have a nice time and enjoy every minute. Just don't give too much of you away – and I'm not talking about dropping your knickers again!'

'Again, I wish I'd never told you!'

'Who else are you going to tell?' Her cousin had a point. 'Remember, first dates are cringey to begin with, but you'll know when it's going well when the conversation flows and you're not embarrassed to eat in front of him.'

'Embarrassed to eat in front of him?' This was a new one on her.

'Yeah, it's a thing. I know loads of people who can't eat on a first date, or a second, or third. The whole putting food in your gob is a big deal!'

'You sound like you speak from experience.'

'I do! I lose pounds when I start dating, just nibble like a bird and then have to go home and have bowls of cereal before bed.'

A bang on the glass of the door gave them both a start. She looked up as Connie's boy, Sonny, squashed his face against the door, leaving a greasy smear from his chocolate-covered mouth.

'Come on, Mum! Dad's in the van and you said we could do crazy golf!' His eyes were wide, whether at the prospect of crazy golf or due to the amount of chocolate he'd consumed, it was hard to know.

'Right there, my love, is another reason to keep your pants on. All I want is a hot bath, a cup of tea and a nap in front of the telly in my pyjamas. Instead I'm off to play crazy golf with that reprobate.'

Her cousin's words were clear and yet the way her eyes lit up at the sight of her son turned them into a lie.

'You and Farquhar can join us if you like?' Connie smiled at her suggestion.

'Yeah, that sounds like fun!' Tawrie let her lip rise in a curl; it was the very last thing in the world she wanted to do.

CHAPTER EIGHT

HARRIET STRATTON

AUGUST 2002

Harriet sat at the kitchen table. Hugo was walking around the harbour on his morning constitutional, a habit of which she heartily approved. The way she breathed in his absence, a reminder that in his presence she held her breath, overly conscious of her expression, demeanour and language. A little on edge. They had always been a working couple whose lives collided in their early morning bathroom visits and of an evening across the supper table, chattering wildly on shared car journeys and at the weekend. This new exile, where she had no job and he was working from home, meant they were together in the little cottage most of the time and it was a stark reminder of how much she had relished the quiet of their village house when he was out and the kids were at school. The moments of solitude that gave her time to think, reset, plan the minutiae of life: what to make for supper, what needed laundering next, a quick check on the calendar that hung on the wall of the utility room. They were gaps in her working schedule that she valued. Here it was different. They prowled around each other, seeking out space, wary, while she did her best to get through the silences that screamed of all they were each trying so hard to contain.

In the quiet of the kitchen and with her thoughts cluttered, she opened her diary. The cupboards were stocked with the kids' favourite cereal, chocolate nestled in their sweetie tin, and pizzas lurked in the fridge. It was a crass attempt to make them want to be here, to delight them at the prospect of this new life simply by providing the junk and sweet treats ordinarily rationed. The equivalent of a magic trick, clever finger-clicking to draw the eye away from something you were not meant to see. This, like all her conversations with the children and the upbeat, optimistic notes she'd popped into their luggage, felt laced with deceit, and yet she deemed it necessary. Not that it made it any easier to swallow.

Their new rooms were tidy: their beds made in their familiar bed linen, toys packed on to shelves, work desks assembled and lamps on their bedside tables. It was easy to make the place look pretty and homey. Her confidence, however, in them settling into this new environment was not high. It was hard not to bring her own doubts and insecurities into the cottage, and Bear was a sensitive boy. The way he'd held on for dear life when they'd said goodbye, in stark contrast to his usual, casual peck on the cheek, suggested he might already be aware that there was more to being shipped off to his aunt's than giving his mum and dad time to get the house ready.

'But why, Mum? Why are we moving? I'm goalie next term for the A team!'

'Because life is an adventure!' She'd offered the salve, a half-truth that in retrospect was demeaning to them both.

The thought of things not working out here, however, filled her with a cold dread that had the power to shake her from sleep in the early hours. To have given up their home, their whole lives in Ledwick Green, only to admit defeat felt like a worse prospect than if they'd stayed put, watched their home life crumble and gone their separate ways. But how would that work? The kids living with her during the week and seeing Hugo at weekends? Splitting the week so it was fair? And where and how would they live? Two bedrooms, two addresses, two birthday parties, two Christmases, two separate lives? It was unthinkable and just the idea of it left her feeling hollow, nausea swirling in her gut.

She did her very best not to harbour such thoughts, determined that they would come out the other side with trust and love restored, determined to work very hard to this end. But what if they failed? What if they couldn't? More specifically, what if *she* couldn't? What if this whole pantomime of upheaval was for nothing?

'Stop it,' she whispered, and closed her eyes briefly, breathing through her nose, knowing such musings helped no one, least of all her.

Her heart yearned for reunion with her children and the thought of all four of them sitting around this very table for supper warmed her. It was easy to picture: the kids chuckling, Hugo goofing around for just such an effect, mouths filled with tasty, warming food, a candle flickering, maybe a board game or two after pudding, with the usual high jinks and accusations of cheating and subterfuge.

Normal life.

Never a regular crier, her sob came without warning. It was a surprise when a rush of hot tears trickled down her face and filled her nose and throat. Her sadness was tightly bound in her chest and it didn't take much to set it free. In this case it was this false image. The idea that they could go back to the suppers of old when she hadn't known there was a fault line running through her family, and that her marriage was a lie. Suppers where her biggest concern had been were her potatoes crispy enough and would Hugo like a second helping of gratin? She grabbed the paper serviette shoved into her jeans pocket, wiped her eyes and blew her nose. Outbursts like this were a reminder of the cruelty of his actions, and the fact that she was left mopping up, trying to rebuild what had been shattered.

She picked up her pen, as her tears ebbed.

Sitting here crying, which is a shame, as it's glorious today: blue sky, gull song and gentle pockets of warmth when the wispy cloud clears. Ellis is coming down on Saturday with the kids. I've missed them so much! I ache for them, to feel their little arms around my neck, to hear them at play (and at war!). To know they are tucked up and sleeping under the same roof will bring me peace.

It felt like a good idea, coming down alone with Hugo, getting the house straight, giving us time to chat, heal a little, plan before the arrival of the human encyclopaedia and her big brother – my sweet babies. They have no idea what we've been through, no clue as to why we've uprooted them from school and are starting over here in North Devon. It feels a little deceitful, but is a decision made with the very best of intentions.

This summer has been the worst of my life.

I have stumbled, physically and emotionally exhausted, hostage to fits of sobbing and the desire to crumple. My thoughts entirely scrambled.

A feeling of desolation akin to grief has engulfed me, weakened me, and I shall never forget being fearful of leaving the house in case I saw Mrs Peterson and fearful of staying in the house in case she or someone else in the know knocked on the door. I felt like a caged bird and I don't ever want to feel that way again. Coming here was the right thing to do.

I never want the kids to know, never want them to think less of their dad, never want them to know the level of despair I've felt. He is, after all, a great dad, the best, and he loves them, of this I have no doubt. I want them to enjoy the family life they deserve, and what better place to do it than here with the beach on our doorstep, clean air, fresh fish, country lanes and all that this kind of life will bring. It's exciting! And importantly, no one here knows us. And no one here knows her.

He cried again last night, but this was different. He hadn't had a drink and I wasn't with him. There was no gentle discussion that led to the tears, no raising of the topic that might cause such a reaction. I was soaking in a tub full of bubbles when I heard him sobbing in the rear bedroom that's going to be Bear's . . . and I liked it. I wanted to reach out and hold him close and tell him it was all going to be okay, but I can't lie, I liked it. Because if he's crying, it means he feels bad, and if he feels bad, it means he's regretful. If he's regretful then it means he loves me, right? It means he too wants to turn back time, and that everything is going to be okay. Does feeling some kind of comfort from his remorse make me a horrible person? I'll talk to Ellis when I see her. She's much better at analysing this kind of thing than I am.

So, Saturday reunion! We've decided to take them on a whistle-stop tour of new school, harbour, beach and then home for supper and their first night in their new home. Bear, once he gets his head around something, is pretty resilient. I'm not worried so much about him physically settling once he sees Hugo and I are okay. But Dilly? I don't know. She may be quiet, thoughtful – she's more like me, takes a while for her to feel comfortable in a new situation. Ellis's presence, her glorious noise, will be a welcome life raft to which we can all cling if things feel choppy.

Hugo says we should get a dog.

He might be right. Is there any situation in the whole wide world where getting a dog does not seal the deal? We'll see. The cottage isn't exactly vast and having to towel-dry a wet, hairy, sand-covered mutt might not be the best idea.

And in reference to a previous entry, I've been thinking: Wendy and Hugo sounds awful! Just awful!

Harriet and Hugo

Hugo and Harriet

Much, much better . . .

Putting down the pen, she wiped away the residue of tears on her sleeve and sat back in her chair. Saturday, just a few more sleeps and the kids would be here. Her face broke into a smile as optimism warmed her from within. What if they succeeded? What if they could? More specifically, what if she could? What if this whole pantomime of upheaval led to a glorious new life here on the North Devon coast?

'Yes.' She smiled as she stared out of the sash window with its darling view of Fore Street. 'What if?'

CHAPTER NINE

Tawrie Gunn

August 2024

Tawrie stared at the sparse contents of her wardrobe. The pitiful number of hangers clanging loosely on the rail indicative of the fact that she didn't go anywhere other than working in the café, pottering in the town, sitting on the beach with a book, or swimming with Maudie and Jago. There were a couple of t-shirts that she'd had since her teens, certain that if she held on to them long enough they'd come back into fashion, a little black dress she'd outgrown, but couldn't bear to part with, and little else of interest. What should she wear tonight? What *could* she wear tonight?

She heard the flush of the loo and briefly considered asking her mother if she might have something she could borrow. A snort of laughter left her nose. They were not that kind of mother/daughter. Not quite estranged and yet hardly close. Tawrie had only really known her as the remote lady who came in late and crept out quietly. She carried the vague memory of her mother dancing with her in the kitchen, scooping her up into her arms and rocking her to the sounds of The Carpenters that Freda loved. In her mind's eye she was small, a toddler, and therefore this couldn't be relied upon.

Their conversations were now rudimentary, functional, cool, and even if it might have been normal to ask for access to Annalee's wardrobe, they most certainly did not have the same taste in clothing. Her own preference was for items that were practical, warm, comfortable and in muted shades. Her shoe collection consisted of trainers, her ancient flip-flops and walking boots. Annalee, on the other hand, wore lace, things in red and jewel-coloured cotton tops with deep V-necks that ensured one bony shoulder was revealed at all times. Short, tight skirts and shoes with the kind of heel that caught in the cracks between paving stones, made it impossible to navigate sand, and frequently buckled on the stairs when she was drunk, resulting in twisted ankles.

For Tawrie, it felt painful to give her attire this much attention; it smacked of a vanity that had no place in her routine, and so in haste, she grabbed her jeans, which were cleanish, an almost matching set of underwear and her rose-pink, long-sleeved sweatshirt that had gone thin over the years but was possibly the comfiest item she owned.

Sitting at her desk she tousled her hair until it was practically dry and full of body and sprayed her décolletage and wrists with the fresh, summery Clinique scent that Connie had bought her for Christmas. She ran her fingers over the mascara wand that sat in a pot but decided against make-up. Not only was she fairly confident that the item was dried and ancient, but also Edgar had, after all, seen her fresh from the sea, swathed in a dry robe with sand-spattered hair stuck to her face. It felt like there was no need for the artifice of make-up – he knew what she looked like. Besides, to present a painted face felt like setting an unachievable standard, and with the hope of many more dates filling her thoughts, she didn't want to have to go through the rigmarole of getting made-up every time she saw him. Far better, she figured, to go au naturel. No shocks, no surprises.

One final smile in the mirror, and as her stomach jumped with joyful anticipation she made her way down the stairs.

'Where are you off to, little love?' her nan called from the sofa, which sat in the middle of the room, facing the TV.

'I'm going out, Nan, meeting a friend.'

'Oh yes, that's right, Connie told me! A bo-oy!' There was no mistaking her excitement at the prospect.

Cheers, Connie.

'It's nothing. I mean, I am, yes, going to meet a boy – a man – but it's only for a chat and . . . and a drink, and that's it. I'll probably be back before nine.'

'You sound a bit flustered over something that's nothing.'

Tawrie hadn't realised her mother was in the kitchen and turned to face her as she came to rest in the doorway, leaning on the doorframe with a cup of coffee in her palms. Her statement lingered like an odour.

'See you later.' She pulled her sleeves down over her wrists and kissed the top of her nan's head before making her way down to Fore Street.

It was a calm night and only the gentlest of breezes stirred the air, which was still full of happy particles at the sunny day just passed. Looking back towards Hillsborough as she made her way up the hill, she saw the faintest tinge of pink on the horizon, a glorious promise of another lovely day tomorrow. It was in moments like these that she remembered how fortunate she was to call Ilfracombe her home.

Sitting opposite the Terrace Tapas with its fabulous deck strung with festoon lights, which she could see from her bedroom window, Corner Cottage looked pretty from the outside. A large wicker lamp shone from the middle window of the upper hallway and more lamplight lit the downstairs windows. It made the place look cosy, warm. She wondered if he'd invite her inside or simply grab his keys, shut the door behind him and off they'd go. And actually, did she want to go inside? Might that be awkward? But if they went out, where would they go? She didn't like the idea of bumping into people she knew – a pretty tall order in a small place like this. Especially if Connie had been as liberal with the information to others as she had been to their nan. It was a distinct possibility. Deep down she kind of liked their enthusiasm, it almost validated her own feelings that this might be something. Or maybe it was just the novelty that had got her family excited, which in itself felt like some kind of pressure.

It was a sad fact that after her one and only semi-serious relationship with Jamie, her ex, her last date had been . . . she did the mental maths . . . nearly two years ago. Living in a small town meant there wasn't much of a pool to choose from when it came to dating and without a large group of single friends, it was hard to go on the prowl in places like Barnstaple where she'd look like a weirdo hanging about on her own on a Friday night. Plus she was so tired at the end of the day that falling into her bed was preferable to heading out looking for love. Or at least that was what she told herself.

Two years ago! It was a little jarring how much time had passed since she'd agreed to go to the Embassy Cinema on the High Street with Sid from the butchers'. Sid was impossibly good-looking, beautifully handsome with perfect teeth and pale-blue eyes. She had felt a little weak-kneed just stepping out with him. Unfortunately, he also had the personality of a pot plant and, as she was soon to discover, an IQ to match. She had thought she could overlook it, concentrate on his eyes, that smile, but after he'd called her Toz for the eleventh time, asked three times in one hour if the woman on screen was the baddie's mother, showered the row in front with popcorn when his great galumphing laugh had caused his body to convulse, she decided, sadly, that no amount of handsomeness in the world could compensate for the rather shallow interior of the boy. He still waved at her enthusiastically whenever he saw her. She was convinced he had no recollection of their night at the Embassy, which was probably no bad thing. Sid was now engaged to Taylor-Marie from Bratton Fleming. She wished them all the luck.

Memories of her last disastrous date caused the first deep stir of doubt as nerves bit. Suppose they couldn't decide where to go? Suppose Ed did invite her inside, but they had nothing to talk about? She shivered at the thought of how awkwardly soul-destroying that might be. Suppose she was dull, boring and he was expecting her to be sparkly, witty, and wearing mascara or something made of lace or red? With only a hundred or so yards between the bottom of the steps that led up to Signal House and the front of Corner Cottage, she didn't have time to make a plan and, at the point when it was still possible to turn and run back home, there was the very real risk that he had already seen her approaching. Linen bistro curtains covered the lower half of the windows, which meant that while she couldn't see in, there was no guarantee he couldn't see out.

'You can do this, Tawrie Gunn. You can.'

She took a deep, slow breath through her nose and rolled her shoulders; it helped pre-swim, yet not so much pre-knocking-on-the-door. Particularly not the door behind which lurked the boy she had built up to be something wonderful in her mind. As she raised her hand to knock, it opened and there he was. Her face broke into a smile at the sight of him. He was wearing another shirt, this one pale blue, but it was similarly misbuttoned. She liked his lack of precision, suggesting he too might have grabbed what came to hand in the wardrobe and shoved it on.

Standing back slightly, Edgar stood against the door, as if it were a foregone conclusion that she would step inside.

'I've had a total nightmare!' he laughed. 'I need to calm down.'

'Oh dear, why?' She stepped into the open space of the sitting room, entered via a wide step up from the small, square hallway where a row of pegs held hoodies and scarves and the stairs to the upper floors wound away to the right.

It was a space that felt weirdly familiar, although she was certain she had never been inside. She guessed it was because, having walked past so many times, the glimpsed interiors and snatched detail had no doubt formed the picture in her mind.

'Do you want the long story or the short?'

'Short, please.' She beamed.

'Very wise. I have been known to go on a bit.' He snorted laughter.

And just like that they were chatting, her nerves melted and she was reminded that there was nothing to fear, no need to turn on her practical heel and run. To be in his company felt like walking with a safety net beneath her, a cushion. It felt wonderful.

'About an hour ago, I realised that I'd invited you over and had no food, no nibbles.'

'Nibbles?' she laughed.

'You know, the nuts, crisps and shit that people put on tables.'

'Well, I like nuts and crisps but you can keep the shit.'

'Noted.' He clicked his tongue against the roof of his mouth. 'Anyway, I decided to run to the supermarket, a very sweaty exercise in itself. I was about to pay when I realised I'd left my wallet in the kitchen. I had to put my goods to one side, a task performed with the accompanying tuts and groans of everyone in the queue behind me, although why or how it affected them I really don't know. With my humiliation complete, I ran back here, grabbed my cash then jogged back to the supermarket to pay, and have only just managed to squeeze in an inadequate shower! I'm still flustered.'

'Nuts and crisps will do that to you.'

'And now I'm feeling the most enormous pressure because I don't know what to put them in!' He stood with his palms splayed, his harassed air suggesting he might be placing similar importance on the evening and that this was not a regular thing for him. It did nothing but bring her relief; she didn't want to imagine how it might feel if her current excitement levels were not reciprocated. 'Honestly, I had no idea there was so much to it! There's a big wooden bowl that I'm guessing is better for fruit, tiny dip bowl things that'll only hold a single crisp, or cereal bowls. Who knew that the simple offering of a snack could be so complicated?'

'Not me.' She liked the easy nature of their chat, feeling any last vestige of nerves flee out of the open window.

'Anyway, I'm waffling. The one thing I have managed to source with confidence is wine. We have red, white and the other, pink stuff.'

'Rosé?'

'That's the fella!' He pointed at her. 'Which can I get you?'

'I'll take a glass of the other, pink stuff please.'

'An excellent choice, madam.' He gave a half bow and she followed him down a step into the cosy kitchen where handmade pine units lined the walls, a round table with four mismatched chairs sat in the corner, and a large linen lamp on the wide windowsill filled the room with a golden glow.

She liked the decor. The sitting-room walls were painted in a warm white, pale-blue linen accent pillows were on a blue-and-cream striped sofa, an oversized raffia lampshade hung from the ceiling and sea-themed artwork was dotted here and there. Clusters of round mirrors reflected the light and a patchwork rug of various blues took up much of the wooden floor. Large navy-and-cream patterned ceramic lamps dominated the corners of the room and wooden side tables were home to all manner of things from ornate shells to crystal-and-brass inkwells, and even a ceramic artichoke. It was magazine beautiful and she couldn't imagine what it must feel like to live among this much order, without the clutter of life in every corner. The clutter of life that at Signal House sat on top of a mountain of dust and was laced into place with cobwebs. Corner Cottage smelled fresh and clean and she liked it very much.

'Here we go.' He handed her a glass of wine and grabbed the bags of crisps and nuts, which he pulled open. Ripping the bags wide for easy access, he placed them on the kitchen table. She took a seat, happy he was leading the dance, as they settled into place opposite each other. She was just thinking that the seating arrangement was a tad prim when he spoke.

'Thank you for coming to this interview. What makes you think you're suitable for the position?' He put on a formal voice and joined his hands at the knuckle on the tabletop.

'It's my pleasure.' She lowered her head. 'I think it would help if I knew what position I was applying for. And also I'm wondering if it might be frowned upon if I sipped wine during the process?' She took a sip of the cool rosé, which was dry and refreshing.

'Funny story, actually.' He dropped the act and sat back in his chair. 'My boss wanted to take on a graduate for a twelve-month internship and asked me to go through the whittled-down list of applicants and conduct the interviews.'

'Pressure!' She knew she wouldn't enjoy doing that at all.

'You have no idea, but put it this way, choosing a bowl for crisps was a doddle in comparison.'

She liked how this felt, as if they'd known each other for an age and meeting up to chat like this was a regular thing. Easy.

'I was quite looking forward to it, the idea of getting away from my laptop, something different. They booked out a couple of days where I sat in the boardroom while these young, eager, hopeful banking wannabes came into the room one by one and did their best to sell themselves to me.'

'You didn't enjoy it? Wielding all that power?'

He shook his head. 'I really didn't. Not when it came to it.' He took a sip of wine. 'It felt desperate, horrible, almost gladiatorial. They were all brilliant over-achievers, far more brilliant than me! They'd been to far-flung corners of the globe, spoke loads of languages, worked for worthwhile charities, and had a raft of top-notch grades. There was nothing to choose between any of them, so did it really matter that one had grade eight on the violin while another was a county tennis player?'

'Wow, makes me realise I've done absolutely nothing with my life.' She spoke half in jest.

'I felt the same and I found it really sad.'

'Don't be so hard on yourself, you have years to learn how to play the violin and improve your backhand.'

'It wasn't that so much.' He gazed at her and she took the chance to study his long lashes. 'They had this burning look in their eyes, as if to fail at this, to not get the internship, was going to crush them. Like it was the only thing that mattered, but I knew we could only take one. The rest of the applicants, all really nice, super-keen, were going to be just that: crushed. And I was the person who was going to do that to them. It made me realise that I don't have a ruthless streak, which I kind of think you need if you want to live that cut-throat life, but I couldn't stop thinking about how it was all such a waste of time.'

'In what way?' She matched his serious tone.

He swallowed. 'I guess I could see that these people had worked hard at school, gone to first-class universities, as if they were in some desperate race and here they were, still racing, still competing, trying to get chosen, to get ahead, taken on. And I knew they'd never stop – elbowing each other out of the way for promotion, grasping for the next rung on the ladder and greasing the steps they'd already taken to make sure those following fell.' He paused. 'I didn't like it, any of it. I knew I found the job dull and unfulfilling and I wanted to take these very clever, dedicated people to one side and say, look, there's more to life than this. You need to be happy; you need to do something that makes you laugh every day. You need to spend your time in a way that means when you climb into bed at night, you feel content and you don't dread the alarm going off the next morning, full of fear or sickness at the prospect of having to get up and do it all again.'

It was odd how much his words resonated, mirroring her own desire to be happy, to laugh, be content.

'Did you say that to them?'

He shook his head and swilled his wine around the glass. 'No, but I said it to myself and that's when I decided to give up my job.'

'To either paint or teach or . . .'

'Yep. Because I looked at them all and saw myself a decade ago and realised that I was stuck. Still racing, not happy, not sad, just looking forward, doing what I thought I had to, earning enough money, and yet not fulfilled, not hopeful. I can't count the times I said to myself that when I reached X or when I did Y then I'd be happy – things would be better, easier. But there was always another X or Y on the horizon and I knew I was never going to arrive. Do you understand that?'

'I really, really do.' She felt connected to him, his words so close to her own experience. In that moment she knew that for them to move forward, for this friendship to deepen, she would need to open up about her life, her past, her mother . . . Shifting in the chair, her skin itched with discomfort. What would he think of her when he knew the full story? She'd go slowly, that was probably the answer. 'It's partly why I swim. It's like a reset. A good, positive thing that makes me so happy, and I do it just for me.'

There was a moment of silence but she felt no need to fill the gap with chatter; instead she was content, calm in his presence.

'Do you sail as well?'

It was a straightforward question, an obvious one, really, when she considered the geographical location of her home. She shook her head and felt a shiver of fear at the thought of going out in a boat, knowing how quickly it could all go wrong and how a family, like hers, could be left struggling with the consequences decades later.

'I've never, erm . . .' How to begin, where to begin? 'I think I may have been out on a boat when I was younger. In fact, I don't know why I said it like that. Yes, I *did* go out on a boat when I was little. With . . . with my dad. He had a little boat called *Ermest* – after the River Erme, another Devon river.'

'So you could have been called Ermest if the mood had taken him?'

'Quite possibly.' She smiled wistfully; it felt nice to talk about the man she only recalled in shadow. The outline of him without the detail. It was also refreshing not to see the pull of distress on Edgar's face at the mention of Daniel Gunn. A look she was used to and was synonymous with her father's name. Unsurprising, really, as all who knew and loved him and every local within living memory knew his story and this melancholic salute was almost mandatory. But not for Edgar, who had no prior knowledge and no embedded rumours; it was another reason to enjoy his company.

'I'm wary of asking further about your dad after the way you reacted on the beach, and trust me, that's not me pushing or prying.' He sat forward, eyes wide, his words urgent. 'I would never want to make you feel uncomfortable or for you to talk about anything that was triggering. So feel free to answer in any way you see fit, or not, nothing matters – we have wine and crisps and nuts, and the night is young.' He pinched several crisps and shoved them into his mouth, an act so unselfconsciously relaxed she felt another layer of reservation strip from her skin.

I do trust you . . .

'I don't . . .' She took a sip of wine. '. . . I don't really remember him.' The words were as painful to say out loud as they sounded in her head and it was a fact she rarely shared, only able to imagine how Nan and Uncle Sten would react to it.

'Because you haven't seen him?' he asked softly, returning to their conversation at Hele Bay Beach.

'He died.' There. She'd done it. Ripped off the Band-Aid. 'He died when I was seven.'

'Oh, Tawrie.' It was almost instinctive, the speed with which he abandoned his wine glass and reached across the table to take her hand. This contact sent a shiver of longing rippling through her whole body. Curling her fingers around his fleshy palm, their first touch, she sat quietly with him, almost in reverence for the news shared, and she was thankful for it, quite certain he could hear her loud heartbeat that filled her head. 'I hate saying it, even now.'

Because it makes it real.

He squeezed her hand a little, the increased pressure speaking more than a thousand words.

'But you have pictures? And I bet other people remember him. I know that for my childhood – not that it's the same, and please don't think I'm comparing my life to what you've been through – but I know that even if memories are a little hazy for me, it's other people's testimony, for want of a better word, that builds a picture, fills in the gaps for me. And so I think I have more memories than I actually do.'

'Pictures? Not many really. A few, yes.' She thought about the mostly blurred photographs of her with her dad on the harbourside or on the beach. Photos snapped, subjects off-centre, taken carelessly, hurriedly, without any awareness of the importance they would have. After all, what did it matter? It was just a day at the beach, a moment with a melting ice cream, a quick hug on her dad's lap post-swim, a towel around her shoulders, her with a lopsided ponytail and a grin minus two front teeth, and him looking young and strong and kind, a day's stubble gracing his chin as he beamed into the camera or smiled at her. 'And it's hard for me to talk to anyone objectively because of, erm . . .' She took a deep breath. 'Because of how he died.'

'How did he? I mean, I don't know if it's okay to ask, I don't want to, erm . . .' he gabbled and withdrew his hand, reaching for his wine.

'No, that's okay.' She kept her eyes on the tabletop, counting the crisps that had spilled from the packet, anything to divert her sadness and allow her to get the words out. One . . . two . . . three . . . three and a crumb. 'He drowned.'

'Oh.' She watched his shoulders fall and his head drop and she understood. It wasn't a neat death. There was little comfort to be taken from it. No slipping away in his sleep or at the end of an illness with his family surrounding him, having had the chance to say goodbye, the event wrapped with bittersweet relief. There was nothing neat about it. Drowning was ragged, uncomfortable to voice, a word redolent with images of struggle and violence. 'Yeah, so it makes it hard to talk to my nan or his brother or my . . . my mum.'

'That must be so difficult.'

'Yes, I think so. And that's why I don't raise it, you know? It's like the first thirty-odd years of his life might have been fantastic, but mentioning him, especially how he died, and it feels like everything that went before is reduced to that one day. And I don't want to put them through it. They've been through enough.'

'I meant hard for you.'

'I guess. But I don't know any different. People say you don't miss what you never had, or in my case what you don't remember.' She twisted her mouth to suggest this might not be true.

'I think they're wrong. I know I miss what I never had.' He spoke slowly, sharing his own confidence, which in some way levelled their emotional investment, swapping secrets, building a bridge of trust.

'What didn't you have?'

'A normal family life is probably the best way to describe it.'

'Jeez, find me someone that did!'

He laughed and drank. 'I guess you're right.'

'I am right.' She chuckled, giving them a route out of the previous weighted conversation, as they both shifted in their chairs and emptied their glasses. Any lurking sadness whistled right out of the open sash window and disappeared over Capstone Hill.

'Do you have siblings, someone you can talk to who knows what you've been through?'

'No, just me. But I have Connie, who's my cousin, but like a sister. She's only a bit older than me and we were raised together. I can talk to her. I don't always choose to, but I could.'

'That's nice. I'm one of six.'

'Six? Wow!' She couldn't begin to imagine.

'Yes, wow, and not always in a good way. I've got three sisters and two brothers.'

'How do you keep track of what everyone's up to?' She pictured the comings and goings of Signal House and tried to imagine six kids running up and down the stairs.

'You don't really. I mean we all get on, but we're not in each other's pockets. I don't see too much of a couple of my sisters. It's complicated. My brothers are twins – a right handful, I find them hilarious.'

'Where do you come in the pack, age wise?'

'I'm the oldest. And therefore the most sensible and the most respected.' He sat up straight.

'Is that right?' She liked the smile that played about his face.

'No, absolutely not! That'd be my sister, who's next in line. She's sensible, studious. She's the one who texts to remind about birthdays, arrangements and stuff; she's pretty organised. Then I have one sister who lives with her mum in Wales, I think. One sister who is only a baby really, and the twins are teenagers.'

He stood and went to the blue free-standing fridge to retrieve the opened bottle of pink stuff. He topped up their glasses and she liked what this suggested; that they weren't going anywhere.

'Do you like Uno?' he asked without a trace of irony as he put the bottle within reach.

'Who doesn't like Uno?' It had been years since she and Connie had played it at her nan's kitchen table one rainy afternoon in the school holidays.

'No one I'd like to know.' His eyes shone as he disappeared into the sitting room and she heard him ferreting in the cupboard of a dresser she'd noticed earlier, painted in a stunning Grecian blue. He reappeared with the Uno box in his hand.

'I propose a tournament. And I should probably warn you that I'm very competitive.'

Tawrie rolled her shoulders and cracked her knuckles.

'Do your worst.' She narrowed her eyes, reached for a crisp and threw it into her mouth, before instantly reaching for another.

CHAPTER TEN

HARRIET STRATTON

AUGUST 2002

The two sisters sat at either end of the wide, comfy sofa in the sitting room in Corner Cottage with their legs curled beneath them, their bodies twisted to face each other. It was always this way – no matter how much time spent apart, within minutes they reverted to their teenage selves, utterly at ease and taking comfort from the mere presence of the other. Harriet took in her sister's soft denim frock with its embroidered collar and skirt, and noted her mismatched socks, her style so very different from her own, which was conservative at best, practical and frumpy at worst.

An image of Wendy Peterson in her sparkly blue top on New Year's Eve flashed in her mind. She'd thought the item gaudy, inappropriate for an early open-house drinks party with the neighbours and far more apt for a night club. Had she said as much to Hugo? Was this bitchy observation part of their post-event analysis while they cleaned their teeth or threw the spare pillows off the bed, readying for sleep? Had she inadvertently expressed her distaste while all the while that sparkly blue top was exactly what he desired – or more accurately, what lurked within it? The familiar creep of cold rejection flooded her veins.

'I love you, Hats.' Her sister toyed with the handle of her dotty mug, filled with Earl Grey.

'And I love you.' It made her smile to hear the loving nickname.

'It's a bloody awful business all of this.' Ellis kept her voice low, like her, aware that the kids might be within earshot and equally aware that this was Hugo's house too. 'How I feel about Hugo has changed, certainly for now and maybe forever.' Ellis paused, letting this settle. 'Only time will tell. I mean, I still love him; I can't just switch it off. He's my brother-in-law, Maisie's uncle. I've known him since my teens and he's been a big part of my life too, and I guess my anger is that I feel a little duped. I'm also mad because Mum was so fond of him and I can only imagine how she'd feel about all this.'

Harriet had thought similar; he was always good to their mother and she had adored him in return.

'But I'm so goddam mad at him!' She spoke quietly through gritted teeth. 'Mad because he's let us all down, done the unthinkable, but maddest of all because he has hurt you and you deserve only the best. I feel naïve in that I thought you guys were on the invincible list. I'm shocked! You two were like the gold standard! What we all aspire to – that chummy lover, best friend, comedy partner vibe that to the outside world made it seem like you were golden.'

Ellis's words struck a chord, in that she knew this was how they had been perceived and also that there'd been no artifice in their actions; it was just how they were, how they lived: happily and in harmony. Or so she had believed.

'I don't think golden exists, not any more,' she admitted.

'Maybe you're right.' Her sister tapped her large silver ring against the china mug. 'I've been through a whole range of emotions in the last couple of weeks, including considering emigrating and taking Dilly and Bear with me so I never have to give them back. I adore them. They've been hilarious, and so sweet! I'd forgotten this lovely stage before they get to grumpy teenager and communicate in grunts. Bear actually wanted to watch TV with me and Dills let me brush her hair!'

She knew her sister was painting a picture, easing her guilt, letting her know that the kids were fine.

'Thank you, Ellis.'

'Any time. I mean it. I'm always on the end of a phone for whatever you or the kids might need.' Harriet noted the absence of Hugo on the list. 'I can pick you up from anywhere, come to where you need me. I have fold-out couches, a larder full of pasta, a deep tub, bubble bath and enough wine to see us through to the early hours. You only have to call me. Any time, day or night. And you can stay for as long as you need. Forever! I mean it.'

'I'll be fine.' She conjured a small smile; her sister's words were well meant, but they spoke of failure, hinting that this emotional rescue service was there for *when* she needed it, not *if*. 'We'll be fine.'

Ellis leaned forward and took her hand, letting their palms fall entwined on to a cushion.

'You're smart, Hats, the smartest and the kindest, and you're beautiful. I need you to know that you never have to put up with a situation that is anything less than you deserve. Never.'

'Do you think . . .' She chose her words carefully, wanting to hear her sister's predictions and yet dreading them in equal measure. 'Do you think we *can* fix things?'

Harriet noted how Ellis took her time responding, her gaze fixed on the bright mug. Her hesitation spoke volumes and her heart sank accordingly. 'It's hard, and I try to walk in your shoes. I do. Nothing has been done to me, I'm only an observer. I've not been injured by Hugo in the way you've been and yet I feel a murderous rage on your behalf. I wake in the early hours shaking, thinking of all the things I want to say to him and to her. How dare he?' She took a beat. 'So I can only begin to imagine how you're feeling.'

'Not rage, not how you describe it. I mean, I do imagine confrontation in my wilder moments, but if I saw her again, I'd probably choose to ignore her. She knows so much more about me than I do about her; the fact that she had a secret, came into my home, touched my things. How does a woman do that to another woman?' She double blinked away the images that formed. 'That knowledge kind of puts me on the back foot. I'd be wary that she might give me more information than my brain can cope with, paint new pictures to taunt me in the night. Yes, I'd ignore her, I would. I'd walk away. Concentrate on putting one foot in front of the other as I have been over the last few weeks.'

'You look . . .' Her sister seemed to be studying her face, and she felt her cheeks flame under the scrutiny. 'You look so sad.' Ellis rubbed the back of her hand with her thumb.

'I am very sad. Sad and disappointed. Even a little embarrassed.'

'You have no reason to be embarrassed, none at all. You've been quite remarkable throughout the whole thing, but that's not a surprise – you are remarkable.'

'I'm really glad you're here.' She tucked her sister's compliment in a pocket beneath her heart.

'Me too.'

'I've felt quite lonely. It's isolating – not being on an even keel with Hugo means things feel out of whack, and not knowing anyone here who I can go for a coffee with or offload to doesn't help.

Mind you' – she took a slug of tea – 'it's not as if I'd have people to chat to back in Ledwick Green. Not now.'

'What're you talking about, you know loads of people there!'

Ellis, it seemed, had not fully completed the complex mental jigsaw of just what Hugo's infidelity meant.

'Yes, but by my reckoning, a third of those will take Wendy Peterson's side: "How dare Hugo mess around with a young divorcee, have his wicked way and then bugger off to North Devon, what a horrible man!" I can hear them saying it over a cup of tea. A third will absolutely love the scandal, letting the juicy details liven up their dreadfully boring lives, making me the centre of that gossip and revelling in the chat about how, where and why it all happened. Raking over my life rather than the dead leaves that gather on their veranda. And the other third will pull up the drawbridge, shield their kids from the unsavoury goings-on at our end of the village, and their view of me will be forever shaded by the event. In fact, not just their view of me, but of us – the kids too – and likely they'll never speak of it or to me again.' She took a slow breath. 'That's the thing about being golden, people want to be close to it, hoping some of it might rub off on them. The stink of an affair is just the same in reverse – people don't want to be close to it in case the stink rubs off on them.'

'Jeez!'

'Yep, Jeez indeed. Welcome to village life!' She raised her mug in a toast.

'Could it be you're better off out of it?' Her sister spoke softly. 'I mean, not the marriage, and it goes without saying that I hate how you've got here, but those people who were your friends, your neighbours, they actually sound like arseholes.'

'Some, yes.' She smiled at her sister's astute summary. 'But there were some I was fond of and some things I will always miss. The house my babies grew up in for starters, the lovely garden I planted.' She pictured her and Hugo dancing in the kitchen, wine in their veins, laughter on their lips, love on their minds. 'Lots of things.'

'Of course. It's doubly hard because everything happened on your doorstep.'

'Worse than that, it happened inside our doorstep, in our home, in our bedroom, on sheets I laundered.' Harriet pinched the top of her nose.

'God, Hats, I could swing for him right now.'

'That wouldn't solve anything.' She couldn't deny it felt good to have this unconditional support.

'No, but it might make me feel better, even if only briefly.' Ellis released her hand and balled her fingers into a fist. It made Harriet laugh awkwardly.

'It's not just in the village. I haven't even begun to think about the repercussions at school. Wendy's son is in Dilly's class.'

She remembered the day after she'd found out about the affair, seeing Wendy's child walk across the playground with his heavy bag across his shoulder, his little tongue out, as if it was an effort to walk, and she imagined him calling Hugo 'Dad' and found herself rooted to the spot, unable to breathe or take a step forward or turn around; paralysed with something very close to fear. Another reason to move away, abandon ship, start over.

'Shit! I didn't know.' Ellis drew her from the memory.

'Yep, then there's soccer club, where we are, or were, a tight-knit group of parents. Church where we sat on several of the same committees. Oh God, Ellis! It goes on and on!'

It felt suffocating, like a weight on her chest, as she laid the facts bare.

Her sister drew breath. 'I guess in answer to your question, I think if anyone can fix things it's you guys. You've always been such great friends, you both adore the kids, you had a good life in

Ledwick Green before it all went tits-up, so you have strong foundations. They've been shaken, yes, but I do believe you can have a good life here.'

'Yes, we did have a good life, but that wasn't enough to prevent him sleeping with Mrs Peterson.' She pointed out the obvious with the familiar twist of horror in her chest.

'I suppose the question is . . .' Ellis took her time. '. . . what do you want to happen, Hats? How do you see it panning out?'

'I guess . . . I guess time will help us get back to normality. We're like strangers sometimes – a lot of the time. A bit awkward, timid, overly aware, and it crucifies me! It's Hugo! My Hugo! And yet I wrap my body in a robe before I leave the bathroom. He used to pop in and pee in the loo while I was in the bath, now he knocks tentatively and asks if I'm going to be long . . . it's cold, different. Unfamiliar.'

'That's awful.'

'It is. It's lonely.' It was the best thing about talking to her sister, she didn't offer platitudes or pithy rationale, but instead validated her feelings, helped her believe she wasn't going crazy. 'I'm even too polite to ask if he had any dreams in case that's a grey area. It's like when you meet a stranger and cherry-pick topics to avoid differences or awkwardness.'

'God, it sounds exhausting.'

'It is. I'm very tired. We don't talk about the old house, not ever. Not the move, the furniture we left behind, the kids' old school – all topics we would and should be nattering about. It's like an old horror movie where there's a monster on the path behind us so we don't look over our shoulders, don't turn around, we just keep looking forward and smiling as if it'll disappear or we reach safety and slam the door so it can't come in – whichever happens first. It feels like we avoid any topic that might take us down that road to where things went wrong: the night he gave her a lift back from the Christmas concert and that, apparently, was that.'

An image of them kissing like teens in his Audi sent a swirl of nausea around her stomach.

'The joke is, I was the one who asked him if he'd mind dropping her off, as I was staying back to stack chairs and sweep the hall to help get the place ready for the drop-in lunch for the homeless the next day.'

'What is it they say, no good deed goes unpunished?' Ellis sniffed.

'I can't stand it! Yes, it's exactly like I've been punished! It's pretty here and the house is great, but I've given up everything. I loved my job, there was talk of promotion, the lab was familiar, I liked the team.' She wiped her face. 'What a price I've paid!'

'You have, my love.'

'And the kids.' Her tears rolled as she thought of them starting over. 'They were settled, happy, and now . . .'

'Aunty Ellis, do you want to come crabbing? Dad's taking us down to the harbour,' Dilly shouted as she clattered down the stairs, interrupting their chat as she raced into the sitting room.

'Well, I'd absolutely love to!' Ellis leapt up, clearly distracting her niece, heading her off at the pass to give Harriet a minute, but also, as Ellis paused to squeeze her arm, Harriet knew it was a ruse to give her space, let her get her thoughts together, compose herself.

'We will probably get chips, Hats, so don't bother cooking supper!'

'Yes!' Bear shouted in response to this suggestion of a treat.

Hugo grabbed his sage-green Schöffel from the back of a chair and winked at her.

'Up for a spot of crabbing, Ellis?' He clapped his hands loudly. Harriet saw him wither under her sister's stare as she walked past him in the doorway. Her loyalty was heart-warming; her sister, her champion . . .

Harriet raised her hand in goodbye and waited until the noise of the foursome carried along the street, heading towards the harbour, and she found herself alone.

A rare moment of peace . . . I've realised that I miss my commute, the time for quiet contemplation that book-ended my working day, I miss the solitude that helped me gather my thoughts. Although I think I'd need a bit more than half an hour on the A4130 to figure my life out right now.

Everything still feels a little chaotic, to put it mildly.

It's so great having Ellis here. She's wise and a good listener. She asked me today what I want and it's made me think: what do I want?

Harriet took a moment, tapping her pen on her teeth while she let her thoughts form.

I guess what I want is to go back to golden. I have a lump in my throat, not only at this truth, but also in recognition that we had it all! And this in turn reignites my distress. Urgh, it's a horrible helter-skelter that I ride day and night. I just want to get off! I want to feel the solid ground beneath my feet. I don't know if it's even possible. I've never thought we'd recover entirely, not really. And I think that's okay. All we need is to recover enough.

Enough so that we can live together and create the haven I believe is necessary for us all to flourish. It sounds dull, pathetic even, aiming for no more than 'enough', but having lived through recent times when my heart has been pulled out of my throat, my reserves are depleted, my very bones fragile, so I can say with certainty that to attain 'enough' would feel wonderful. I've given up on the dream that nothing less than forever would do – I gave up on that the moment he stood in front of me and confessed.

I've been going outside more. I was trying to get match fit before the kids came home, joining Hugo for his strolls around the harbour and now, when the mood takes me, I sit on the high front doorstep in the sunshine with a cup of coffee. I like to watch the world go by. I study other couples, surreptitiously of course. I stare at them through my sunglasses, either as we walk or I sit. I listen to the snippets of their conversations and it makes me smile to hear the gentle teasing, the idle chit-chat about supper plans, visiting friends, facts about their families, illness, worries, the weather. These fragments of other people's lives help remind me that when a relationship works, it really is all about the small stuff: a good lunch, holding hands, lifts to the pub, the details of a shared life that bind you. Maybe golden was always too hard to maintain, maybe a small, adequate love will work.

God I hope so.

There's one couple in particular who have caught my attention.

I don't know their names, but I see them nearly every day. It seems they are outside more than they're in. Always together, engrossed in one another, come rain or shine, as if the whole world exists just for them and whatever is going on around them is merely the backdrop to their love affair. I feel drawn to them, admiring of their apparent devotion and envious of it too. He has thick curly hair, a stocky man, kind eyes, handsome, and she's petite, dark hair too, but straighter. She has big brown eyes and seems coy, smiling gently, as if her happiness is a precious thing, a secret that she carries close to her chest. They fascinate me. Forever arm in arm or hand in hand. If they slow or stop, she places her head on his shoulder. As if only this level of contact will do. They are like one person, split down the middle.

Golden . . .

My heart lifts when I spy them. I eavesdrop as we pass them on the quayside, or they pass us, or we walk slightly in front of or behind them. There are lots of us walking a familiar route along the harbour, back up past the fish and chip shop, around Capstone Hill and then doubling back to the seafront, up Mill Head and back to Fore Street. It's a pleasant walk with enough places to stop and take in the setting sun or to admire the crash of foaming waves on the rocks or to do a double-take of the dark shapes that draw your eye out to sea. Shapes and activity that suggest dolphins and whales so we screw our eyes tight to see better.

This golden couple, they wave subtly, nod and smile in the way you do when faces become familiar but are not fully acquainted, and I notice that they always keep walking, even when we are still, as if, while happy to see us, they have no intention of engaging, of diluting their perfect walk, arm in arm, shoulder to shoulder, like they have everything they need.

They laugh a lot, like teens, unabashed and doubled over.

Hugo was with me a couple of nights ago, sitting on the step at the front of Corner Cottage, taking in the night air, when they walked past, almost oblivious of our presence until I called hello, and only because it felt rude not to. They almost jumped, jarred from the bubble they'd created.

'Hi!' The woman smiled and nodded; her handsome man lifted his eyebrows in greeting.

Hugo and I watched them walk past and away down Fore Street and when they disappeared from view, he reached out and held my hand. It was almost visceral, instinctive and I let my hand rest inside his. It felt like a breakthrough, an action once so automatic, so commonplace that I didn't used to notice it, or at least gave it no credence, but in the absence of so much of our closeness, it really felt like something.

I was reminded of the early days in our relationship when such a gesture could floor me with desire, could scramble my thoughts and fill me with a longing to sit like that forever, hand in hand while we planned our future, painted a picture of the life we wanted to lead, a life lived together: two children, nice house, safe jobs, all bound with unwavering love.

He leaned close to me and whispered in my ear, 'I'm so sorry, H. I am so, so sorry.'

There was something in his tone, his manner and his thwarted expression that moved me greatly. This wasn't the first apology he'd made, far from it, but it felt different, sincere. They weren't just words, but instead suggested that he'd reached a point where he was ready to put it all behind us and move on, weary of the silent analysis, the personal dissection, the knife edge on which we teeter.

I think he's right; the constant quiet stoking of the embers does neither of us any good. We came inside and we had sex. An act that's been bubbling in the background like lava, too hot to touch, to consider – something to be feared. I'd imagined what it might be like, resuming our physical connection, as we did our best night after night not to stray from our sides of the bed, as if a river itself ran down the middle and to fall in would mean we drowned. My head full of all the hideous comparisons of his love affair, the physical union between him and someone who was not me, which still, despite admission and proof to the contrary, almost feels unbelievable.

Like many things in life that take on far greater significance in the pondering than the doing, it wasn't the big deal I had imagined. The fact it's been so long and I feel the need to write it down, sums up what a milestone it was. But the sex was quick, flat and average. But it's a start, right? I chose not to tell Ellis about this in case it gave the impression that we are healed and we are not. We really aren't.

In the immediate aftermath and ever since I've noticed a difference in Hugo.

It's as if he's had a mental checklist:

End things with Mrs Peterson

Confess all to Harriet

Pack up our home

Organise to rent it out

Find a new home

Move to the seaside

Apologise

Get the kids settled

Have sex

Carry on as if nothing ever happened . . .

And as we rattle through his list, his confidence that we are going to be okay, that he is forgiven, grows.

I know it has to be that way, but it bothers me. There has to be movement, of course, momentum to make change, and yes forgiveness, otherwise we are truly stuck. Stuck in this perpetual middle ground, this no-man's land of reflection and pretence and walking on eggshells, and with a boulder in my gut made of all that I swallow to keep the peace.

So what bothers me? It's the simple fact that he's got away with it. Because it isn't fair.

I'm aware this makes me sound like some bitter crazy who wants an eye for an eye. I'm not, but how does it happen like that? How can it be that he takes a sledgehammer to our life, my happiness, the security my children have enjoyed and have a right to? Then abra-cadabra! A quick change of postcode, a bottle or two of plonk, some timely tears and voilà! We are repackaged and sailing on.

I don't want him to suffer, of course not. That would make me a monster. I know that peaceful resolution, friendship, love and communication are the best things with which to line the walls of our home, but what if I can't? What if I am truly stuck and I start to resent the path he has put us on? What if I cannot let go of the hurt, the duplicitous nature of his affair? What then? I have just this one life – my mother used to remind me that this was not a rehearsal – and so I guess Ellis is right: the question is, how do I see it panning out?

'Mum?'

At the sound of her son's voice at the front door, as ever left on the latch, she slammed the book shut and popped it on the end table with her pen on it, as if the mighty pen was as good as any lock and key.

'In here, Bear!'

Her son darted and jumped on the spot as excitement spilled from him. He was an open book, this boy of hers, and she loved him for it. 'Have you swallowed jumping beans?'

'Mum, erm, is it okay if we go to the island, the one out on the horizon?'

'Lundy?' She'd spied it offshore on a clear day and read about it in every bit of tourist literature relating to the area.

'Yes, Lundy! Dad says there's a boat, like a ferry, and it leaves in half an hour. People are already queuing, but he said I had to come and check with you first!'

'Yes, of course, that sounds like fun!'

'An actual island, Mum! You can only get there by boat! It's small and not that far. We're going to take pasties and erm, erm, we're going to walk to the end of the island and have our pasties, then go exploring and then come home!'

'Wow!' Bear worshipped his dad and she wasn't proud of the flicker of envy that sparked in her chest. 'That sounds like an amazing adventure! Have you checked for rain?' The sky looked a little overcast.

'Dad said there's no such thing as bad weather when you're exploring.'

'I see, right.' She thought Amundsen, Scott and Shackleton might disagree. 'Are Aunty Ellis and Dilly going with you?'

'No, Dilly said it sounds boring. She wants to come home and read her book and Aunty Ellis said she might get seasick and she needs gin, so she's staying.'

'Of course she is.' Her heart flexed with love for her sister and for her little bookworm. 'Well, you guys have a great time, can't wait to hear all about it!'

'Can I take some crisps too?'

'Of course! The perfect picnic; it's a rule in Ilfracombe, you know, that you can't have a pasty without a packet of crisps too.'

'I love you, Mum.'

The way he looked at her before dashing from the room brought her to tears. Her sweet boy, unaware of what they as a family had lost, unaware of what they as a family might still lose.

'Oh,' Bear shouted from the kitchen, 'Dad says we need our waterproof jackets.'

'They're on the coat pegs.'

'We're going on an adventure! Lundy Island!' Bear continued to jump around as he stashed bags of crisps in his pockets and grabbed their coats.

'Have the best time!' She beamed. His reply was the slam of the front door.

Why did it bother her that Captain Marvellous had got away scot-free? What did she want? Punishment? That the kids would side with her? Kind of! Not that she'd ever say it and not that she wanted to think it!

And did she really? How would making Hugo suffer help her anyway? A miserable husband would only add to her own misery. No, he was right: they had to keep things neat, upbeat and with forgiveness at the core, for all their sakes. But still, it rankled a little.

He had won. Had he won? I mean, yes, they'd moved away from Ledwick Green, but had he paid his dues? And what kind of person did that make her if she wanted some kind of levelling up, some kind of debt to be paid?

A human one. The answer came to her now.

A human with a heart that was figuring out how to untangle itself from the barbed wire in which it now found itself snared . . .

A human whose emotions and wants were steeped in confusion.

CHAPTER ELEVEN

TAWRIE GUNN

AUGUST 2024

The early sun was showering Ilfracombe in a golden glow. The only thing brighter and more joyful was Tawrie Gunn's mood. From the moment she announced she really had to leave, to this point where Edgar now lingered on the top step of Corner Cottage as she dawdled on the one below, was an age. Hours, in fact. Neither of them, it seemed, was in a hurry to put an end to this date. Dusk had slipped to evening, which had become night, and as they had sat on the sofa, chatting, laughing, swapping wine for tea and crisps for toast, dawn had broken. Their encounter had been chaste, and all the more exciting for it. It was uncomfortable, the thought of leaving, exiting the bubble they had created – a space that might have been in the middle of Fore Street, but felt like a secret bolt-hole for them alone. They had idled in an alternate universe where all was wonderful and the future hung like a bright thing, tantalisingly within reach.

Her reluctance to leave was unparalleled, even if it was only to head home to grab her swimming kit and then, after her dip, to go off to work. What she wanted to do, however, more than anything, was stay beside him, keeping him within reach and in sight, unwilling to waste a second. These were new feelings and the strength of them was more than a little frightening. But mostly wonderful – entirely wonderful, in fact! Connie's warning about 'men like him' had been well heeded, but right now, as she stood within touching distance of him, she felt almost smug at how right things felt.

'Do you have to go?' He reached out and let a lock of her hair slip through his fingers. 'I've got bacon.'

'Bacon? Well, why didn't you say!' She made out to walk back inside. 'I really do have to go, sadly. I have a thing about lateness and I can't miss my swim.'

'Obviously!' he laughed. 'Is it my imagination or did that whole night last about an hour?' He smiled at her, taking in her face from this different angle, which she found simultaneously thrilling and terrifying. Would this light show off her large pores, was her scalp greasy?

'Not your imagination.' She smiled. 'It was like we put it in a microwave and *ping*! Here we are.'

'And now you've got to go and I have to eat bacon alone, and I'll probably finish off the crisps. Plus, there's lots I still want to say! *So* much to talk about!' he enthused, as if he'd just woken from a deep and restorative sleep and was keen to tackle the day.

'I'm sure you'll manage. And Ed, thank you for . . .' She hesitated, knowing this was not a simple, single date, unsure of what words could both adequately describe her happiness without freaking him out with her enthusiasm. 'I don't know, I guess, thank you for a great selection of nibbles and for my first and possibly last ever Uno tournament.'

'You never stood a chance, to be fair. I'm an Uno master.'

'Well, good for you!' she laughed.

'Do you want to go for a drink?' His suggestion was as surprising as it was welcome.

'What, now?'

'Good God, no, it's breakfast time! What kind of offer would that be?' He pulled a face in mock horror.

She gave a small smile, thinking of the times she'd come down the stairs to find her mum at the table, a coffee in a mug, a cigarette simmering on the edge of an ashtray and a small shot glass full of vodka.

'A scary one,' she admitted.

'I was thinking tonight we could go to the pub, or the Terrace Tapas.' He pointed to the restaurant and bar immediately opposite. 'We can sit outside, have a couple of cocktails. Do you have plans? Or I could open a bottle here at home, if that's not too dull two nights in a row? We don't have to play Uno if you're still smarting from your defeat? Or we could go for a long walk? Whatever, anything, I just need to know I'm going to see you.'

She bit her lip to avoid saying that two, three hundred nights in a row she would jump at the chance, dropping any plans without hesitation. And Uno or not, she couldn't care less how they spent their time as long as she was next to him.

'Home?' This word resonated. 'Well, you're certainly making the most of your holiday let! And no, I don't have plans.' She laughed, as if this idea was what fuelled her absolute delight. Whereas it was the fact he was arranging to see her again, taking her for a drink. She felt a rush of joy spread through her veins. This was what happened to other people, this was how men treated women who were shiny haired and giggly, not a slightly moody waitress who only owned jeans and was in love with the sea.

'Oh.' He looked over his shoulder into the pretty interior. 'It is a holiday let most of the time, but my family own the house. In fact, we do – my sister and I. Don't know why I didn't say, didn't want to sound . . .'

Tawrie tried to speak but the words cued up on her tongue got buried under an avalanche of nervous excitement. Did this mean he might be sticking around?

'All right then.' She twisted to leave before taking one last look at him. 'I think a long walk would be nice. About seven?' she suggested, as she shoved her hands in her jeans pockets and tried to calm her flustered pulse.

'About seven. Come and knock for me!'

'I will.' It felt wonderful, unifying, to already have in-jokes, a history, no matter how brief.

Without warning, he reached out and pulled her to him, and it happened.

He kissed her.

It was sudden, unexpected and all the more exciting because of it. She had thought he might at various points throughout the evening, but there was a reticence that she found sweet, respectful, despite being desperate to take things up a notch.

It was a wonderful kiss.

Their first and one she would never forget; the start of *them*, the beginning. It was a kiss given chastely and without embarrassment, as though it was the most natural thing in the world to lean in. A tiny peck that turned into something lingering, open-mouthed, wet-mouthed, soft-lipped, and gloriously life affirming! Each moment of contact an electric shock of bliss that evoked teenage lust and a desperate, desperate desire for more. Her fingers roamed his bare arms as he stroked her neck and she placed her hands in his hair and felt the solidity of his form beneath her touch as the fire built and built . . .

Right there on the doorstep, anyone could be passing! She moved backwards and found it hard to breathe, to find words, quite overcome and entirely consumed by the physical contact.

She felt him watch her leave.

'Hope the day passes as quickly as last night!' he called, and she thought she might burst.

He had kissed her.

She had kissed him!

And it felt wonderful!

This was not merely a vague hope that lived in her imagination, nor was it the fanciful imaginings of another life while she swam, or one of the daydreams that comforted her before sleep claimed her; this was Edgar telling her that he too wished he could magic time forward until they saw each other again. Edgar, *Ed*, who part-owned this lovely house on Fore Street. A house she had walked by a hundred thousand times without knowing how significant it would become. Ed, who just might be sticking around. She felt a little dizzy, a little out of sorts; this no doubt due to the heady and complex emotions that filled her right up and the fact she'd polished off three large glasses of the other, pink stuff on an almost empty stomach, and hadn't slept.

'Tawrie?'

'What?' She stopped outside the table tennis club and looked back to the step on which he perched, leaning on the doorframe, his arms folded, as if there was nowhere he'd rather be. She put her hands on her hips in a mock huff. 'What?' she called again.

'Just . . .' He smiled at her and she got it. *Just* . . . for the sheer joy of saying the other's name out loud. *Just* . . . in anticipation of the evening ahead. *Just* . . . in memory of that kiss. No matter that her loins had gone into overdrive and she wanted nothing more than to run back inside and take the kissing malarky upstairs, she was also aware of Connie's wise words:

'*You're sweet, lovely, slightly grumpy, serious-faced Tawrie Gunn and I don't want you to get hurt . . . Just don't give too much of you away . . .*'

And she hadn't. The most intimate part of their evening was when Ed had grabbed a wool blanket and thrown it over their legs as they lay on that wide, comfortable sofa.

◆ ◆ ◆

Having managed to grab her kit without disturbing the other two Gunn residents of Signal House, her ride down to Hele Bay Beach was swift. She waved to Jago and Maudie who were already pulling strokes a little way out in the bay.

'Morning, fellow Peacocks!' she yelled, and heard their laughter by way of reply. It seemed only natural to share the joy that wanted to explode from her. The water felt warm today – of course it did – and as she let her shoulders dip beneath the surface she closed her eyes.

'Here I am . . . here I am, Dad,' she whispered. 'Where to start? I have news, I guess. The man I told you about, he and I . . . I can hardly get the words out! We spent the evening together, well, longer, actually. And it was sweet and easy and I think I would have been happy sitting on that sofa with him for eternity. I know it sounds crazy, impossible! We've literally only just met and yet, I hardly dare say it, it feels like something incredible. I wish you'd felt that, I wish you'd had it. I can't imagine Mum staying sober long enough for you to have shared what we did last night. And my heart breaks for all that you missed out on. I would so love for you to meet him. I really would.'

'Are you going to bob around all morning, Ms Gunn, or is there swimming to be done?' Maudie came alongside and cut her chat with her dad short.

'To be honest, I'm rather liking just being still.'

'I get that. Sometimes it's the best way to clear the head. And there's no better place to do it than right here in the water. Aren't we lucky?' The old lady cupped a handful of water and splashed her face, which was wrinkled, sun-damaged, freckled, and beautiful with all the life it spoke of.

'We are. Very, very lucky. Especially me right now. I think . . . I think I might be in love, Maudie.' She had to tell someone. Had to let the news out!

'Tawrie! Oh well, that's absolutely marvellous! Good for you! Is it with the young man you were chatting to on the beach?'

'Yes.' Her smile a visceral reaction at picturing his face. 'I feel daft saying it – dramatic even. Like some infatuated teenager. Even I don't think it's possible! But it's how I feel.'

Maudie turned in the water to face her. 'Never feel daft about it, Tawrie. It's a story not everyone gets to tell: how they started, when they started and how they knew.' It was almost instinctive, the way her eyes sought out Jago as he swam through the waves. Tawrie couldn't help but wonder if a long love was possible for her and Ed, and the very thought sent a ripple of joy right through her.

'How did you and Jago start and when did you know?' She was curious.

'It was a very, very long time ago, when dinosaurs roamed the earth!' They both laughed out loud; she loved this woman's humour! 'Oh, Tawrie, so much has happened in our little lives, lots of things that I probably should remember but have forgotten, but meeting him . . .' She closed her eyes briefly and lay back in the water. Tawrie did the same and the two bobbed alongside each other like plump, recumbent starfish on a rock. 'Every detail is etched in my mind like a photograph. Even the scent of the gardenias that my mother had cut from the garden and put in an earthenware jug on the hall table. If I close my eyes I can smell them.' Maudie closed her eyes again and inhaled deeply, as if doing just that. 'Our parents were friends and my mother mentioned that Jago Bray was coming over with his mum, and honestly, my heart sank. I wanted to go and see my friends, play tennis, not make polite conversation with some ghastly boy my mother was introducing me to. I knew for a fact that if she liked him then I most definitely would not! Besides, I had my eye on Gerald McIntosh from the youth club.'

'So what happened?' Tawrie trod water and let the waves soothe her muscles and ease her spirit.

'What happened is that in he walked and he was smiling, and I got this feeling in the pit of my stomach. It was powerful, surprising, and in my mind I said, "There you are!" Like . . . like . . .'

'Like you'd been waiting for him, you just didn't know it.' Tawrie spoke softly of her own experience.

'Yes. Exactly like that, Tawrie, and here we are, a thousand years later, and I still don't like to be apart from him. I would still rather sit somewhere with my hand in his than anything else on earth. We take care of each other.'

'I can see you do, every day, and I love how you laugh together and at each other.'

'We do. Laughing is important. It helps get you through the tough times, the challenges. We've learned that taking care of each other isn't only a physical thing; it's not just going to fetch a blanket.'

Tawrie pictured the moment Ed had tucked the blue wool blanket around her legs, making sure she was warm, taking care of her, and her stomach rolled with pure happiness at the memory.

Maudie wasn't done. 'Driving safely, preparing food, giving medicine, they're all important, but it's about taking care of each other's mental health too. Not easy in this world with all its pressures, but we've always made sure we don't add to the burden, we're kind to each other. We're reliable. We provide a haven.'

Tawrie felt the sting of emotion that swelled in her throat. It was a beautiful sentiment.

'And I wish for you every bit of love and luck that the universe can gather. I want it all for you, Tawrie. You are a smashing young woman.'

'Thank you, Maudie.' Her words were as touching as they were sincere. 'What happened to Gerald McIntosh?'

'Who knows?' Maudie laughed and pulled through the water, off to swim alongside her great love. 'But he missed out on me and for that alone we should pity him, because I'm quite wonderful!'

Yeah, you are! Tawrie watched as Maudie caught up with her lover of a thousand years.

Tentatively she walked through the front door of Signal House, unsure, in that moment, if she wanted to face the other Gunn women. It was different to confiding in Maudie, who was a little removed from the situation. She was wary of filling Freda with expectations that might set the gossip train in motion, knowing that would only feel like a pressure, because despite her strength of feeling and earlier conversation with Maudie, it was still early days. Very early days. And when it came to her mother, she didn't want her involved in any way, knowing her knack of sarcastically stomping on the roots of anything that brought Tawrie joy, whether intentionally or not. Her mother's behaviour was also unsavoury, grubby, and she didn't want what she and Ed shared to be sullied by association. Not that this realisation made her happy; it didn't. Quite the opposite, in fact.

Her nan was washing dishes in the kitchen and for a moment Tawrie watched from the sitting room, through the wide doorway where the door was permanently propped open as the older woman plunged her hands into the deep dome of suds in the sink before lining the plates up in the wooden rack that graced the draining board.

'Is that you, Tawrie?' Freda called over her shoulder.

She should have known any plans to avoid detection would fail miserably. 'Yep. It's me, Nan.' She walked over and placed her palms on her nan's shoulders. The woman turned her head and kissed the back of her hand. An act so loving, so tender that, with thoughts of her mother's sordid habits still lingering in her mind, Tawrie greatly appreciated.

'Where've you been, love, out for your swim?'

'Yep, just got back.'

'And how was your date? Connie's already texted to ask if I've seen you yet!'

It might, she realised, already be a little late to stop the gossip train from leaving the station.

'It was lovely. Really lovely. We sat and talked and laughed and I'm seeing him again tonight.'

'Tonight?' Freda whipped round and placed one bubble-covered hand over her mouth. 'Goodness me! That's a bit keen, isn't it?'

'I guess.' She shrugged, going for coy, trying to hide the flames of delight that she was sure shot from her.

'Is he lovely?' Her nan looked at her earnestly. 'Cos he needs to be.'

'He is lovely.'

Freda nodded and reached for Tawrie's hands, which she held in both of her soggy ones.

'You deserve the best. You're the most wonderful granddaughter; your dad would be so proud.' This was the trigger for her nan's face to crumble with distress. In a practised response, Tawrie stood tall and swallowed her own surge of sadness, being strong for her nana, allowing the old woman to metaphorically fold her into her lap.

147

'I've got to go and get changed for work, Nan, will you be okay?' She hated leaving her like this.

'Course I will. You go get ready, little love. I'm going to do my crossword.'

As she trod the half landing, her mother came out of her bedroom.

'You coming in or going out?' Annalee asked as she leaned on the wall; her whole body seemed to wobble with the effort of staying upright.

'Both.'

With no more than a cursory glance to take in the state of the woman, she dashed to her room to get ready for work.

Looking out of her bedroom window over the harbour, her mood was further elevated by the sight of her very favourite kind of day. It was not yet seven thirty and the sky at this early hour was pink – pink! Sugared-almond coloured, the air already warm. It did something to her spirit to look out and feel the anticipation of the day ahead softening her bones and putting a smile on her face. It never occurred to her to take a picture, knowing that a photograph couldn't truly capture the marshmallow palette nor the feeling that came with it. Plus, it was a view so perfectly preserved in her mind's eye, a single image would only fail to do justice to the shift that came immediately after or immediately before; it was a scene that fluctuated in colour and subject, a hypnotic movie.

It was a feeling no doubt enhanced by the happy, intoxicated state in which she found herself. This girlish lightness to her footfall, the flutter of joy in the base of her stomach, all down to the fact that she would see him again tonight. She was also certain that, just as she thought about him, so he was thinking about her. It wasn't logical or rational, but Maudie was right: she *knew*.

Do you have to go? She liked to replay this in her head. Not only to capture his voice, which was clear and just the right level of deep, but also the way he had looked at her and she at him. It had been intense, gut-stirring, and spoke of an interest that one date should ordinarily be no basis for. But there was nothing ordinary about any of it.

She had spoken sincerely to Maudie when she'd used the word love. *Love!* Or at least how she thought love should feel: warm and like coming home, fascinating and raising more questions than it answered. But how could she feel like this after two conversations and one date? It was crazy! Irresponsible. Literally madness! Her of all people! She didn't do this, didn't feel this! She was practical, level-headed, the person who paid bills, cared for Freda, wrote letters, bolted the door, and checked on her mother to make sure she wasn't going to vomit in her sleep, or that the man she was trying to sneak up the stairs wasn't an axe murderer. And yet there she was: giddy. That word in itself reserved for flighty teens and romantics, the butterfly girls who flitted from beau to beau.

Tawrie was not and never had been one of those, and she hardly recognised herself, as she stood in the window of her bedroom, looking out over the pink blush of a summer morning. She could see his face dancing in the clouds, hear his voice above the call of the gulls and if she closed her eyes . . . She shivered, as if able to recreate the way she had felt when the universe saw fit to make them collide. Aware of how it sounded, making her utterly, utterly certifiable, she was also unable to deny that it was an important collision, a life-changing event for her. Excitement surged in her veins and hope and happiness had a new name and that name was: Ed!

'Taw?' Her mother called from the green bathroom on the half landing, drawing her from her delightful musings, as she rushed to get changed for the start of her shift.

'Yep?'

'I've got the shits and there's no loo roll, can you grab some from the airing cupboard?'

149

And just like that, real life was restored.

◆ ◆ ◆

'Morning, Needle! Early start?' she called as she passed the King Billy where Needle was loading crates on the pavement.

'Yep, got a delivery.' He looked up. 'What in the world?' He clutched his chest and leaned dramatically on the wall. 'I thought you were Tawrie Gunn. I mean, you look like her, you sound like her, a bit, but you can't possibly be her, because you're smiling and chatting so I know you're an imposter! Where's that sour-faced, half-hearted hand wave that you give as you walk on by?'

'Very funny!' she tittered, knowing that if her mother's shits hadn't dented her mood, Needle's sarcasm wasn't going to come close.

'I'm pulling your leg, Taw, but I have to say it's good to see you looking happy!'

'It's good to feel it!' she confirmed.

'So what's all this in aid of? You won the lottery?'

She stopped and looked at the man she had always known, as an image of Ed topping up her wine glass before counting out the Uno cards floated to the fore of her mind. Then that kiss! Oh that kiss on the step . . .

'I have kind of, yes.'

'Well, in that case, lend us a fiver?' He winked. 'Oh and don't forget to—'

'I know, I know' – she waved as she walked away – 'ask Connie if she'll go out on your bloody yacht!'

'Atta girl!' he called after her. 'I'll wear her down, you know! Or I'll die trying!'

CHAPTER TWELVE

HARRIET STRATTON

AUGUST 2002

Harriet sat at the kitchen table and thought about how much she would miss her sister. Ellis had left the day before and Harriet had taken it particularly hard. Her sister's very presence – willing ear, unfailing support and love – had made the biggest difference, made Harriet feel less alone.

'You're up early?' Hugo spoke the half statement, half question, as he stood in his shorts and his old rowing club t-shirt.

'Couldn't sleep.'

She glanced over her shoulder and did her best to let her eyes crease into a smile. The look that said, *All good here, nothing to worry about; let's just carry on!* A look that she had perfected over the last few weeks but one that was built on foundations of deceit. It was a look that was growing harder and harder to make convincing.

'Kids are still zonked out. Late night last night – that competitive Uno battle got them riled. It makes me laugh how Dilly is such a stickler for the rules and Bear's just happy to win a bit, lose a bit; for him it's the fun in taking part.'

'Mmm.' She nodded, feeling this was preferable to dissecting his words, wanting to point out that yes, Dilly was a stickler for the rules, as was she. *Don't cheat at Uno. Don't cheat on your wife. Don't cheat your family out of their lovely, lovely life.* It felt easier to say nothing, better not to start the day in a way that would be challenging, hostile.

'Thought I'd go for a run up around the Torrs.'

The Torrs was a nature reserve and one of the four main hills of Ilfracombe that provided a spectacular view. He liked to run it alone, music on, said it helped clear his head, and this she more than understood, envying him the opportunity for escape. She found recently that no matter what she did her thoughts were cluttered.

'Sure.' In truth she wanted him gone, out of sight, relishing the prospect of an hour of quiet this early in the morning, a chance to try to clear *her* head.

He leaned in and pecked her on the cheek. A hard kiss that saw their cheekbones clash. It was unpleasant almost, and certainly unwelcome. Her instinct was to yell, '*Don't fucking kiss me! You kissed her with that mouth! Don't you dare!*' It happened like this sometimes, when she had time alone to overthink and hurt steered her down a dead end where, trapped, the temptation was to howl and pounce like a creature snared. Of course, Hugo would only wonder where this reaction had come from. The aftermath of such an outburst would scare the kids and this thought alone was not enough to justify it. Instead she pushed her feet into the floor and ground her teeth together.

His low hum as he went off to locate his trainers spoke of how oblivious he was to it all. Her whole body shook.

The front door closed quietly behind him and she heard him greet Andrew the window cleaner who rattled up and down Mill Head with his ladder.

'Lovely morning!'

She heard Hugo's chat through the window. It might have been a lovely morning for him, but for her . . . Sinking down into the leather armchair that felt like home, she reached for her diary, wanting to exorcise her thoughts and try to calm the volcano of anger and hurt that bubbled in her gut before the kids surfaced and came foraging for Sugar Puffs.

◆ ◆ ◆

It was mid-afternoon. Harriet wasn't used to feeling this nervous. She brushed her hair for the third time and resprayed her perfume. It was very different from slinging on a backpack and going off to meet her friends in Ledwick Green with the kids in tow, where they'd scamper off and do their own thing, while the grown-ups talked about school life, drank coffee, shared a cookie, and moaned about how little time they had in their busy lives, before arranging to do the whole thing again. Soon.

This felt a lot more formal, a bit like a test, and she so wanted to pass, knowing it would be that much easier come September if the kids knew at least one person when they started at their new school. She had no idea if Bear and the little girl who was going to be in his class next term would play nicely or even get on. Plus, she had never met the mother – suppose *they* had nothing to talk about? To be trapped with someone with whom she had zilch in common was a torturous prospect. A wave of unease washed over her. This was another challenge she would not be facing if Hugo had not royally buggered up their lives.

She was trying her best, really trying, yet these thoughts of recrimination just kept sneaking up on her.

Bear's new teacher had suggested a meet-up. It felt very much as if she were being forced into her own play date and her adrenaline was pumping. It wasn't that she was anti-social or even that she didn't miss the companionship that came with being known in her community; it was more the awkwardness she knew she'd feel when it came to all the ordinary and anticipated questions that could get asked:

'So, what made you move to Ilfracombe, Harriet?'

'Funny thing, actually; my husband had an affair with my neighbour, Mrs Peterson, and we more or less ran away in the dead of night. Can I get you a cup of tea?'

'How are you finding your new house?'

'Claustrophobic, smaller than I'm used to, but also, I suspect, because I'm sharing it with my husband who had an affair with my neighbour, did I mention that? And quite honestly, even if this room were the size of a football field, I'd still feel his proximity. Do you take sugar?'

'Let me introduce you to some of the other parents and people who live close by, it'd be good for you guys to meet people. What do you say?'

'Maybe one day, but not yet. As I said, my husband had an affair with my neighbour and we're on shaky ground when we're alone. I can't stand the thought of having to pull together and smile broadly to impress strangers. How about a biscuit?'

It was fair to say she wasn't relishing the prospect.

A knock at the front door removed further opportunity for dread. She dug deep and found a neutral smile that was neither too forced nor too keen.

'I thought it was you!' The woman smiled and Harriet felt all her worry over the encounter disappear. 'I said to Miss Knox, I'm sure I've seen a new family in Fore Street. I'm Annalee by the way.' She touched her dainty fingers to her chest.

'That's us! The new family! I'm Harriet. Please come in!' Self-consciousness cloaked her as she recognised Annalee as one half of the couple she was a little in awe of, spying on them discreetly when possible.

'And this is Tawrie.' Annalee placed her hand on the slender back of her daughter who stood a little awkwardly to one side, her leg twisting, head down, as if she'd rather be anywhere else.

'Hello, Tawrie, it's lovely to meet you. Let me give the kids a shout.' She popped her head around the bottom of the winding staircase. 'Bear, Dills! Tawrie is here! Please come through.' She ushered them into the open-plan sitting room with steps that led down to the kitchen. 'We're still not quite straight, please don't look at the random boxes or piles of clothes waiting to find a home.'

'Oh goodness me, Harriet, please don't worry about that. We live with my mother-in-law just further down the hill and I've been there for nearly ten years and the place is in chaos! I'm still unpacking!'

Harriet liked her voice, her calm manner, her kindness.

'What do you like doing, Tawrie?' The girl was shy, her eyes cast downward and her shoulders hunched forward.

'I like the beach.' She was sweet, young for her age.

'And how lucky are you, having so many beautiful beaches right on your doorstep!'

Bear and Dilly burst into the room and she watched Tawrie slink back towards her mother, as if the woman herself was a safe harbour.

'Hi!' Bear waved.

'Hello.' Dilly stared at her, her reading book still firmly clenched in her hand, suggesting this was a very unwelcome interruption.

'Bear and Dilly are starting at your school in September.' Annalee tried to grease the wheels and Harriet was grateful.

'Do you want to play Uno or we can go on my Nintendo?' Bear asked confidently and Harriet was so proud of his manner and attempt to get to know the girl, aware of how much he missed his old mates, his old house, and that he'd probably rather be playing football in his old back garden.

'Sure.' Tawrie replied with so little enthusiasm, it didn't bode well for the playing of Uno or any other activity.

'We can play in my room.' Dilly pointed upstairs and the three trooped up.

'She's quite shy,' Annalee explained.

'She'll be fine. Bear and Dilly will fight and she probably won't get a word in, or Dilly will read a book and Bear will bore her to death with his Pokémon card collection. Would you like a tea or coffee?'

'Oh, tea would be lovely.' Annalee was smiley and Harriet warmed to her.

'I'd offer you something stronger but it's probably a bit early. Plus, I don't want you to tell Miss Knox that I encouraged you to hit the bottle at three in the afternoon!' She spoke half in jest.

'I actually don't drink – well, very rarely. I'm not too good at it. One glass and it's a headache all the next day.' Annalee blushed as she shook her head. 'I can't be doing with that.'

'Sounds like you need more practice!' she joked, liking the woman's honesty.

'Dan, my husband, always says I'm a very cheap date!' Annalee joked back, and Harriet liked her instantly. 'So what brings you to Ilfracombe?'

This was the one question she had been dreading and at the sound of it, she felt a narrowing of her throat, along with the threat of tears. It was as mortifying as it was awkward.

'Oh my God, Harriet, I didn't mean to pry. I hope I haven't upset you! It's none of my business why you came here. I feel awful! I was just—'

'No, no.' She took a minute to catch her breath. 'It's nothing you've done, Annalee, things are just a bit . . . Oh, I'm so embarrassed. I'm not usually like this!' Grabbing the kitchen roll, she tore off a square and shoved it under her nose and wiped her eyes.

'Don't be embarrassed. We all have days like this.' Annalee placed her hand on Harriet's back and just this one small act of camaraderie, of kinship, was enough to set those darn tears flowing again.

'It's been weeks like this unfortunately.' She sniffed.

'Why don't we sit down?' Annalee calmly took control as the two sat opposite each other at the kitchen table. Harriet put her elbows on the tabletop and cried for a minute.

'I'm quite good at keeping it all together, until I'm not and then, *blurgh*! It just all tumbles out, like someone pulls my plug.'

Annalee smiled at her. 'You'll probably feel better after a good *blurgh*!'

'I hope so.' She smiled at her sweet guest.

'It really is none of my business, and I'm not prying, but what I will say is that Ilfracombe is a good place to be if you want to get away from the world. It's small enough to hold you in its embrace, big enough to give you space and there's not much a walk around the headland in a brisk wind can't cure.'

'You walk a lot, don't you? I've seen you and your husband.'

'Yes, that's where I recognise you from. I thought you might be holiday renters at first, but you kept popping up. I said to Dan that I thought you might have moved in, and here we are!'

Harriet noted the way her face lit up at the mere mention of her husband.

'Here we are, with me crying into a soggy bit of kitchen roll!' She held up the near-shredded evidence and they both laughed.

'This is the first time I've been inside this house.' Annalee looked around the kitchen. 'It's lovely!'

'Well, it will be when we're finished.'

Conversation was easy and Harriet could see that Annalee was the kind of woman she could call a friend.

'And you're right, we do like a good walk. Partly because it's how we get out of the house. Living with my mother-in-law is great, but we need that escape, if you know what I mean.' She rolled her eyes.

'Goodness, I can't imagine living with my mother-in-law – lovely though she is,' Harriet added with comic effect. Again they both giggled.

'Freda's great, that's Dan's mum, a real character and very good to us. Don't know how we'd manage financially if it weren't for her opening up her house to us. She's amazing, brilliant with Tawrie, but still, Dan and I crave alone time. On the plus side, we have a built-in babysitter, so we *can* go out walking!'

Harriet remembered what that felt like: to want nothing other than to be with Hugo, holding Hugo, kissing him, talking to him, uninterrupted . . .

'I'm so glad you came over, Annalee. Recently, I'm not too good with meeting new people but I'm trying very hard not to pass this on to the kids, telling them with false bravado that it'll be fun! All the while my stomach churns with nerves and I dread having made the arrangement in the first place. I can be quite shy; things have . . . things have made me quite shy.' It was all she could give away. A hint that she might be struggling but without the detail that would decry Hugo or set tongues wagging – the very thing they had moved away from Ledwick Green to avoid.

'Me too!' Tawrie's mum leaned forward. 'I used to be worse – wouldn't say boo to a goose – but Dan . . .'

There it was again, that look.

'. . . he's incredible. And I think, if someone like him wants to be married to me, then I can't be that bad. I might have something to say after all!'

Harriet noted the sweet blush on her cheeks, and tried hard to smother the unattractive stab of envy that rose in her throat.

'Well, I think you have plenty of lovely things to say.'

'You too, Harriet.'

The two shared a look of understanding.

'Now, how about that cup of tea?'

'Yes! Smashing!' Annalee clapped her small hands together.

Their guests stayed for a little over an hour, enough time for Harriet to feel the seedlings of friendship sprout and for Bear to decide that he didn't want to spend time with the girl again.

'She can't even work the controller! And she doesn't like football!' he had moaned.

Harriet had laughed softly. These, according to her boy who was yet to leap on to the threshold of teen life, the two most valuable assets a friend could have. Tawrie had sadly failed on both counts.

It was now early evening. The kids were in bed – Bear no doubt playing a computer game and Dilly with her head in a book – and Hugo was watching a movie in the bedroom. Harriet put a call in to Ellis who failed to answer. Disappointment at this fact was far more galling than it would normally have been, such was her turmoil, her fragility, her loneliness. A quick glance at the clock confirmed it was probably getting close to supper time in her sister's house, and so instead she reached for her diary and sat coiled in a corner of the sofa.

Met the lovely Annalee Gunn today, my neighbour.
A woman infatuated and desperately in love with her

husband, Dan. I cried like an idiot. She was very sweet to me. I like her. She brought her daughter Tawrie, who according to Bear was the worst playmate, her inability to play on the Nintendo 64 and her lack of interest in football consigning them to never be friends! At least he and Dills will know someone when they start school, even if it's just to nod at in the corridor or to stand next to in the lunch queue. Maybe I'm worrying too much, trying too hard to engineer what should be a natural process. Urgh! It just feels like a big deal because they were so happy at their old school and I hate how unfair this all is. And here we are back to that . . .

Her phone rang.

'Sorry, Hats, I was just in the tub! All okay?' Her sister sounded breathless, rushed.

'Yes, all fine, just checking in.'

'Good, you know I worry less if I've heard your voice.'

'Well, here I am.' She smiled at her sister's mothering.

'Kids okay?'

'Yep, in bed.'

'I wish Maisie was; she's out with an unsuitable boy who has a car! I feel so old – one minute she's trying to balance building blocks and now she's out in a car with a boy who wants to snog her face off!'

Harriet laughed out loud, but the thought of Bear and Dilly doing similar was worrying. Luckily it felt a long way off.

'You used to be that girl.' She liked to remind her sister.

'And that's precisely what's worrying me! The poor boy doesn't stand a chance!' They both howled. 'Although Maisie is much more sensible than I ever was.'

'In fairness that's quite a low bar.' She ribbed her sister in the way that only she could.

'Hugo still upset?' Ellis's tone had switched to one of concern. Harriet had told her about his crying alone in empty rooms.

'Not so much,' she whispered, deciding not to confide how his gaiety was like an invitation to bite, aware that Ellis had little time for Hugo right now and not wanting that to worsen. The realisation that she was shielding him, protecting him, was conflicting. 'At least I haven't heard it. Things are ticking along, and yes, I'm aware how pithy that sounds, but it's the truth.'

'I was thinking . . .' Her sister paused and Harriet listened hard, as if conscious that Ellis's next words might be important.

'Thinking what?' she flared, impatiently.

'Don't know if I should say.'

'For goodness' sake, just say it! You can't lead with that and then not say!' she tutted and heard Ellis take a breath.

'I've been thinking a lot about why Hugo has been crying, upset. It's not like him.'

'Well, thanks for that, Einstein. In case you hadn't noticed we are going through something a little out of the ordinary.' She sighed.

'All right, calm down. This is why I'm thinking twice about saying anything!' Ellis snapped.

She felt the beginnings of a headache as her sister voiced her justification, and rubbed her temples. 'Ellis, I'm tired. Just say it and then I can go to bed.'

'Do you think . . .' Her sister swallowed, nervously. '. . . do you think he's distressed because he is genuinely remorseful, regretting every act that has brought you to this point? Or is he crying because he feels trapped, wants out, or even because he's missing Mrs Peterson?'

Harriet opened her mouth to speak but no words came. Instead, she made a noise that was almost a strangled whine. 'I . . .' She stared at the pen in her hand and felt her body shaking. The thought was too monstrous, the consequences of this being true too horrendous to contemplate.

'Hats, are you still there?'

'I just . . . I can't even begin to . . .'

'Just forget it.' She got the distinct feeling Ellis was trying to backtrack.

'How can I forget that? Do you think that's true? Did you see something or hear something?' With every shred of confidence in her own attractiveness destroyed, her stomach felt hollow.

'No, nothing. But I only look out for you, Harriet, you and the kids, and I know what type of man Hugo is – never overly emotional and certainly not a crier. It's been on my mind and I just want you to be sure, because I understand forgiving him once, if that's what you want to do and you think you guys can recapture what you had, but if he were to mess you around a second time . . .'

She knew her sister's concerns were born out of love, but they cut no less deeply for that.

'I'm too tired to process this, Ellis.' Her headache turned up a notch.

'I don't want to put horrible thoughts in your head, but I want you to be sure – you *need* to be sure – because this is a crossroads and the choices you make and the path you choose have consequences for you and for Bear and Dills.'

'I know that.' She closed her eyes tightly and willed her sister to stop talking. 'I need to go. I'm getting a dreadful headache.'

'Call me tomorrow, promise me?'

'I promise you.'

'I love you, Hats, never forget it.'

'Love you too.'

She sat for a while on the sofa with her sister's ugly suggestions whirring inside her skull.

'Penny for them?' Hugo caught her unawares as he stood in the doorway.

'Just . . . thinking.' She shrugged and smiled, going overboard to prove the inconsequential nature of her musings. Still pretending, bottling up the fizzing tangle of thoughts and hoping she could keep the cork from exploding!

'I'm going to grab a glass of red, would you like one?'

'No, no thanks. I've got a bit of a headache.' She was reminded of her earlier chat with Annalee, who didn't drink. Harriet was certainly less inclined to do so now the kids were back under their roof.

'My movie is halfway through if you want to join me. I could try to catch you up?' he called from the kitchen.

'No, but thanks. I might read for a bit.'

'Cheers!' With a cheery face, he raised the glass of wine and made his way back up the stairs.

The diary fell open at the last page she had written and she let her pen dance across the page.

> *I know Ellis's words will stay with me . . . she's got me asking questions, like why Hugo felt the need to stray in the first place? Is it something I did or didn't do? I mean, let's face it, I talk about us being happy before, content before, hopeful before, but how happy, content and hopeful can he have been if he chose to have sex with Wendy Peterson, and what if when I talk about that life before, I am actually only referring to how I felt? It's possible, if not likely, that we were in fact not as happy as I believed, or wanted to believe. And if this is true, then could it be that too was just pretending?*

'I've come for the bottle! Who am I trying to kid?' His voice took her by surprise. 'I'd only be up and down the stairs twice more and having to pause the movie is a pain in the—' He watched as she closed her diary quickly. 'Okay, woman of mystery! What *are* you writing?'

'Just notes, jottings. It helps me order my thoughts.' This was almost the truth.

'Can I help order those thoughts in any way?' His cheery grin all but gone.

'I've been thinking . . .' She decided not to divulge Ellis's part in her doubts. 'About why you made the choices you did and I guess I still feel gutted because if you hadn't . . .'

He leaned on the wall by the door.

'I think what you want is not only my apology, which I've given many times, but you want me to take all the blame for the situation.' He kicked his heel against the wainscot, his expression one of mild irritation, as if the red wine had stripped him of his mask. Or maybe the easy false nature of their exchanges since the kids had been home had given him mistaken confidence that he no longer had to try quite so hard. Either way it was sobering and galling in equal measure.

'What do you mean by that?' It was a match to kindling and her hackles rose.

'I mean, Harriet, that you want it to be solely my fault that this marriage has hit the rocks.'

'Are you kidding me right now?'

'No, I'm fucking not!'

His language and tone were incendiary and she was aware of a rising tide of fury that she did not want to erupt with the kids in close proximity; they'd already had to leap for safety once when they left Ledwick Green.

'Follow me,' she instructed as she jumped up from the sofa.

'What?' He looked at her like she'd lost her reason.

'I said, follow me!' She moved closer to him and spoke through gritted teeth and made her way to the smallest room in the house where it was possible to talk privately.

CHAPTER THIRTEEN

Tawrie Gunn

August 2024

At the sight of Edgar standing in his open doorway, glancing comically at his watch, she sped up, jogging the last few steps.

'You're late!' Edgar tutted. 'And I thought you said you hated tardiness.'

'I do. And give me a break, it's only five past!' She had once again found herself in a quandary with so little to choose from inside her wardrobe, opting finally for a plain white tee, which had gone a little grey over the years, and her jeans.

'Hey' – he held up his palms – 'it's not me that set the rule.'

Reaching down, he took her hand and helped her up the steps. Closing the front door with urgency, he pulled her into him and kissed her hard on the mouth. It was as if nothing would do other than this close and urgent contact, suggesting he too had been thinking about it all day. Almost picking up where they left off, it was an act that was at once new and exciting, yet also the most natural thing in the world.

'That's better.' He ran his hand over her hair and looked into her face. 'This is weird, right? Like really weird?'

'What bit?' She blinked, as happiness fizzed in her veins.

'The whole "known you for five minutes, but feels like a lifetime" thing. Is it just me?' He kissed her again.

'No. It's not just you.' She made the delightful confession.

'I don't know whether to be excited or shit scared.' He spoke softly.

'Both.'

'Yep, both.' He held her close and she inhaled the scent of him. A smell that was still a little unfamiliar, yet gloriously intoxicating.

'I need to sort things, Tawrie. It's a lot.' His expression was thoughtful and she loved how seriously he was taking this new coupling. It gave her confidence.

'It is a lot!'

'I need to sort things so we can make plans so we can . . . so we can . . .' he stuttered.

'So we can what?' She leaned back to properly see his face.

'Go forward, if that's what you . . .' His shyness was attractive.

'Yes, it's what I . . . No doubt.' She placed her hand on her stomach, trying to quell the feelings that threatened to burst from her.

Squashed into the hallway, she was aware of something fundamental shifting in her world. She swallowed and tensed and it was in this second that a portal to a place she had always doubted existed opened up right in front of her. A moment when she felt just like the women who chattered in the café about 'him indoors', their 'other half' or their 'bloke'. Women like Nora who looked at Gordy as if he had just fallen from Planet Fantastic; women who had heeded the call, submitted, agreed to share their life with a human who was not a relative. And it was nothing but thrilling, exciting and wonderful with all the possibilities it suggested. It was a realisation, an acceptance, and she was ready. More than ready.

He exhaled slowly and only then was she aware that he'd been holding his breath, confirming for her that her response meant as much to him as his suggestion had to her.

'That makes me very happy.' He kissed her again. This time it was gentle and brimming with intent, and it sent a surge of longing right through her core.

She smiled at his simple summary, not only in delight at their easy reunion, but also in anticipation of their walk and the whole night ahead. It was an exchange that she knew would invite further analysis when she was alone, something to ponder as she waited tables or scraped food waste into the bin, or idled in the shower or swam at Hele Bay Beach. Words, plans almost, that would keep her warm when any cold wind of doubt whistled in via her rattly sash window or through the gap at the bottom of the front door.

'I thought we could go to Woolacombe and walk the beach right round to Putsborough? Do you fancy it?' His eagerness was infectious.

'Yes, great. Haven't done that for a while.'

'I'll drive.' He grabbed a bunch of keys from the wooden hooks that hung on the wall. At least one, she noted, was a door key. She felt a stab of anxiety about the home he had in London – a place she couldn't picture, a routine of which she was ignorant – and she wondered how, whatever this grew into, things would pan out if he stayed in the city. Simultaneously, she wondered if this quiet, harbourside life would suit him when the sun was absent and the shops were shut for the season. This was no doubt what he meant about sorting things out, untying the knots of his current life.

'I'm parked in Ropery.'

They made their way down Fore Street. Tawrie's stomach jumped at the sight of her nan putting the rubbish into the wheelie bin that lived in the bin store at the bottom of the steps that led up to Signal House. It felt way too early to be introducing him to family, way too early for publicly acknowledging they even spent time together. It felt like a pressure, putting a stake in the ground that she knew came with expectations, at least from her excitable kin. Not that there was much she could do about it. Without time to second-guess it, her nan shouted.

'Tawrie Gunn! There you are!'

'Hi, Nan.' With little point in trying to avoid it, she decided to bite the bullet. 'This is Ed. He's staying at Corner Cottage.'

'Hello Ed, love. I'm Freda.' Tawrie noted the way her nan studied him from top to bottom, fully aware that he was so much more than Ed from Corner Cottage.

'Lovely to meet you, Freda. We're just off to Woolacombe for a walk on the beach if you want to join us?'

Tawrie was dumbstruck – happy he'd been sweet enough to invite her nan along, but also worried, in case the old lady said yes.

'Oh, that's very kind of you, dear, but I've just made a cuppa.' She pointed up the steps. 'And also my programme's on in a bit. But you two have fun!' Her nan winked at her, an act that smacked of approval. 'See you later, Taw. Love you, my girl!'

She felt her heart swell. 'Love you too.'

'And come up any time, Ed, kettle's always on!' Freda hummed softly to herself as she trod the stairs.

'I will!' Ed seemed taken with her nan, as they watched her disappear up the steep steps. 'She's fab!'

'Yep.'

'Why's it called Signal House?' he asked as they made their way down the street towards Ropery car park.

'Ah, well, that's up for debate. It's a ramshackle old place, a couple of hundred years old and in need of TLC and a big injection of cash. But we love it. There's a small, odd-shaped room on the top floor, almost like a lookout, and rumour has it that it's where signals were passed across the rooftops on dark or foggy nights.'

'Ooh, that sounds nefarious. What were they signalling about?'

'Well, if the Gunns had anything to do with it I doubt it was to talk about the weather!'

'I hope it was piracy, or smuggling barrels of grog or treasure!'

She laughed at the distinct excitement in his voice and the way his eyes had lit up. 'What are you, a child?'

'Find me a man who doesn't love pirates and treasure and I'll show you a man who is tired of life.'

'That sounds like a t-shirt slogan.'

'Okay, negative Nelly, sorry if I find the whole idea exciting.' He drew breath, as they stepped down into the Ropery car park. 'But have you properly checked the attic and cellar for trapdoors, hidden treasure, secret tunnels, buried scrolls, signs in the wall, that kind of thing?'

'Oh my God! Trapdoors and hidden treasure? You *are* a child!'

She secretly loved how enamoured he was with the idea of Signal House, the family HQ that was as much a part of the Gunns as any living, breathing relative.

'Here she is! The silver dream machine!' He patted the roof of a slightly battered, ancient silver Seat Ibiza with a rear window taped shut with gaffer tape and several rusted dents peppering the bodywork, and opened the passenger door.

'She?'

'Yes. She has a chassis of extreme beauty. Almost a classic. And within her confines lurk some of my funniest memories.' He didn't crack a smile and it made her laugh out loud. This was what he did.

'Do I want to know?' She pulled a face. It was inevitable that she wondered if these best memories involved a girl who wasn't her. Not that there was a darn thing she could do about it, but she very much hoped they would make better memories that were even funnier.

'Have you ever laughed so much you can't breathe, sung so loudly your voice goes hoarse, and had to pee in an old plastic Coke bottle because of a traffic jam so bad you feared you'd miss your own graduation?'

'Yes, yes and no.' She climbed into the front seat, choosing not to comment on the various stains that lurked on the upholstery.

'I've said too much already,' he whispered, looking left and right with spy-like theatricality, and this time they both laughed.

It felt exhilarating to be tootling the lanes that ran along the coast in Ed's car. Although in fairness, she'd have found traipsing up the High Street with him to buy milk or going to the dentist just as much fun. The novelty of being with him, the discoveries still to make, greater than any trip. Even in his battered car that was almost a classic.

The car park in Woolacombe was quiet at this time of evening. Still with the day's residual warmth lingering in the air, and the sky clear and blue, surfers sat on their boards and bobbed on the shoreline with no real waves to speak of. Their camaraderie, no doubt cemented in the unified love of the surf, was palpable even at this distance. It reminded her of Maudie and Jago, her fellow Peacocks, and how they had become such an important part of her routine.

'I'd love to learn to surf,' he commented as they trod the sand-covered stairs that took them down past the Beachcomber café. 'I think it's a really cool thing to do. I've never been cool, but I reckon I'd feel cool if I was a surfer, and that's halfway there, right?'

'Absolutely, and you're in the right place to do it, here. Croyde, Saunton, you're spoilt for choice.'

'I don't think I've ever met a stressed-out surfer. I think putting on that wetsuit and holding that board must be like magic that strips away the worries of life. I mean, they could be running on high octane, frantic all day and then *bam*, they step into waves and it all melts away. At least that's what I think.'

'I think it's more than that. The gathering in vans for warm drinks post-surf, the sitting in all weathers looking out over the ocean, taking a minute. I always think it looks nice, inclusive. And I know how much my morning swim centres me, calms me.' She wanted to know him at a deeper level, understand him, this man she was falling for who was still, in so many ways, a stranger. 'Do you have many worries in life then, Ed?'

'Not compared to some people.' He stared at the sand. 'Shall we sit here for a while?'

It was hardly the big hike she'd anticipated, as they made their way along the wide beach and sat on the soft sand, staring out at the breathtaking view. Not that she would have changed a thing. They sat close together, mere inches between their shoulders; any greater distance would have been less than satisfying.

'This really is something.' He threw his head back and exhaled, letting the last of the sun's rays kiss his face. 'Have you never wanted to move away, Taw, go up to the big smoke? Wake up with a view of a skyscraper?'

She stared at him and ordered her thoughts, in case he was fishing, thinking, like her, of their next moves, of what the future might hold if this pace and strength of feeling were to continue.

'It's complicated. I love waking up at Signal House and looking out over the harbour. I like to be here on the beach, any beach really. It suits me and I can't imagine not having it on my doorstep.'

'Fair point.'

'But recently, I don't know.' She kicked at the sand with her toes.

'Tell me.' He spoke in a way that was calm, encouraging her trust.

'Recently' – she took a deep breath – 'I keep thinking of what comes next and how the last decade has gone by so fast. I've always liked the idea of becoming a midwife, but never felt able to, erm, to leave, not really.' Her face flushed. In her mind, admitting she was anchored to her home, her family, still smacked a little of failure or dire inaction.

'Why not?' His expression was one of interest, far from mocking, which she might have expected from someone less empathetic.

'I like to be close to my nan, she's . . . she's been through a lot. And I know that I make things better for her and my mum too, I guess. I'm like the sticker after the dentist, the sugar after the medicine.' She gave a short laugh, but the truth was sharp and hard to swallow, like a stick in her craw. 'I know things would be harder for them if I wasn't there.'

'So not only sugar after medicine, but a sacrificial lamb too, giving up your own dream and happiness. Sorry, that sounded really judgey. What's it got to do with me?' He looked anguished, at no more than the thought of overstepping the mark. It was endearing.

'I am happy.' She pressed this truth. 'I am. Content in many ways. There are worse lives.'

'There are.' He smiled, looking out over the wide sweep of the beautiful bay.

'I guess it's an age thing where I'm starting to realise that I don't want the next decade to whizz by just as quickly without achieving more.'

He twisted to face her, concentrating on what came next in a way that made her stomach bunch with longing. She folded her hands into the hem of her t-shirt.

'Losing someone in the way you lost your dad is awful – it must change how you feel about everything. Distort a regular life.' His voice barely more than a whisper.

'It does. It did. And it is awful – for me, Mum, my nan, all of us.'

'Yes, but it's not too late, never too late.'

'It's not that easy, though, is it?' She needed him to understand the bonds that kept her tethered.

'It's not.' He swallowed. 'And I understand. But wouldn't your family want you to set your goals and go for it?'

'They would, definitely, but it's how *I* feel that's the stumbling block.'

There was a beat of quiet while he, like her, stared at the moving sea as if reflecting. It was, however, a comfortable silence.

'I know you said memories of your dad were sketchy, but there must be some that stuck?'

'Yes, one or two. But it's like I only remember bits of him, and not as much as you'd think.' Her voice was low as she whispered the private sadness. 'I don't know if I've blocked a lot of things out, but it's almost like my grief reset my mind in some way. I don't remember too much about my early childhood at all.'

'So what do you remember about him?' She liked how he was trying to get closer to the man who had meant so much to her.

'I remember him singing when he was in the bath, loudly! I remember the feel of his chin on my cheek when he kissed me goodnight and he hadn't shaved. I smell nail polish sometimes when I think about him, which is odd. And I remember he used to bring me a big punnet of cherries in the summer and we'd eat them together on the terrace and spit the stones into the flower bed. Like we were rebels, laughing and spitting stones when no one was looking.' She smiled at the memory, the scent of fresh cherry now strong in her nose. 'I don't think there has ever been anything quite as beautiful as those glossy red cherries with their delicate green stems, sitting in a white china bowl on the table and what they represented – that he'd thought they were perfect for me – and what they represent now – one of the strongest and loveliest memories of time spent with my dad. A time when I didn't know what it felt like to have a blanket of sadness thrown over Signal House. Happiness. Security.'

'I love that. And of course you have your mum too?' He was joining the dots.

'Uh-huh, she . . .' How to phrase it. 'We're not exactly close, not like I am with Freda. My mum drinks a lot.' She hated that she had to share this, a negative. A reason for him not to like her: a minus point, a burden, something problematic, a dark cloud that hung over her rosy life. But what was the alternative? Hide her mother away? If only that were possible.

'Don't we all, given half the chance.' His tone was jovial.

'No, Ed.' She cut him off, this the one aspect of her life where there was no room for humour or excuse. 'Not just a lot, more than a lot. She's . . . she's an alcoholic.' It wasn't a word she used often; the connotations too difficult to jostle with.

'I'm sorry, Taw.' His body stiffened and he sat up straight, as if awkward to have misjudged it. 'That must have sounded flippant. It's a horrible disease, it really is. It affects so much more than just the person drinking.'

'Mmm.' She was disinclined to match his empathetic tone. Too many thoughts and experiences had filtered through the bedrock of despair for too long. Was it her mother's drinking that encouraged her dad to seek solace on his boat? How happy could he have been living with someone like that? It was a hook on which to hang her anger and it had always been this way.

'It can't be easy for you.' He placed his arm across her shoulders and she sidled even closer, resting her head on his chest, liking the safety of it.

'It isn't, but I'm used to it.' She shrugged, wanting to change the subject, as she felt perilously close to opening up about her feelings towards Annalee, and that was not where they were at. Yet.

'So, I know you said your dad drowned.' He spoke reverentially. 'Was it in a pool, the sea? If you don't want to talk about it that's fine, of course.'

It was an odd topic, as everyone she knew and everyone she mixed with knew the details and she was therefore unrehearsed in having to voice the tragedy out loud.

'He had a small boat, a little wooden sailing dinghy. It was his hobby, his pride and joy. If he wasn't in it, he was cleaning it, repairing it or painting it. As I mentioned before, she was called *Ermest* after the River Erme. He was pretty obsessed with rivers and the sea.' She smiled. 'He and my Uncle Sten had always sailed together since they were kids. One Sunday morning, my dad was on the quay waiting for his brother, but Sten got held up, so Dad went out alone and he never came back.' She gave the simplified version. 'He used to put his keys and wallet in a little Tupperware box on the seat and it was there in the boat when they found it. The boom was loose, flailing. The water was quite choppy. They think it probably hit him on the head and he fell overboard, maybe knocked him out or whatever. It doesn't make any difference, it ends just the same.'

'Tawrie.' He pulled her even closer to him, holding her tightly. She closed her eyes and let the soft fabric of his jersey brush her cheek. It was a place she wanted to stay. 'You must miss him.'

'Every day.' *I miss the shape of him on the stairs, sleeping with a feeling that I was safe because my family was complete, sleeping soundly and deeply because he and Annalee had their hand on the tiller, not me. And so I get into the sea where he rests, part of him, and I let the water hold me and I know it's him, close to me.* 'It changed everything. Uncle Sten gave up his office job and bought some land – he felt so guilty, still does probably. He thinks that if he'd not been late that day and had gone out with my dad then it wouldn't have happened, but I think it's pointless to feel that way. My nan lost half of her heart and even though my gramps had only died three years before, this was worse for her, way worse.'

'Her child.'

'Yes.' She snuggled in closer. 'And it made me want to stay close to where he died, close to my family, our home, his home. It's complicated.' She sat up and wrapped her arms around her shins, hoping that physical containment might help keep her emotions at bay.

'It's funny, isn't it, the things that happen that shape our lives, and yet are nothing to do with us – accidents or decisions made when we were young and it's like we are at the tail end of the flip. We feel the force of it but are powerless to change things. Passengers on a journey where the coordinates are set by those in charge – our parents or whoever.'

She turned to look at him. 'Did you lose someone?'

He shook his head. 'No, no.' His tone vigorous as if he was aware they were not comparing like for like. 'But my parents divorced and it was huge for me. The start of living under two roofs, having two Christmases, two sets of clothes, two home addresses, two step-parents, one house with a cat, one with a dog, one that was vegetarian, one where meat was served at every meal. One where my sister lived most of the time and the other where I did. Then new babies popping up. A fractured family, or a normal family, I'm never quite sure. But certainly different to the one I felt I wanted.'

'It sounds complicated.' She liked that he was confiding in her.

'It was complicated, it's still complicated, but it's also great a lot of the time, and I remember those days vividly – happy times. But you know that feeling in your stomach that you've been cheated somehow, like if only they'd not been so rubbish, your life would have been a bit easier? Does that sound ridiculous?'

'No, I get it.' Of course she did, not only was her own mum rubbish most of the time, but the what-ifs surrounding her own dad's passing were many. *What if Annalee had been a sober wife, would he still have sought the escape of a day on* Ermest? *What if Sten hadn't been late? And her biggest secret, the thing she never shared: what if he wasn't really dead, but had merely run and was now living a secret life on Lundy?*

'I'm being unfair,' he sighed. 'My parents are wonderful, both of them, genuinely. I mean, they're very different and I'm closer to my mum, but my dad's not a bad person, it's just that . . .'

'It's just that what?' she urged.

'It's not the same, is it? It's never the same, having to negotiate new partners, new siblings, half-siblings. It's a lot. It's always been a lot.'

It was her turn to take his hand and keep it warm inside both of her own. Their breathing was in sync as they looked out over the wide stretch of sand as the sun sank on Woolacombe Bay. The silence was cathartic.

'This is the life, Ed.' She smiled.

'It is, isn't it? This really is the life!' He tilted his head back, allowing her to study his profile while he sought out the last of the rays.

'No.' She shifted on her bottom, which had gone a little numb, and curled her legs beneath her. 'I mean this is the one life we have, this is it! So when you said did I not ever want to wake up in the big smoke with a view of a skyscraper, the answer is I try not to think too much about it on a day-to-day basis, but sometimes I re-evaluate and remember that you're right: it's not too late.' She swallowed and he lowered his face to look at her. 'I think we all need to do more of what makes us happy rather than what we think we should. And I'm realising that more and more.'

'God.' He wiped his face. 'That's the dream, right? Doing more of what makes us happy rather than what we think we should.' He looked a little overcome with emotion. Her heart flexed at his level of understanding.

'I speak to so many visitors, people who come into the café, who tell me they're a teacher, an estate agent, a police officer or whatever!' She let her hands rise and fall. 'And they say their dream is to move down here and be by the sea, to sit on the beach like this, to live simply, learn to surf, make friends, sit on the harbour and watch the world go by. And it makes me want to weep because this *is* the life! This is it! There's not another one cued up. And they go back to wherever they've come from, grabbing slices of happiness from their days by the sea and longing to be here. It must feel like punishment. I want to say to them, why not now? Why not today? You need to prioritise your happiness and not do something because you're expected to or happen to find yourself on that track. Jump off! Start over! Because if losing my dad and watching my mum live her life through the neck of a bottle has taught me one thing, it's that life is short. It's too short, Ed. And in those moments I understand that I am good at giving the advice but not so good at acting on it.'

'There's no shame in being loyal, in feeling responsible, in loving your family so much you want to make everything better.'

He got it and she could barely stand to look in his eyes, wary of what else he might read in her face, as the desire to be held by him was almost overwhelming.

He took a moment to speak, his eyes studying her face and she felt the intensity of it. She wondered if this might be the moment he kissed her again, and she braced for it, trembling in anticipation and with a swirl of nerves in her gut, wanting him to do it, wanting more. Instead he looked away.

'I do get it. It's not always simple, is it? Not always possible to pack a bag and jump track, otherwise everyone would do it.' For a second she wondered if he might cry and wanted to know what thoughts could have caused this in the kind, glorious human who she was falling for.

'But that's the thing, Ed, everyone *can* do it! I'm not saying it can be done without some hard choices being made or without consequences, but anyone can do it if they're brave enough. That's my issue – I'm just not brave enough.'

'There's always more to it than bravery. You're right: every decision has a consequence.' He blinked and she would have given anything to know what rattled inside his head. With more time under their belts she might have had the courage to ask him. 'So come on, tell me three things I don't know about you that you think I probably should.'

She wriggled again to get comfortable on the sand, relieved for the lightening of the mood.

'Oh gosh, erm . . .' She looked skyward as if this was where inspiration might lurk. 'Oh, I know!' She clicked her fingers. 'I share my birthday with my mum and my nan, we were all born on September the fourteenth.'

'That's mad!'

'It is, and we all celebrate together. We have a party down at Rapparee Cove called the Gunn Fire and everyone's invited, and it's become a kind of thing, far bigger than our birthdays! But it's lovely – we just sit around, eat, drink, chat, dance, and there's a bonfire of course.'

'That's amazing. September the fourteenth, you say? I'll put it in my diary. If I'm invited?' He batted his eyelashes at her. It made her laugh. Not only his antics, but the thought that he'd be there. It was a plan, a future plan and her stomach folded with happiness at the prospect of it.

'No one's really invited, not properly, it's much more organic. Everyone discusses it and everyone looks forward to it and everyone turns up!' She shrugged. 'That's it.'

'I can't wait!' He rubbed his hands together and his enthusiasm for this tradition filled her with joy. 'Okay, two more things.'

'Hmmm.' She tried to think. 'I can whistle loudly, like really, really loudly.'

'How loud?'

'You know when you're in public and someone whistles so loudly that everyone turns to stare and dogs howl and kids cover their ears?'

'Yep.'

'It's that loud.'

'Impressive. How did you learn to do it?' He tilted his head.

'I didn't, I could just do it! I think it's like being ambidextrous or colour blind, you're just born with it. It's a skill.'

'It sure is. And far more useful than being colour blind. Can you do it now?' He braced himself.

'Nope. It'd probably break all the bulbs in the street lights along The Esplanade, if not the windows in the houses, your ears would bleed. It wouldn't be pleasant.'

'Wow! It's like a superpower!' His eyes were wide.

'It really is.'

'Right, final thing.' He scooched closer on the sand and she liked the proximity of him. It helped her say out loud the hardest of things. She took a long, slow breath, wanting to share with him the thing she had never shared with anyone before, another secret that bound them close.

'I talk to my dad.' Pausing, she glanced at him, checking out whether his reaction was one of support or scorn. It was, unsurprisingly, the former.

'Of course you do. I think that's quite standard.' He placed his hand on her leg and she felt the heat from his palm radiate through her whole body.

'Yeah, but not just the odd "I miss you" or anything like that. I mean I . . . I give him an update every morning when I get in the sea. I tell him my news, what I've been up to, all kinds of things.'

'So, you've only been talking to him like that since you became a Peacock?'

Despite the intense nature of their discussion, she wanted to laugh as he called her a Peacock. She shook her head.

'No, I used to talk to him before, but it'd be while I sat on the bench having a break from the café, staring at the sea, or if I went for a walk around Capstone Parade and looked out over the water.'

'So always with the sea as your focus?' His expression was intense, suggesting he wanted to understand and found nothing amusing in it. It gave her the confidence to continue.

'Yes. Because . . .' The next words shrank back from her tongue and she swallowed.

'Because what, Taw?' She felt the increased pressure from his hand, gently squeezing her leg.

'Because I . . . I think he's *in* the water.' There, she had said it.

'You think his spirit lives on in the water or it reminds you strongly of him?'

She could see he was trying to better understand.

'No, Ed. I know it's not true, not really, but it makes it easier for me to picture him living under the sea. Like, in a specially adapted cave or able to breathe under the water. I imagine that he might have sunk to the bottom of the sea and was saved by kelpies and now lives in a cave on Lundy with a special breathing apparatus that he can't leave because he'd drown. Married to a mermaid, with new merchildren, my replacements; half-kid, half-fish.' She could see he didn't know whether to laugh or commiserate and she understood. 'Or . . .' She took her time. 'I also think he might actually live on Lundy. More to the point, I think he might be hiding on Lundy.'

'Lundy?'

'Yes.' She looked out to the island that sat on the horizon. 'Just over there.'

Edgar's eyes darted to the island and back to her face.

'Why do you think that, how does it help?' His eyes were mournful and gently she shrugged her leg free from his hand. She didn't want to be pitied, didn't want him to see her as many in the town did, *that girl, bless her* . . .

'Because he went out in his boat. And he never came home and we never found him, and no one saw his body, we didn't bury him or burn him. We had a memorial service but there was no "him" to bury or burn and so . . .' She closed her eyes and ran her palm over her face. 'I think he might not really be dead. Even though I know deep down he is. It's complicated.' A quiet, wry laugh left her lips, a mask to her embarrassment at having spoken so candidly. 'It's had the biggest impact on my life.'

'Of course it has!' he interjected.

'When it happened, I kept waiting for the facts to sink in, for it to feel real and I'm now twenty-eight and it never has.'

'Do you want me to take you to Lundy?' His offer was beautiful, sincere, and moving because of it.

'No, but that's the kindest offer. Thank you.'

'It'd be easy, we could hire a boat, go on one of those trips that leave from the harbour.' His enthusiasm for the trip grew.

'I can't, Ed, but thank you.'

'Why can't you?'

'Because' – she drew on every bit of courage she possessed to make the admission – 'because if I go to Lundy and find he's not there, then I know it's true, don't I? If I go and he's not there, then

I know he's never coming home and somehow that feels worse. Because when things feel like too much at home or it's a hard day in the café, I think about' – she swallowed – 'I think about him coming back, think about my daddy coming home, and it makes things better.'

He didn't laugh, didn't judge, but simply reached for her hand.

'Do you speak to anyone about it, about how you feel?'

'No, because I'm okay! I have a great life, a happy life, really. There are just things that I find hard, too hard – like going out in a boat. I don't want to. And I can't bear anyone being late. It bothers me. I know we've joked about it, but I try wherever possible to be on time because if someone says they will be at a certain place at a certain time and you're relying on them, it's really shitty when they're not there. It makes you feel . . .' She paused, seeing shadows of the day her dad was lost, hearing her mother wailing and her nan sobbing. And while not able to fully recall the detail, which was like a photograph out of focus, blurred, she could remember quite clearly how much of it had felt.

He was supposed to be home by four.

That's what he said, four or five at the latest.

Why isn't he home?

Have we called the sailing club?

Has someone checked if his boat is in the harbour?

Can someone call Sten?

She shivered as the breeze picked up and carried across the sea to lift her hair and cool her skin.

'Shall we head back to Corner Cottage? Go get some hot chocolate?' He stood and reached down for her hand to help her stand.

'Yes, please.'

He didn't let go of her hand as they walked back along the beach, towards the steps that would take them up to the car park.

'I never got to hear the three things that I don't know about you.' She looked up at him.

'We'll pick it up at home, how does that sound?'

Home.

'It sounds good.'

CHAPTER FOURTEEN

Harriet Stratton

August 2002

With shaking hands, Harriet closed the door of the smallest room in the house, the laundry room, and switched on the tumble dryer. Not to drown out their conversation entirely, but certainly with the intention of masking it. Plus, she figured the whirring sound resonating throughout the cottage would give Bear and Dilly the impression, should they venture downstairs, that there was nothing to be concerned about, no drama lurking beneath their little feet on the floor below.

It was unpleasant how close she was to Hugo in the relatively confined space. Not that she found him unpleasant but she would certainly have preferred more distance in light of the conversation they were about to have. She leaned on the white china butler sink, he by the window, putting no more than thirty-odd inches between them, the space made smaller still in light of the topic. But this small discomfort preferable to alarming the kids.

'So.' She decided to begin, harnessing the anger that sparked in her veins. 'You think the issues we have in our marriage are *my* fault?'

'No, I never said that.' He shook his head.

'Because, and please do interject if I've got the wrong end of the stick entirely, but I thought it was because you were having sex with our neighbour while I scurried around Waitrose on the hunt for hummus?'

'Why do you do that?' He narrowed his eyes at her, as if trying to see her, really see her. She could smell the tang of red wine on his breath and found it repellent.

'Do what, Hugo?'

'Try to be funny, while being so fucking mean, so cutting!'

She took a deep breath; maybe he was right. Deciding to turn down the meanness, she would try to speak plainly without the edge. The point of this chat was, after all, to make progress. This, she knew, would be a hell of a lot easier to do if the red-hot poker of anger and indignation was not shoved firmly up her arse.

'Okay' – she held up her palms – 'let's start again. Why don't you tell me how you feel I'm responsible for what we're going through, or at least tell me my part in it?' She folded her arms tightly across her stomach.

He took his time in forming a response and this, too, bothered her more than she could say.

'I know I'm the one that had the affair.'

Bravo! Wisely, she kept this to herself.

'I've admitted it, told you everything there is to tell, agreed to move and I've been working hard to help us heal, to figure out how we go forward. I mean, here we are, in Ilfracombe, our fresh start!'

'Yep.' She could barely contain her contempt for the fact he wanted points for admitting the affair, as if unaware, or choosing to ignore, the *reason* for their move.

'But I think it's useful to look at the reasons why I made the decisions I did.'

She felt her jaw tense. *Useful?* He sounded irritatingly officious, as if he were about to conduct a post-implementation review, or garner lessons learned after a project.

'For the last few years, H, you've been so focused on your job, the kids, the house, whatever else is popping up next on the calendar. It's like you have to slot me in. I've felt redundant. I was never the priority for you. Never. And Wendy . . .'

It was rare for him to use her first name. When unable to avoid mentioning her at all, he would say 'her' or 'she' as if aware that to use her name made a connection, gave her status, both of which were like knives in her gut.

'. . .Wendy was all about me. And it reminded me what it felt like to have someone put me first.'

It was as if all the air had been sucked from the room and she was hit with an overpowering sense of claustrophobia. Fearing she may pass out, unable now to prioritise what the kids may or may not hear, she opened the laundry room door and made her way across the kitchen to the open-plan sitting room. Gulping great lungfuls of air, she walked backwards until her legs touched the leather chair and slumped down, as the strength finally left her. She was appalled by his admission that basic flattery and a little attention had been all it took to divert him from their shared life, to knock him from the pillars of commitment on which their future had rested.

Hugo, having followed her, wasn't done. He sat on the couch opposite and rested his joined hands on his knees, his head down, tone earnest, calmed a little.

'I guess I never realised when we got married, when the kids came along, that I would slip further and further down the list, and I guess being with her was a reminder of what it felt like to be considered. It wasn't that I wanted *her*, per se, but I wanted to be someone's priority. It felt good.'

She bit her lip, trying to think of the last time she had put herself first. It was far easier to recall all the times she hadn't; turning up at many a school event without having had time to wash her hair because she'd been too busy making cupcakes for the bake sale, hours and hours of homework and reading with the kids instead of taking a hot bath, gluing masks for Halloween until the early hours, or packing jars of sweets for the Christmas tombola while yawning at the end of a hectic week. Giving Hugo the last of the vegetables, an extra helping of apple pie or the spare pillow, always thinking of his needs/wants before her own. The big things too: only inviting her beloved family every other Christmas as he found it all 'too much', turning down the offer of promotion four years ago, which would have meant relocating to Edinburgh, because despite it being a huge whack of salary and an opportunity for her to write her own scientific paper, Hugo and the kids were settled and that was how she understood compromise. And this before she got to the daily sacrifices she willingly made for her kids, or how she'd packed boxes, locked up their family home and was now in this cottage in a town where she didn't have one proper friend and was clinging on by her fingertips.

'I know it sounds selfish, H.'

She couldn't help the snort of sarcastic laughter that left her mouth. *Ya think?*

'But I don't think it is selfish to want more. I mean, I fucked up badly, I know I did, but I feel that if we'd had better communication, if we'd made more time for each other . . .'

She could hardly stand to hear any more and kept her voice low. Another sacrifice to spare the kids hearing the row, when all she wanted to do was scream from the roof!

'I remember—' She coughed to clear her throat of the plug of sadness that had risen unexpectedly there. 'I remember when we were at university and we'd spend nights in that single bed in my room. It was so narrow, we practically had to lie on each other, until we devised the perfect way to sleep; me halfway down the bed, you on your back, legs wide, me in the gap, head on your stomach, so close . . .'

'So close,' he echoed.

'I'd never felt so safe, so comfortable, so happy and I knew that if I got to sleep like that every night, *every* night, then we'd be happy forever.'

'And forever would not be enough,' he whispered, completing the phrase they had coined and used sparingly and with great intent throughout their marriage.

She ignored it, knowing that to give it credence right now might throw her off track. She needed to stay focused, to rip off the Band-Aid, to stop pretending.

'If I think about those two young lovers with their lives in front of them, they're hard to recognise; it's like looking at people we used to know, but have lost touch with.' The accuracy of this was a moment of realisation for her, another jab of sadness. The first being a little more than a jab, actually, more of a right hook that caught her squarely on the jaw when she'd found out about him and Mrs bloody Peterson. 'And for the record, it seems you might have forgotten that you only admitted your affair because I figured it out. Who knows how long it might have gone on otherwise? And if it had finished, run its course, would I ever have known? I mean have there been others?'

'Jesus, no! What a thing to say!' He raised his voice a little, adamant.

'Also . . .' She knew her maelstrom of thoughts wouldn't settle until she'd addressed all the points that he'd raised, lodged now in her chest like thorns. '. . . you used to say, "I love how smart you are, how hard you work." We'd plan to take over the world! You liked that I never rested, was independent, busy.'

He nodded. 'Yes.'

'Yet listening to you just now, it seems like the very things that attracted you to me are the very things that you now dislike, the things that have irritated you, the things that *drove* you into Wendy's arms.' She accentuated the verb she used sardonically and felt her lip flinch at the use of the woman's name.

'No, I just—'

'I was never one of those girls with a small handbag.' She cut him short. 'Or one with the latest clothes, high heels, a sparkly top and a big laugh. I was quieter, thoughtful, and that's how I've behaved for our entire marriage. I don't think I've changed.'

'You think I've changed?' He lifted his head.

'Erm, if not changed, then maybe got a little bored, wondered if the grass was greener.' It was easy to be direct when she spoke her truth, no longer treading on eggshells, guarded.

'Doesn't everybody?'

That her reply to his question was slow in coming spoke volumes. 'No, Hugo. Not everybody.'

'There it is again, that blaming voice, that tone.' He placed his hand over his mouth, as if this physical barrier might prevent the words slipping out that he knew were only damaging them further.

Harriet sat back in the chair and folded her hands into her lap. It was a moment of reckoning; Hugo's words were branded in her thoughts. His casual admission of how he had been 'lured' into infidelity with no more than a kind word, was incendiary and with it the realisation that they never had been and never could be stable. Picturing a small cage, she mentally placed it around her heart and locked it tight, knowing that if she could so misunderstand her marriage, misjudge her family life, and mistrust her husband, then nothing else in life could be taken for granted. She had never felt so alone, so dangerously on the edge, and she realised how easy it would be to fall.

What came next was delivered calmly, clearly, and she did her best to control the emotion that threatened to hijack her composure. It was important she got her phrasing right. Important that he listened. There was a beat of weighted silence before she was ready to speak. Hugo's foot tip-tapped gently on the floor in anticipation.

'In case you're wondering, or wonder in the future, at which point I decided to walk away from this marriage, the moment I knew I was done, the second the plug got pulled on all those remaining feelings that meant we might be in with a shot: it's now. Right now. This is the moment, Hugo.' She gestured towards the floor, a visual that she knew would live in her mind to concrete the moment in recollection. She saw his mouth fall open, his shoulders slump. 'Not that it will matter in years to come, not at all. Everything we have, everything that concerns us and keeps us awake in the early hours, will be no more than a tributary of indifference that will trickle into the sea, and these past few weeks and how we got here will merge into one murky area of shade in our lives.'

'Are you—'

'Joking? No. No, I'm not.' She felt the wave of nausea, despite her outward serenity.

'So this is it?' He spoke as if this might help the facts sink in.

'This is it.'

'We can't just give up!'

'I'm not just giving up. If I had wanted to give up, I would have packed a bag the day I found out or I'd have stayed and carried on in Ledwick Green, hauling this sadness quietly inside me. That would have been giving up. We tried. I tried. I almost needed the clarity of coming here, away from our normal life, to get my head straight.'

'I . . . I don't want us to.' His lower lip wobbled, and it was hard to see. 'I can't stand the thought of us not being—'

'That's the thing, Hugo. It's no longer about what you want or what you can or can't stand. It's not even about trying to reach the compromise that I've held in my thoughts, strived for. A goal, if you like, since I first found out.'

'Please, H, please!'

'No.' She shook her head, not wanting him to pointlessly plead and knowing it would be better for him, upon reflection, if he did not. With her tone still level, her demeanour calm, despite the desperate avalanche of sadness that tumbled inside her. 'No. It's . . . it's gone. It's really gone, whatever it was, whatever we had – love, I guess – it's been gone for a while.' Her throat narrowed at the admission. 'That love was slashed and burned when you slept with her, when you slept with Wendy Peterson. I thought the roots might reseed, that it might be recoverable. That we could renovate our love, repaint, upcycle, go again. I believed, wanted desperately to believe, that it was a blip, an anomaly, but your words about how we live, the things I do that are wrong—'

'Not wrong, just . . .' he interrupted, as if it might make a difference.

'Okay, not wrong, let's say, distasteful to you. That list, your views . . . I can see that it wasn't a blip; it was an escape from the cage you see yourself living in, a way to break through the walls of dissatisfaction that have hemmed you in. I don't and have never wanted to be your jailer.'

'It's not like that, Harriet. I love you.' He sank down on to the floor in front of her, one hand on his heart, the other on her knees. He sounded a little breathless, overcome. 'I love you.'

She stood slowly, edging him out of the way and coming to stand in front of the sitting room window with its view down Fore Street, deliberately not looking as he sat on the floor, giving him a chance to stand and restore his dignity.

'I love me too, and that's why I need to walk away. In setting you free, I'm setting myself free from a situation I didn't know I needed to escape. But it's the right thing to do.'

'What about the kids? What about all the reasons we moved here, gave up our home, unsettled them?'

Turning to face him, she nodded. 'This will always, always be all about the kids. Every decision I have ever made has had the children at the heart of it. That won't change, not ever.' This to remind him that her way of life meant never putting herself first. 'I thought we could patch things up, thought we could start over, but we can't. I can't. The kids will be fine, eventually, because it will be their normal. And I for one can tell them how suddenly things can shift, even when you least expect it and you have to learn to live with a new normal.'

He put his hands on his hips and his stance and expression changed a little. It was familiar, and easier to deal with somehow; the way he switched gears from humble to defensive, depending on how things were going. It took all of her strength to continue, not knowing when she might next have the opportunity to speak so candidly. 'I have to think about the long term and the message I want to give them. I don't want Bear thinking it's okay to treat people in the way you've treated me and there be no consequence, and I want Dilly to know her worth and not to put up with any shit because her partner tells her that's all she has any right to expect.'

'Are you enjoying this?' This, too, a familiar pattern; how his frustration now bubbled over into anger.

She stared at him, noting his less than attractive physical traits. Part of the process, she guessed. The start of the emotional disentangling from the man who she had always thought was her future.

'No. What I enjoyed was the life I had and not knowing I had anything to worry about. I enjoyed all of that. I'm not enjoying this, the dismantling of our lives, of our kids' lives and all that comes next.'

'You're using that voice.' He gave a short burst of laughter that didn't reach his eyes. 'The one you keep in reserve for talking to idiots, people you hold in low regard, officious pricks with clipboards, or when talking about your father.'

'I know the one, and it's nothing personal, Hugo. It's just part of the barrier I have to put up to keep myself together, to stop me from losing it. To stop me from unravelling.' It was taking every ounce of strength and every fibre of her being to remain calm and not sink down to the floor and weep.

'You need to talk to the kids.' His words were clipped.

'*I* need to talk to the kids?' She narrowed her eyes, wondering why the responsibility was deemed solely hers.

'Yes, I mean this is your choice. Your decision.'

'Yes, it is. Like deciding to clamber up on to a raft, forcing everyone to get out of the sea, to spoil the fun, when you're the only one who's seen a great big fucking shark circling!'

'So, am I the shark?' She hated the glint of confidence in his eye, as if he was happy she'd bitten. It didn't bode well for the calm, grown-up strategy she pictured for their future.

'Well, I certainly feel like the bait. Dangling, swallowed up and left in the dark. But yes, I'll talk to the kids. If that's what you want.'

Hugo moved quickly, turning towards the staircase and it was all she could do not to jump up and physically restrain him. How dare he do this, in this moment! In this way! It was cruel, a shit trick.

'Dilly, Edgar, can you come down for a minute please, guys!'

There were two things about his yelling that bothered her most. The way he had used their son's real name, almost suggesting that his childhood was coming to an end, time to use this grown-up name, and also his disgusting timing. The kids were readying for sleep, safe in their rooms, still getting used to their new home. What would have been the harm in letting them rest until the morning, to have this last night of peace before they had to hop on to that bloody raft? And forcing the issue, the timing; putting her in an unenviable position just to prove his point. Harriet knew she would never forgive nor forget his actions right now.

'You can be a fucking prick, Hugo,' she whispered, loudly enough for him to hear, as their little feet thudded down the stairs. It was harrowing, knowing her children were about to sit down on the sofa believing they lived one life, but by the time they stood again, they would be living quite another.

CHAPTER FIFTEEN

TAWRIE GUNN

AUGUST 2024

'So, hot chocolate?' Ed asked as he put the key in the front door of Corner Cottage.

'Yes, please.' Tawrie followed him into the kitchen. She swallowed nerves before voicing her thoughts, reflecting on what she'd shared on the beach. 'I don't tell many people about my life, how I feel, and about what's going on. How I am.'

'Well, I'm glad you can talk to me.' He turned to hold her eyeline as he filled the kettle, before grabbing two blue-and-white dotty mugs from a dresser in the corner.

'I don't know what's happening here, Ed.' Her mouth felt dry.

'What do you mean?' He stopped foraging for hot chocolate in the cupboard and faced her.

'I mean . . .' Anxiety soup sloshed in her stomach. 'I mean you and me. I'm not used to feeling like this. This doesn't happen to me.' It felt imperative to voice her worries, to find the clarity that would help her sleep without the jumble of thoughts about this man and where she stood. She was still quite unable to believe her luck.

'But what if it has happened to you? What do we do then?' His voice was steady as he fixed her with a stare.

'I guess . . . I guess I'd be worried that it wasn't reciprocated. It would be mortifying to feel this way and for it to only be one-way traffic.' Her relief at having spoken so plainly was immense. 'I don't know what I'd do then, apart from run away,' she half joked.

'To Lundy?'

'Possibly.' She smiled.

He took a step forward and sat at the kitchen table. She followed suit. 'So, Miss Gunn, this is your second interview for the position.'

She laughed, but actually wanted to stay on track. Ed sat up straight.

'I can tell you, categorically, that it is very much reciprocated.'

'It is?' she whispered, wondering how actual butterflies and rainbows weren't firing out of her navel.

He licked sweat from his top lip. 'But it's not straightforward. And so first, I want to tell you the three things you don't know about me.'

'My heart is racing; I only like straightforward. Can only really deal with straightforward.' And just like that her butterflies and rainbows were back to anxiety soup.

'Hear me out, okay?'

'Okay.' Her voice was small and she reminded herself that if the need arose, she could be back at Signal House and in her room in less than five minutes.

'First thing is that my parents divorced when I was about eight. Everything for me, as I mentioned, has been separate since then. Two houses, two bedrooms, two Christmases, two birthday cakes, two dressing gowns stuck on the back of two hooks on the back of two bathroom doors, two pets – one dog, one cat – they couldn't even agree on that!'

'I don't know if it sounds like fun or a nightmare.'

'Both, depending on what I was going through, my age, how well my mum and dad were faring, their partners, the arrival of my step-siblings – all the usual stuff.'

'There have been times when I was growing up when I'd have quite liked an alternative home to run to, a different parent, different bedroom, different view . . .'

'Yep, it had its advantages and there are some people who don't have one stable home, so I know I'm lucky in some ways. But it was tricky. Up until they divorced, my life was pretty perfect. And so I think I compared it to that a lot.'

'How was it pretty perfect?' She liked idea of living perfectly.

'We lived in the house where I was born. Home. Traditional Christmases, Sunday lunches, great holidays, summers in the garden with a paddling pool, lots of laughter and then *boom*!' He touched his fingers together and let them splay apart like a firework. 'My dad had an affair.'

'Oh!' She didn't know what to say.

'I didn't know it at the time, but I found out after a few years; my aunt let it slip – not in a malicious way – and it really affected me.'

'That must have been so hard for your mum.'

'Yep. It got much harder, but initially, they tried to start over, a new place, a new house. And I was bitter, I guess, because I hadn't realised when we packed up our old house in Berkshire that we were packing up so much more than clothes and stuff. We were packing up the only life I'd known. I thought it was temporary and that we'd all go home eventually, but actually, everything was temporary from then on.'

'Where was your new house?' She was curious as to where he had called home.

He sat back and smiled at her. 'This was our new house. Here. Corner Cottage, Ilfracombe.'

'Are you kidding me?' She jumped in her chair. 'You lived here?' She pointed at the wall, trying to make sense of it. 'You were my neighbour? How come I don't know you? I've always just lived down the road! Where did you go to school?' The fact that their paths might have crossed was as exciting as it was odd.

'In fairness, we weren't here for long. We were supposed to be; this was our big new start, but it ended up being for no more than a few weeks and we left just before school started and went back to our *old* school, as though nothing had happened. And I guess for most of the kids in school not much had happened, but for my sister and me . . .' His eyes misted and she wanted nothing more than to hold him. 'Things quickly got very complicated. My dad moved back into the family home, the one we'd all vacated, and we were there during the week and it was shit, really. He was a mess, couldn't cope, didn't cook, laundry was hit and miss and all the things I'd taken for granted, things my mum did and the way the house felt—' He swallowed. 'It was a lot.'

'I can imagine. So where was your mum?'

'She moved in with my Aunty Ellis, who's great. A spare mum, you know? Always been there for me. She was about forty minutes away and every Friday, Mum would pitch up and collect us from school, and it was always so good to see her, but also horrible too because it reminded me that it was an odd situation. We'd then go to Ellis's house for the weekend, but I often had homework or a sports fixture or wanted to see friends. Plus, we were always on a timer, which felt desperate. Monday morning was always three sleeps away and that meant going back to my dad's.'

'You must have felt torn?'

'I did. I do. But then it got even more complicated when my dad moved Wendy Peterson, the woman he'd had the affair with, into our house. So she then kind of tried to step into my mum's shoes in every sense and I couldn't stand it. I was so mad at him for the way he'd treated my mum. I felt like it was all his fault and I found it hard to get over.'

'Jeez!' She could only imagine.

'Yep, Jeez! Dad and I fell out quite badly. I was rude, angry.'

'You were only a kid.'

'I was, but I still said some pretty hurtful things. My sister Dilly took my dad's part and stayed with him and Wendy, and I went to live with my mum full-time in her new flat, which was closer to school. And that was all good until Mum met Charles Wentworth and they eventually moved into their present house and had my twin brothers, Rafe and Louis. And then my dad had my little sister, Aurelia.'

'With Wendy?'

'No.' he shook his head. 'With Sherry.'

'Sherry?' She was confused.

'Yes, Sherry who worked in the coffee shop, who he was with briefly. Briefly enough to have a baby with.'

'So he's with Sherry now?' She was trying to keep up.

'Nope.' Ed shook his head. 'He's now with Ramona who he met on a murder mystery weekend and they have Riley, my baby sister.'

'I'm a bit confused.'

'Try living it.'

He rose from the table, re-boiled the kettle, heaped the hot chocolate powder into the mugs and topped up with hot water, stirring vigorously, before passing one to her.

'Thanks. I see what you mean now, about being at the mercy of other people's decisions.'

'Yep.' He retook his seat. 'I left home the moment I was able after uni and you know the rest. Oh, well actually, you don't know the rest – I still have two things to share.'

Her relief at this point was palpable: if this was what he meant by not straightforward, not traditional, then she could happily deal with it. Disjointed families were her specialty.

'I am so split in two that I even have two names . . .'

'What?' She bit her cheek, praying, praying, praying he was not about to reveal that his name was something mad like Sebastian Farquhar, knowing she'd never live it down and Connie would laugh for a lifetime.

'Yeah, it's true. My name is Edgar, Edgar Stratton, and my dad has, for as long as I can remember, only ever called me Ed, but my mum calls me Bear, my childhood nickname that stuck, for her at least.'

'Bear?' She laughed. It didn't suit him at all.

'Yep. My sister calls me Bear, and Ellis, a couple of others, but not many people.'

'God, we are really laying it all out here on the table tonight!' She swung her arm in an arc and as she did so, knocked Ed's full mug of hot chocolate over the table. It ran in a river over the table-top and soaked the arms of his shirt and dripped on to his jeans. She gasped, mortified not only by her clumsiness, but the potential damage to table and floor.

'Ouch, shit! Hot hot!' He ripped off his shirt and unzipped his jeans, pulling them down quickly until he stood in his boxer shorts.

'Ed! Oh my God, I'm so sorry! Are you hurt? Look at the table! I'm such a klutz!' Jumping up, she grabbed the cloth from the sink and wiped up most of her spill.

'Don't worry, it was an accident. I'll pop this in the washing machine.' He balled his jeans and shirt and walked to the laundry room.

Instinctively, Tawrie threw the cloth in the sink and followed him into the relatively confined space. It was cosy, intimate, and it mattered little that there was no soft mattress or music or a cold glass of whatever. There was no more than thirty inches between them as he leaned on the sink and she stood by the window. They moved at the same time. It was visceral, desperate, and all-consuming as the two sank down on to the blue-and-white striped rag rug. Urgently, they pawed at skin and in a frenzy of kissing, he removed her clothes. The new couple, giddy with anticipation, laughed in the moment that would set a new precedent and from which they would emerge changed. Suddenly Ed stopped and, bracing his arms, hovered over her as she reached up to touch his beautiful face.

'Just so we're clear' – he kissed her fingers – 'the feeling we were talking about earlier, the one that's reciprocated. It's love, right? That's what's happening here?'

'Yes,' she whispered, as tears of joy trickled across her temples and soaked into her hair. 'I love you.'

He kissed her then and stared at her as if seeing her for the first time.

'And I love you, Tawrie Gunn. I do. It would be so much easier if I didn't, if I hadn't met you yet, not while my life is so . . . complex.' He shook his head, and she understood, knowing how tricky it was to navigate a less than conventional family. Not that she cared, not that she cared about much in that minute. 'But I do. I really do.'

The morning light crept gently across the ceiling as she woke in the arms of the man she loved! *Loved!* It was exciting, life-affirming and the most glorious feeling she could imagine.

'Morning.' He yawned, pulling her towards him. 'Tawrie.' He sat up slightly and she nestled against his chest.

'What?'

'I . . . I can't think straight!' He gave a nervous laugh.

She understood, knowing that to be wrapped in this bubble of love was indeed brain-scrambling. She felt drunk without having consumed a drop!

'It's okay, I understand.' She kissed his chin. 'This is such a lovely room.' She stared at the eaves of the bedroom, once an attic, liking the irregular shapes. 'But sadly I have to go; I need to get to Hele Bay.'

'Course you do, little mermaid. Actually' – he sat up, leaning against the wooden headboard – 'that would be a better name for your swim group. You know peacocks can't swim, don't you?'

'Not at all?' The thought made her laugh. Of all the swimming creatures Maudie and Jago could have chosen.

'Not at all, they'd sink like stones!'

'Think I'll keep that to myself.'

'So this swimming malarkey, why are you so hooked?' He wrapped his arm around her bare shoulders and pulled her close to him, her head now resting in the slight dip between his chest and throat. She could feel his heart beating against her cheek.

'It's weird really. I've always liked cycling, pottering around on my bike and walking – hard not to like walking when you live in Fore Street.'

'True.' He chuckled.

'Then I saw a couple of videos online of people wild swimming and it wasn't so much the swimming but the way they looked when they got out of the water: just exhilarated! Happy! Rosy cheeked. And some wild swimmers who come into the café to cosy up after their swim, they had this air about them, and I thought, I could do with a bit of that! And it's turned into my favourite thing.'

'I get it.' He sighed.

'So come on, what's your favourite thing?'

'This!' He squeezed her tightly. 'This is my favourite thing!'

'I wasn't joking, I want to know!'

'I'm not joking!' he countered.

'But I mean, you've done this before?'

'What? Sex?' he shrieked. 'Are you suggesting I'm a novice?'

'No, not that.' She felt her face blush. 'I mean this!' She pointed back and forth between them. 'This whole loving thing, which sounds odd but I don't know how else to say it.'

'Where to begin?' He closed his eyes and wiped his face with his palm. 'Why, have *you* done this before?' He pulled away slightly and looked at her.

She took her time, knowing this history sharing was important, more stepping stones to help them along the way. 'I've had a couple of boyfriends, one serious-ish, Jamie, who I was with when we were at school and then for a few years after. But it just' – she made a dull pop noise with her mouth – 'fizzled. He's a fisherman, part of the lifeboat crew and he's happily married with a little one. I still see him, it's fine. He's nice. And then the usual crap dates that don't go anywhere that are part of the checklist.'

'The checklist?' A wrinkle of confusion formed on the top of his nose.

'Yeah, you know, all the things you need to do before you become a fully formed grown-up.'

'I am unaware of this checklist, and therefore decidedly concerned that I might not be ticking off all that's necessary before I can claim entry into the world of grown-uphood.'

She loved his humour.

'Things like falling off a bike, eating so much sugar you feel sick, collecting something obsessively – like football cards or friendship bracelets – and then losing interest just as quickly.'

'Check, check, check!'

'What did you collect?' She was curious.

'Cricket balls.'

'Cricket balls?' She laughed.

'Yep, although I haven't strictly lost interest in them. It all started when I found one in a ditch in the village where we lived and it felt like such a lucky thing, a really great day. I thought, if I could find a beautiful, hand-stitched, leather-bound cricket ball then what other wonderful things might happen in my life? I was so delighted with it that my dad gave me another one and then I got one for my birthday and then Christmas and so on, and I had quite the collection. I loved them. I still love them. But haven't added to my collection in quite some time.'

'That's sweet. And then of course there's the more serious life events to tick off, like voting.'

'Check.' He nodded.

'Missing a train or a flight.'

'Check.' He grimaced.

'And it's not so much the missing it that's the life lesson, but how you recover, what you do next and how you get out of the scrape,' she explained.

'Nice. I like that.'

'Erm, what else?' She thought hard. 'Breaking a bone – always better to get that out of the way as a kid and there's actually nothing cooler than walking into school with a plaster cast.'

He laughed loudly, as if he could relate.

'Sleeping under the stars.'

'Camping? I've done that too.'

'No, Ed, specifically not camping, but more coming to the end of the evening and finding yourself in a field or on a beach or in a back garden and looking up at the sky and lying there until morning, watching the movement, the light, the shifting darkness.'

'I've never done that.' He kissed her shoulder.

'I've never done that either, but it's on my to-do list,' she confessed.

'I could talk to you for hours and hours . . . and we need to, it's important.' He looked a little tense and she wondered if he, like her, was already dreading their parting, even if it were only for a few hours.

'You have! And now I need to get going!'

She swung her legs to the side of the bed and sat up, looking back as Ed sat with his arms behind his head.

'Hurry back. I need to see you tonight. We can talk some more, really talk.' He swallowed. 'And I've got crisps. Fancy an Uno tournament? I need the opportunity to maintain my crown.'

'Oh well, if you've got crisps . . .' Leaning over, she kissed him hard on the mouth, a down payment on the evening to come.

'I want to say I love you,' he whispered. 'But it feels new and I'm still nervous.'

'It's the same for me, but you can say it. In fact, I'd like you to say it.' She grinned.

'I love you, Tawrie.'

'I love you too.'

With time ticking on and keen to grab a shower before her swim, she practically ran down Fore Street and up the steps towards home, glancing back at the cottage on the corner where her lover lay, knowing reunion would be sweet. Nothing could dampen the high she felt, nothing could dilute the bubble of pure happiness that filled her up!

As she put her key in the front door and wondered how much to share with her nan, a sharp, acrid tang filled her nostrils.

'Sweet lord! What's that smell?' She placed her hand over her nose and mouth and made her way into the sitting room.

'What smell?' Her nan turned to face her, sitting up straight on the sofa.

'It's disinfectant or bleach or some kind of cleaning fluid?' It was strong, noxious, and overwhelming.

'Oh yes, well.' Her nan fiddled with the edge of her dressing gown and Tawrie could tell she was stalling. Tawrie's heart sank; the very last thing she wanted to do was embarrass her beloved nan.

'What happened, are you okay?' She kept her voice soft, not wanting awkwardness to have any part between them. If her nan had had a little accident, Tawrie wanted her to be comfortable in the knowledge that not only was it okay, but that she'd always be on hand to clear up, sort it out, make things better . . . Because she was tethered to this house, this town, this family of Gunn women. What had Ed said, *a sacrificial lamb.* The thought came with a new ping of loss, as if aware of all she would not experience if she didn't spread her wings . . .

'I'm okay yes, love. All okay.' Freda sounded a little indignant.

'What aren't you telling me?' she asked softly.

'Nothing!'

The way her nan averted her eyes told her differently.

'I'm worried about you.' She leaned forward and kissed the crêpey cheek of the woman she loved.

'No need to worry, love. It was your mother, she . . . she . . . well . . .'

'What happened?' All the joy of the night just spent was now replaced with something edging close to fury. 'What happened, Nan?' she repeated, sitting next to her on the sofa.

'I think she had one or two in the pub.'

'Really, you surprise me. And I think we both know it's never one or two.' Her teeth ground together, picturing her mother propping up the bar, nipping outside to top up her nicotine levels, before sauntering back into the pub to top up the booze. 'So why have you doused the place in bleach just because she was in the pub?' This would not be the first, nor the last time that Annalee had expelled bodily fluids that flowed from her in a tide of booze. Sick, shit, piss; the old wooden floor had seen it all, as had much of the stair carpet. To put Freda through such a ghastly experience in her absence made her blood boil. It was the first time in years that Tawrie had not been on hand to make things better, to clean up, and she knew her anger was wrapped tightly in guilt.

'She . . . she wasn't very well when she got back. I did what needed to be done, used an old towel and put it in the bin.'

Her nan looked at the floor and Tawrie knew she was only getting the tail end of what had occurred. Jumping up, she took the stairs two at a time and knocked forcefully on her mother's bedroom door, each knock in time with her hammering heart.

'Mum? Mum?' She rattled the door handle before walking in, giving her, or anyone who happened to be lolling next to her, the opportunity to cover up. The room was in semi-darkness as the heavy curtains were still drawn. The air was sour, the stench overwhelming. The disgusting tang of wine, vomit and cigarette breath was so potent she could almost taste it. Her stomach rolled with nausea as she made her way across the carpet, littered with dirty clothes, discarded heels, used tissues and crumb-laden plates, trying not to breathe in. She yanked the curtains open and threw the sash window up to let the fresh air whip around the room.

'Wassgoinon?' Her mother lifted her head from the pillow and propped herself up on her elbow, squinting to avoid the daylight. Her eyes were no more than tiny shrunken holes in her emaciated face, her make-up grotesquely smeared over her cheeks, the remnants of carmine lipstick streaking her lip and chin, short hair sticking up in spikes.

'What happened last night?'

'What?' Annalee sat up and rubbed her face, her lilac bra strap falling off her narrow shoulder.

'Something happened and Nan had to clear up your mess! I went out for the first time in God only knows how long, and you couldn't keep it together, not for one night?' She folded her arms across her chest and gripped the material of her sweatshirt with her shaking hands. How, how could she swan off for a life with Ed or to train as a midwife if this was the chaos that ensued when she was gone?

'Stop shouting at me!' Her mother placed her face in her hands and took deep breaths.

'I brought you a glass of water.' Her sweet, sweet nan walked in and hovered by the bedside cabinet, holding the drink out and struggling to find a place to put it down among the detritus littering the surface. Eventually, she nudged an overflowing ashtray to one side and popped the glass next to it. Tawrie knew the glass of water was a prop and that she more than likely had appeared to dilute the tension, head off a row.

'Thanks.' Annalee, Tawrie noted, avoided Freda's eyeline.

'Can you tell me what happened last night, Nan?' She wanted not only to hear the detail, but also for her mother to hear it too, as clearly, with a skinful and a fuzzy head, her memory might not be the most reliable.

'I was asleep and I heard your mum come in. Not too late.' Freda glanced repeatedly at her daughter-in-law, as if aware of humiliating her or breaking a confidence. Despite the dire situation, Tawrie could only admire her misplaced loyalty. 'I think she fell over. There was a bang. It woke me up and then she started being ill.'

'Vomiting?'

Her nan nodded.

'Well, that's nice!' She smiled sarcastically at her mother who continued to hold her head.

'Please, Tawrie, just . . .'

'Just what, Mum? Shut up? Stop going on? Or isn't it about now we get to the apology and tears stage? Honest to God, people ask me why I didn't go off and become a midwife and it makes me laugh. How could I go and study? How can I concentrate on anything when my mind is always half here, wondering what you're doing, whether you're safe, if Nan is okay and worrying that she might be having to clean up after you!'

On cue her mother's thin shoulders heaved and fat tears fell down her face.

'There we are!' she boomed, entirely fed up with the whole circus, the empty apologies, the meaningless tears that she had witnessed time and time again; tears that only a change in behaviour would legitimise. Not that she was holding her breath.

'I am sorry! I *am*!' Annalee did her best to shout, as if this might give her words credibility, but her voice was thin.

Freda sat on the side of her bed and to Tawrie's irritation, she saw her reach out to pat her mother's leg over the blanket.

'I am sorry!' Again, Annalee sobbed.

'Are you, though? I get you don't give a rat's arse what happens to you and you clearly don't give a shit what effect your boozing has on me, you never have.' She paused to let this sink in. 'But you should be ashamed of how it affects Nan.' Annalee finally looked at the old woman perched on the mattress. 'You woke her up and she had to set to, clearing up your sick and whatever else she isn't telling me.' Her nan's look downward suggested this was probably accurate. 'Picture it, Mum, Nana Freda on her hands and knees in her nightdress, mopping up your wine and vodka sick, the smell of it, the *worst* job, and she did that for you! Again! Downstairs stinks!'

'All right, Tawrie.' Her nan spoke firmly and held her gaze. 'That's enough.'

It was hurtful that her nan even partially seemed to be siding with Annalee, and with high emotion spinning around them, she decided the best thing to do would be to get out of the room and get out of the house. There was no time for a decent swim, not now, not without it making her ridiculously late for work, and that was unfair on Connie. She knew, however, that she had to cycle down to Hele Bay Beach and tell Maudie and Jago that she was okay. Missing her swim for the first time since joining the Peacock Swimmers would only worry them and she cared about them far too much for that.

She did her best not to look at Corner Cottage as she cycled past, didn't want Ed to see her in a state of high agitation, angry all over again that her perfect night had been hijacked by the events waiting for her at Signal House. It was so bloody unfair! Picturing the neat, cosy interior of Ed's house, she wished she could have stayed cocooned inside it, safe in his arms with untested words of affection bouncing off the walls. Despite the dire welcome at home, her spirits lifted at the thought of her new love and all that lay ahead for them. It was impossible not to feel excited, although this was tinged with dread at the thought of having to expose him to her grotty, grotty homelife as far as her mother was concerned.

She wished she could rewind to the point where she'd woken up in the attic room and held on longer to the feeling in her stomach that the world was a wonderful place full of infinite possibilities.

It really had been a perfect night. Time had lost all meaning, as they sat with legs touching, holding hands briefly, his fingers reaching out to move hair from her face, as they laughed and chattered.

'Taw?' he called after her, and just to hear his voice was enough to send her happiness into cartwheels. She turned on her bike and there he was. Just the sight of him enough for a punch of lust to whack her in the stomach and erase the stench of bleach and dys-function that lingered in her nostrils. 'I've been waiting for you to go past on your bike. Do you want me to come with you for your swim? We can chat on the way.'

His keenness to accompany her, to be with her was electric! She couldn't wait to be seen with him, for him to meet Connie, to introduce him to Uncle Sten, for Freda to make him that cuppa. Just as wonderful as the way this crazy, fast, head-spinning love felt was the thought of all they were yet to experience.

'That's so sweet, but I'm not going to swim, just off to tell Jago and Maudie that I can't make it but that I'm okay. I'm running late.' She pulled a face.

'And you hate being late.'

'I really do.' She smiled.

'Tawrie?'

'Yes?'

'I need to tell you my third thing. The third thing you don't know about me.' His smile played nervously about his mouth and he took his time.

'Go on then, make it quick!' She looked up into the face of the man who had professed his love, and her heart flexed at the mere sight of his mouth moving and the memory of his lips softly grazing her skin.

'No.' He shook his head. 'It's not a quick thing or a by-the-way thing, it needs a longer chat. It's important.'

'Okay, well, after work?' She loved making plans; the thought of another evening spent in his arms was enough to fill her with joy in anticipation of the day and night ahead. This love felt a lot like a secret and one that, she knew, lit her from within.

'Yes, after work.' He stared at her face, his eyes creased with kindness and something else. Concern? It was to be expected; to have expressed love so quickly, no matter how confident she was

213

of her feelings, left her a little vulnerable, exposed. It had to be the same for him.

'I'll come knock for you.' She laughed as she pedalled off to find her fellow Peacocks, wondering how it was possible to spend mere minutes in his company and forget entirely that she had just rowed with her mother. It was what he did – made her feel that all was right with the world.

CHAPTER SIXTEEN

Harriet Stratton

August 2002

Harriet knew she'd never forget the way her children listened to her every word, their expressions fraught as they sank back into the sofa, eyes wide, looking smaller and younger than ever.

'And so that's it.' She paused. 'Daddy and I will never ever stop loving you, but we're going to be friends instead of married. It will all be fine . . .'

All she had wanted to do was scoop them up and hold them close. She had felt every part of her body tremble and did her best to keep her voice steady.

It had hurt her heart to be the bearer of such news, but this, she knew, was preferable to leaving it up to Hugo, who might let his anger, his defensiveness, colour his tone or choice of words. He stood just outside of her peripheral vision, but she could hear him breathing, feel his closeness and wondered if he was there to offer support or watch her suffer. Possibly a bit of both. Having known him since their university days, she knew he could carry a grudge when things didn't quite go his way. One evening during Michaelmas term, when they were students, they'd stumbled across the labelled keys of Spencer, who rivalled Hugo for captaincy of the rugby team. He had picked them up, and before she could suggest handing them in at the porter's lodge or taking them to Spencer's study room, he'd launched them way into the distance, where they landed in a wooded area on the boundary of their halls. She had thought it a shitty thing to do then and still it rankled. Harriet wasn't hypocritical enough not to recognise that she had suppressed her horror and readily married the man, but this vengeful streak didn't exactly fill her with hope for a smooth transition into the next stage of their lives.

'Where will, erm . . .' Dilly began, before running out of words and scratching at an invisible spot on her pyjama leg.

Harriet understood, knowing that with so many questions, so many worries, it was hard to make your mouth settle on one and ask plainly.

'You don't need to worry about a thing, Dills. I promise you.' This the first lie. 'Daddy and I will always work together to make sure that things are the best they can be.' The second. 'We know it's a lot, it's a lot for us too' – this the truth – 'but we will always be a team. It will all be okay.' Lies three and four.

'Can I go and finish my game?' Bear asked, his face red, mouth thin, a recognised precursor to crying that made her heart twist, knowing he wanted to do so alone in his room.

'Of course, love, and if you have any questions, in fact, *when* you have—' He ran up the stairs before she had the chance to complete her sentence.

Dilly loped after him and Hugo followed. Her leather chair offered some comfort as she sank into it, running her hands over the arms that her mother had touched as she tried to order her thoughts. What did come next? Her shoulders shook – not from the cold but with fear at the prospect of packing up once more and heading out into the unknown. She ran her hand over her face; everything in that moment felt a little insurmountable and she wished she could curl up somewhere alone.

Suddenly, there were shouts and a scuffle of activity outside, a disruption of some sort, the detail of which evaded her and had ceased by the time she popped her head out and glanced down Fore Street and then Mill Head, as much to breathe fresh air as anything else. Probably pub-goers on their way home, making merry and living in the minute, now spirited away inside the closed doors of the neighbourhood. How she envied them. She couldn't remember the last time she'd enjoyed the heady escape of a good night out. And just this idea was enough to cause a page to fall open in her memory, bookmarked for easy access.

Thank you, doll, I feel gorgeous!

Making her way outside, she sat on the wide top step and stared up at the inky night sky. Stars shone brightly and she closed her eyes, offering up a wish that whatever came next would not be too hard on her or her beloved children, and even on Hugo. A vicious emotional tussle was more than she could contemplate, knowing exhaustion would reveal her bravado to be just that if there were to be a war of words.

As she climbed the stairs to bed, she wondered for the first time about the sleeping arrangements. What would happen now they were no longer trying to patch things up? The thought of spending the night with Hugo under the same roof but in separate beds was jarring. The thought of being under the same duvet, worse. The only other times this had happened was when illness had made it prudent to do so or one of the kids had had a bad dream and she'd camped on their floor. She stood in front of the big mirror of the family bathroom looking in the direction of Capstone Hill with its zigzag paths leading up to the summit, and ran the tap, washing her face with foaming cleanser and cold water – part of her nightly ritual. How quickly the fracture in their marriage had fallen into a crevasse, on the edge of which she and her little family now teetered, staring down.

'God, Harriet.' Hugo came into the bathroom with urgency. 'It's awful, just—' He looked distressed, and in truth she preferred it to the toxic combination of frustration and anger that had reared its head earlier.

'It is awful,' she agreed. 'It's new. Very raw and strange, but we'll find a way to navigate it; we have no choice. I was just thinking that we need to do so calmly. We'll come together and—'

'No, no!' He shook his head and walked forward, his breathing fast, his eyes dilated, his expression concerned. 'Something terrible has happened. I've just got off the phone with Jack.'

'Jack from the pub?' She knew he liked to pop in for a swift half on his way back from a walk.

He nodded. 'There's been an accident.'

'Oh no!' Her gut jumped in anticipation. 'What kind of accident?'

And as he told her what little news he had, she felt a weakness in her knees, aware more than ever of the frailty of life.

It had been a long and restless night. Her plans for sleep had been hijacked by the terrible events unfolding. Up early, she'd wandered down to the harbour, a pashmina wrapped tightly around her shoulders.

Now she sat at the kitchen table, the room bathed in dim lamplight as she sipped hot tea, hoping this might be the remedy to the shudder of her limbs. The quiet of the streets was eerie; it was like a ghost town. On this summer morning it seemed that people had chosen to stay indoors, windows closed, TVs muted, the volume on their radios turned to low. There was no chatter, no dog bark, no engine roar, no horn toot, nothing. It was an odd phenomenon in this vibrant quarter, unnerving.

The only noise of which she was now aware was the collective heartbeat of grief, which echoed through the town and hovered like a cloud. As tangible as smog and just as oppressive. Having placed her diary on the seat next to her, Harriet sat at the table in the kitchen and laid her hand on its cool surface, taking solace from its solidity when it felt as if the world were spinning.

'You okay?'

She looked up with a start; she hadn't heard her husband come down the stairs. He looked tired, as she no doubt did as well; they had a lot to process.

'Yes,' she lied.

'The kids are sound asleep.'

'Good.' Only half listening, she did her best to engage, to be present.

'It's just awful, isn't it?' He shook his head.

'Really is.' Her tears gathered.

It had been hard work over the last couple of months, putting in the effort to mine the glue that would keep them together. The endless hours spent analysing and trying to understand how they had reached this point and where they might go from here had left her emotionally and physically exhausted. Their decision the previous evening proved that the glue was brittle and all that work had been in vain. On top of this, the accident. A bucketload of sadness dumped on her and every other doorstep in Ilfracombe, a reminder that what they shared and how they lived was fleeting. It was a mudslide of distress that made no allowance for how far they as a couple had come, the healing they had managed and the foundations they had tried hard to rebuild. It was a fierce, fast deluge that washed it all away.

And here she sat at the table, pushing her body down into the chair, trying to stay upright, to feel stable, as her thoughts got stuck on what came next. Her husband stood before her. It was like watching skin and tissue fall from bones, leaving nothing but the ashen, skeletal remains of their marriage exposed, raw, and entirely irretrievable.

'Can I get you anything to eat, toast?' His demeanour told her that he too was entirely affected by the situation.

'No, thanks.' Her stomach rolled with revulsion at the thought of taking food; her hollow gut and the subsequent jitters felt preferable, matching the shaky nature of her thoughts.

'I'll go have my shower. If that's okay?'

'Sure.' She watched him creep from the kitchen, trying to make the least amount of noise, to be the smallest he could, and she understood. She pictured their bed, and knew that if the kids were still at Ellis's house, she'd crawl beneath the duvet, sink into that soft space and hide away for as long as she was able. But she was needed, on guard for when her kids awoke.

Reaching for the diary she'd secreted in the table drawer, she took her time, writing slowly, methodically, honestly.

Don't know where to start . . . what a terrible, terrible couple of days. Sometimes something comes along that floors a community, that derails the normal and changes the shape of a place, and such a thing happened yesterday.

I've felt caught up in it while also trying hard not to hijack another person's misery – someone I barely knew. I couldn't stand for anyone to think I was trying to claim a part. But the truth is I feel so very sad for the man, a stranger to me really, and his family, sad for the whole town.

Dotted around the harbour this morning were flowers in jam jars and on the steps of cottages, or bunches with their bases wrapped in wet cotton wool, interspersed with candles whose flames flickered mournfully in the growing light of day. Sorrowful, beautiful beacons that made me weep. I pictured families behind the front doors, gathered in clusters, kids held close, couples holding hands or with arms around backs, heads forward, noses pressed into sleeves and tissues pushed into eyes. Finding solace where they could in the arms of those they love and this for me amplified the realisation that my safe harbour is smashed to smithereens on the sharp rocks of betrayal.

The whole town is quiet; the atmosphere has gone from crackling with the joy of summer to feeling muted and toned down. Even the gulls sit quietly on rooftops, as if aware that this is a time for stillness.

The news spread like a lit fuse . . . travelling along its twisted, looping route, gathering gasps and cries as it went. The worst kind of gossip, each fragment of news added to, as more information came to light and the bigger picture revealed itself.

There's been an accident . . .

A man went overboard . . .

Probably hit his head . . .

Not exactly sure who . . .

He was sailing alone . . .

They can't find him . . .

They've found his boat . . .

He's obviously dead . . .

The man who married Annalee, his mother Freda owns Signal House . . .

An Ilfracombe family . . .

They have a little girl . . .

How will they get over something like this?

And that's how I found out it was Daniel Gunn. This is the information that floated through the open window, over the phone, gleaned from Hugo's chats with Jack, and from the whispers I overheard in the harbour, as those that knew and loved him struck matches with which to light their candles.

Shock doesn't come close. How my heart aches for sweet Annalee, and for Dan too, the handsome man. I feel for his family: his kind mother, and most of all for that little girl, Tawrie, whose daddy is not going to come home.

I cannot imagine that family's pain. I know what it's like to have the plug pulled on your world, to feel your heart cleaved open, but Hugo is in the shower right now. He is here! In the face of what the Gunn family are going through, our bump in the road and what comes next pales into insignificance.

I have the French doors open, as is my habit, and the morning air is warm and still. The place feels different. Only yesterday it was buoyant, so much so I felt I could look down at the street and see a carnival. It's as if the whole town weeps. But no one will ever weep as hard or as long as Annalee, the woman with the sparkle in her eye as she walked with her arm linked with that of the man she so loved. I shan't ever forget her happy, happy face: a woman who looked like she had the whole world at her feet and was loving every second of it. How I envied her and how I envy her still, knowing that the strength of feeling she will carry in her heart is something I can only dream of.

I hope they find Daniel Gunn.

I hope they get to lay him to rest and say their goodbyes.

I hope his daughter finds peace, safe in the knowledge that her parents adored each other and that she was made in love.

CHAPTER SEVENTEEN

TAWRIE GUNN

AUGUST 2024

'Bloody hell!' Connie pulled a face of utter disgust as Tawrie waltzed into the Café on the Corner and grabbed her apron and notepad. 'I can't deal with that smug, happy face all day, it's enough to make me puke! I suggest you think miserable thoughts and start frowning a bit.'

Tawrie could feel the love in her cousin's ribbing.

'Envy is a terrible thing, Con! Anyway, you should be happy for me!'

'I am, but I just can't deal with that sickly lovestruck smile. So wipe it off your chops and we'll all have a better day.'

'Well, aren't you a little ray of sunshine?' She tied her apron around her waist.

Connie turned her attention back to the grill. 'So I guess we can assume you had a nice time last night with Sebastian?'

Tawrie leant on the countertop and let out a dreamy sigh. 'I feel like a teenager. I'm literally all of a dither. It was . . . it was . . .'

'Two bubble and squeak with fried eggs, both with bacon and one with beans!' Gaynor called over her shoulder. 'Morning, Taw, you all right, me darlin'?'

'Oh, she's fine, Gay. About to tell me all about her night of passion with Sebastian!'

'Ooh, I'll hang around for that then, I do love a bit of love.'

'Honestly, you two! There's nothing to tell!' She squirmed while her cheeks ached with the width of her smile.

'Oh, you dirty cow!' Connie brandished the cooking tongs in her direction.

'What're you talking about now?' She shrank back towards the wall.

'I know that look! I think there's everything to tell! Just wait till I tell Nan what her little Tawrie Gunn's been up to!' Connie tutted loudly.

'What's Tawrie Gunn been up to?' They hadn't heard Needle come in, and yet there he was with his reusable cup in his hand, awaiting his morning coffee. His words were offered generally but his eyes fixed on Connie.

'Wouldn't you like to know!' Connie shot him down.

'This one might be in love!' Gaynor mock whispered, loud enough for them all to hear, while pointing at Tawrie.

'Well, that's a turn-up for the books, although I knew something was going on, what with her new happy face. That's how I got my nickname, cos I notice things. Sharp as a needle!' He tapped his temple.

Connie turned with the tongs in her hand. 'That's not why everyone calls you Needle, Needle.'

'Isn't it?' He stared into the face of the woman he wanted to take out on his boat.

'No, love, it's not cos you're sharp. It's because you're a prick.'

Gaynor let out a laugh and Tawrie felt a flicker of sympathy for the man.

'I know you're joking.' He smiled. 'And to be honest, Connie, my love, you can call me anything you like, cos if you are talking to me in any way, about anything, then I know I'll be happy.'

'Oh Connie! You got to admit he's a trier and God loves a trier.' Gaynor grabbed a Diet Coke from the fridge and whisked it out to the back.

'Well, maybe he can take God out on his boat then?' Connie sucked her teeth and turned her attention back to the grill.

Tawrie left them to it, knowing nothing, not even their bickering, could dampen her mood. She approached the woman sitting alone at a table. She was about her own age, but beautiful, elegant, with long blonde hair carelessly slung over one shoulder and denim cut-offs that showed off her tanned, endless legs. A dainty, thin woman, definitely built for sitting on a pretty seat while improving her needlepoint. Her movements were languid, her limbs rangy, her build narrow, refined. There was no way she came from a long line of log-shifters, hole-diggers, net-menders, barrel-hefters or fish-gutters. A quick glance down at her own sturdy thighs and she felt the cruel twin daggers of comparison and self-doubt simultaneously threaten her confidence. It was an observation that ordinarily would deflate her good mood, but this was no ordinary day and she was still aglow!

With one hand supporting her head and her elbow resting on the table, the woman scrolled her phone with her free hand, suggesting she might have been sitting there for a while, waiting.

'Hi there, what can I get you?' Tawrie smiled and waited with her pen poised.

'Hi, erm . . .' The woman flashed her impossibly white, impossibly straight teeth. 'Do you have any herbal teas?'

'We have peppermint or chamomile.'

'Do you have any others?'

'Other than the ones I just told you we have?'

'Yes.'

'Connie?' she yelled over to the counter where Needle had just made his exit.

'What?' Connie called over her shoulder.

'Do we have any herbal teas other than peppermint or chamomile?'

Connie looked up from the grill. 'What is the lady looking for exactly in terms of tea?'

Tawrie recognised her cousin's subtle sarcasm, which seemed to be the order of the day.

'Oh!' The woman sat up straight and beamed. 'Do you have anything with ginger in it? I like anything with ginger.'

Connie shook her head. 'No. No, we don't.' She smiled almost imperceptibly at Tawrie and went back to the bangers, which were starting to sizzle.

Undeterred, the customer continued. 'Okay, erm, what about anything fruity: rosehip, blackcurrant, apple?'

'Did you hear that, Con?'

'No, what?' Her manner was decidedly less patient.

'Can you check the chamomile and peppermint teas and see if they have anything fruity in them?'

Connie abandoned the metal tongs, wiped her hands on her apron and grabbed the slightly dusty boxes from the shelf before scouring the small print.

'Nothing fruity, I'm afraid.' Connie replaced the box and reached for her tongs.

'Sorry about that.' Tawrie smiled at the woman who twirled the ends of her hair between her fingers. She was nicely dressed, pairing a long-sleeved white shirt with her cut-offs, and with a tiny turquoise choker at her neck.

227

'Okay, so . . . in that case, I'll take a coffee, do you have decaf?'

'Yes.' There was no need to check.

'Fab, so, decaf coff for me and a black tea for his nibs.'

'Black tea?'

'Yes, he's lactose intolerant, and late!' She gestured to the empty chair opposite.

'No worries. I'll leave the menu with you in case you want to order when your friend arrives.'

'Thank you.' The woman was sweet, sincere and a bit posh.

'Right, Gay' – Tawrie leaned on the counter – 'can I please have—' She was about to put her order in when she was wholly distracted by the rather handsome visitor who appeared at the door.

'Oh marvellous, that's all we need! Another lovebird to clutter up the place! She's working, you know!' Connie brandished the tongs – her new weapon of choice – in his direction and laughed as Tawrie stared at her man, come to visit her in the café. She was actually delighted. It seemed that he too found the thought of no contact until this evening utterly unacceptable.

'Well hello you, couldn't keep away?' She took a step forward and watched as he took a tentative step backwards; it made her stomach drop. There was something about the rise and fall of his Adam's apple, the way he exhaled, that made her ears ring and the blood rush from her head. She pushed her foot into the lino-covered floor and let her arms fall by her sides, willing him to spit it out. 'What's up?'

'I . . . I got a, erm . . . I got a . . . text, a text from, erm . . .' He wiped the sweat from his top lip.

'Spit it out!' She found his behaviour confusing and concerning in equal measure.

'I got a text, telling me to be here. I texted back, but she didn't reply . . .' He swallowed. 'I don't have time to explain, but I . . . I have a girl, a someone. A . . . a girlfriend.'

228

'What?' Her voice croaked as the ground rushed up to meet her. It was as if he spoke in a foreign tongue. Unable to process his words, she felt numb, rooted to the spot and wasn't sure whether she wanted to vomit or sob. Her legs shook and she felt the floor tremble beneath her as she sought clarification, leaning now on the countertop.

He looked over her shoulder and exclaimed, 'Oh fuck!'

It was the first time she'd heard him swear like this and it didn't suit him.

'You all right, Taw?' She heard Connie ask behind her.

'I don't . . . I don't know what to say.' It was all she could manage as her heart leapt at the sight of his greying complexion. He stared ahead, looking into the café, while she kept her eyes on his face.

There was no need to ask who he was looking at; she knew before he spoke, could tell by the look on his face as he stared, unable to tear his eyes away from the pretty, dainty woman with the tanned legs who liked herbal tea with ginger. Alerted as she was by the rosy flush to his cheeks and nose, the way sweat broke on his forehead and the rather harried way he shoved his fingers into his hair, and knowing in her soul what was about to unfold, guessing at the words yet to be spoken, Tawrie's heart felt like it was being squeezed and her pulse raced loudly in her ears.

'I . . . I don't know what to say,' she repeated, quieter this time, hoping that if she whispered and he responded in kind, she might not have to hear the words that she was confident were about to slice her heart into pieces and wash away the pillars of confidence on which she had stood since meeting this man.

'It's . . .' He spoke deliberately, seemingly his lips were stuck to his dry teeth. 'It's Petra. Petra, erm, she's my, she's the . . . I didn't know she was coming, I—'

'Bear!' The woman jumped up from the table, clearly delighted to see him. She trotted the length of the café and practically leapt into his arms. He held her fast and Tawrie wondered if she were actually there watching as the two slid together, faces touching, lip to lip, nose to nose, arms entwined, or whether she were invisible, disappeared altogether, spirited away into nothingness, which would explain the hollow void where her stomach used to lurk and the slight ethereal echo of all sound.

'What . . . what are you doing here?' Edgar managed, as he placed the woman gently on the linoleum.

'I missed you!' Petra spoke the simple truth as she stared at him. 'And what kind of a welcome is that?' She prodded his chest. 'I thought I'd come down and surprise you but didn't know where the house was. I knew it was close to the harbour, so I thought I'd come here, grab a cuppa, message you and voilà!' She curtseyed.

Tawrie could barely look him in the eye as Ed turned towards her.

'This . . . this is Petra.' His voice shook.

'Hi! I'm Petra. Bear's fiancée.'

'Fiancée? Wow!' The words coasted out of her mouth on forced laughter. 'Congratulations to you both!' She grinned even though her preference would have been to sob.

'Oh, thank you! I'd show you the ring but it's still being properly sized at the jeweller's.' Petra cupped her hand over her mouth as if sharing an aside. 'His great-grandmother's ring, and let's just say she had rather sausagey fingers!'

'Ha!' Her laughter was an odd sound, staccato and loud.

Ed tried to hold her eyeline but she looked away, concentrating on Petra's dewy complexion, that great cascade of thick hair, and her bright smile.

'I don't know your name?' Petra took a step closer and Tawrie wished she had a smaller nose and that she'd brushed her hair.

'This is Tawrie, she works here in the café.'

230

This time Tawrie looked up and stared right at him. Was that her introduction? Was that who and what she was to him? Apparently so. She felt the embarrassing tightening of her throat and knew that she would take any action to avoid crying here in her place of work, in the town she'd lived her whole life, in front of these two.

'That's me, Tawrie who works here in the café. But I guess you'd rather gathered that, as I've just taken your order.'

Ed looked like he might faint.

'Cute!' Petra wrinkled her nose. 'Tory as in David Cameron? Carrie's fancy wallpaper, Boris, and his chums, tiny Rishi?'

'Yep. Yes that's me. That's it. Tory. True blue.' She grimaced.

'Wow! That's quite a name.'

'Isn't it just?' She threw her head back and tried to match Petra's stance. 'And Bear, that's an unusual name too!' Again she grinned at the man who had held her hand while she told him about the loss of her dad; the man who had told her he loved her not three hours since.

'It's a-a nick-nickname, not many people call me it.'

'A nick-nickname, I see.' She held her ground, recalling how he had said something similar as they'd got to know each other, making, she now knew, false confessions. 'Well, there we go.' She took a deep breath, entirely disinterested in his explanation. He was a liar and she felt like a fool for having believed anything he'd said. Not that this revelation made it hurt any less. 'Anyway, I should be, erm . . .' She pointed in the general direction of the grill, where Connie stood with her mouth open, the sausages all but blackened. 'I just need to . . .' She pointed out the door and Connie nodded. This time with no sarcastic commentary, no jibe, just a look of either horror or abject fury, it was hard to tell.

'Take your time.' Her cousin gave a brief nod. 'Do you want me to come with you?'

Tawrie shook her head, knowing they were busy and with her gone things would quickly turn to chaos.

'Nice to meet you, Tory, hope to see you around!' Perky Petra threaded her arm through Ed's and clung on like they were about to run a three-legged race as she steered him towards the back of the café, where their drinks would arrive any second.

'Oh, you will.' She smiled at the woman. 'Ilfracombe is a small place. It's hard to avoid people, even if you wish you could.' Her eyes lingered briefly on Ed's and she wanted to scream at the sadness that lurked there. How dare he pretend he was bothered! His only regret, she was certain, was having been exposed as the shit he was.

'I'm going to order us salad,' Petra informed him as the two walked to the back of the café.

Stumbling out of the building, Tawrie did her best to remain upright as she made her way to the benches that overlooked the harbour. Ordinarily it was a place for quiet contemplation, reflection or rest. Today it was a lifesaver. Collapsing down on to the wooden seat, she kept her head down and her gaze fixed on the floor, trying to sort the jumble of thoughts that whizzed around her head, as sadness kept a vice-like grip on her throat and she fought for breath.

'Oh my God! Oh my God! Oh my God! I can't believe it! You're such an idiot, Tawrie Gunn.'

Putting her hands over her face, she did her best to make sense of what she now knew. Put simply, she had been used and lied to, and the very worst thing, apart from shagging Ed while his pretty girlfriend had no clue, was that she had been so willing, eager! She'd even dropped her knickers the first time she spoke to him. Although even that didn't seem quite so funny now.

What was it Connie had said? 'Don't let him in. Don't let him get to your heart.'

Tawrie had agreed that she wouldn't, but she had lied. The lure of him and all he represented had been greater than her ability to think rationally.

She wasn't sure how long she sat there but she wanted to be sure he and his fiancée had left the café before she returned, and she was confident Connie would call and give her the nod. The thought of having to see them again, holding hands, cheerily chatting . . . She bent low and breathed deeply through her nose to try to stem the rising nausea.

'Tawrie!'

To hear his voice over her shoulder was a surprise. She sat up straight, still in shock, still trying to make sense of the news, to comprehend the worst kind of betrayal, to recognise that she was an idiot. A naïve idiot.

'Tawrie, please.' He spoke softly and sat next to her. Just the scent of him, the proximity of him, was enough to open up the channel of distress as her tears fell. 'Please don't cry.'

It felt easier to ignore him. She watched his hands grip, flex, and regrip his fingers, suggesting he might want to take her hand, but thankfully knew better than to try.

'What do you want? Why're you here?' she managed through her tears.

'I told Petra I was going to the loo.'

'Lying to her too.' She gritted her teeth.

'I told you I needed to sort things, so that we could make plans—'

'And in my naïvety,' she interrupted, 'I thought you meant redirect your mail, cancel your London gym membership, bring more clothes! Whatever! But not in a million years did I think it involved a partner!'

'I-I wanted to tell you, I really did. I tried, but . . .'

'But what?' she sniffed. 'When did you try, and what could you possibly say to justify being such a shit?'

'I was going to tell you tonight, that was my third thing, but I didn't want it to sound trite, I promise—'

'Oh well, a promise from you is all I need to convince me!' She snorted her derision and wiped her face.

'I know how it looks . . .' he began.

'Do you?' she fired. 'We were in bed together only a few hours ago.' She pointed up towards Fore Street. 'We spoke about everything from cricket balls to first loves, going through a bloody checklist! And at no point did you think it might be a good idea to mention that you're getting married?'

Frustratingly, her tears fell harder.

'I'm not getting married.' He swallowed.

'Oh, right, it's just that I think you'll find that's what fiancée means!'

He rubbed his eyes and she noted the slight shake to his fingers. 'It's all a fucking mess.'

'It is. A mess of your making!' she spat. 'I feel like such an idiot. I believed everything you told me!' This was the hardest thing for her to fathom: how she had fallen and how quickly. 'I've got to give you credit, you were very convincing.'

'You can believe me! I love you! I do.'

Those words were no longer the key to a portal in which she could see her future. She looked out over the water and let her pulse settle.

'Do you know, this is where I was sitting when I first saw you.'

'I thought it was at Hele Bay?' His mouth twitched briefly, as if he were happy in the memory.

She shook her head. 'No. I was standing right here. It was like I was aware of you before I actually saw you, and when I did,

I remember thinking, *there you are.* As if I'd been waiting for you, waiting for you without even knowing it.'

'It's the same, the same for me, but—'

'But what, Edgar, Bear, Ed, whatever your bloody name is?'

'It's such a mess!'

'Yes, so you've said.' She sucked in her cheeks to stop a sob forming.

'I need to tell you—'

'No, no you don't need to tell me anything.' She cut him off. 'I want you to leave me alone. Please just go away.' Her veins ran cold with humiliation.

'Tawrie, please, I want to explain, I need to—'

'I said go away! You don't *need* to do anything. Don't you think you've done enough?' She was unaware of just how loudly she had yelled until Needle came alongside.

'Everything all right here, Taw?' He stood with his shoulders back, chest out, as if prepared to go toe to toe with Ed, and she was strangely glad he was there. Despite having him witness her distress, it felt good to have the support of someone who knew her, knew her family. Here in this little town, where she belonged and Edgar Stratton did not.

'Everything's fine, thanks, Needle. Just saying goodbye to this wanker-named blow-in.' She found there was nothing rewarding in having spoken so foully about the man she loved, nor the expression of hurt that flashed across his face. 'You'd better get back to your fiancée, your decaf coff might be going cold.'

He looked from her to Needle and then at his watch, before walking slowly, shoulders hunched, back to his fiancée, who thought he was in the loo.

'You all right, love?' Needle placed his hand on her shoulder. His kindness was almost more than she could stand.

'I will be. I'm going to go home for a bit.'

'Want me to walk you?' He bent his head and looked into her eyes; sweet, kind Needle who might not be sharp, but was lovely.

'I'll be okay, Needle, but thanks.' She turned and walked away, although with her thoughts spinning like a tornado, tears clouding her vision and with the collapse of the adrenaline-fuelled happiness that had been holding her up, tiredness now lapped at her heels and her footsteps faltered.

Ed turned to look at her as she passed him at the café entrance, making her way up Fore Street.

She kept her gaze firmly ahead, willing her robust legs to move faster, as she fired off a text to Connie.

JUST NEED AN HOUR

Her cousin's reply was swift: a single kiss.

Having made it to the top of the steps, she spied her nan in a deck-chair, reading the paper in the sunshine with her broad-brimmed straw hat hiding her face.

'Here she is! All okay, little love?'

Standing in front of the big old house, she felt unable to move, rooted to the spot and not sure where to turn, what to say or do next. There was a new feeling now: acute embarrassment and shame that she had dared to think she might have met her soulmate and would now have to admit it was a sham.

'What's up, darlin'? Thought you were at work?' Freda folded the paper into her lap.

These words were enough to pull the ripcord on her distress, which she had managed to keep tightly packed in until that moment.

'Oh Nan!' Running forward she flopped down on the grass in front of her and placed her head on her lap. Her tears came thick and fast and with her eyes tightly closed, she wished she could wake up from the whole horrible nightmare.

'What on earth's the matter, Tawrie Gunn? This isn't like you! What's happened, love?'

'He's engaged. The boy you met by the bins, he's engaged to a girl with thin legs and she's ordering him salad!' Her sobs upset the rhythm of her breathing and she welcomed the feel of her nan's palm on her scalp.

'There there, little maid, don't cry. Don't you cry. He's not worth it. They never are.'

'I thought he-he was different.' She hiccupped. 'He made me feel different! But it wasn't real. None of it! He's a liar.'

'I tell you what we're going to do.' Her nan sat forward and threw the newspaper on the floor. Tawrie sat up to face her, her eyes stinging with tears. 'We're going to have a cup of tea and you're going to wash your face and then we're going to go down to Corner Cottage and we shall tell him what an arsehole he is!'

'I'm not going to do that.' She laughed at the thought. 'I'm never going to speak to him again. I can't.'

'Well, I'll go then!'

'You don't need to do that, Nan; I don't want him to know how upset I am. And I don't want to upset his fiancée, it's not her fault.' She felt the start of a headache.

'Well, I mean this' – Freda pointed her slightly bent finger with its nobbled, arthritic knuckle – 'if he or anyone else gives you any grief then you tell me and I'll bloody sort them out! Or I'll send your Uncle Sten to sort them out! He got all his judo belts when he was little. They both did.'

And just this reminder of her dad as a boy was enough for Nana Freda to reach for the tissue that lurked up her sleeve.

'Thanks, Nan, but I'll be okay.'

Tawrie hoped this was the truth as she trod the stairs, ignoring her mother's closed door and what had occurred behind it earlier – a literal shit-show that now paled into comparison with her own woes. She stopped on the half landing to stare at the middle window of the upper hallway at Corner Cottage.

It helped to say it out loud, to help the facts percolate.

'You have a girlfriend, Ed. A fiancée! Someone that isn't me! Another woman who, I guess, will never know we had sex last night. And you were telling the truth about one thing: it is a bloody mess.'

She felt the twin blades of regret and shame slice through the image of the two of them on the floor of the laundry room and then, later, entwined on the wide bed beneath the eaves of the attic room. Where she had felt so safe.

She pushed the door open to the cluttered bedroom in which she'd always slept and lay on the bed, tortured by images of her and Ed eating crisps from the packet, drinking 'the other, pink stuff' and playing Uno, as wave upon wave of tears filled her nose and throat. Her interior monologue was mournful. *Of course this is how it ends for me, for us. What did you expect, Tawrie? This, right here in this room, is the life you have always had and it's not going to change, not now. Not ever!*

Lying on her front, she buried her face in her pillow and wished she could curl up and shut out the whole wide world, just for a while.

CHAPTER EIGHTEEN

Harriet Stratton

August 2002

Harriet folded the towels, still warm from the dryer, and placed them on the kitchen table. She returned the carton of milk that had been left by the kettle to the fridge, then set to with a sponge and spray cleaner to make the surfaces sparkle. Anything, in short, to keep her hands and mind busy. Her breathing came in shallow pants and her pulse raced. She felt flustered, light-headed, overwhelmed. Bracing her arms on the butler sink, she exhaled slowly and closed her eyes, trying to calm down.

'It's okay. It's okay, Harriet.'

She whispered the self-soothing mantra, wishing more than anything that she could see her mum. In that moment, all she wanted was to fall into the embrace of the woman who had raised her, to know again the unique solace and protection that her encircling arms could provide. There never had been and never would be anywhere like it. This, however, was no time for tears and she sniffed them back down her throat, afraid that if she gave in to the distress that beckoned, she might just drown in her sorrow.

She sat at the kitchen table. It was too much, all of it. Her showdown with Hugo and the death of Daniel Gunn were more than she had the capacity to cope with right now. Not that she knew Daniel, no more than someone to nod to, but it was as if the collective sorrow of the town seeped through the very bricks of Corner Cottage and mingled with her own private sadness, magnifying both. She was uncharacteristically nervous about the children surfacing, not sure what questions they might ask or how they might be feeling. Dealing with the fallout of that while doing her best to reassure them was also a lot; more, in fact, than she felt she had the emotional capacity to deal with.

Hugo walked into the kitchen, his hair still wet from his shower.

He sat upright in the chair opposite hers. It felt like an interview, giving the occasion a formality that only added to the weighted atmosphere. She declined to offer him a drink in the way that would once have been automatic, as if she were already mentally clocking off. These small things highlighted the state of before and after in which they now lived.

'How're you feeling?' he asked.

She was stumped as to how to answer without breaking into a long, long soliloquy. 'I'm okay. I can't stop thinking about Annalee and what she must be going through. I wonder if they've found his body yet?'

'I haven't heard. Maybe they won't.' He added the unsavoury possibility and again her heart flexed for the Gunn family.

'God, I hope they do. It'll bring closure.'

'Yes.' He took a beat. 'So what happens now, Harriet? What happens to us?' He looked awful, like a man who hadn't slept, a man who awaited his fate. It brought her no pleasure, knowing her face held similar clues.

'What happens now?' She stared out of the French windows with the view over Fore Street. 'I guess the first thing we need to figure out is the road of least discomfort for the kids. I expect they'll have questions. They will, of course, have questions,' she qualified, 'and it's best we have our answers lined up. We don't want them to worry that no one's steering the ship.'

This was, as ever, her priority and she knew it would be his too. He gave a stiff nod, his mouth tightly closed. His silence encouraged her to fill the quiet, to keep talking.

'And then I suppose we need to be practical and think about where we're all going to live, where the kids are best in school.'

'Jesus Christ, another school? Another house? Another move?' He shook his head and bit his bottom lip and it bothered her. Just like that, his manner was sharp.

'Maybe not,' she said as an idea came into focus. 'Maybe just go home, go back to the house the kids love and tell Mr and Mrs Latteridge that there's been a change of plan, that we're no longer renting, let the kids go back to what they know – school, everything.'

'Back to what *we* know,' he corrected.

There was nothing pleasant about knowing she was going to dash his look of hope, but she had little choice in that.

'Back to what *you* know.' Her words were weighted with intent, but of one thing she was certain, even though the idea itself was a dagger in her breast: she would not, could not go back to that bed, that room, that house in that street where Wendy Peterson, who lived a few doors down, had pissed on everything she held dear. 'And just a reminder that I was happiest when I didn't know I had all of this to worry about and so were the kids. This is of your own making, Hugo. You did all of this, so please don't get angry with me.' Her words were strong, her back straight and yet inside she quaked with fear.

'So what are you suggesting? I live there with the kids and you go where exactly?' He looked and sounded startled.

Her thoughts raced and settled on the obvious solution. 'I guess I could stay with Ellis, have the kids there half the time.'

'Seems like you've given it quite a lot of thought.'

She pushed her thumbs into her closed eyes, as if this might relieve the pressure she could feel building.

'I really haven't. I'm flying blind, like I have been for the last few months.'

'So are you suggesting that you would rather have not known? Would it have been better to let it run its course while you jogged on as normal?'

'No. I would rather you hadn't done it and I could have "jogged on" with my life, which felt pretty perfect!' She rubbed her forehead. Was this what it was going to be like now? Verbally running round in circles that were as exhausting as they were futile? 'I'm tired, Hugo, too tired to do this with you, in this way.' She spat out the verbal olive branch and hoped he might grasp it.

'I guess it was always going to be like this, wasn't it? You were always going to have that ace up your sleeve.'

'It doesn't feel like an ace. Nothing about this feels like winning.'

She kept her voice low, aware that the kids were upstairs. It was a surprise to realise that he was crying again. His tears came suddenly and he swiped angrily at them as they gathered on the stubble of his cheeks. Ordinarily she'd have reached out, taken his hand, held him close, grabbed some kitchen roll, but there was nothing ordinary about this.

'You're right, Harriet, no winning, only loss. I've lost so much. The house, the village, our friends, my reputation, the way my kids will feel about me when they inevitably find out.' She couldn't deny this truth. 'And you—' He gulped back a sob that sounded wet, heartfelt and spoke of sorrow. 'You've been my very best friend for over half my life and I've lost you, haven't I?'

'I think so. Yes,' she whispered. Her mouth trembled and it took all of her strength not to sink to the floor.

'Fuck!' He wiped his eyes and rubbed his hands on his jeans. 'Fuck!'

'What did you think would happen?' Her comment was made calmly and without any intended facetiousness.

He took a moment, drew breath, and shifted in the chair, running his fingers through his hair, and doing his best to remain in control.

'I didn't. I didn't think you would ever find out and I got caught up in the . . . the . . .' He looked into the middle distance as if struggling to find the right word. '. . . the secrecy. It was quite intoxicating. The sex was okay, no more. It was more about the adventure, the illicitness.'

'The lying,' she clarified, uneasy with the palatable coating he wrapped the words in as if to make them easier for them both to swallow.

Hugo nodded.

'I trusted you. Always have. And I don't believe there are degrees of trust. It's either implicit or it's not, and I trusted you. I trusted us. I thought what we had was solid. I thought it was enough.'

'I guess that's why I thought I could get away with it.' He was direct, a little cool, and she knew him well enough to recognise that this was what he did when cornered: he tried to hurt in order to mirror his own pain.

She was actually grateful for his candour but no less cut by his words. She felt sick and swallowed the bile that rose in her throat.

'I don't really know what to say, H, none of this feels real for me, any of it. I fucked up so badly.' And just like that his shoulders fell and he was back to crying.

She sat quietly, waiting for the moment to pass, wanting to get back to the planning stage while they had a moment, before the kids came down.

'So this is really happening? Us living apart, the kids divvying up their time, is that the plan?' he asked again, looking up at her through bloodshot eyes, and she felt the shift in their exchange, if not a shift in their relationship. He was asking her, not in a rhetorical sense, but because she now had the power.

Her words, when they came, were wrapped in sadness. 'I meant what I said: I don't believe there are degrees of trust.'

'And now you don't trust me.' He completed her sentence.

'No, Hugo, now I *can't* trust you. That's the thing. And so we need to speak plainly, but calmly. We need to make arrangements, so that we can get it straight in our heads and explain it rationally to the kids.'

'So what exactly do we do now?' He sniffed. 'Instruct lawyers? Get a divorce?' His face again crumpled. 'Jesus!'

'Yes.' An image of her lying in her student bed, her head flat on his stomach, his fingers lingering on her skin. Sleeping so soundly . . . She blinked it away. 'Yes, we instruct lawyers. We get a divorce.'

'We're that couple.' He sniffed again.

'We are now that couple.' She confirmed the horror of it.

'Dad! Dad!' Bear came running down the stairs. 'There's a seal in the harbour! I was hanging out of the window and a lady shouted up, she's just seen it! Can you take me?'

'Of course I can, sport! Just need to go to the bathroom. Meet me by the front door in two minutes, tell Dilly!'

She watched as Hugo jumped up and Bear ran off to find his sister. It was a reminder that no matter what came next, they would both always love their children more than anything, anyone. All this excitement over a seal. She was glad of the distraction, aware of the fact that her family was on a timer. Few would be the days they would all be together. Instead it would be the kids with one adult missing, or a new adult, or they'd meet at Granny's house, or a thousand other scenarios that would be different from this – the four of them, living under one roof. It was Harriet's turn for tears. She felt swamped by sadness for all they would be denied in the future and all they had lost.

Her husband was right about one thing: nothing about this felt like winning.

Dear Diary – haven't written that phrase for a while. I tend rather to launch into it, but right now I feel like I need a friend and so 'Dear Diary' it is, like we're mates, chatting. Although I must admit, it's a fairly one-sided conversation.

Hugo has taken the kids seal-spotting in the harbour and I'm glad. Not only is it a chance for me to be alone, to catch my breath, but also, I hope, an event that might help shift the focus a little from the death of Daniel Gunn. I figure that for Annalee and little Tawrie, if their friends and neighbours are even momentarily distracted, it might help them move forward, even if only a bit.

It's been one helluva few days.

Truth is, I'm in a tailspin, hanging on by a thread. And in the absence of a friend close by and not wanting to eat up so much of my sister's time, I've come to look upon you as a confidante of sorts. I'm thankful for this ritual. A steadfast thing in the choppiest of seas. And boy do I need the ritual right now.

4.25 a.m., that's when I woke with a start, sweating as if emerging from a nightmare, my skin clammy, heart pounding, nightdress rucked around my hips and my throat dry.

How to describe it?

Like getting hit by a bus

No, not that.

Like being shot

No, not that either.

She took a moment, closed her eyes and tipped her head back in the chair as she tried to recall exactly how it had felt, sitting up in the bed and doing her level best not to howl out loud, as her husband slumbered soundly by her side. There had been a short discussion and, on her part, much thought, on the most appropriate sleeping arrangements following their decision to call time on their marriage. Yet when the time for bed came, both, felled by the news of Daniel's death, had fallen exhausted into the double bed. Close together, yet miles and miles apart.

It came to her.

She sat forward and tucked her hair behind her ears, pen in hand.

I woke with a start and it was like an ice pick of realisation hitting my chest. Pointed, painful and specific. Not the first time I've felt it. The first time was when I was in the bedroom of our house in Ledwick Green. The night I found out my husband was cheating.

It was May, a pleasantly warm evening. I'd just put away pants and socks in the chest of drawers and sprayed my neck with perfume, for no reason other than I was passing the bottle that sat on my dressing table. I was about to draw the curtains, gripping the inner edge, when Hugo's car pulled up in the driveway. He drove in, as he always did, facing the house, and I saw him unclick his seat belt.

My first thought was to hurry downstairs and crank up the stove, encourage supper to cook quicker, and to shove the peas on to boil. Planning for a regular supper with my family, thinking of his rumbling tum, just like any other night. Only it wasn't to be a regular supper and it certainly wasn't like any other night.

It was the first night; the first time I had unwelcome knowledge that would change the course of my life, of all our lives.

It was also an ending; the end of family life as I'd known it.

The end of loving him in the way I had.

It was also a beginning too. But just what was starting it would have been hard to say.

I only happened upon him as I stood there. Perfect timing, as they say. I wasn't waiting or looking or stalking or suspecting, doing nothing more than drawing the curtains to keep the soft glow of the street lamp at bay. I sometimes wonder what my life would be like today if I had not discovered his affair. It's a thought that scares me: the idea of carrying on oblivious – smiling, cooking, working, sleeping, loving – while the whole time he snuck out, lied and betrayed me, betrayed us. I then have to remind myself that this was how I lived before this night of revelation and I had been happy in the dark. Happy and ignorant. But that's the trouble with knowledge, once you have it, once you're informed, there's no going back to happy and ignorant. There's just no going back.

I watched him release his seat belt and was about to pull the curtain when he leaned forward to end a phone call. His mobile sat in its holder on the dashboard and he lingered, just for a second. No more. His hesitation in that moment was the cypher to crack the code of a puzzle I didn't know I had to figure out.

I was transfixed.

The fact is, I've known Hugo since university. I've known him skinny, muscled, fat. I've known him with a mop of curly locks, I've known him balding. I've known him to hit rock bottom when one or two bad financial decisions left the coffers empty, and I've known him to dance around the kitchen when the big wins have come in. I've known him happy, sad, up, down and I've loved him through it all.

I know his peculiarities, his quirks, tics, traits, likes and dislikes, and I know with certainty that he hates, absolutely detests, talking on the phone. A marvellous raconteur, he can natter for hours face to face, especially after a good supper and in front of a fire or sitting side by side looking out to sea on a blanket as the sun sinks and dusk steals the warmth from the day. Oh yes, in those situations his conversation and energy for connection is boundless, but when it comes to the phone . . .

'Bloody thing. I don't want to be connected or available 24/7 – just because you can be doesn't mean it's good for us! Impossible to hide!' That's what he always said.

And yet, as I held the tasselled edges of my Susie Watson linen drapes, my mind on the cauliflower cheese that was bubbling in the oven and the bacon waiting to hit the skillet (butcher-bought, of course, freshly sliced and wrapped in wax paper, tied with string) I saw that something life-altering had been hiding in plain sight.

That was the other ice-pick-in-the-chest moment.

For no more than a single second he paused, reluctant to end the call, wanting to eke it out, to hear the voice on the other end of the line, to linger longer than was necessary on the driveway in his two-litre, shiny, metallic cocoon of deceit, connected to a call that might have lasted his whole journey home. Company for him as he navigated the twisty lanes to the place where his family waited for him.

My stomach turned over and I couldn't move. Mesmerised, staring, hunting for other clues. He was smiling, happy, in a new shirt, with a recent haircut, the slow, easy pace of a man satisfied in every sense.

He climbed out of the car and looked up and when he saw me there was the vaguest flicker of unease about his eyes. As if he'd been caught, unmasked.

We ate supper. I remember Bear babbling on about a Pokémon movie and Dilly took an age to eat, forking tiny morsels into her mouth reluctantly and it really irritated me. I think I snapped at her to eat up or don't eat at all, and Hugo stared at my uncharacteristic outburst. I remember feeling hot shame spread over my face, but at so much more than the fact I had shouted at Dilly. Although yes, that too.

My suspicion was that I'd been duped.

That I'd been displaced.

He'd chosen someone else.

I was certain of it.

I could feel it.

I then spent an hour or so in the bath, drawing up a list of possible women: Claire from the pub. Always breezy and forward, her humour full of double entendres, saucy and obvious.

Bear's French teacher. Ms Duvall, who is sultry, sexy and with a voice like liquid chocolate and a tiny waist. I'd heard Hugo joke to Frank next door about dabbing on extra cologne for parents' evening and how he wouldn't mind detention with Ms Duvall. I'd laughed. He'd spoken brazenly in front of me, so obviously it had to be a joke, right? But what if it wasn't?

My mind raced and made illogical leaps. I was so in the dark.

The girl on reception at the gym – I couldn't remember her name? Lois? Or Lou? Super-fit. Young, strong, with a no-nonsense approach; she always seemed to have time to chat to Hugo but never to me.

Or any number of faceless candidates I'd never met at his workplace. He was, after all, a partner at the accountancy firm, and some level of power, no matter how small, was attractive to certain women.

I never thought it would be Wendy Peterson. Never in a million years! Wendy who lived further down the lane and liked to show her cleavage. Divorced Wendy with the convertible who had garden ornaments that we, as a couple, had secretly mocked, laughing at her lack of taste.

I sat next to him on the sofa as he flicked through the channels. The kids were asleep. I'd stacked the dishwasher, washed up the supper things, the kitchen was clean and tidy.

There was no pre-chat, I asked him outright: Are you having an affair?

His reply?

What a bloody ridiculous thing to say to me! No!

But he was lying.

I wanted to believe him, aware of how much easier life would be for us all, but I didn't.

I thought we were immune to infidelity, he and I, because we were built on a bedrock of trust. Affairs were what happened to other people. I figured that because of our long history, our buoyant sex life, our communication, our great kids, our lovely, lovely life that it wouldn't come knocking on our door, but I was wrong.

So yes, that was the first time I felt the ice pick, and this morning, as I sit here in this cosy kitchen, I feel it again, but this time it's for very different reasons.

The pain is the same, the grief too, but this time it's me who has caused the ripple.

I woke with a start at 4.25 a.m. and a clarity to my thoughts that has been absent for the longest time. A clarity that is as welcome as it is terrifying.

I thought loving Hugo enough would mean we could conquer anything, rebuild.

I had no idea that when trust is the thing that's broken, there isn't a glue in the world that can piece it back together, no matter how hard I try.

Maybe it's just me.

Maybe others are successful in brushing off the insult, the injury, but not me.

Mine is a scientific brain and I have analysed the facts, sorted the data, and come to the conclusion that this experiment – moving to a new place, living in a new house, and making new neighbours, starting afresh – it has failed.

We have failed.

And right now I feel angry that we took the step at all.

And no matter how hard I try not to, I see her face every time he makes a phone call and a small part of me wonders if they are in touch.

I imagine his hands on her body when his fingers graze my skin.

I picture him ending that call and the way he looked . . . caught. And every time it's like a knife in my gut.

I can't do it any more.

Annalee Gunn is in my thoughts, of course. Mrs Annalee Gunn. I remember the way she looked at her husband as

*they walked around the harbour, entirely engrossed in one
another, come rain or shine, as if the whole world existed
just for them and whatever was going on around them
was merely the backdrop to their love affair.*

*And I know that it's the way I used to look at Hugo, and
it's the way Hugo used to look at me, but not now.*

Not ever again.

So I guess the question is: what the hell do we do now?

*Hugo is right: another school, another house, another
move and then we separate and we get a divorce. It's easy
to write. Simple and straightforward, the words on the
page making no allowance for the dissection of the whole,
the cutting of the emotional ties, the breaking of the routine and the way the heart will jump at the prospect of
separation. All of those things much, much harder . . .*

The sound of Bear's feet thundering up the front steps and
through the front door brought her to the present.

'What are you doing?' he asked, kicking off his trainers.

'Just scribbling in my little book.' She hated the thought of
her words being discovered, deciding there and then to hide it
somewhere and let it gather dust. She pictured the small wardrobe
built into the eaves in the attic room on the top floor, with its loose
side panel. That would do. She'd pop it in there, out of sight and
out of mind.

'Did you see the seal?'

'No, it had gone.' His expression was crestfallen. 'Dad and
Dilly are coming.'

'What would you like for breakfast?' She did her best to control the break in her voice, knowing that the decisions she and Hugo would make in the coming days would affect him and Dilly in ways that were unthinkable only a few months ago.

'Sugar Puffs, please.'

Harriet stood and her boy fell against her and she held him fast. Her beloved son. And there they stood, as she hoped and prayed that in that space, in that moment, he would know the unique solace and protection that her encircling arms provided.

CHAPTER NINETEEN

Tawrie Gunn

August 2024

With leaden limbs, fatigue-riddled bones and a cloak of sorrow about her shoulders, Tawrie cycled slowly. Hele Bay Beach was quiet when she pulled up and placed her bike and duffel bag in her favoured spot. It was rare and deflating to look out over the water and not feel the rush of excitement at the prospect of striding in. Not even the sight of glorious sunshine spreading over the water could lift her. Never could she have imagined that to walk into the big briny and feel its embrace would seem like a chore. Her heart just wasn't in it, but she was damned if she was going to let someone like Edgar Stratton spoil this for her too.

Images of his laughing face and his words, offered so sincerely, had plagued her throughout the night, and she knew that if she hadn't heard from his own mouth that he had a girlfriend, she would not have believed it. Her experience of him and the trust quickly built, based on nothing more than instinct, had led her to believe that he was the real deal and that her feelings were indeed reciprocated.

A quick glance along the shoreline and she spotted Jago, already in and pulling through the water. Maudie was a little way off to his right.

There was no sign of Ed, something she had hoped for and dreaded in equal measure. Practising in her head how she would ignore him, while thinking of all the questions she wanted to fire at him. It was a quandary. She longed to see him, the love drug residue still lingered in her veins and fed the craving. At the same time, the prospect of seeing him and not being able to touch him because he was not hers was galling. A realisation that caused her stomach to grip with loss.

With her swimming costume on, wetsuit left at home on this warm day, she strode into the water and felt the frustrating sting of tears; she waded further until the water lapped her thighs and still those tears just kept on coming. With her head now in her hands and her goggles dangling on her wrist, she knew there was no point putting them on only to have them fill from her leaky eyes. Her shoulders shook as frustration and fatigue combined to make her do something that the darkness, rain, and wind had failed to do: look back at the shore, where her dry robe nestled invitingly on her bike, and wonder if she had the strength to swim at all, or whether she should give up and go home, just for today.

The water chopped against her and she took this as the push she needed to get on with it. Further still she ventured, until gentle waves lapped her shoulders and neck and she closed her eyes, letting the ocean soothe her.

'What's wrong with me, Dad?' she whispered, swallowing the salty mass of distress that gathered at the back of her nose and slipped down her throat. Pulling her arms through the sea, she moved swiftly out into deeper water before slowing, eyes closed, the sun on her face as she opened her heart to the body of water where she felt most at home.

'Why is it never my turn? What did I do? Should I have put mascara on?' She sniffed. 'I don't wear make-up because I don't look like Connie so I don't see the point, and I would hate anyone to think I was like Mum, always with a face full of the stuff. I don't want anyone to think I'm like her.' Her tears added salty drops to top up the ocean. 'I really liked him, more than I was supposed to after such a short period of time. I couldn't help it. I loved him. I love him. He felt like mine, and I know that's a ridiculous thing to say for a grown woman – romantic, fanciful even – but it's the truth, he did. And I liked the way it felt; in fact, I loved it.'

'It's okay, take your time . . .' The voice was soft, kind.

Dad?

She took a sharp intake of breath and opened her eyes towards the sound coming from the ocean. It was of course Jago who had come alongside her and spoke again. 'Who are you talking to, Tawrie Gunn?'

She turned in the water. 'Oh! Jago! I didn't know you were there.' Her humiliation was complete.

'I didn't want to interrupt you; sounded like you were having quite the chat.'

His kindness was like flicking a switch that made her tears surge.

'Be steady, Tawrie, nothing is worth crying over, dear.'

At the sight of the kindly old man who was most definitely not her father, she cried harder, sinking down into the water, crying and bobbing like a lost seal pup. The disappointment of the voice not belonging to her dad was more than she could or would ever confess.

'I'm . . . I'm oka-ay.' She stuttered.

'It's horrible to see you like this! You are always so sunny! So delighted to be a Peacock! It gladdens our hearts. We look out for you every day and when we see your bike appear on the slipway, it makes us so happy!'

She found his sweetness and the sentiment he expressed profoundly moving.

'I can't help it.'

'I don't want to pry and you don't have to tell me a thing, but is it because of that young man? Maudie said you were quite keen.'

Tawrie nodded. 'I was. More than quite keen.' She could picture Maudie mouthing the understatement. 'But not as keen, apparently, as his fiancée.'

'Fiancée? Oh, what a rotter!' Jago shook his head, spitting water that had trickled into his mouth.

She couldn't disagree.

'You know, dear, I remember everything about the early days with Maudie when we first met – everything. What she wore, what we said, the things that made us laugh. Although in fairness most things made us laugh; we were quite the giddy young things.'

This she could relate to: the giddiness.

'I wasn't only excited for what was happening in that moment, but also for everything that lay ahead. I knew very quickly that it was her. That she was who I'd been waiting for.' This phrase was so reminiscent of her experience, it was at once a validation of her feelings and a devastating reminder of what had slipped through her fingers. 'And even though we've been together for a hundred and fifty years' – he rolled his eyes comically, his face lapped by the sea as a wave came in – 'I still feel like that. I'm still happy, excited to be with her, even though what comes next for us, at this stage in our lives, is without doubt the toughest part of any love affair.'

She felt the boulder of sadness in her throat, picturing her beloved dad, knowing how devastating and unrelenting grief could be.

'And that's what you need to hold out for – someone who makes you feel like that.'

'Thank you, Jago.'

'Not at all. Maudie isn't the only one with advice, difference is I don't feel the need to give mine every five minutes.' He winked at her. 'Shall I tell you a secret?'

'Yes please.' She was cheered by their interaction, the closeness. It was odd yet perfectly comfortable, bobbing about in the sea with her fellow Peacock.

'I'm not deaf. Or at least not as deaf as she thinks I am.'

'Jago! Why would Maudie think you were?' She was perplexed.

'Because I let her think it, my dear! For the last decade or so at least, my beloved wife has spoken with complete candour, confident that I can't hear a word. I know all her secrets. I know where she hides her chocolate stash, songs that remind her of former crushes, I know that when I slurp hot tea it maddens her to her very core. I know that when our daughter says she'll ring and doesn't it cuts her to the quick. I know that she farts when she thinks I'm occupied with something. I know she makes up the lyrics to songs, filling in the gaps with nonsensical words. I know she gives me the fattest chop, the crispiest potatoes, the largest glass of whatever we're drinking. I know she loves me and I know how to amend my behaviours to make her life better. And all this I know because she speaks freely, confident in the knowledge that I can't quite hear.'

'I love how much you two love each other.' She felt the beginnings of a smile; it was impossible not to find this fact wonderfully life-affirming.

'Morning, darling.' Maudie swam over, breathing hard, her chest heaving, muscled arms steadying herself – she was a strong swimmer.

'Morning, Maudie.' She leaned back and let the water coat her hair.

'Goodness me, was there ever a more mournful greeting! What's the matter, Tawrie? You've lost your sparkle today!'

'I have a bit.' She hadn't planned on crying again, and yet those darn tears broke their banks regardless.

'Now, now whatever is the matter?' She saw Maudie exchange a look with Jago and his subtle long blink.

'Just feeling a bit sorry for myself,' she confessed.

'Anything to do with that young man?' Maudie was a woman with her finger on the pulse.

'He's a rotter, Maudie! I've just told Tawrie as much,' Jago piped up.

'Well, I'll tell you what I've always told my daughter.' The old lady took her time. 'If someone doesn't want you then they're not the person you thought they were and therefore what you miss about them, or the life you imagined with them, doesn't exist. Because they are not the right person. They're a fraud and who wants to be lumbered with a fraud! Do you understand?' She spoke plainly, as was her way.

'Kind of.' She didn't want to think of Ed in those terms, didn't want to accept that he just didn't want her. The wanker-named liar.

'I'm losing the morning, better get on.' Jago lifted his hand and pulled away, satisfied there was little he could do or add.

Maudie stared at her. 'Right, get a grip, Tawrie. Take control of your emotions because you're going to need them. You need to present as strongly as you can.'

'I know.' She nodded and gave a false smile, something she was quite adept at: digging deep, finding a smile, and standing firm and calm while her nan and mum fell apart. 'I'm fine,' she lied. 'I'll do a couple of laps and head in.'

'You might want to rethink that.' Maudie jerked her head towards the beach as she swam off.

Tawrie turned in the water, sending a bow wave out around her. Her heart jumped in her chest. There he was. Sitting by her bike with his knees up to his chest and his arms wrapped around his shins. He was wearing the pink linen shirt and she could guess that the buttons would be askew. Her thoughts were jumbled. Her body, it seemed, had forgotten that they were estranged, and the familiar flame of attraction leapt in her stomach and radiated along her limbs, before her brain put the lid on it, extinguishing all possibility of physical contact.

'*I want to say I love you.*' That's what he'd whispered and it had felt like magic.

'*It's the same for me . . . I'd like you to say it.*'

It felt surreal, recalling this exchange while staring at him from the water, trying to figure out how they had tumbled so far, so quickly from that perfect moment.

Having made her way over the rocks and up to the wet sand, self-consciousness slid over her sea-slicked skin. It felt exposing, him seeing her in her swimming costume, especially after the intimacy they'd shared, now made shameful in light of his deceit. She decided to act as if he were invisible, ignoring him completely. To be this close to him was uncomfortable, unbearable, almost. Not that she intended to let him know this.

'Tawrie,' he began, standing now as she reached for her towel and rubbed her wet hair. 'I don't know what to say, but I know I need to speak to you. I've hardly slept.'

As she concentrated on getting dry and changed, invasive and unpleasant thoughts popped into her mind with imagery she could have done without. Had Petra climbed into that double bed in the attic room, lain her head on the pillow where Tawrie had slept and stared at the ceiling? How had Ed felt about it, a second bedfellow in such a short space of time, the sheets barely cold after they'd spent the night entwined and making promises he had no hope of honouring?

Gathering her dry robe from the bike she took a few steps to the left and pulled it over her head, rolling her wet swimming costume down to her waist, as ever welcoming the feel of the soft fleece lining against her skin. Her gaze she kept on the ocean, watching as Maudie and Jago took their last strokes of the morning swim.

'I guess I thought . . .' She heard him swallow. '. . . I thought I had time to think of what to say, trying to find the time when things were perfect, knowing I was going to shatter it, trying to figure out how to tell you that—'

'That you're a liar?' Still she didn't look at him, but not speaking, not giving in to the words cued up on her tongue was a lot harder than she'd thought it would be.

'I'm not, I'm not, I—'

'It doesn't matter how you dress it up or try to justify it. You're engaged to be married to a woman who wears your sausage-fingered great-grandmother's engagement ring, when the adjustments have been made that is. You must have been texting her, calling her and her you. I mean, of course, you guys are engaged after all.'

'Taw.' The sound of her name on his lips was like a punch to her throat.

'And all while we drank wine, held hands, scoffed crisps, played bloody Uno, walked on the beach . . . while we kissed. And we kissed a lot. Even when I slept with you.'

'I never meant—'

'Never meant what? Never meant for me to find out? What was your plan, *Bear*? To piss off back to London after a summer fling and leave me stranded, filled to the brim with all your bullshit?'

'It wasn't bullshit, none of it. It's complicated, I—'

'No! No, it's not complicated. You lied to me! It's actually very, very straightforward.'

'I didn't.' He sounded close to tears and she took small comfort from it.

'You did, you lied through omission, which is the same as telling a big fat lie!'

'It's . . . it's not . . .' He spoke softly.

'Oh, but it is! It's exactly the same, and the worst thing is that I fell for it! I fell for it all!' She placed her palms on her forehead where the beginning of a headache was brewing. 'All that bloody detail about hating your life, wanting to teach or paint, and never once dropping into the conversation the fact that you are engaged to Perky Petra! I feel like such an idiot. You made me into an idiot. And you know what? I have enough going on in my life without you throwing rocks into it as well.'

'The reason I came here, apart from hating my job, which is true, is that I never wanted to get engaged, not to her. I thought I'd put some distance between us to figure all my shit out and then you just came into my life out of nowhere! She's great, really lovely and we've been together for six years and she wanted more—'

'Why are you telling me this?' She felt torn, wanting him to shut up while actually craving the detail.

'Because it's important!' He lunged forward and gripped her by the tops of the arms. 'It's important. And if you want me to sod off and not bother you again that's fine, but I won't be called a liar.'

She shrugged free, laughing in the face of his insistence when the exact opposite was the truth.

'I didn't know how to tell her that things were moving in the wrong direction. She's a nice girl, a great girl, and I didn't know how to say that while she was daydreaming of pageboys, marquees and flower arches, I was trying to figure out how to end things. I've never felt so trapped in my life! What started out as a suggestion from her, no more than a joke over dinner, all got very real very quickly when my stepmother got involved. The next thing I knew, they're making plans, looking at fucking dresses and my dad had got his gran's ring out of the attic!'

'None of that is relevant. None of it. That's how you got to that point in your life and good for you, but it's what came next that bothers me. You told me you loved me, you slept with me, you let me fall in love with you! I'm twenty-eight, Ed, not a kid, and I've never, ever felt so shitty. And trust me, the bar was already pretty high.'

'I never wanted to make you feel like that. I couldn't bring myself to say it out loud. You and I were in this brilliant bubble and I knew mentioning Petra would burst it and I wanted to stay inside it forever. I didn't want to risk scaring you off.'

'Scaring me off? You've done more than that. You've hurt me! Hurt me deeply!' She cursed the croak to her voice.

'And that's the hardest thing for me to reconcile. I didn't speak plainly to Petra for fear of hurting her and not knowing how. I hid the truth from you for the same reasons. I feel like shit. Absolute shit. I didn't plan any of it, I didn't. You just happened to come along when I was trying to figure out my life and my next steps, and it's like—'

'Don't. Just stop. I just don't want to hear it! Your weakness is cringe-inducing. And I guess the good news is, you were worried about hurting us both but now you don't need to be. You can go back to your fiancée and she'll be none the wiser. You can omit the truth with her too.' She pulled on her trainers and righted her bike.

'Are you okay, Tawrie?' Maudie called as she and Jago walked up from the shoreline.

'I will be, Maudie. See you tomorrow.' She spoke plainly, no false smile, no platitude to ease the atmosphere, just the truth. It felt good.

'I'm not weak and I'm not a liar! I mean it, Taw.' Edgar, it seemed, had no intention of shutting up and she felt shards of guilt prick her conscience that she'd been so harsh. 'I didn't plan it, but meeting you has made me think about what I want and where I want to be and—'

'Well, let me help you out.' She slung her duffel bag over her shoulder and stared at his face, his handsome face, with the floppy fringe that hung over his forehead. 'What you want is to marry your fiancée, who seems very nice, and who I feel very sorry for because you're lying to her too, and where you want to be is London, so do me a favour and sod off back there as soon as possible. Please, just go away, for all our sakes.'

'Please, Tawrie, I just want to be with you, be near you!' He pawed at her arm as his tears mustered.

It was more than she could take. 'You don't understand!' She cared less now that tears sheeted her face, or that talking was difficult with this particular level of distress altering her voice, the rhythm of her breathing. All attempt at control was abandoned as her sorrow spilled from her. 'Loving you was like going to a different place, a place I doubted existed. I wanted to stay there forever. It was wonderful. It was winning. It was all the good things I thought it might be.'

'Tawrie.' He took a step towards her and she took a step back.

'And now it's gone and it's worse than having never been there at all because I know that it exists, and I know that I've lost the key and I can only go there in memory, like . . . like with my dad. It's the same; I can't see him or feel him or touch him, I can only remember little bits – like his singing, the scent of nail varnish and bowls of fucking cherries!'

'Tawrie—'

'Stop saying my name! It's not yours to say any more. I'm no part of you and you're no part of me. You're someone else's. You're fickle and false, a liar, and that's that.'

'T—' He started but clearly heeded her warning and thought better of it. His tears didn't have the same impact as they would have only days before. Before Petra had pitched up. 'I'm not fickle or false and I'm not a liar.'

'Oh no? You keep saying that as if it might make it so. Like father like son! Isn't that what they say? I sat and listened to you tell me how bitter you were about how your dad treated your mum and his whole catalogue of misery and bedhopping, and then you do this!' It was a low blow and she knew it. 'I slept with you; you said you loved me!'

'I am not like my father, I'm not. I think—' His voice was raised now, jaw tense, eyes blazing.

'It's irrelevant what you think. What matters is what I know!' she shouted.

'What you *think* you know!' he implored. 'But that's the trouble – you make your mind up and that's that!'

'You don't know me! Just like I don't know you!' she spat.

'I know that you can't fully grieve because you think your dad might live on Lundy and is hiding from you!' His return attack was well aimed and lodged in her breast. To hear her greatest secret spoken so freely in anger was something she knew she'd never forget.

'Fuck you, Edgar, fuck you!' Her voice was gravel thin, she cursed without caring that Maudie and Jago might be close enough to hear – it was all too late for that.

'You need to face what happened and free yourself, you need to . . .' He calmed and swayed slightly, and for a brief second she feared he might fall.

'You need to stop talking before I lose it!' She turned on her heel as fast as she was able and wheeled her bike up to the road, moving quickly, determinedly, doing all she could to get away from him.

'Tawrie!' he yelled.

'Just go back to London and live your split-down-the-middle life. I hope everything works out for you both.'

As the wheel touched the road, she jumped on to the saddle and raced home back to Fore Street, her sight clouded by the tears that fogged her vision.

It felt good to have told him to go away and yet no matter how strong she had sounded, how firm her outward stance, her insides were shredded with sorrow.

◆　◆　◆

'God, you look like shite.'

Connie's observation, voiced as Tawrie walked into the café to start her shift, did nothing to help ease her flagging confidence. She knew, however, that this whip-smart ribbing was preferable to probing questions about how she was doing, why her eyes were a little red, her demeanour a little off. She knew that kind of investigation might lead to a total breakdown, here in public, and a tear-soaked admission that her heart was about as scrambled as the eggs Connie ladled on to hot, buttered toast. Her plan was to keep it together, get through the day and collapse tonight on her own time.

'Thanks, Con, that's exactly what I needed to hear.' She let her lip curl in distaste at her cousin's remark.

'Who got out of the wrong side of the bed this morning?' Connie pulled a face, trying to cheer her up, but at the mention of getting out of bed, her mind flew to the cosy attic room and again she felt winded at how quickly her life had turned from a fairy tale to rat shit. Her shoulders slumped and her cousin's expression turned to one of concern. 'You okay?'

It hurt knowing Connie had been right all along; Sebastian Farquhar wanted nothing but fun, and he'd got it.

'I saw him this morning, he came down to Hele while I was swimming.'

'So what did he have to say for himself?' Connie spat.

'I can't . . .' She grabbed her apron and notepad and was about to go through to the back tables when Connie grabbed her arm.

'Oh, Taw . . .' This time her voice was full of love, brimming with kindness.

'I'm okay,' she managed. 'We can talk later. I just can't go into detail; I don't want to cry any more.' She kept her voice small.

'All right, honey. But I'm here. You know that. And what you need is time with Sonny, he'll cheer you up – he's collecting football cards and needs help putting them into this book thing.'

'How would that help me?' She was confused.

'It definitely would. Plus I need a babysitter tonight.' She beamed.

'Sure, not like I've got anything else on. Where are you going?'

'Nowhere.' Her cousin looked away and she guessed it was a date, as if the subject was too touchy to share.

'I'll look after Sonny, happily. Course I will.' She breathed in through her nose and went to work.

'Tawrie!'

The temptation was to keep on walking, to make out she hadn't heard her name called from the door. The voice, however, was one that had replayed in her mind all night, as torturous thoughts interrupted her much-needed sleep.

With as upright a posture as she could manage, in spite of wanting to sink to the floor, she turned slowly to face the future Mrs Edgar Stratton.

'It's me, Petra! We met yesterday, Bear's fiancée!'

Petra stood in the doorway with an open smile, bright-eyed and with her skin aglow. It seemed Ed was right, she was a nice girl, a great girl, and Tawrie wanted nothing more than to disappear through the floor, and yet it wasn't Petra's fault. Civility felt like the best option. It was that or give the woman the full facts that would, she was certain, leave his fiancée feeling even more wretched than Tawrie did, and she couldn't do that to this sweet stranger.

'Yes, of course I remember you. How can I help?' She looked through the open door and into the street, praying that Ed wasn't accompanying her. The very thought left her feeling cold. Thankfully he was nowhere to be seen.

Gaynor, tactful as ever, tried to help, creeping up behind her, her voice soft, kind. 'Want me to deal with the young lady, Taw, so you can take your orders out back?'

''S'alright, Gay. But thank you.'

'Thing is, Tawrie,' Petra continued in her breathless, energised way that was as guileless as it was endearing. 'Bear's gone for a hike and I wanted to grab some breakfast and whatnot to take back to the house. We only live up on the corner.' She pointed over her shoulder, as if this might help her locate where 'we' lived.

Yes, I know it. Walls painted in a warm white with pale-blue linen accent pillows on a blue-and-cream striped sofa, a patchwork rug and ornate shells dotted here and there.

'Anyway, I'm rubbish at cooking, shopping and all that, so I thought I'd pop down and stock up!'

'Right.' She moved through the café to behind the counter, wanting to put as much distance between them as possible. Petra followed her.

'I'm a real stickler, actually. He can't eat dairy, oh, and we try and be meat-free, nothing with sugar in, not too much salt or anything overly processed. So as long as it fits with all that, I'll take whatever you have!'

Tawrie felt her tongue stick to the roof of her mouth and words were not immediately forthcoming. She pictured the evening spent gorging on crisps and wine and recalled his shared sentiment of the merits of a good pasty, the coffee they'd drunk with milk and, for him, sugar . . . more lies, even his eating habits a sham. Who was this man? Grabbing a menu, she held it out.

'May I draw your attention to the vegan breakfast options right here.' She used her pen to point to the wild mushroom ragout on sourdough toast drizzled in parsley and garlic oil with roasted vine tomatoes on the side and all sprinkled with seed mix.

'Oh, that looks delish! I'll take two large helpings to go! Fab! Thank you.'

'No worries. Did you get that, Con? Two large vegan breakfast specials to go?'

'Got it.' Connie nodded and kept her head down.

Tawrie kept her eyes fixed on the woman as she fished in her pocket for a credit card. It wasn't like she had a choice. There was something exquisitely painful in studying her competition. Not that it was any such thing. Petra was the marvellous woman he would marry, whereas she was merely . . . *What are you, Taw, or more accurately, what were you? A blip? Someone to waste the day with while he idled away the summer weeks. Yes, and yes.* In a way it was a good thing, because had it been a contest, Tawrie could see that she'd lose. Comparison left her wanting in every way. Not only was Petra perfectly narrow about the shoulders, but her skin was unweathered, eyes bright, her laugh a tinkle, like glass, and not the throaty braying that Tawrie had been chastised for on more than one occasion. If this girl were fine china, Tawrie was cement. If she were a flower, Tawrie was a sturdy oak. And on it went, until it felt easier to look at the card machine and wait for her to pay, anything other than look into the pretty face and know that whatever came next, she could never be like Petra, who seemed to have it all.

It was a relief when, gratefully jostling her vegan breakfasts in her dainty hands, the woman left the café.

The day ground on and Tawrie's mood didn't lift. She tried her best, chatting to Nora and Gordy who popped in for a cup of tea and a wedge of soft carrot cake to share, two forks. She liked them, enjoyed being in their company, their happiness was ordinarily infectious.

'So when's the big Gunn Fire, Tawrie?' Nora asked as she stirred her tea. 'We couldn't believe it last year. We'd taken Amber for a wander and stumbled across this festival! Right there in Rapparee Cove! It was amazing!'

'I'm surprised you remember it, Nora. I seem to recall rum was your tipple of choice and then you danced around the fire with Needle and a couple of the lads from the RNLI!'

'That sounds about right.' Nora beamed at her. 'And I fully intend repeating the activities this year. My sister Kiki, her new partner David and our nephew Ted will be here. They're coming down for a holiday. Ted makes out he's happy to hang out with us old fogies but he's a proper teenager and only really wants to be plugged into a device with a screen.'

'Can you blame him?' Gordy chuckled.

'It's in about four weeks.' She smiled weakly, having allowed herself to picture the event with Ed by her side. That too was now dashed and her enthusiasm for the whole event was sadly lacking.

'It'll be wonderful!' Nora grabbed a fork from the table and cut away a chunk of carrot cake. 'This will be the last fattening thing I eat before then. I want to get into my white jeans.'

'I bet you a pound it won't be!' Gordy looked at his wife adoringly and it was like a bolt through her throat, witnessing this much love when her heart was so sore.

◆ ◆ ◆

'How are you doing?' Connie asked, wiping the countertop as the clock ticked towards closing time.

'Bit numb.'

'Get yourself off home. I can finish up here.'

'It's okay, Con, it's not fair on you – plus, don't you want to go home and get ready? What time do you want me over?' She was, however, grateful for the offer to leave early. The truth was, for the first time ever, she was nervous about walking up Fore Street, wary of wandering the harbour, fearful of seeing Ed and Petra, of putting any more images that would torture her thoughts into her mind.

'Around seven?'

'Sure.' She tried a smile.

'I didn't want to be right about him, you know. I was only ever half joking. I was over the moon to see you so excited.'

'I know.' And she did.

'I've never seen you look so happy and I'm angry that he led you up the garden path. I could clock him one. Honest I could, and Needle's ready to tear a strip off him.'

'He's lovely, Needle.' She spoke her thoughts out loud.

'What makes you say that?' Connie stopped cleaning and held her gaze.

'I just think he's kind, constant and he's there for you. There for all of us.'

Her cousin blinked and looked up along the harbourside towards the pub where Needle held court.

'I suppose he is.' She looked back at Tawrie and smiled. 'So you reckon I should go out on his bloody boat?'

'Well, it'd shut him up if nothing else!' She pointed out the obvious.

'You might be right, Tawrie Gunn.' Connie tucked her hair behind her ears and stuck out her chin. 'You just might be right.'

◆ ◆ ◆

'Only me, Nan!' she called as she closed the front door behind her and walked through to the kitchen where Freda was unpacking groceries into the cupboards.

'Have you had a better afternoon, darlin'?'

'Yeah, fantastic!' She ran the tap for a glass of water. 'I've loved it. I love coming home with feet that feel like they've been shredded, hair that smells like bacon and aching legs. I hate people with their inane bloody questions: "Does the steak pie have meat in it?" "Is it okay if we take the macaroni cheese without the cheese?" "Do you have sushi?" I mean, Jesus! Read the menu, eat off the menu, pay for what you eat, that is literally all they have to do and yet it's always so complicated!'

'Not such a good afternoon then, love?'

She let out a long sigh and knew that what ailed her could not be taken out on her nan. 'Sorry, Nan. It's just that the world feels a bit shitty right now.'

'I understand, little maid. I do.'

'Anyway, I'm babysitting for Sonny tonight so I've got that to look forward to.'

'He's no bother, lovely lad.'

'He is, Nan. I guess I'm just a bit out of sorts.' She was about to explain how Petra had come in to order take-out and how it had made her feel, when the sound of the front door being flung open and hitting the wall caused them both to turn. Tawrie's heart thudded as Uncle Sten ran in, flustered and breathless, his cheeks flushed. 'Oh God, them bloody steps!' He fought to catch his breath, bent double as he addressed the floor, his hand over his heart. 'Glad you're both here. It's Annalee . . .'

The panic to his tone was enough to make her stomach drop to her boots. That and his manner of entry lit the touch paper of long-forgotten memories. It happened this way sometimes – snippets of the very worst day came back to her quite vividly.

Things she had overheard as she sat on the sofa wrapped in a crochet blanket, trying not to eavesdrop on the adults while her heart beat fast and her tears refused to come. Feeling like she should be crying but not knowing how.

RNLI crew are still out looking but they're losing light . . .

They've found his boat . . .

Oh good Lord, they've found his boat . . .

Nothing. No sign of him . . .

The spar was flapping about, untethered and it were proper windy . . .

They reckon he's gone overboard . . .

The light's fading, they'll resume the search at daybreak.

Shaking her head from these memories, Tawrie turned to face her uncle.

'What's happened, is she . . . is she okay?'

He stood upright and she saw that his face carried a look of pity.

'I'm not sure, love. She's fallen down the stairs that go down to the Harbour Beach. Her head's proper gashed and her teeth are in a state. Her face is a mess. I said I'd run her up to the A&E but there's an ambulance on the way, which is probably best. Reckon you should come too. She's not on her own, she's with the gang from the pub. They brought her up to the top of the steps.' He panted as his breathing settled and he made for the front door, as if time was of the essence.

'They shouldn't have moved her.' She tried to digest the information that came thick and fast and knew this much to be true. Her world moved in slow motion as it occurred to her that she might have lost her mum.

Sten raised his arms and let them fall as if it were literally out of his hands.

'I'm coming.' Freda reached for her soft suede bag that carried her essentials like phone, purse and mints.

'No, Mum.' Sten spoke softly. 'We don't know how long we're going to be at the hospital and it's better you're here. Don't want to take over the place, do we?'

'I guess not.' Freda looked less than happy with his suggestion. 'But if you think I'm not coming down there to offer comfort or help in any way then you'd be wrong, son.'

'Fine.' He nodded as he turned to Tawrie. 'You ready, love?'

'Yes,' she managed, her voice sounding strangely disconnected. 'Can you let Con know?'

Her nan nodded.

'Mum, we'll run ahead, take your time, don't want two falls on our hands.'

'I'll be fine!' Freda snapped as Tawrie followed her uncle down the steps at speed and quickly passed the entrance to Ropery car park, where to her mortification she spied Ed climbing into his silver dream machine. Petra was ensconced in the passenger seat. Not that Tawrie had time to think about it. At least he was taking her advice and sodding off back to London. It was one less thing to worry about, knowing she wasn't going to bump into him any time soon.

'We've brought her up to the top, Sten!' Calvin, one of her mother's drinking buddies, called out, as they rounded the back of the closed café and made their way across the cobbles to the harbour wall where the stairs were steep and the drop long. Tawrie sped up as she spied her mum lying on the ground. There was a small crowd gathered around her and someone had placed a rolled-up anorak under her head as a makeshift pillow. Elbowing her way through, she dropped to her knees and smiled into her mother's face. Her mother who was bashed and bleeding, but very much alive. The relief was palpable.

'Hey, Mum. You're going to be okay. Everything's going to be okay.'

It was shocking to see her face up close: her lips and eye were badly swollen, and her hair was stuck to her forehead with blood, which also ran from her nose. It was distressing and horrifying in equal measure and Tawrie felt the iron jaws of disgust and duty clamp around her throat, even as her heart flexed with sadness at the pitiful sight.

Her mother was shaking and Tawrie whipped off her hoodie, leaving her in a t-shirt, as she wrapped the thick top, still warm from contact with her skin, around her mother's body.

'Let me through!' Her nan bustled through and sat on the floor on the other side of her daughter-in-law. 'You listen to me, Annalee Gunn' – Freda spoke through a mouth contorted with tears – 'you get yourself better, my girl, cos there's only four weeks till the Gunn Fire and we need you in top form, do you hear me?' Her voice was reed thin over vocal cords pulled taut with distress.

Annalee tried to talk, tried to sit up, but Tawrie pushed her back down. 'You need to lie still, Mum. You don't know if you've broken anything. You need to stay still.'

'We've called an ambulance!' Calvin yelled.

'Yes, nice one, Cal,' Sten said.

Annalee reached out and gripped Tawrie's arm with a bloody hand – one of her false nails had been ripped off and taken her original with it. Injuries to her body were not uncommon – nothing like this, of course – but always, it seemed, alcohol anaesthetised her against the pain. Tawrie bent low so she could hear her mother's words, whispered from a mouth disfigured by swelling and clotted with blood.

'Smshhhhhhtuuuuummn.'

'I don't know what you're saying, Mum.' It was a nonsensical ramble and Tawrie was none the wiser. She looked at Freda with the hope that she might have more of an idea but her nan shrugged.

'Smshhahahhhtuuuuummn,' Annalee tried again.

Tawrie sat up a little and held her mother's eyeline. 'You can tell me later. Don't try and talk now. The ambulance is coming and you're going to be okay. I'll stay with you, I promise. Nan's right here too.' She spoke as gently as she was able, not wanting others to hear her mother's incoherent speech, and wary of getting too close to her mouth where the foulest stench of wine and vodka-infused breath was enough to make her want to vomit. Any remaining lumps of her heart were now pulverised. This was her mother, her *mummy* . . . She felt protective, distressed, concerned, and this was all underpinned with fury at the fact that Annalee's wounds were effectively self-inflicted. She had fallen publicly while inebriated and the whole town would be talking about it. It wasn't so much that the gossip bothered her, but rather that it was her mother's reputation, or what remained of it, that was to be brutally dissected, or worse, made the butt of jokes from Barnstaple to Croyde. It was heartbreaking.

'Are you all right, little one?' Her nan reached out and ran her palm over her arm.

'Yep.'

'You've had better days though.'

'I have.' Keeping her eyes low, she didn't want to acknowledge the gawpers and gossips who gathered around, drawn to witness the misery of a fellow human. She wondered what it must have been like on the day her dad died. The spectacle . . .

Sten's shout brought her back to the present. 'It's here! I can hear it!'

The sound of the ambulance siren seemed to cause greater interest and the crowd at the top of the steps had grown. Tawrie hated how exposed her mother was and felt torn up inside at how many bore witness to her frailty, her disease.

Annalee lay back with her eyes closed and Tawrie again whispered to her, 'It's going to be okay, Mum. The ambulance is here and they'll get you sorted. I won't leave you. I'll be right by your side.'

The paramedics pushed the crowd out of the way and were swift in their actions, checking Annalee over, giving her a jab for pain relief and putting her on the stretcher and into the back of the ambulance.

'I'll go with her.' She followed the stretcher and climbed up into the high vehicle as her mother was secured with straps.

'I'll drive and meet you at the hospital, so we've got a car there!' Uncle Sten yelled, heading to his truck.

'Please let me know how she is and what she needs and what's happening.'

She raised her hand in acknowledgment of Freda's yelled request and welcomed the kiss her wonderful nan blew in her direction.

'And don't leave Tawrie on her own!' This time Freda pointed at her son.

'As if I would!' Sten shouted over his shoulder.

As the doors of the ambulance closed, Tawrie's pulse raced.

Her nan was right. She'd had far, far better days.

CHAPTER TWENTY

Harriet Wentworth

August 2024

Harriet Wentworth was scrubbing the bath. Bent over with the sponge in her hand, her back twinged as she completed the hated chore. Despite her best efforts, and even having resorted to bribery in the past, her teenage sons Louis and Rafe seemed immune to the desire to clean the dark ring of dirt that gathered in the tub. Not that her husband was much better! Thankfully, they were all barred from the en-suite shower room she claimed as her own. The only person allowed to use that was Dilly, her darling daughter, when she came to stay, which was a rare occurrence now she was joined at the hip to Parker, her beloved. Harriet smiled. She really liked Parker and hoped his family were welcoming Dilly in Boston. Her daughter had followed her English professor over there for love and was now about to give birth to Harriet's first grandchild. It hardly seemed possible! It was difficult to picture Dilly as anything other than her little bookworm. Her boys found it hilarious that their mum was also going to be a grandma, and Charles too had voiced his concern on what it might be like to sleep with a gran – she'd chased him out of the bedroom with a raised slipper. She might be a grandmother-in-waiting but she was still rather nifty on her feet.

'Harry!' Charles bellowed up the stairs as was his custom, using the nickname he'd given her shortly after they'd met. 'Bear's here!'

'Oh fab! Coming!' Her face broke into a smile as it did whenever her eldest child returned home. He'd texted to say he was inbound, hence the emergency tub scrub in his honour. Not that she was short of kids – when the twins weren't playing rugby, talking about rugby, watching rugby, or checking stats on their various devices about rugby, her house was full of the actual rugby team, muddy knees and all. The fact that they didn't live in the largest or grandest of houses was neither here nor there; her house was, apparently, the one people liked to congregate in. Not that she minded. In fact, she loved the chaos, the chatter, the laughter. It meant life! A quick glance in the mirror on the landing confirmed her rather dishevelled appearance, hair grey at the temples – not that she had time to fix it and not that Bear would give a fig either way.

'Coming!' she yelled again as she raced down the stairs, wiping her damp hands on the thighs of her jeans. 'Hello, darling!' She smiled at the sight of her floppy-haired boy who sat with his back to her on a stool at the kitchen island. Charles caught her eye and she noted his look of concern, his gaze a little lingering, as if giving her a sign she was quite unable to decipher. He did this a lot, as though he could telepathically relay what he was trying to say. It was maddening. She knitted her eyebrows in confusion as he reached into the fridge and pulled out two bottles of cold beer.

'Here we go, mate.' Her husband plonked the bottles down on to the island as Ed turned to greet her.

'Oh, love!' Her heart twisted at the sight of him and suddenly Charles's message came through loud and clear: *Bear is upset. Very upset.* His eyes were red raw from crying, his nose snotty. 'What on earth? What's happened?' Walking forward, she cradled him to her. He might be a grown man of twenty-nine, but he was still her son, and this was what she did best – administered love where and when she could.

'I've really messed up, Mum.'

'You have? How?' Her thoughts raced as she tried to figure out what possibly could have caused this level of distress. Had he bashed the car, rowed with Petra, got fired? Nothing insurmountable, she was sure; it was just a case of holding him close and finding the solution. 'What's happened, love?' she pressed, wanting the information right this minute to stop her thoughts from racing.

'I've . . . met someone.' It was not what she'd expected to hear and her mouth fell open as the significance of these three little words sunk in.

'You've met someone?' Charles was slow on the uptake and she fired a look at him. He slunk back on his stool and sipped his beer.

'A woman.' Bear clarified for his stepfather.

'A different woman to the one you're engaged to?'

'Yes, Charles! Obviously!' she tutted and rubbed her son's back as he actually laughed.

'I bloody love you, Charles.' Her son sniffed.

'The feeling is entirely mutual, boy, even if it takes me a wee while to catch on!' He raised his bottle in a toast. Despite the flair of love she felt for this man, she chose not to comment, hoping that for her son, this meeting of 'a woman' did not mean infidelity. She knew too well the cold cut of pain such an action could cause and still, after all these years, felt the lance of betrayal at the thought. She pictured Petra, who had always seemed a little besotted.

'Come through to the sitting room, darling. We can sit in the comfy chairs and you can tell me all about it.' She thought this might be the best and most private place to talk.

'I'll do the dishes and I'll keep the human wrecking balls out when they come home,' Charles offered. She was thankful for this sweet, sweet man she had married nearly sixteen years ago.

'Come on.' She walked slowly with her hand on his back, turning to mouth *Thank you!* to Charles as they left the room. He blew her a kiss in reply. It landed on her cheek and was soft and inclusive and spoke of unconditional love.

Bear settled on one end of the squidgy sofa, which took up a large chunk of the square room, and she clicked on the lamp that sat on the side table, before taking a seat at the other end and folding her legs beneath her.

'What's going on, Bear?' she asked gently, while her whole being itched with the need to hear the detail.

'I don't know where to begin.' He bit his lip as if to quell further tears and she was so powerfully reminded of the little boy who had wept when she'd packed up a bag and headed off to stay with her sister, promising with her whole heart to be back in three sleeps, that it almost took her breath away. Nerves fluttered in her stomach, not a familiar feeling when addressing her boy, but that was by the by. The thought that his behaviour might echo Hugo's was as unsettling as it was worrying. The topic itself enough to take her back to that time she chose not to revisit. Not ever.

'Start at the beginning. And take your time.'

Her son took a deep breath and wiped his eyes. Displays like this were rare for him in recent years, and from this alone she understood the magnitude of his feelings. It was hard to see him so distressed, but at the same time she rather admired his openness. This was in itself a world away from Hugo's shady secret life of infidelity, which, the first time it had happened, had come as the greatest shock, but thereafter was no more than a rather sad expectation. It was, she thought, an uncomfortable way to live. And one that she, long after she had extricated her life from his, still felt the consequences of.

Like those moments when Charles, her beloved Charles, was late or didn't answer a call, and the breath caught in her throat, not necessarily thinking that he too might be a philanderer, but aware of how these things came out of the blue, like a barking dog coming at you in the dark. No matter that it was tethered or friendly, it made your heart jump just the same. And that tiny nagging sliver of self-doubt that if she hadn't been able to stop Hugo from straying, why was it going to be different with any other man? What exactly had she done wrong? Had she inadvertently driven him to it? And if she didn't know, how could she avoid doing it again? All this before she started on the deep gash that ran across her heart and her trust, a cut that had only ever partially healed, so deep was the injury. An injury sustained in a battle she had never believed she would have to enter – the shock of it as great as the fight itself.

'Let's start with Petra,' she suggested.

Having watched him struggle, she offered the prompt and spoke the name of the sweet girl who Hugo and Ramona seemed positively dotty about.

'It all happened so fast, Mum.' He took his time.

'The engagement?' she queried, not quite understanding as the two had been dating on and off since they were twenty. Nothing about it felt rushed.

He nodded.

'Petra's mother came to stay with Dad and Ramona for the weekend.' Harriet chose not to voice how this sounded 'cosy', knowing it was pure jealousy on her part which was neither attractive nor founded. She could, of course, make more effort with Petra's mother and invite her over, as long as the invite didn't have to include Ramona. She found the woman to be impossibly loud and opinionated. This too she kept to herself.

'They were all drinking wine, Dad was in his element, Petra and I were joining in, and it was great. And then Ramona said wasn't it about time we tied the knot, took things up a gear – I don't know exactly what she said, I can't remember. It was more a joke than anything and I think I agreed and laughed, and the next thing I know' – he gave a slow blink – 'Ramona's opening a bottle of champagne, Petra's mum is crying and texting her friends and Dad's ferreting about in that attic to try and find Granny Stratton's ring!'

'So . . .' It sounded ghastly and bloody typical of Hugo, running headlong at a hundred miles an hour no matter the consequences. It was a thing she'd loved about him in their youth, a wild and exciting adventure, but when stability and a clear plan were needed, it was the very opposite of endearing. She was aware of treading carefully, delicately, as expressing a personal opinion that might alienate Bear could have a disastrous effect. Plus, if there was any chance of him smoothing things over with Petra, she needed to leave all pathways open. 'Is it that you don't want to get married at all, or you have doubts about Petra or are fearful of the change, or . . . ?'

'I did want to be with Petra,' he confessed. 'I figured even though marriage hadn't really been on my mind, it kind of made sense. We've been together for a long time and all our friends have been saying it's the next logical step and Jack and Fi have got married, so . . .'

His lukewarm tone and mild justification was alarming. There was none of the unbridled joy or eagerness for this shared future that she believed was an entry-level requirement for such a step, only confirming the doubts she'd felt when she'd heard the news a month or so ago. Petra had squealed her joy, while Bear, his face pale, stared at his fiancée as if in shock.

'And Petra was so happy and that made me happy and I thought it was enough.'

'Your happiness is just as important, more important to me because you're my son.'

He gave a brief nod. 'And then I started to feel the most overwhelming sense of burden, like this huge weight crushing me from the inside out. I could hardly breathe!' He placed his hand on his heart, in the way she'd seen Hugo do. Was this how he had felt? 'I didn't want to go to work, I didn't want to go home, the flat felt like a prison and so I quit my job. Told Petra I needed to go and get my head straight, and she was great, supportive.'

'Yes.' Harriet was glad of this; Petra was a lovely girl.

'As you know, I went to Ilfracombe and then . . .' He looked up towards the ceiling and his shoulders slumped, as a smile formed on his mouth, this followed by the trickle of more tears.

'Then what, Bear?'

'Then I met someone, a woman, who has smashed my world into a million pieces. Everything I thought I knew and everything I thought I wanted is on the floor in fragments and I know the only way to build back up again, to construct my future happiness, is to do it with her.'

'Wow! That's . . .' She had so many questions it was hard to know which one to lead with. 'That's quite the statement!' She was torn, knowing all too well what it felt like to be the one discarded for something new and shiny.

'It is, but it's the truth. Not that it matters; she doesn't want me. Not now. Petra turned up and told her we were engaged and at the very least I now know I can't marry Petra, can't be with Petra, and yet I've lost the woman I love. And that's the bones of it, Mum. As I said, a bloody mess.'

It was a lot to take in. He sounded romantic, fanciful, and yet Bear had always known his own mind and she either trusted his judgement or she didn't – there were, in her view, no degrees of trust.

'Does Petra know?' she asked softly.

'She knows I can't marry her.' His lip wobbled again as a precursor to tears. 'I haven't told her the full story; I don't want to be cruel and I figured it best to go one step at a time.'

'Oh, love.' She reached for his hand and gave it a squeeze. 'Is she with her family or her friends?' She couldn't stand to think of the girl heartbroken and alone, knowing very well what that felt like, able even now to recall the desperate, hollow ache of rejection that still had the power to jump up out of nowhere and jab her in the chest.

'Her mum's on the way and Fi is with her right now – they've been close since uni. We drove back earlier and I dropped her at the flat and I told her as gently as possible that I couldn't marry her and she was obviously upset and it's so shitty to know I've made her feel that way.'

'Regardless of what else or who else is involved or what happens next, you've done the right thing in telling her. She deserves your honesty.'

Reflection over the years had taught her that one of the hardest aspects of her marriage collapse had been Hugo's lack of transparency, having to peel layers away until the truth was exposed. How much easier, kinder on them all, if he had had the courage to be open, truthful, allowing her to see the full picture and make decisions accordingly. She wanted Bear to be different, would guide him to be different.

'I know that, Mum. And then I just wanted to come and see you.'

This the biggest, best compliment that made joy bloom in her chest. Their closeness hard won after her and Hugo's separation. Long after the ink had dried on their divorce papers, Hugo's spontaneity and lack of strategy meant she often had to step in and reassure her kids that all was going to be well. It irritated her at the time, but she could see the result sitting in front of her – the trust of her son – and it was worth every second when she'd cursed her ex-husband as a new crisis loomed. Her words had always been conciliatory, reassuring – keeping things as positive as possible for the children's sake, as they'd long ago agreed.

'Wendy's moving in? It'll be fine!'

'Sherry's having a baby, well isn't that exciting!'

'Ramona means well, she's fun!'

And every time her reassurance was needed, her kids looked little again, sitting on the sofa in Corner Cottage while she told them things were going to change. How she hated that these moments were so clear in her memory – jagged things with which she tried to grapple, but still had the power to send ripples of sadness right through her.

Harriet twisted now and came closer to her boy. Again she held him close and let him weep.

'Bear!' Rafe came crashing into the room and stopped short at the sight of his big brother sobbing in his mother's arms. 'Oh shit! Has someone died?'

'No, darling.' Harriet released Ed, who sat up straight and wiped his face. 'No one died. Bear's just going through something a little tricky and he needs our love, our support.'

'Have you got cancer?'

'Rafe, no!' she tutted. 'People can be upset without it being death or cancer! Although of course those would be two very good reasons to be upset.'

They shared a moment of understanding at the blunderbuss that was Rafe Wentworth.

'Do you want a beer?'

Her eldest laughed at the offer from her fourteen-year-old who was not allowed to drink and had never, to her knowledge, offered a guest a beer. 'No, but thanks, mate. I'll come out in a bit, just chatting to Mum.'

It warmed her heart to see her sons so caring of each other, thankful every day for their easy camaraderie.

'We could watch the rugby sevens; I've got it recorded!' Rafe's face lit up at the prospect.

'I'd love that,' Bear lied and she loved him for it.

Once Rafe had closed the door, Bear seemed a little more relaxed, as if his tears had been cathartic.

'What's he like?' Bear chuckled as he wiped his face.

'A nightmare! They both are!' She smiled, full of love for this second round of motherhood, a gift that arrived when she'd least expected it.

'I've never experienced anything like it, Mum. This girl . . .'

'So what happened? How did you meet? Tell me all about her.'

Harriet felt a stab of worry. Bear was a reliable, kind and gentle man, yet this seemingly all-encompassing, impetuous infatuation was so redolent of Hugo it was worrying. The last thing she wanted was for her son to lead a life like his dad, where the newest, shiniest thing was the most appealing and damn the consequences or the trail of destruction he left in his wake. Not that Bear was like his dad in that sense, but she'd be lying if she didn't admit this was a concern. It was, however, impossible not to feel the power in his words, and she was keen to learn about this woman who had smashed his world into a million pieces.

'I was up early and went for a wander down to Hele Bay Beach.'

'I know it.'

She felt the familiar shiver whenever she thought about that town in North Devon and that terrible time in her life when loneliness and devastation had been her constant partners. How her weight had plummeted, and Ellis, her lifeline, had offered advice down the phone, and all the time she was smiling so hard that she thought her face might crack while her heart broke. It was an act she continued until she met Charles. It wasn't until he told her quite plainly to stop smiling when she felt like crying; to be open, vulnerable, and to know it wasn't a weakness, but was, in fact, a strength, that she was finally able to confront the fear that if she took her hand off the tiller, the whole family would flail against the rocks. It was a lovely way to live, safe in the knowledge that he understood all humans were flawed, fallible. Yet still, there was that paper cut of worry that she was in some way to blame, and just the thought that she might at some point in the future find herself once again on the edge of the abyss was almost more than she could stand.

She focused now on Bear.

'I hadn't been to Hele before, but walked out towards Hillsborough, dropped down over the headland and there was the bay. It was really quiet and there were a couple of people swimming and . . .' He paused and looked directly at her. 'And I know this is going to sound weird and if it was someone saying it to me, I'd think it was bullshit, but I kind of felt her before I saw her. She walked out of the water and came towards me, and it was like a firecracker going off in my chest. I could hear this sound, like a note, like music, like . . . I don't know, clarity. Yeah, like clarity, as if the fog cleared in my mind. And this is the crazy bit,' he qualified, 'after one chat, which was unremarkable in content really, I'd have gone anywhere with her. Anywhere. I wanted to hold her, to talk to her, to be with her. And she's been in my mind and behind my eyelids ever since.'

'Bear!' It was fascinating and she had no doubt about his strength of feeling, yet his quick-fire switch from Petra set alarm bells ringing.

'*Are you having an affair?*'
'*What a bloody ridiculous thing to say to me! No!*'

Hugo's first denial, a lie that came so easily – and all that had followed.

'I even sounded out her situation, one of the first things I ever said to her was, "You swim alone? You don't drag your partner down here on dark, rainy mornings?" Trying to suss out whether she was married or single or whatever. I know I'll never forget a single minute of the little time we've spent together. It's like we fit together. Talking to her is so easy. We just natter away and if we're quiet for a minute, that's fine too. There's not a drop of awkwardness. It felt entirely right to be with her. Every bit of it. Everything just as it should be as if I was in the right place with the right person and so was she.'

'Wow, it sounds beautiful.' And it did, but that was no guarantee of a solid future, of happiness, which was all she wanted for her son.

'It is. Have you ever felt that way?' He looked at her earnestly.

'Truthfully?' She took her time. 'When I met your dad, we were babies really. Teenagers who thought we knew it all! He was very romantic, he'd say the most wonderful things to me and he was so much fun – I don't need to tell you that!' She pictured him, hogging the dancefloor, arms wide, shaking and moving with abandon, ignoring the tuts and elbows of the more sedate dancers. 'We fell into our relationship and it was lovely, really lovely. A happy time for me. Then marriage and you and Dilly and our fabulous house in Ledwick Green, and I had no reason to question whether we were truly happy or whether we'd make it, because I assumed both of those things.'

It felt odd, she'd never spoken in detail like this to him or Dilly, not really. But it was time. She controlled the nervous flutter in her throat.

'When things went wrong and we moved to Corner Cottage, I can't describe the level of shock for me, how hurt I was. Every step

I took I did slowly, as if I couldn't even trust the ground beneath my feet to hold fast. It was like living on a trapdoor that I knew at any second would open up and I'd drop for eternity. Freefall.' Even remembering it sent a chilly quiver through her limbs. 'And that's the thing about these spontaneous heart-led decisions: they are exciting, physical, wondrous, but you need to be sure, Bear. You need to be certain that what you feel is the real deal and not just some distraction or worse, an alleyway that allows you to run from commitment to Petra.' She watched his face fall. 'The more people you rope in to the equation, the more people get hurt.'

'I know that.' He swallowed.

'It was only when I started to come out the other side that I realised that maybe we weren't truly happy and accepted that we weren't going to make it. I think it says more about me than it does about Dad.'

'He was the one who cheated.'

There was no mistaking the hurt that echoed in his words; he clearly didn't recognise his behaviour as mirroring his father's in any way.

'Yes, but I guess the question is why, and that's a complicated thing for another day, I think, Bear, darling, Hugo is not a bad person, and he's a terrific father in many ways. We were just different people, on different pages, if not reading different books entirely.' She gave a wry laugh. 'And we ran out of love. That's it.'

'And with Charles?' He kept his voice low, his eyes darting to the closed door.

'Charles and I are truly happy. I love him very much. Also a great dad.' She smiled. 'And I think the difference between Hugo and Charles is that Charles and I are really, really good friends. Best friends, in fact. It's different, but good different. I treasure him.' She paused. 'But that instant thunderbolt, musical note of clarity that you describe so well . . .' She shook her head. 'No, I've never had that. I guess I envy you a little bit, not that I want any more than I have, but it must feel . . . amazing.'

'It does.' A smile briefly split his face, replaced by a look of hurt. 'I cheated on Petra. But it didn't feel like cheating. In fact, sleeping with Petra again, which I didn't, would have felt like cheating.'

'Well, I think cheating sucks.' She tried to keep a note of neutrality. 'I've been on the sharp end of it and it's awful, soul-sapping.' She spoke openly, wanting to drive home the harmful nature of his actions.

'I'm not like Dad!' he pressed, his distress evident.

'I don't think you are,' she levelled. 'Not as a person and not in your intentions, but I have to be honest and say that you need to be aware of how decisions you make set you on a path. Your dad wasn't a serial cheater or womaniser – whatever you want to call it – not when he only cheated with Wendy. One indiscretion, that was all. But I guess the thrill and the ease of it became attractive to him. I don't know, and I can't speak on his behalf. It's unfair. I just don't want you to hurt or get hurt.'

Bear looked deep in thought.

'You're not a bad person. Quite the opposite.'

'Thank you, Mum.'

'What's her name?'

His face broke into a smile at the mere prospect of saying her name. 'Tawrie Gunn. Her name is Tawrie Gunn.'

'Oh my!' To hear the name after all these years was like stepping back in time. With her hand at her throat she thought about that day when she and Tawrie's mother had stepped over the threshold.

'What's wrong? Are you okay?' He leaned forward, staring intently.

'Tawrie Gunn!'

'Do you know her?' His voice had gone up an octave.

'I don't know her, but I have met her, once. We were staying in Corner Cottage when her father was killed in an accident.'

'Yes, yes I know about it.'

'You had a play date with Tawrie before her father first went missing.'

'What? Are you kidding me? That's insane!' His mouth fell open, eyes lit up, and his body jumped, as if delighted by the thought.

'No, I'm not kidding. I haven't thought about it for yonks, but I seem to remember the play date was a bit of a disaster and of course it all got overshadowed by what came next.'

'That's . . . I don't know what to say!' He ran his palm over his face.

'I had a coffee with her mother. She was sweet, I remember, and then when I next saw her, it was when I was leaving Ilfracombe, heading off to stay with Aunty Ellis, and you, Dills and Dad were going back to the house in Ledwick Green. She stuck in my mind. Annalee, that's her name, Annalee Gunn. She was so pretty and she and her husband were so into each other, like the rest of the world was an inconvenience.'

It was only after she'd spoken that she recognised the similarity between what she'd seen and what Bear described. His eyes were wide, gaze intent, as if the discussion of this woman who he claimed had stolen his heart had given him a glimpse of something so wonderful she lived behind his eyelids.

'I only saw her that one time after and she looked very different. She'd got old and frail and hollow and broken overnight. I didn't know what to say or whether to say anything. You were all in the car and I caught her eye as she walked up towards the slipway. I reached out and rubbed her arm and she nodded once, as if even that was more than she could manage. And that little girl. Tawrie, your Tawrie.'

'Yes.' He nodded. 'My Tawrie. Although not my Tawrie right now. She told me to sod off to London and not to go back. She thinks I lied through omission, and I did, technically.'

'There's nothing technical about how the heart conducts itself, that much I have learned. It's an emotional, illogical thing that will heal in its own time.'

'What helped your heart to heal?' He looked up at her, his eyes mournful.

It didn't fully . . . She coughed to clear her throat and stop these words from escaping.

'Time. That was it, really.' She let the words settle. 'After the initial hurt, when I found about Hugo and Wendy, came anger, then a small amount of bitterness, jealousy even.' It wasn't easy to admit. 'Then when I realised that I couldn't change what had happened, couldn't reset, I felt powerless, which was a horrible feeling. Also getting so wrapped up in my hurt that it took me a while to fully process the fact that I didn't actually want to go back to someone who didn't want me, and so if I didn't want him, if I *accepted* the new direction my life was going in, then why did I need to be so angry? I didn't, was the truth. It meant my load was lighter, my thoughts clearer and then I met Charles, as if the universe was telling me I was ready.'

'Was it easier between you and Dad once you'd met Charles? Like you had your ally?'

'I suppose. I mean we've never really revisited that time, had the conversation, and there are still things that, I don't know, erm . . . things.' She stumbled on her words, wondering how to explain that sometimes she still had the breath knocked out of her with naked fear of all that might or could happen again. And how the memory of that hurt was enough to make her want to curl up and hide. It felt impossible to phrase without it sounding like she expected Charles to cheat, which she categorically did not. It was more like a muscle memory, like one scalded who is wary around hot water. It felt a lot like unfinished business, she suddenly realised. 'I guess things became more civil between us, but easier? I'm not sure.'

There was a moment of silence before Bear spoke.

'I can't settle, Mum. I'm exhausted. I need to go back to the flat and sort things with Petra. We need to unpick our lives and I owe her a longer conversation than a quick chat in the car and while I was carrying her bags up to the front door. I want to tell her everything calmly, so there's no surprises lurking, and I want to make sure she knows that I'm there for her and how much I've really loved our love and our friendship. She's great. She's just not for me. And I'm not for her.'

Harriet was struck by his maturity. His empathy and his desire to end this relationship with kindness, knowing it would make all the difference in the future, help Petra, in time, reach acceptance too. It was a balm to some of her concerns.

'I'm so proud of you, Bear. Truly proud of the person you are.'

'Thank you.' He stared at his feet, still a little awkward at accepting the compliment.

There was a knock on the door as Charles entered, wearing an apron that was splattered with what looked like tomato sauce and she couldn't help but admire a slice of red onion that nestled on his scalp.

'Need a bit of help, Harry!' He pulled a face. 'Tried to make pasta sauce and the whole saucepan has exploded.'

'So I see.' Her gingham apron looked ruined.

'Yes, you'll also see it on the work surface, the stove, the wall and one or two major splats on the ceiling.' His expression was part sheepish, part highly amused.

'How, Charles, how?' She stood up and prepared to get scrubbing.

'I don't know!' He laughed. 'One minute I'm adding oregano and the next I'm diving for cover.'

She turned to her son who looked a lot better than when he'd arrived, with a little colour in his cheeks and a more upright demeanour. 'Forget what I said about me treasuring this husband of mine.' She laughed. 'The man is a complete doofus!'

CHAPTER TWENTY-ONE

TAWRIE GUNN

AUGUST 2024

With the window open, bringing some relief to the stagnant air, Tawrie drew the curtains to keep the daylight at bay, hoping her mum might find some rest in sleep. She lifted the chair from behind the old desk, creeping across the carpet, sidestepping the clutter of clothes and crockery that made for a tricky obstacle course, before placing it down beside Annalee's bed. Her mother's eyes were closed. It had been a long, long night for them all.

The bedroom door opened and Freda crept in with a mug of tea.

'You look exhausted, love. Was it busy at the hospital?' she whispered.

'Thanks, Nan.' She took the mug into her hands and held it close to her chest, a warming thing against her heart where a chill lurked. The hot drink was restorative nectar. 'It was busy when we arrived, then quiet for much of the night while we waited for her to get X-rays done and checked over and things.'

'It's good she sleeps.' Her nan peered at Annalee.

Her mother was a pitiful sight, sitting propped up in the middle of the bed, leaning back on her pillow mountain. An insubstantial slip of a thing who looked as if she might float away, had she not been weighted down by the duvet and blanket that Tawrie had folded over her legs. Her tiny body sustained by little more than alcohol fumes, and her wobbly head loose on her thin neck. It tore at her heart to see Annalee so frail. The cut across the top of her right eyebrow, now artfully stitched, and her split and swollen top lip only added to her sorry state.

Tawrie chose not to share how her mother had railed against the doctors who tried to examine her, had practically fought with the paramedic who wheeled her into the A&E department, and how she and Uncle Sten had spent the best part of the previous twelve hours apologising on her behalf, and offering profuse thanks to everyone they encountered, as if their gratitude could somehow balance Annalee's blatant lack of grace.

It was conflicting. The pitiful sight that evoked such compassion, yet knowing the reason for such a disaster was her drinking. This edged with anger that it wasn't the first time she'd been called upon to come to Annalee's rescue, and she would bet her final dollar that it wouldn't be the last.

The whole ghastly event coupled with a night spent wide awake, wired, had made Tawrie wrestle with some uncomfortable truths. She had thought being in close proximity, on hand, meant her mother wouldn't come to real harm. Yet she'd only been yards away from her when that tumble could have ended with a snapped neck and there wasn't a darn thing Tawrie could have done about it. This realisation that she couldn't, no matter how much she willed it, keep Annalee Gunn safe – or her nan or her dad, for that matter – was as enlightening as it was galling. But the fact was, these grown-ups were responsible for their actions, not her. And if she accepted this, then didn't she also have to accept that she was the only person responsible for *her* actions. And if this were the case, then it also followed that the only person holding her back was herself. It was a lot.

She saw with absolute clarity, as she watched the hands of the clock go round and round on the wall of the accident and emergency department, that if she ever wanted to get out of the middle lane of mediocrity, if she ever wanted to achieve her dreams, be like the nurses who bustled along the strip-lit corridors, she had to act. Her happiness and her future lay in her hands, not anyone else's – especially not in Ed Stratton's.

The thought was at once scary and liberating.

'Connie's been calling and texting.' Freda's words made her focus on the now. 'She said don't worry about last night and don't worry about going in today. She's called Jan in to cover your shift.'

'Okay. I'll call her in a bit.' It was a relief to know that she too might be able to rest, for a while at least. It was a reminder that she was also due down at Hele Bay Beach for her swim, and the last thing she wanted was to worry Maudie and Jago. Opening Facebook on her phone, she left them a message on the crappy Peacocks page, knowing they probably wouldn't get it until they got back from their dip, but it was the least she could do. If only they were mobile-phone savvy – it would be so much easier if she could call them.

'I'll leave you to it, darling. If you need me, I'll be downstairs.' Freda creased her face into a gentle smile of understanding.

'Thank you, Nan.' She sipped her tea.

The thought of failing to turn up for her swim, breaking her promise to take a morning dip every day during the season, was galling. Especially as it was not down to her own actions. Tawrie hardly ever felt sorry for herself, but in that moment, as she grappled with images of her mother raging against getting out of the ambulance, swearing at the kindly nurse who had tried to tend to her cut head, and the mortification of her singing loudly while the walking wounded sat in silence around her, she did. But none of these incidents were quite as mortifying as when she had threatened to injure Tawrie, who had suggested it might be best, when they got home, for her to go straight to bed. She felt the weight on her shoulders of all she carried and it pushed her down and down.

The truth was she was tired. But it wasn't anything a quick nap could cure; hers was a fatigue born of years of responsibility and she had almost had enough. Actually, no, she had had enough.

She felt low, missing Ed – or rather missing what she'd thought she had with Ed. Maudie was right when she'd said that if someone doesn't want you then they're not the person you thought they were and therefore what you miss about them, or the life you imagined with them, doesn't exist. It was perfectly succinct but no less hard for her to swallow. All she had to do was repeat it until it sank in: Ed and the life she had imagined did not exist! What she needed to do now was pull up her big-girl pants and go grab the life she wanted. It sounded so easy in her head.

Annalee stirred and Tawrie wondered what it must have been like for her dad, having to put up with his wife's desperate shenanigans. She wondered if things had been this hard for him. Quickly her mind fled to a familiar thought: what if he'd found it too hard, what if he'd had enough of her mother's erratic behaviour and so had taken his boat out, stowed his wallet and keys . . . ? It was no surprise that in this low moment this thought again bubbled to the surface, stoking the embers of her unhappiness, her regret, her anger.

She didn't know who she could ask. Certainly not her nan, who had lost her son, and not her mother, who just might have been the cause. Uncle Sten? They rarely spoke of anything at a deeper level and Connie, she was sure, would be just as much in the dark as she was. It was a mess. The whole thing was a bloody mess. Daniel

'Dan' Gunn might have died in 2002, but she was still dealing with the repercussions of it here in 2024.

Annalee opened her eyes. Tawrie could tell by her blink and focus that she was no longer sloshed.

'How you doing?' she asked softly.

Her mother nodded and sat up in the bed.

'You don't have to sit and watch me.' Her voice was scratchy; she sounded beaten.

'I know I don't have to, but I want to. You took quite a tumble yesterday.' It wasn't clear just how much her mother remembered.

'Yep.' Annalee wiped a tear that ran along her temple and soaked into the pillow.

'They've stitched up your head and your mouth is a bit of a mess, but other than that, just bruising.'

Her mother ran her fingers gingerly over the fresh wound on her scalp and forehead, as her tongue probed her swollen lip and her tears fell harder. Tawrie looked away from the finger with the ripped-off nail, the nail bed exposed, bumpy and bloody. The sight of it was enough to make her own finger throb.

'I don't want you to sit there, just go. I'm okay.'

'You don't look okay. You look sad and a bit beaten up, so I'm going to sit here and finish my tea.' She raised the mug.

'As you like,' Annalee huffed, closing her eyes and pushing back against the headboard, reminding Tawrie of a petulant toddler.

'*As I like?*' The words were like a lit match to the balls of angst and frustration that lined her gut. 'Nothing is as I like, Mum. It's odd, isn't it, how everyone in the pub, all the regulars in the wine bar, they all tell me how you have them howling. "She's so outgoing, really funny, a right old hoot!"'

Her mother opened her eyes and stared at her.

'Yet all I get is this woman.' She pointed at her mum. 'This woman who slopes around the house, quiet, morose, thoughtful and broken. How come you save the funny, outgoing, hoot of a woman for strangers?'

'I can get her right now if you want, all I need is a bottle of vodka and an eighties' playlist.' Annalee looked away and Tawrie took a beat, reminding herself that her mother was only recently out of hospital.

'I want to help you, Mum. I want to help you not get into a situation where you fall down the steps in broad daylight and we have to spend the evening in the hospital. Because honestly? I'm done.'

Annalee wiped angrily at her tears, as she did whenever Tawrie attempted to broach the topic, which she had periodically over the years – usually after an event that seemed to bring things to a head.

'I know we've had this conversation before and it all boils down to the fact that it doesn't matter how much I want you to get help, you have to want it too. It's you that will have to do the work, and I can't imagine what it must feel like, what a huge mountain it is for you to climb. I can't do it for you and neither can Nan, it's down to you.'

Her mother laughed once and folded her arms across her narrow chest. And whether it was because she was tired or because her heart was newly broken, or maybe because she was utterly, utterly at the end of her rope when it came to Annalee's behaviour, Tawrie saw red.

'What's that laugh for? I'm sitting here trying to rouse you into action, for your own good, for you! And you just don't give a shit! You don't give a shit what this is like for Nan, you certainly don't give a damn what it's like for me and it seems you don't care that you could have snapped your neck yesterday, crashing down those steps as you did.'

To her intense irritation, her mother shrugged, confirming exactly what Tawrie had said.

'You're unbelievable! It's not that I want thanks for sitting with you all night, although that would be nice, but to be so bloody indifferent is just—' She felt the rising tide of frustration in her throat, all thoughts of going gently on her mother now vanished. 'I'm going through my own shit right now and I have no one to talk to, no one!' Her voice cracked and Annalee met her eyeline. 'I loved someone.' It felt good to say it out loud. 'Actually, I *love* someone, but it's going to come to nothing. He's engaged to someone else, and it feels like I've been kicked, kicked really hard in my chest and I can barely take a breath and I want to lie down, curl up, hide and be warm. I want to . . . disappear.'

'No, you don't, love.' Annalee sniffed. 'You don't, not really.'

'And how would you know how I feel, Mum?' she challenged.

'Because I've had my heart broken, believe it or not,' Annalee snapped.

'Yes, but how would you know how *I* feel? You don't know me, don't know me at all.' It didn't feel good to state, but it was no less truthful for that.

'What are you talking about, of course I know you!' Annalee shook her head at the absurdity of it all.

'But you don't, do you? Not really,' Tawrie pushed.

'What are you getting at?'

And then it happened.

The volcano of honesty that Tawrie had regularly smothered with short replies or by removing herself physically from a situation, dousing the flames of truth that had been bubbling in the base of her gut for as long as she could recall, came firing out. All of it.

It was as if someone had lit the fuse and there was no going back, no slowing down and no time to offer things in a considered manner.

'I have no . . . no memory of you.'

Annalee laughed out loud. 'No memory of me? I don't get it, I'm right here.' She tapped her fingers over her heart as if she had to make sure she was present. 'I'm right here.'

'No, Mum, you're never right here. You're always planning your escape, hatching a plan to get to the pub, or into some bloke's car or on to a beach, on a jaunt, a jolly, away, away from me.'

Annalee's eyes brimmed. 'No, no, Taw, never away from you.'

'Yes. Always away from me and then always returning drunk, slurred, blurred, gaze askew, clothes twisted, not present, stumbling up the stairs to bed, sometimes alone, often not. And I tell myself that you're a grown woman who can do what she wants with whoever she wants. I'm not your jailer or your judge, but one thing I know for sure, is that . . .'

'What?' Her mother's voice no more than a whisper, her pitch dismissive. 'What do you know for sure?'

Tawrie found it easier to look towards the window where a gentle breeze brought the curtains to life. 'I know that if I was a mum and my child had lost their dad, I'd be there, with her, holding her, telling her everything was going to be okay.'

Annalee too turned to face the big window with a view of the ocean, like her daughter, it seemed, taking comfort from the possibility of escape. Tawrie could make out the tremble to her frame.

'What if you knew it *wasn't* going to be okay? What if you knew nothing was going to be okay ever again?'

'Then all the more reason to stay close and hold them tight.'

Annalee now faced her. 'You think you have all the answers.'

'No, no I don't think I have any of the answers.' This was her truth. 'I sometimes think if it wasn't for Nan—' She bit her tongue, there was a fine line between honesty and cruelty and Tawrie Gunn had never been cruel.

'I think that too. What would we do without her?' Annalee gave a forced, ugly smile and wiped the tears from beneath her eyes where thin remnants of mascara pooled, mixed with dried blood.

'All my memories from before Dad and after, they're all of her, with you on the edge, stumbling in and stumbling out.'

'You have no idea! None at all!' her mother shouted.

'I know you're always pissed and wobbling upstairs, or downstairs or tripping out of pubs and spraining your ankle on kerbs, blacking your eye on walls, or falling down the bloody steps to the beach or shitting yourself so Nan has to scrub up your mess! I know all of that! And I know I sit in my room or work in the café instead of doing what I think I'd be good at just so I'm close enough to come and mop up after you! You think that makes me proud? You think I like being your daughter?'

'Get out!' Her mother extended her damaged digit towards the door. 'Get out, now!'

Tawrie stood, welcoming the chance to get out of the room, to get away from the woman who invoked such a reaction, and to calm down.

'I don't know who you think you are, Tawrie, but you have no right to speak to me like that!'

'No right? And what rights do you have? You're not a mother, not in the way I deserved. And I wonder if you were a wife in the way that Dad deserved.' Her mother's eyes grew wide and her swollen mouth fell open. Tawrie had gone too far and she knew it, but the bull was battering the gate and in one more sentence it broke free entirely and came charging. 'Did he get into that boat to get away from you? I mean, is that why he sailed all the time? Jesus, can you blame him? Look at the state of you! If I could escape I bloody would! And do you know what? I just might!' She practically bolted across the bedroom floor, cracking a china plate beneath her foot, and stomping on clothes, cigarette packets and empty beer cans as she went.

Annalee's sob was loud and visceral. It made Tawrie gasp as she slammed the door behind her.

Leaning now on the banister at the top of the half landing she did her best to catch her breath as her tears fell.

'I might.' Eyes closed, she spoke into the ether. 'I just bloody might run from this bloody house and the view of Corner bloody Cottage, and Ed bloody Stratton, and the bloody café and all the bloody misery!'

'Have you finished your bloody tea, darling? I came to get the bloody mug.'

She hadn't seen her nan in the stairwell, who saw fit to emulate her outburst.

Their laughter was sudden and welcome. It was mere seconds before this turned to tears and Tawrie sobbed as her nan put her arms around her and held her close. It felt as if a volcano bubbled inside her. Rocks of pain, hurt and desperation were rising on the lava of regret. What scared her most was how unsure she was that she could keep it contained.

A hot shower had done much to restore her sense of calm. Guilt over her exchange with her mother sat at the forefront of her mind, a jagged boulder around which all other thoughts and ideas had to circumnavigate. It had thrown her and left her spent. It felt very much like she had reached a crossroads and was looking for a signpost. Did she have the courage to put herself first? This quandary on top of the sleepless night, preceded by another sleepless night, and the news that the feeling of euphoria that had gathered up and whistled her along was based on nothing true.

Connie did a double take as she walked in.

'Didn't think we'd see you today, my love.'

'Yet here I am!' She made her way to the sink and without further discussion, grabbed the scouring pad and a heavy pan and began to scrub, running the hot tap and dousing everything in suds.

'Is your mum okay?' her cousin asked casually from behind the fridge door where she wrapped a block of cheese.

'Oh, she's peachy!' She gave a false grin and a double thumbs up, before turning her attention back to cleaning the pot, scouring it hard on its blackened base and working mercilessly on the blobs of hardened food that clung on like limpets at low tide.

'Hello, Taw! Didn't expect to see you, my lovely!' Jan smiled as she handed the order to Connie.

'And yet, as I just said to Con, here I am!'

'Ignore her, Jan,' Connie interjected. 'She's pissed off at the world and it appears we are today's lucky recipients of all that anger. She's taking her frustration out on the washing-up and us apparently. So tighten your apron strings, I think we're in for a rocky old shift!'

'Blimey, better hide the glasses,' Jan suggested.

'And the sharp knives!' Connie winked and Tawrie couldn't help the thaw to her demeanour. It was almost impossible to be in the company of these women, this loving community, and not feel the benefit of it.

'That's more like it, an actual smile!' Her cousin came up behind her and slipped her arms around her waist, resting her pretty head on Tawrie's shoulder. 'It'll all get better; it'll all get easier. Your heart will heal. But I don't need to tell you that, do I, Tawrie Gunn? You're a survivor, a bloody warrior woman! You've got this. And as for that arsehole Sebastian Farquhar—'

'No!' Tawrie shook her head, her voice firm. 'Nope. We are not going to mention his name. We are not going to discuss him, and we are not going to analyse events or think about what might have been. He's like early morning sea mist: forgotten by lunchtime. Okay?'

'Okay, my love. As you wish.' Connie whistled as she went back to the fridge.

Instantly she regretted snapping at her cousin, knowing her frustrations went way further than anything Connie said or did, and to react like this was as unfair as it was out of character. She paused with the scourer in her hand, understanding that what she needed to do was heed Maudie's advice and get a grip, take control! She stood tall, knowing that now was the time to galvanise her thoughts and make a plan.

CHAPTER TWENTY-TWO

HARRIET WENTWORTH

SEPTEMBER 2024

As was her evening habit, Harriet watered the roses in the back garden, standing with the hose at a particular angle, and using her thumb over the end to get the right level of spray, she stared at the tiny, hypnotically beautiful rainbows that appeared in the mist. With a rare few days' holiday her time was more or less her own and she loved idling in her cottage garden.

Bear's visit a month ago had thrown her. Not that it wasn't wonderful to have his company, to hear about his life – it was – and she was of course more than thrilled that their closeness meant he could confide in her. It was more that she was worried about him, having rarely seen him so distraught nor so resolute. The thought of him getting hurt was more than she could stand. She was also disturbed by what had risen to the top of her thoughts as they raked over old sand. She rarely, if ever, thought about Ilfracombe and that life-changing summer. It was easier not to. That, and she was far too busy with life in the present day and all that her career at the research lab and being mum to the twins threw at her. And that was before she considered that in approximately six weeks, she would become a grandmother to a baby girl, who with any luck would be born in the image of her mumma, with fingers that grasped for a book the moment she was able. The idea alone was enough to make her smile.

There was a new thought that sat in her mind like a pebble in her shoe. The matter of Hugo, that terrible summer. She was conscious of the fact that it had been years since she'd had a meaningful conversation with Hugo, particularly about a topic that was like kryptonite to her. She was fearful still of it being raised. They had interacted little outside of the handing over of the kids and the odd chit-chat about due dates for his babies and how they were faring. Small talk. It felt easier to keep a little distance. But right now it bothered her; was it unfinished business or was it best to let sleeping dogs lie?

It had taken her a long time to recover from the way her marriage had ended. Not only the loss of him and the dismantling of their little family, the rewriting of the rules she had taken for granted, the fragmented nature of their living arrangements and the way her heart ached at every single goodbye. But also the damage to her faith in humanity, which ran deep, maybe deeper than she'd realised. It was when she finally began to heal that Charles had come into her life, quite by accident, when Ellis had dragged her along to a lecture on 'The Art of Ancient Greece', given by none other than Dr Charles Wentworth, esteemed classicist. Dragged was an often misused exaggeration, but in this case entirely true, as she'd dug her heels into the pavement and pleaded with her sister that they do anything but this. The future lovers had met in the crowded lobby beforehand, only for Harriet to roll her eyes as he smiled at her. Yet she'd liked his worn tweed jacket and his heavy-framed glasses. A little different.

'Can you think of anything more tedious than an evening with some old bore waffling on about statues and artifacts? I could be at home watching paint dry!' she'd laughed. 'I'm Harriet by the way.'

'Lovely to meet you, Harriet. I'm Charles, by the way, and I'm the waffling bore you're consigned to listen to, although there's a bit more to it than statues and artifacts.'

A sweet man who could not have been more different to Hugo – he made her feel safe. He was kind and open. But what if Hugo had not been the problem? What if . . . ?

'Penny for them?' Her husband crept up beside her in the garden.

'I was just thinking about you, actually, and the night we met.'

'I don't like to think about it.' He looked quite serious.

'Why not? What a terrible thing to say!' She made out to spray him and he jumped back accordingly.

'It's not a terrible thing to say,' he countered. 'I don't like it because I think about the many opportunities, the infinite possibilities that existed on that night for us not to meet, not to chat. Imagine if you hadn't been so very forward.' He laughed and she joined him. 'And then if you hadn't hung back at the end because Ellis needed the bathroom? All those little acts that meant I found you. I hate to think of the fickle hand of fate, cruelly keeping you from me. I can't imagine not having you, not having the boys, not having this.' He let his arm rise and fall in an arc that indicated their whole world, their home, their haven.

'Or maybe it wasn't fate,' she suggested. 'Maybe it was written in the stars, preordained, meant to be and so it wouldn't have mattered if we chatted or not, we'd still be here, right now, we'd have just taken a different route.'

'But you don't believe in all that nonsense!' He stared at her, his lovely face breaking into a smile.

'No, but whatever it is, I thank my lucky stars for you.' She wrinkled her nose at her beloved.

'And I for you, Mrs Wentworth. Do you think Bear is still desperately in love with the girl he met in Devon – Tawrie? Or do you think this last month away from there has given him perspective?' He voiced her own thoughts.

'I don't know, he seemed pretty fixed on the idea of her. More than that, entirely dedicated to it. I'm glad he's taken some time out, though. Apparently Petra moved her mother in and Ramona visits a lot, so he feels a little . . .'

'Yes, I've been in the company of Ramona and Petra's mother, and I must admit I felt a little . . . overwhelmed?' He fished for the right way to phrase it. 'They can be a bit of a noisy twosome, like the boys when they gang up!'

'But with much less rugby chat,' she quipped.

'Yes, and then when you throw a wine-soaked Hugo into the mix.' He pulled a face.

Harriet couldn't disagree. When Hugo had moved Wendy Peterson into their old family home in Ledwick Green, it hadn't been as gut-wrenching as she might have anticipated. In the beginning, when news of his infidelity was raw, it would have been an axe to her will and motivation. By the time he'd rather sheepishly informed her of the development one night when she'd dropped Bear and Dilly back home for his half of the week and was about to return to the flat she'd rented only a stone's throw from Ledwick Green, eight months had passed, and everything had calmed. It still smarted, she'd be lying if she said otherwise, but gone was the visceral throb of rejection, the utter pain of deceit. Instead, she was more concerned with how the kids would cope seeing Wendy at the stove or Wendy on the sofa or Wendy in the bathroom. And how she'd cope when Wendy opened the front door when she came to collect the kids or dropped them off.

Thank you, doll, I feel gorgeous!

She shivered.

And pretty much like anything that's dreaded and takes an inflated position in the mind, in reality it had been a fairly innocuous transition. Wendy, in a matter of weeks, went from the woman who had taken a weapon to her life, to Hugo's girlfriend; the woman Harriet gave instruction to about how to reboot the pilot light on the boiler and let her in on the trick of kicking the dishwasher door to make it work when it gave up the ghost mid-cycle. The children also seemed to take it in their stride. Figuring they'd take their lead from her, she spoke only positively about the new set-up when they were within earshot and it did the trick. Then, just like that, Wendy was out and Sherry was in and her kids slid back to square one; another resettling with a new woman and a baby to boot.

'I've been thinking about Hugo a bit.'

'In what way?' His casual tone spoke volumes about how secure he was in this marriage.

'Just . . .' She took her time. 'I don't know. Things I might want to say, to ask, things that have stayed with me.'

'I guess only you know if these "things" need exploring, darling.' He used air quotes, to emphasise her vagueness. 'If there's something that bothers you that you want to get off your chest then do it. Or maybe with so much time having passed and so much water under the bridge, it might be like picking at an old wound for no reason.'

'Yep, that's the dilemma.' She liked how he always guided, never instructed, this patient man she so loved. 'When's Bear back from Ellis's?' As ever, she'd lost track.

'This evening. Apparently he and Maisie have been drinking wine till the early hours and dancing to nineties' club hits in the kitchen, while Maisie cries over lost loves. Ellis has had to remind them that she's way too old to be dealing with teenage angst at this time of her life, and so are they! I think she'll be glad to see the back of him! Do you want me to cook?' he offered casually.

'Good Lord, no! Please, please don't do that! I can't stand the thought of having to redecorate.' She walked over and kissed his cheek. 'Though we could get a takeaway? The boys would like the treat.'

'Great idea.' He stood and cleared his throat in the way he did when he had something to say.

'What is it love?' she prompted.

'I suppose . . .' He rocked on his heels. 'I just get the feeling that since Bear has raised the topic of Ilfracombe, you seem a little bit . . . preoccupied. And of course you're worried about him, we all are. But whatever else is filling up your head, I just wanted to say that I do understand, or at least I try to. I . . . I've always been aware that it's a time and place in your life that you avoid, in every sense, and that's a shame. It's like . . .' His mouth moved and his eyes roved the sky, as if finding the wording was tough.

'It's like what?' she asked softly, dreading and welcoming his thoughts in equal measure.

'It's like a boulder in the fast-flowing river of our lives, and it always has been. We climb over it, we swim around it, we avoid it as if to get close means we might dash to pieces upon it. I don't like it. I don't like having this thing between us. It's not necessary. I guess what I'm saying, or trying to, is that maybe it's time you revisited both the place and the time? You might find it freeing.' He reached out and stroked her face. '*We* might find it freeing. Because no matter how deeply I love you, if there's even a thin coat of armour that you wear as a shield close to your skin, around your heart, no matter how tiny, almost invisible, it's still a barrier between us.'

'I . . .' To hear this from the man she loved was like a knife in her gut. 'I don't . . .'

'You don't have to give me details, you don't have to *explain*,' he stressed, 'but you do have to have everything clear in your thoughts; you owe yourself that.'

'I owe us that,' she whispered, barely trusting herself to get the words out. It had been a revelation, his awareness of the fear she had thought she held in secret; she felt exposed, afraid, and relieved all at once.

He nodded. She concentrated on her roses, a great prop to channel her emotion and help hold back the tears.

'You're right on both counts.' He knew her inside out. 'I do avoid the place, the topic. I was always happy to let the rental company deal with the holiday lets and whatnot, but never felt the need to go back. I fear it might be too painful. As you say, the opening of old wounds and all that.'

'Also . . .' He took a step towards her and smiled into her face, a lingering look of love that warmed her still after all these years. 'I've always thought the way you coped, having your life torpedoed by things outside of your control, is remarkable. You are remarkable, but also . . .'

'Also what?' she asked with a nervous crack to her voice.

'I suspect there are elements that you hide, hurt that you mask, fears you don't share, a brave face that you paint on that you don't have to.'

'We all do that, don't we?'

'To a degree, but I think you need to face it head on, face it all. I think maybe you should . . .'

'Should what?' She lowered the hose to hear better.

'Should go back, lay some ghosts to rest. And maybe it would be good to take Bear. He needs closure one way or another when it comes to this girl. We don't know if he's fallen for her or whether she's an escape hatch that's taken him away from marrying Petra, which he clearly felt press-ganged into, either way.'

'You are wise, Charles, wise and kind. I feel very lucky to have you.'

'Quite right too. I'm what's known as a catch, Mrs Wentworth!' He did a clumsy twirl and she felt a rush of love for him.

'Maybe I'll ask Bear.'

'Maybe you'll ask Bear what?'

They both turned at the sound of her eldest coming out of the back door from the kitchen and into the garden.

'Welcome home, son!' Charles boomed.

'Thanks, Charles. Louis let me in then threw a rugby ball at my head.' He rubbed his scalp.

It was a relief to see he looked a little less pale, a little recovered.

'He was probably trying to hit your chest; his aim's a little off.' Charles pulled a face. Their laughter only added to the convivial atmosphere as they stood in the sunny garden, where the unexpected warmth of the day gave way to a slight chill in this changeable month.

'What are you thinking of asking me?' Her son clearly keen to know.

'I was going to ask you if you fancy a trip.' She moved the hose along to water the other flower bed.

'A trip where?' He stood with his hands on his hips, looking so much like his father it was striking. 'I've only just arrived!'

'A place that will allow you to take a moment, a place you can breathe, get your head straight away from the hustle and bustle of life, away from the gossip. A place where you might have left a piece of your heart.' *A place where I might have too . . .*

'Corner Cottage?' His mouth seemed a little dry, his words sticky.

'Yes, Corner Cottage.' She tried to imagine stepping over the threshold for the first time in all these years and her heart beat a little too fast.

317

'But you don't go down to Ilfracombe.' Her son pointed out the obvious.

'No, I found the thought too painful, too many ghosts, but I think maybe Charles is right, it's time we laid them to rest. Plus I want to show you something.'

'What do you want to show me?'

'Ah, you'll have to wait and see.'

'I want to go, Mum. It's taken all of my strength over the last few weeks not to jump in the car and go find Tawrie, but she was so angry, so hurt and I get why. I think she meant it when she told me to sod off.' The crease at the top of his nose and the inward curve to his eyebrows spoke of the distress he contained.

'I think it'll be hard for you to settle until you've spoken to her. I also think it will be easier to talk to her now some time has passed and things are a bit more transparent, especially with Petra. I also know that in the heat of the moment, when people are backed into a corner, they say things they don't necessarily mean and only time allows it all to flatten out.'

'Okay.' He took a deep breath and bit his lip.

She laid the hose on the ground and turned off the outside tap, before kissing her boy on the forehead. 'It'll all be okay, Bear. It'll get better, easier. Your heart will heal. But I don't need to tell you that, do I, Edgar Stratton? You're a wonderful, strong man! You've got this. And any woman – Ms Tawrie Gunn or anyone else for that matter – will be very lucky to have you.'

'Thanks, Mum.'

She noticed how just the mention of Tawrie was enough to bring a lump to his throat and she hoped and prayed that taking him back to Corner Cottage was the right thing to do for them both.

'When should we go, do you think?'

She shared a lingering, knowing look with Charles.

'How about tonight after supper? What is it they say? No time like the present? We could drive in the dark and chat on the way, make it part of our adventure.'

'As long as I can shower before we leave and freshen up. Oh, and I get to choose the music. I think a few hours of non-stop ABBA might finish me off!' His smile, however, was faltering and she understood, aware as she was of the enormity of going back to face Tawrie.

'I can't promise.' She winked, thinking about what she might need to pack for a couple of nights away and trying not to think about those first nights way back when the kids were little and she and Hugo had spent a week or so surrounded by boxes and chaos, under the misapprehension that once they had restored order in their new home, they would be able to do the same in their marriage. 'But life's not that simple.' She had meant to think it, only aware she'd spoken out loud when both Charles and Bear looked from one another to her. 'Right then, supper!' She spoke with gusto, keen to distract from her embarrassment. 'Pizza or chippy?'

'Chippy!'

'Pizza!'

Charles and Bear spoke in unison and she was thankful for the laughter that followed. It was a reminder of all that was good in her life right now and a picture she would carry in her mind as she made the journey to the south-west.

It was dark when Bear, yawning and flexing his aching back, parked his rusting old banger in Ropery Road car park. Harriet was glad of the darkness, a shield of sorts. It was odd to be back: comforting, familiar and wonderfully evocative, taking her instantly to the time when her children had been young and wanted nothing more than to run on wet sand with a bucket and spade, and hold a drippy ice cream at the end of the day. Yet there was no denying the tremble to her limbs, a reminder that this was where her marriage had imploded and she had been set adrift.

Gripping her hastily packed holdall, she followed her son up the slight incline of Fore Street. The street was largely untouched, a few buildings in much better condition than she remembered, a couple worse, but the meandering shape of the pavements, the thick, whitewashed walls, towering town houses and squat cottages – the soul of the place – was exactly the same.

The darkness was softened by Victorian street lamps and the festoon lights that criss-crossed the buildings, meaning she walked under a canopy of warm light. Dilly had once marvelled at them, and as Hugo carried her home on his shoulders, she'd asked if they were fallen stars. The thought of her daughter made her smile; her beloved bookworm who in a few short weeks would have a child of her own – she was full of excitement at the prospect, but still wondered if she'd ever get used to the idea.

Inhaling now, she took in the scent of salt air, real fires, fish, beach life and the history of three hundred years. She thought about the footsteps of everyone who had trod Fore Street. Including her younger self, who had lugged suitcases and collapsing cardboard boxes stuffed with kettles, books, lamps and other items that had evaded capture by the removal men, which she'd hastily grabbed and shoved into the back of their roomy saloon on the day of the big move.

If, over the years, she'd envisaged a return, in her mind's eye it had been very similar to the momentous journey she had taken over two decades ago, when the sun had been high in the sky, gull song heralded her arrival, and the pretty harbourside town nestled in its higgledy-piggledy formation from the top of the hill right down to the water's edge. Arriving at Corner Cottage, she would, as before, throw the windows open and take a minute to appreciate the light that streamed in through the wide sash windows. Back then, amid the chaos of a new move, and with her mind heavily laden with all she wrestled with, she had still been quite overwhelmed by the beauty of her surroundings, while from the vibrant harbourside, ripples of laughter and the warm scents of holiday had wafted up to welcome her. This time it was quite different, though. She was a different person with a different life, a new family even! This trip was about rounding off the edges of an unfinished work – a reckoning of sorts.

Corner Cottage, on the junction of Mill Head and Fore Street, a house they had bought in haste and abandoned as quickly, looked just as she'd expected from the photographs sent by thankful families who had enjoyed a holiday there, or the newly snapped images from the rental agent.

It was meant to have been a new start for their little family, but with divorce looming, no intention of selling the house in Ledwick Green, and without the first clue as to how things might pan out, they'd figured it would provide an income, which they would divide equally, as well as being a wonderful nest egg for the kids when they grew up. The little house on the corner might look pretty much as she'd expected, but nothing could have prepared her for how being here felt, as the memory of her emotional turmoil came flooding back so powerfully, it almost knocked her off her feet.

'It's beautiful, isn't it?' Bear, oblivious, stood at the front of the cottage and looked down the street, which had an ethereal quality at this hour and in this light.

'It really is.' The slight quaver to her voice belied her steady response.

She watched as her son's eyes wandered along the street and then rose, settling on the looming silhouette of Signal House. It was hard to imagine how it must feel, being this close to Tawrie and with so much left to say, but not being able to say it.

'All good things, my love,' she whispered.

'God, I hope so, Mum.'

She caught the high emotion in his voice and it confirmed that being here was the right thing; he needed closure, one way or another.

As did she.

Watching now as Bear pulled the key from his pocket, she felt her stomach jump. A key that once held so many possibilities, entry into a new life, a new beginning . . . Without further time to think, he was in and had flicked on the light in the small, square hallway, as she climbed the steps to the front door.

The interior was different, beautifully updated by Dilly and now in a soft palette of pale blues, creams and navy. It was very beachy and yet tasteful, she approved. A new oversized sofa looked inviting and bookshelves groaned under the weight of all the books her daughter had read while recharging here. Some things were familiar: her grandmother's old card table, which still sported the vintage china lamp that had once been in the sitting room at Ledwick Green, and next to that, a little shabbier, a little softer, sat the old leather club chair where she had spent so much time.

'Welcome home.' Bear's voice jolted her into the present and she smiled at him. 'Do you want a hot drink or is it too late?' He glanced at his watch.

'Never too late for tea. Thank you, darling.'

'I'll go put the kettle on.' He disappeared into the kitchen, walking with the confidence of a man who knew the space and had made memories here.

She sat in the leather chair and placed her hands on the worn arms, closing her eyes briefly.

I love you, Harriet. I love you, always you. Only you. I love you so much this is killing me!

It was surprising to her, how fatigue had ushered in the hand of nostalgia and she could clearly hear Hugo saying these words, recalling how very desperate she had felt, how torn.

'Is it odd for you, Mum, being here? Bringing back some memories, I bet?' Bear called out.

'Yes and yes, but I guess that's rather the point, isn't it?'

Standing, she went to join him in the cosy kitchen, which was the least altered. The freshly painted walls kept the room bright. But the hand-built old pine units, the wooden floor and of course the wide sash window that gave a great view of Mill Head, the street on which the building sat, were just the same.

'And I thought you were here to help nurse my broken heart or help me find a way to glue it back together. Which it will, I hope, if Tawrie will just hear me out.'

'Who knows, Bear? Maybe she's missed you desperately, or maybe' – *like me* – 'she has come to see that life is too short to be with someone you can't trust, and if she can't trust you . . .' She let this trail and his expression fell.

'I think I'm prepared for that but it's a thought that kills me, honestly, Mum.' He took a deep breath and popped teabags into mugs. She took a seat at a table slightly smaller than the one they'd left behind; still old and with a scrubbed top it was a fitting addition that was better sized for the space.

They had spent many an hour at that old table, she and Hugo, sitting either side of the worn wood that was no more than three feet wide and yet represented a gulf of miles and miles they'd had no hope of traversing. Not that she'd fully understood that in the beginning. Just being here took her right back to then. She half expected to hear the thunder of little feet on the stairs and for Dilly to appear, book in hand, and for Hugo to walk in, dark half-moons under his eyes, his gaze one of avoidance. A chill trickled through her veins as she remembered what it felt like to not be enough and to have no real clue as to why she had been discarded. She rubbed her arms, trying in vain to warm a place that touch couldn't reach.

Bear placed the mug of tea in front of her, topped up with the milk they'd picked up from the petrol station when they'd stopped en route for fuel.

'We can get up early, if you like, Mum, and go and see whatever it is you want to show me! The suspense is killing me.' He looked like an eager child, rubbing his hands together.

'Oh, it's not a place.' She took a restorative sip.

'What is it then?' He sounded a smidge disappointed.

'It's a thing and it's right here in the cottage.' She swallowed the flutter of nerves, unsure if she wanted to revisit the words written by a different version of herself – one who was afraid, hurt. She was unsure if showing her son was a good or bad idea. But either way, she was entirely committed.

'Well, if it's here, show me now! What are we waiting for?' He pushed away from the table.

Reluctantly abandoning her tea, she slowly trod the stairs with Bear close behind. New cream carpet throughout the upper floors had cosied up the place and the middle landing was wider than she remembered, partly due to the fact that in her mind's eye it was cluttered with badly labelled removal boxes, which had taken an age to sort out. Again, she saw how his eyes were drawn to the wide sash window on the middle landing, staring down Fore Street and almost stooped towards the view, as if his whole being longed to run right out of the front door and go wake that girl! She prayed he wasn't going to get hurt, remembering fragments of the lovely Annalee, and hoping her daughter carried the same kindness. She thought also of sweet Petra, wondering if she lay awake feeling the stab of rejection, and, knowing what it was like to get caught in the crossfire of someone's infidelity, her heart went out to her.

Finally up to the top floor, the attic room where she noted the bed was unmade. Gingerly, she walked over to the small cupboard with a louvre door, which cleverly created a hanging area within the boxed-off roof space.

'You want to show me the little wardrobe?' He looked perplexed.

Ignoring him, she opened the door and bent down, placing her hand on the right side panel, one quick push and out it popped. She assumed it had been installed in case of pipe maintenance – or perhaps to hide documents or valuables. It was something Hugo had discovered quite by accident as he'd rummaged around getting better acquainted with their new home. With her arm fully extended, she ran her fingers around behind the panel until, with relief, they touched the firm plastic of the Tupperware box. It was dusty and she wiped the close-fitted lid with her fingers. It was both wonderful and petrifying to have the box in her possession.

'You stashed sandwiches up here?' Bear stared at the loot in her hands with barely disguised disappointment. 'I mean, how desperate were you for a midnight snack? And I hate to be the one to break it to you, Mum, but they might have gone off a bit in the last twenty-odd years. I must admit I was hoping for a stash of rubies or an illegal haul of whisky, something vaguely valuable!'

'This is my treasure. My truth.' She spoke softly and held the box to her chest as she made her way back down the stairs.

They both glugged the cooled tea and stared at the box, which was discoloured and had taken on an unattractive orange hue.

'What is it? I mean, I can see it's a book.' He pointed.

Her son had always had this level of impatience.

Holding the corner of the lid, she peeled it away from the box and there it lay. Its glorious green cloth jacket was remarkably well preserved, bar a couple of age spots, and to see it again, aware of what it had meant to her and how it had saved her sanity at a time when to talk freely was not always possible, was, to say the least, emotional.

'Don't cry.' Bear reached out and squeezed her hand. In truth she hadn't realised she was until he said it. 'What is it?' he asked, softly this time.

'It's my diary.' She wiped her face on her sleeve.

'I vaguely remember it. I didn't know I did until I saw it but I can almost picture you with it on your lap holding a pen.' He stared at the cover.

'It's the only time I've ever kept one. Ellis thought it might be a good idea, get it all down on paper, help me analyse my thoughts, keep track.'

'And did it?'

'Erm . . .' She thought for a moment. 'Yes. I was quite lonely, very lonely, in fact. Things with Dad were . . .' She let this hang. 'And I took solace in scribbling away.' She let her fingers rest on the little book that had been so much more than she could adequately express. 'I'm a bit nervous, actually.'

'Nervous?'

'I can't remember exactly what I wrote, but I know it was written from the heart and I expect it will perfectly capture that time in my life when I felt everything was spinning out of control. Just seeing it takes me back; I've never felt so lost, so scared of what my future might hold.'

'Oh, Mum.' He touched her arm. 'Are you going to read some tonight, or wait until tomorrow when you're less tired and you'll have the beautiful view of Capstone Hill to distract you?'

'That's the thing, darling, I don't think I can read it alone.' Carefully, she lifted it from the box, the weight of it comforting and familiar. 'Can we read it together?'

'Really?' He pulled a face and she understood. He was quite rightly wary of what this book might reveal about his parents' marriage.

'It's up to you entirely, but I think it'll give you an insight into honesty and love and how to treat the people you want to be with. It'll give an insight into your dad and me and I hope it has lessons about communication and openness. And I hope it brings me closure. Helps me understand what we went through, so I can finally shut it away for good.'

'Back in its box.' He tapped the Tupperware lid.

'Back in its box.'

'Well, now I'm nervous!' He laughed awkwardly.

'Don't be, but I want you, Dilly, Louis and Rafe to understand that every choice we make, every decision we settle on is a tiny footprint towards our own destiny, and before you know it, all those tiny footprints have made a path and it's the one you walk. So make a path that's honest, sincere and leads to all good things.'

'Wow!' Her son sat back in the chair and exhaled. 'And there was me thinking it would be just pages and pages of Dad getting a good pasting.'

'There's probably a bit of that,' she confessed. 'Maybe more than he deserves, maybe not! It's hard not to add hindsight to any life event.'

'I'm not sure I want to read it, Mum.'

'And that's fine too.' She meant it.

'It's just that it's taken Dad and me quite a while to reach this ledge, where we sit quite comfortably. He knows that one false move and I'll run all the way down the mountain and I know that if I take him to task on all that irks me, he'll scamper to the top and block the route.'

'It sounds precarious.' She was happy they could talk so candidly, yet sad for the state of the relationship between him and

327

Hugo, recognising it as similar to the way she had handled the breakdown of their marriage: avoiding him other than when absolutely necessary and boxing away the whole episode. She hoped the ledge on which Bear rested was firm and steadfast; it would do them both good to rest awhile.

'It is, really.' He yawned; the day was catching up with them both.

'The truth is, I wrote in a state of high emotion so maybe it's not entirely balanced, but it was authentic for me at the time. I now know that there's so much more to a marriage than one action, one slip, one lie, or even two. It takes two as they say . . .'

'The other being, "Call me Wendy, not Mum! You already have a mum!" Peterson.'

It felt a little cruel to laugh at his accurate impression. It was also easy now to pity the woman who had been on the receiving end of infidelity when Hugo had taken up with Sherry in a short-lived whirlwind of sex and destruction that had culminated in the birth of Aurelia and had left Wendy emotionally in tatters. Harriet had taken no pleasure in watching their relationship unravel – there was no sense of schadenfreude, no feeling of justice or karma, more worry about what message Hugo's behaviour would send to her kids, to their kids. This was why the diary was so important. A first-hand life lesson.

'Your dad has never read it, of course, and I'm quite sure his version of events would be different, but that's life, right?'

'Yes, and what is it they say? History is written by the winners?' Bear held the book up like a prize.

'I said to Hugo once, and I'll say it to you, nothing about our split, our divorce, ever felt like winning.'

'Until you met Dr Charles.' He smiled with obvious affection for the man.

'Yes, darling, until I met Dr Charles.' Her smile matched her son's. 'Anyway, it's nearly midnight. Time to call it a night.'

'God, is it really?' Bear held up his phone and she saw his eyes widen. 'September the fourteenth.'

'Yup.' She stood and rinsed the cups under the tap and placed them on the sideboard, as she had done many times before.

'It's Tawrie's birthday. And her mother's and her gran's,' he informed her.

'Well, that's quite something!' She tried to work out how old Annalee would be and how long it was since she'd seen her – at least twenty years.

'That means it's the Gunn Fire tonight.' He looked thoughtful.

'The Gunn Fire?' She was curious. 'What's that?'

'A party where no one needs an invite, Mum, luckily for me.'

Again she sent a silent prayer over the chimney tops that she hoped might land in Tawrie Gunn's ear. *Please be kind . . .*

His actions were slow as he reached out and took the book under his fingers, sliding it across the tabletop, until he could grip it easily and opened it up. Without preamble or discussion, he read aloud:

July 2nd 2002

A diarist!

Who even am I?

I jest but there's truth in it. I hardly recognise the person sitting here in this pretty sitting room . . .

He paused to look up at her. It was jarring and confronting to hear her words spoken by her son, and she was suddenly wary of what else was about to be revealed.

'I thought we were calling it a night?' She stifled a yawn.

'Or you could put the kettle on?' He smiled and turned back to the page.

◆　◆　◆

It was an hour later that Bear fell asleep with his head on the cradle of his arms on the tabletop. Carefully, she removed the diary from beneath his hand and took it into the sitting room, finding the leather chair familiar and comfortable. She ran her fingers over the cracked leather of the arm. It felt only right to be reading it here where so much of it had been written. Most of it was nostalgic – painful, yes, but with the glorious benefit of knowing how things had turned out for her, it was as if she carried a cushion to protect herself from the written truth, recognising that her fear of being alone had helped to curate some of the content. There was one conversation that had stuck in her mind and she now remembered the evening so clearly.

Hugo had explained her role in their demise, leading her to the conclusion that the very things that first attracted him to her were the very things he had come to dislike. It had felt unjust and cruel then and time had not changed her mind. The revelation that he had simply felt the grass might be greener and had wandered, almost without question, down the road of infidelity, his actions casual, seemingly unconsidered, had only added to her distress. His casual admission of how he had been 'lured' into adultery with no more than a kind word was incendiary, and with it the under-standing that they never had been and never could be stable. It also made it likely that nothing she could have said or done would have prevented his decision to stray.

Harriet sat back in the chair and folded her hands over the diary in her lap. That evening had been a moment of reckoning; the point at which she had pictured a small cage and mentally placed it around her heart, locking it tight, knowing that if she could so misunderstand her marriage, misjudge her family life and mistrust her husband, then nothing else in her life could be taken for granted. A tear fell down her face at the memory of how alone she had felt and how dangerously close to the edge, realising how easy it would have been to fall . . . Her tears were also for a new realisation: it had felt entirely necessary to construct the little cage that kept her safe at a time of vulnerability, when she was fearful of what the future held; what hadn't occurred to her until this evening was that she had failed to unlock it, forgotten to remove the contraption that stopped her heart from being fully open. What had Charles said?

'No matter how deeply I love you, if there's even a thin coat of armour that you wear as a shield close to your skin, around your heart, no matter how tiny, almost invisible, it's still a barrier between us.'

'Oh, my love!' she whispered into the darkness. 'It's time I found that key.'

CHAPTER
TWENTY-THREE

Tawrie Gunn

14 September 2024

'It's my birthday! Oh, it's my birthday!'

Tawrie smiled at the sound of her nan yelling loudly downstairs, hoping that when she got to seventy-four, she'd have a similar level of enthusiasm for the day. In fact, it wouldn't go amiss right now. She'd smile broadly anyway, knowing it meant a lot to Freda and knowing that if her plans became a reality, this time next year things might be very different. Swallowing the lump in her throat, she grabbed her duffel bag and raced down the stairs.

'Well, whaddya know? It's my birthday too!'

'Twenty-nine! How is that even possible! I must have blinked and look at you, Tawrie Gunn, look at the beautiful woman you are!'

'Hardly!' She ran her hand through her locks, which needed to feel the slosh of a good shampoo, and over her skin, which was sun burnished in places.

Freda pulled her into a tight hug. Annalee's absence was obvious, but that was just too bad. And why, after all, would today be any different? Her mother would, as ever, be languishing in bed, no doubt nursing a headache and letting her body settle after a night of soaking it in booze.

A month after her tumble down the stairs and their subsequent row, there had been a shield of discomfort that sat between them at every encounter. This, Tawrie found, was far harder to live with than the vague indifference that had been their norm for as long as she could remember. When in the kitchen, she noted how Annalee would approach quietly, and after spotting her, scurry back upstairs like a scolded mouse. When contact was unavoidable, they passed awkwardly on the stairs, or looked towards the floor as they crossed at the bathroom door. A small, almost imperceptible nod was the standard greeting if their paths collided in the street.

For the first time, Tawrie wondered if her absence might encourage her mother to seek help. If she wasn't on hand for every eventuality, could that be the thing that forced Annalee to take control? She could only hope so. Either way, she knew it was time to make the changes she needed for her own happiness, time to forge her own path. It was a prospect that was equally terrifying and thrilling.

'Excited for tonight?' Her nan released her and looked into her face.

'Yep!' she lied. Her energy for the Gunn Fire wasn't what it usually was, not with the lingering hurt of Ed wrapped around her heart and the acute disappointment that this year she had thought she might arrive at Rapparee Cove with a partner to dance with around the flames, one who might help her home afterwards. She fully accepted what Maudie had said – that he was not 'the one', because if he were, things would have turned out very differently. Yet, even with this level of understanding, her heart didn't hurt any less.

'But first my swim.' She kissed her nan on the cheek. 'I'm not working until mid-morning – Connie said no rush – and then we'll do cards when we have cake later, like we usually do.' It was only in recent years that she'd understood the ritual was more than likely to allow her mother to sober up and be present for the exchange of birthday cards around the kitchen table. Birthday or not, there was no way Annalee would let an event like this get in the way of her drinking.

'See you later, birthday girl!' Freda called.

'See *you* later, birthday girl!' She double-pointed at her nan. These jokes never got old.

Tawrie pedalled up Fore Street and gave a start at the sight of the honey-coloured lamplight coming from the landing of Corner Cottage. Was he home? Her heart skipped and she held her breath when a woman's face appeared at the window, an older woman in a nightdress who with her arms wrapped around her trunk, looked wistfully down the street. Just like that Tawrie's heart rate settled and she kept her gaze onward. It wasn't surprising he'd rented the cottage out – that was, after all, the norm and it had, she'd noticed, been empty for nearly a month. It was closure of sorts and she did her best to embrace it.

'New beginnings. I'm not going to fret over him today. Not on my birthday,' she whispered, determined to keep her maudlin thoughts and reflections at bay.

Her arrival at Hele Bay Beach was not without fanfare. She cackled with joy as she parked her bike.

'Happy birthday!' Maudie carried a helium balloon towards her, a big red heart. Tawrie howled her laughter. Jago stood by his wife like her assistant but his face was split by a smile that shouted affection. 'Okay, Jago, one . . . two . . . three . . .' She counted her husband in and for what felt far longer than the seconds it took, her fellow Peacocks sang 'Happy Birthday' to her very loudly, slightly off-key, and even included a couple of 'Hip hip! Hoorays!' for good measure at the end, which only prolonged the ordeal.

Tawrie found it both endearing and mortifying in equal measure and was thankful the beach was empty.

'Wow! Thank you! Thank you so much! And will you look at that! Can't remember the last time I had a balloon! It's ace, thank you both so much!'

'We've made you a cake too. Come back to the cottage after our swim and we can have hot chocolate and a big slice.'

'I will, thank you, Maudie.' Reaching out she pulled the woman into a hug, before tying the bobbing balloon to her handlebars. 'And thank you, Jago! You guys are the best.' She then hugged the lovely man who had given her such good advice when it felt like her heart might break and she couldn't seem to stem her tears.

'Right!' Maudie clapped. 'Birthday or not the water awaits!'

The three walked with purpose down to the shoreline, every bit as proud and upstanding as the peacocks they represented.

An ostentation, no less.

Tawrie pulled away in the water and quickly got into her stride, breathing in time with each stroke. It was one of those swims when her body fell into an easy rhythm and she felt at one with the sea, taking as much comfort from it as she ever had.

Here I am, Dad . . . Here I am on my birthday. I wonder what the day was like for you? Nan has said it was the best day of your life when I came along, but she says a lot of things, I'm sure, just to make me feel better. Over twenty years without you and one day soon, I'll surpass the age to which you survived. That'll be strange. All the time I think about how different my life would be if you were here. One loving parent would make all the difference. I think I'd be less lonely. And that's all any of us want, right? Not to be lonely. Anyway, I have news, big news. I guess, I've decided . . .

'Tawrie! Tawrie!' Jago shouted with such urgency, it was a jolt to her system that halted her in her tracks, prematurely ending her chat with her dad. She stopped swimming, breathing hard, and turned in the water to locate him. Her overriding thought was that one of them must be in peril and she quaked at the thought, knowing how easy it would be to open a mouth, let the lungs fill with water and sink to the bottom like a stone. It wasn't a pleasant thought, but one she'd had often enough nonetheless – never with the intention of doing so, but rather as a terrible reflection on how she had lost her dad.

'Look! Look!' Jago yelled, pointing towards the horizon. Instantly satisfied it was not a crisis, that neither he nor Maudie were in trouble, she held her salt-water-wrinkled palm over her eyebrows and stared ahead.

A sharp intake of breath and her mouth stayed open, entirely rapt by the sight that greeted her, followed by Maudie and Jago's excited yelps and chatter.

There was one, two, three, four! *Four!* Four dolphins breaching the water in a glorious arc, the colour of slippery wet grey beach slate. Droplets of seawater, each one a tiny prism, fell from their glistening bodies as they leapt and re-entered the water with such agility she felt like a cumbersome thing in their ocean. She'd seen dolphins around the coast before, of course, but this display, this welcome so close to her was a greeting on another level entirely. It was a gift. The very best gift on this, her special day, and her tears gathered at the pure privilege of it. Surely something of this beauty and magnitude on today of all days was a sign!

As Tawrie felt the ripples of their breach and re-entry surround her, she knew it was a once-in-a-lifetime moment, one that she'd remember forever, and she was thankful that Maudie and Jago were part of it, knowing how special it was for them too. A reward of sorts for taking to the water every day and gratefully sharing this space with these beautiful creatures in the place that was their home.

'I can't believe it! I just can't believe it! What a thing! What an incredible thing!' Jago shouted, making his way over to his wife. Tawrie watched as the two embraced like hand-holding otters, and a lump rose in her throat.

'Thank you, Daddy,' she whispered, letting the water lap over her shoulders. *Thank you . . .*

◆ ◆ ◆

Connie was washing her car on the cobbles on the quayside with a bucket of water by her side.

'Car washing? What's the point of having Sonny and washing your own car?' she laughed, masking the flutter of nerves in her chest. She had worked at the café for nearly ten years; this was not going to be easy.

'Have you met the kid? He goes to school in odd shoes, how could I trust him with this beauty?' Her cousin ran her hand over the shiny paintwork of her beloved van. 'Anyway, happy birthday, Taw!'

'Aww, thanks!'

'Excited about tonight?' Connie asked enthusiastically as she re-soaked her sponge and doused the windscreen.

'Yep.' She nodded.

'Is that it? "Yep". Jesus, I've had people show more joy when I give them the bill!'

'Well, you are very reasonably priced.' She smiled at her voluptuous cousin who even managed to make cleaning the bird shit off her windscreen look sexy. 'How come you're out here?' She pointed to the Café on the Corner.

'Jan and Gay can handle things; we've got too much to do! I've cancelled your shift – we need to get ready for tonight!'

Tawrie laughed, delighted to have this day off and looking forward to celebrating in the way she'd been doing since her birth. Her heart might be bruised, but it was still her birthday and that meant celebration. But first, she had to talk to Connie and her stomach churned at the thought, aware that once she'd told her, news would reach her nan's ear and then her mother's. She exhaled slowly.

'There's a lot to do – we want a roaring fire and cushions!' Her cousin beamed, as if the idea was a novelty. 'Lots of cushions!'

'So what can I do to help?' She pushed up her long sleeves.

'Plenty later.' Connie wrung out the sponge and let the water trickle along the floor towards the drain. 'Twenty-nine, Taw, it's quite the age!'

'Thanks, I think.'

Connie stopped cleaning and stared at her. 'There's something I want to say to you. No' – she put her finger over her lips as if mentally regrouping – 'there's something I *need* to say to you.'

'Sounds ominous!' She pulled a face. 'And actually, there's something I want to say to you.'

'Okay, you first.' Connie indicated with the sponge and flicked water in her direction.

She drew breath, trying to remember what she had settled on when having the conversation in her mind; it had seemed so much easier in her head.

'Go on then! We haven't got all day!' Connie urged. 'What did you want to say?'

'What it is . . .' She blew a breath out nervously. '. . . is that I'm leaving the café. I'm giving you my notice and I'm going to college. I'm going to become a nurse, a midwife, specifically. I'm going to do it.' She waited to see how Connie would react, while feeling good to have said it out loud, her words coasted out on pure relief!

'You're *leaving*?' Connie stared at her.

'Yes, I mean, not immediately. I need to sort dates, but I have an offer of a place, and I haven't even told Nan yet, but that's the plan. I'm going for it.' The two women locked eyes. 'Say something!'

'My darling cousin, sister to me, lifelong friend.' Connie toyed with the sponge in her hand. 'I think that's bloody marvellous!' The quiver to her bottom lip suggested otherwise.

Tawrie put her hands on her hips. 'Well, that's charming! You could have at least tried to talk me out of it, told me you'd miss me, how valuable an asset I am, anything!' Humour right now was the mask she reached for.

Connie started to laugh.

'It's not funny! It's a whole change of life for me, a huge step!'

'Yes, it is, my love. And you're right, you can't work in the café any more.' Connie put her sponge in the bucket and came to face her. 'I love you, Taw, we all do. You're a smart woman who's been hiding away in this little corner of the world, serving bacon sandwiches and cups of tea to fill your time. You're right, you need to stop doing that and think about what you really, really want to do with your life, where and how you want to live it. You've always said you wanted to help bring babies into the world. And now you're actually going to do it!'

'Well, I hope I can. I've said a lot of things in my time, including that I wanted to marry Harry Styles. Don't think that's likely now.'

'But that's the point, Taw. Nothing is likely unless you chase it, unless you make it happen. I think you'll be a brilliant midwife.' Connie sniffed the emotion that pooled in her eyes. 'This is it, little Tawrie Gunn, you're setting yourself free. I'm so proud of you.'

'Thank you, Con.' Her throat tightened with emotion, unable to imagine not spending each day with Connie and the gang. She watched now as her cousin straightened and cleared her throat. 'Nan will be okay, won't she, if I'm not here all the time? And . . . and Mum?'

'They will. They will be fine. They were always going to be fine – or not. And you hanging around, hovering with your emotional first-aid kit wasn't going to make a bit of difference. That's the truth, my love.'

'That's what I figure. It's taken me a while, but that's where I'm at. I need to let go.' Looking out over the sea, she knew the responsibility she felt for her nan and mum weren't the only things holding her back. *Where are you, Dad?* The question leapt into her thoughts.

'You do, you need to let go.' There was a beat of silence while this sank in, before Connie shifted on her feet, exposing her nerves. 'Okay, here goes, now I have to tell you something.'

Tawrie had momentarily forgotten that her cousin also had news. She hated the mounting tension and wished that whatever it was Connie had to say, she'd just spit it out.

'Sebastian Farquhar is waiting for you on the bench by Verity.'

Connie flicked her head towards the Verity statue that dominated the quay and Tawrie's heart jumped.

'What? *What?*' She tucked her unruly hair behind her ears. A third of her wished she weren't wearing a dirty t-shirt, a third wondered if it would be a good or bad idea to go and see him and a third thought she must have misheard, as this was ludicrous. 'How, when did . . . ? Oh my God, why? I mean . . . I don't think I can see him! I don't know if I want to!' She turned in a circle like a dog chasing its tail until Connie reached out to steady her, holding her still with her hand around her forearm.

'He came by this morning. I told him to go away.' Tawrie knew her cousin was taming the actual words she used. 'He said he had to see you blah blah blah and that he'd be on the bench by Verity at eleven o'clock.'

'What's the time now?' She felt a rising sense of panic. Supposing she was too late to see him, supposing he'd already gone? And equally horrifying was the prospect that he was still there waiting and she would have to face him.

'It's seven minutes past.'

'Shit! I need to think!'

'You need to do whatever your heart tells you to, Taw.' Connie let go of her arm. 'It's really that simple.'

'Nothing about this is that simple!' Her gut churned and she thought she might actually vomit right there on the cobbled quayside where she'd first seen him all those weeks ago. 'I'll go and see him and tell him not to come back; I think that's for the best. Closure.'

Connie kept her voice level. 'This is something you and Farquhar need to sort out, one way or the other. But I will say that I've never seen you so happy as you were when you thought things were rosy between you, and it's been a long time since I've seen you so low when they weren't. And the way you've bounced back over the last month has been incredible; it shows strength and I'm proud of you.'

'Thank you, Con.' Just the idea that he was mere minutes away from her at that very moment was almost more than she could stand. Her heart jumped as she mentally wrestled with what she might say to Ed. It was a lot.

'You've got this; you're amazing!' Connie reached for her sponge.

'This just might be the shittiest thing to do on my birthday!'

She cursed the warble to her voice and made her way along Broad Street, heading towards the mighty brass statue of Verity that towered over the pier. As she walked along the quay, Nora and Gordy were coming in the opposite direction with Amber, their beloved golden Labrador.

'Hey Tawrie, how are you? What a day!' Gordy looked up at the blue sky where clouds were no more than wisps and the air was still.

'Happy birthday!' Nora tutted at her husband, who seemed unaware of her special day.

Tawrie loved Nora and Gordy, was always pleased to see them, but over their shoulders she could make out the pink linen shirt of the man she was going to meet, a man, she noted with relief, who was prepared to wait a while for her, and a man with whom she needed to have a final conversation, a decent goodbye that would free her to go off to college without the many what-ifs that crept into her thoughts in the wee small hours. She willed Nora to speak faster.

'My sister and nephew are arriving any minute – we're all so looking forward to the Gunn Fire. I'm bringing baklava – we used to live in Cyprus and I think I've finally mastered it! And if it's no good we'll wait till everyone's had a drink or two and then bring it out.'

'Oh Nora, that sounds fab, can't wait to taste it!' She smiled. 'Anyway, see you in a bit!' She didn't want to be rude but was in no mood to stand chatting. Hurrying past, she slowed as she walked along the pier, minding she didn't trip on the gaps between the concrete planks, as she was wont to do, just in case he was looking.

Again she felt the swirl of nausea. It had been easy to dismiss their brief encounter as no more than a fanciful diversion, something she had built up in her mind, imagining the glorious connection to fuel her own fantasy. The reality, she suspected, was nothing more than a lukewarm dalliance, for him at least, and it was vital she remembered this if she had any hope of keeping her dignity. This self-instruction, however, was a darn sight easier to adhere to when she wasn't about to come face to face with him, the man who had made her heart skip, her brain muddle and had filled her with something that had felt a lot like happiness.

It was as she stared at the back of his head, sitting on the right-hand side of the bench with his arm stretched out and resting along the top, that he turned to stare at her over his shoulder, as if he'd sensed her arrival.

The pier wasn't deserted, nor silent, there was the usual toot of car horns, the call of gulls, the chatter of visitors and the sound of waves breaking on the slipway and against the harbour walls. And yet the two stared, eyes locked, as if they were alone. Her initial reaction was to cry: the sight of him as profoundly moving as it was desperately sad for all that had passed. She tensed her jaw and pushed up under her nose with her thumb, managing to keep her tears at bay. Her eyes never left his and she watched as he turned slowly, wiping his own nose and, she could see, tensing his jaw.

Stepping cautiously past him she caught his scent, clear and distinct, and one that had filled her dreams since the first time she'd seen him. He was familiar, attractive and captivating, yet also a stranger. And a liar. Not a person to trust. A shape-shifter who had deceived her into thinking he was the one, when all the while he was someone else's. Her strength was in recognising it and knowing that this was goodbye.

She sat in the middle of the bench, a position she chose carefully, not wanting to seem churlish by going to the far end, yet nor could she risk a sightseer plonking down between them and ruining all attempt at conversation. This felt safe. Next to him but not too near.

'Hap—' He coughed, his voice hollow, raw. 'Happy birthday, Tawrie.'

'Thank you.' *He had remembered.* She kept her eyes on Verity, the magnificent statue that dominated the entrance to the harbour standing at over sixty feet tall. Tawrie loved everything about her: Verity the pregnant warrior woman, holding her sword aloft in one hand and scales of justice in the other, standing on books that represented truth. The allegory wasn't lost on her.

'You look wonderful. It's so good to see you in person and not . . . not just in my head.' She knew what he meant but stayed silent.

'There's a lot I want to say,' he continued. 'So much I've imagined saying to you and yet now here you are and I've gone blank. I can only think to give you clichés that I know you won't want to hear.' His voice alone was enough to warm her, to draw her in. She moved a little to the left.

'Probably not.' She was at least grateful for his insight.

'I came back with my mum; we got in late last night.'

She nodded. So it was his mother she had seen in the window. A woman who under different circumstance might have been important in her life. It was an odd thought.

'Tawrie—'

'Look,' she cut him short. 'I've come to see you because it felt rude not to and I think we need a goodbye that's calmer, and final. I didn't want you pitching up at the café and it being awkward or anything.' Her words carried the tang of realisation that he could turn up at the café whenever he felt like if she no longer worked there. 'So yes, I thought it would be good to say goodbye properly. To wish you well.' The tremble to her mouth said more than her words, and a glance at his face told her he felt the same.

'I've been in limbo; I can't sleep, I can't eat.' He didn't seem to be listening.

'That's really nothing to do with me,' she countered, recognising her own behaviour in his confession. 'I just wanted to see you one more time and leave things . . . neatly.'

'It's everything to do with you, though.'

'It's not, Ed. Not any more.' To say his name was electrifying; an image of the two of them in that big bed in the attic flashed into her mind. She blinked furiously. 'You were the only one holding all the cards.'

'I know that's what you think.'

'Because it's the truth,' she countered calmly.

He nodded, his expression mournful. 'I guess so. It's just that . . .'

'What, Edgar?' She used his full name, putting distance between them; this one word indicative of a formality she neither felt nor wanted.

'You only see the world through your lens.'

'Doesn't everyone?' She glanced at him and he was beautiful. She hated the disloyalty of her gut that folded in want.

'I don't think so, and what I mean specifically is that you're immersed in your own world, safe, small, and I'm not knocking it, not in any way—'

'Sounds like you might be a bit.'

'No, it's just that it seems to me . . .' His tone was measured, his turn for defensive action. '. . . that you've been hurt, that you have a lot going on and so you keep your drawbridge up, never deviate from your routine, head down, eyes low, trying to get through life without getting bumped into or pushed off track.'

'Again, Edgar, doesn't everyone?'

'No.' He shook his head. 'Some people want the challenge of things being shaken up a bit; they don't want to tread gently or predictably, they want to take the rough road and learn as they go.'

'Maybe I'm just different to you. Plus, your observations are based on knowing me for a nanosecond.' No matter that it felt like a lifetime.

'I do know you. You know I do.' She felt an upturn in her mood at this. His defiance, his insistence. 'I think we have a pretty similar outlook; I just think it's easier to live your best life when you're open.'

She pulled her knees up and held her arms around her legs. 'I was open to loving you. I was open to it all.'

'Taw, we can't say goodbye, this can't be it.' He looked close to tears and it killed her.

'I think it has to be.' She cursed the crack to her voice. 'I'm agreeing with you. It's easier to live your best life when you're open.' She spoke earnestly. 'I only came here to say goodbye. Closure.' Her throat hurt, the longing for him made no allowance for this truth. She bit her lip, not wanting to remember nor remind him of that beautiful encounter when they'd got merry and laughed their way up the stairs to the room where she had woken feeling desired, happy, whole.

'You have every right to feel the way you do.' He held her eyeline. 'But I'm not a liar.'

'I think . . . I think you've lied by omission, not giving me the full picture is lying,' she whispered, her eyes gazing out to sea.

He nodded, and this was agreement enough. 'I'm sorry.' He twisted to face her. 'I'm so very sorry.' His words were warming, welcome. 'But I didn't know what to say or how to say it. Have you ever got caught up in a situation that you wanted so badly to last forever that you kind of believed it and to shatter it felt too painful, so you went along, hoping the universe might help put everything in place? Even though you know deep down you're ballsing things up spectacularly, and it'll come and bite you eventually.'

'Funnily enough I do know how that feels.' He was describing their whole, brief relationship. 'And actually, Ed, I don't blame you, not really. I'd choose Petra,' she joked, even though the words were like glass in her mouth. 'She's probably from a loving family and her mother is not living at the bottom of a bottle of vodka, and she was probably conceived in love; she knows how stuff is supposed to work! I'm not like that. I'm damaged. I come from damage. I'm pretty sure my own dad went out alone to escape my mother's shite. He never stood a chance, did he?' She cursed the tears that pooled. 'I'm not going to end up like him or her. I'm making changes to my life. I understand that I can't fix things here, can't continue to be the sacrificial glue that holds everything together. People are still going to fall down steps and get lost at sea no matter how much I smile or make tea or quietly tiptoe up the stairs night after night. I have to build my own life. As do you. I don't wish you any harm, Ed.' Her voice broke. 'The opposite, actually; I hope you and Petra will be happy together.' It was hard to say, but no less genuine for that.

'Taw—' He tried in vain to interrupt, but she had found her stride and was not going to quieten her voice in case she lost her nerve.

'I'm sure she knows about being loved and loving someone, and what to do and how to act, and I'm sure her drawbridge is lowered. I bet she didn't drop her pants on the floor the moment she met you, and if she had I bet they wouldn't have been her old grey, never to be seen, usually saved for a period pants, that she keeps meaning to throw out! I bet they'd be pale and lacy! I can't even get my knickers right!'

Her chest heaved with all it expelled. Her speech was fast, her breathing irregular and her desire to cry strong. It was as if someone had pulled the plug out of her emotional tank and out it all came. All of it, whether she wanted it to or not.

'Tawrie, please—'

'Please what?' She turned to face him. It was hard to get the words out with her throat narrowed with emotion. 'You keep saying that, but I only wanted to say goodbye, for us to end calmly. You look gutted but you can't choose someone else and be devastated. That's not fair on any of us. That's not how it works.' She paused, her next words were whispered and he listened, closely. 'The news that you're getting married landed like a dagger in my chest. And I don't know if I'll be able to see you in the street in the summer and wave politely, thinking of what might have been while you visit Corner Cottage with your wife.' She drew breath, her words genuine and ones that crawled around her thoughts when there was a lull in her day. 'Which, incidentally, if I stand on the little stool in the bathroom and look out of the window, I can see the roof of. Or if I look from the landing I can see the bedroom window. How do I do it, Ed?' She hated this open admission, it wasn't what she had intended, but she couldn't stop. It was too much, all of it. 'How do I switch off how I feel? I think going away is the very best thing for me for a million reasons.' She stood to leave. There was no point in continuing this exchange.

'Sit down. Please, Taw. Just sit down. *Please.* Just for a minute.' He pointed at the bench and she sat, feeling she owed him this at least, his chance to get a neat goodbye. 'I've told Petra, and I moved out the day we left here.'

She wished she didn't feel the flicker of joy at this news. It did Petra, innocent in the whole deception, a great disservice and was confusing. This was supposed to be goodbye.

'Is she okay?'

'Yes, I think so. Her mother has moved in. I've been staying with my aunt. I want to show you something.' He twisted on the bench to face her and she took the opportunity to stare at his lovely face.

'What is it?' Despite her best resolution, she was curious.

He reached into the confines of his backpack, resting against the bench, and pulled out a couple of sheets of folded paper.

'I'm in no mood for reading a letter, and if it's a birthday present of some kind, then I don't really want one from you, Ed, and I mean that kindly.' It was too painful; the thought of having a memento to pore over in his absence, inhaling the paper for the faintest whiff of his touch in her low moments. Even the thought was pitiful.

'You're going to want to make time to read this.' He squished up next to her, his thigh touching hers, his arm alongside her arm, and just this physical proximity was enough to send a shiver of longing through her bones.

'I really don't want to, Ed.' She knew that any words of promise would only haunt her in the quiet hours and make her question her resolve; words that might pluck the string of loneliness that provided the saddest background music to her life.

'They're not my words.' He ran his fingertips over the flimsy sheets. 'They're my mum's.'

'Your mum's?' She turned to face him, his mouth closer now and she felt her gut bunch with a visceral longing to kiss him.

'Yes, from her diary, when she and Dad moved down and my sister and I were sent to stay with my aunty for a bit. That summer I told you about.'

That summer . . .

'It was such a weird time for Dilly and me, unsettling, odd. We were told it was our forever home.' He swallowed. 'I remember they'd tried to recreate the bedrooms we'd left and I was just happy to be back with my mum and dad, and over the moon to be by the seaside. Until it all went pear-shaped.'

'What happened?' It was still an odd thought, that had his family stayed, he would have been a boy on her doorstep, like Needle, always there.

'What happened is all in her diary. I've read it – we read it together, and I wrote some paragraphs out. You have to see them.'

'I'm not looking at words from your mother's diary! That's like . . . no! It's such a personal thing. I'd hate the thought of anyone looking at something I'd written in confidence.'

'Do you write a diary?' He stared at her.

'No, but that's not the point.'

'The thing is, Tawrie Gunn, it's not only her story of that summer, it's mine, and it's yours too in places.'

'What d'you mean? How is it mine?'

'I want to read you something.'

He was making little sense. 'Ed, I haven't got time, I need to . . .' Her mind couldn't think quickly enough of a place or chore on which to hang her lie.

'What you need to do is listen. Trust me.' He fixed her with a stare before unfolding the paper and coughing gently to clear his throat.

With the sheets balanced in his right palm, he took his time, reading slowly, as each word painted a picture that took her right back, the description enough to help her remember, and her face broke into a smile.

'"Met the lovely Annalee Gunn today, my neighbour. A woman infatuated and desperately in love with her husband, Dan. I cried like an idiot. She was very sweet to me. I like her. She brought her daughter, Tawrie, who according to Bear was the worst playmate – her inability to play on the Nintendo 64 and her lack of interest in football consigning them to never be friends! At least he and Dills will know someone when they start school, even if it's just to nod at in the corridor or to stand next to in the lunch queue . . ."'

There was so much to mentally unravel; she put her hand over her mouth, laughing while tears gathered.

'She met my mum! She said she was lovely!' It was a surprise to hear and strangely comforting too. 'And that bit about my dad, read it again!'

Tawrie sat forward, concentrating on every nuance.

'"A woman infatuated and desperately in love with her husband Dan."'

'Wow! Oh my goodness!' She couldn't help the tears that now trickled down her face. It was bizarre to hear about them as a couple, something she'd never witnessed first-hand, and new information too, another facet of her dad's life that helped build a picture. And it wasn't what she had previously envisaged. Any mention of him when she had so little actual memory was like unpicking the stitches that kept all her hurt contained and out it came now, leaking through her eyes.

'Yes, wow! And I'm sorry I thought you were a terrible playmate, but honestly? That still holds true for me if you have no Nintendo 64 skills . . .'

'I remember it now, Ed. I remember coming to Corner Cottage. I thought it was familiar when I walked in, but I couldn't put my finger on it. But that was it – I came to your house for a play date.'

'I remember it too.'

'Is there more about my dad, any more about my parents?' She hardly dared ask.

'Yes.' He handed her the sheets of paper, the words painstakingly written out in his uneven script. 'I think you should go someplace quiet and read it. I've read the whole thing and it's helped me understand my life and a bit of yours too.'

'Thank you, Ed.' She took the gift and placed it on her lap. It was the very best present on this, her birthday.

'Let me know when you've read them, maybe we can talk then?' he asked with so much hope it took all of her strength not to fall into him.

'Come to the Gunn Fire if you like.' It felt like the right thing to do, an invite for this man who had taken the time to write out these pages by hand and had waited for her here on the bench by Verity. She stood and stared at the sheets of paper in her hand. Nervous and excited in equal measure.

'I might just do that.' He beamed.

CHAPTER TWENTY-FOUR

Harriet Wentworth

14 September 2024

'There you are! I was starting to worry!' Harriet called as she leaped up from the leather chair, relieved to hear the knock on the front door and knowing he'd hear her, remembering how chatter used to float through the timber as strangers passed by. 'Oh!' It was a surprise to see a young woman standing on the step. She knew instantly who it was, as if the folded sheets of paper in her hand weren't clue enough. 'Tawrie!'

'Yes.' She nodded. 'I'm sorry to bother you.' She looked a little awkward, standing on the top step, her eyes clearly red from crying.

'You're not bothering me. Not at all. Happy birthday! Bear told me.'

'Thanks.' The girl looked down; Harriet got the impression she wasn't having the best day.

'I was actually just getting a little bored, thought Bear would be back by now, but he's off on a trek up to the Torrs and then walking around the reservoir, apparently. I remember it's beautiful, the view down over the town.'

'It is. I don't do it often enough; you don't do it when you know you can, do you?'

'I guess not. Come in! Please, come in!' Harriet hoped it was the right thing to do, inviting her inside without knowing how their mid-morning rendezvous had gone. It felt a little risky, but if reading her diary had reminded her of one thing, it was that when true love came knocking, you had a duty to usher it in. Charles had shown her how to love again, how to trust, and the thought of Bear and Tawrie not being given their shot was almost more than she could stand.

Tawrie hesitated but stepped inside and looked towards the stairs, her eyes double blinking as if in memory.

'This is rather odd, isn't it?' She thought it best to cut to the chase. 'First of all, as I'm sure you know, this isn't the first time we've met. In fact, the last time I opened the door to you and walked you through into the sitting room you were only a little girl! I can picture you then as plain as day. You were shy.'

'Still am a bit.' The girl smiled awkwardly. 'I didn't know, or at least I didn't remember until . . .' She lifted the paper on to which Harriet's son had transcribed certain sections of her diary.

'Yes, which brings me to the second odd thing: you've read bits of my diary, know some of my deepest darkest thoughts. Bear asked, of course, before he gave them to you and I could tell it was important to him.' She hoped this was a prompt to encourage Tawrie to be open about her feelings too.

'Yes, I feel . . .' The young woman tried to find the words.

'A little awkward?' Harriet cut in. She knew *she* did.

'No, not at all.' Tawrie shook her head. 'A little in awe of you! Absolutely in awe! Is it okay to talk about, that . . . that . . . time?'

'Yes.' It was an easy answer, despite the girl's hesitation. 'I mean, for years after I would have given anything not to talk about it, but now, with the glorious benefit of hindsight . . .'

'I hope you don't mind me saying this, Mrs – Mrs, erm . . .' She blushed.

'Please, Tawrie, call me Harriet. I mean, you've been inside my head, literally, so I think we're way past Mrs Wentworth!' She tried to lighten the moment.

'Harriet, thank you.'

She liked her nature: open, unassuming, sweet – very much, in fact, like Bear. She was pretty too, naturally so, her stance confident.

'I was going to say I think you're incredible; remarkable. Ed has told me bits of what happened, I hope . . . hope that's okay to say,' she stuttered. 'I don't know how you got through it, how you did it. I mean, I've had my heart kind of, well . . .' Again that blush and Harriet could see that Bear's feelings, not least surrounding the complex nature of their beginning, was a shared thing.

'So I guess this brings us nicely to the final odd thing,' she interjected. 'The fact that my son says he's in love with you after only knowing you for five minutes!' She laughed, trying to make light of a situation that felt precarious to say the least. It was, however, the elephant in the room and it felt right to mention it. 'In fact, he said that after one unremarkable chat with you, he would have gone anywhere with you. He just wanted to be with you. It really struck me. I don't think I've felt that way, never had that flash of something that had the power to knock me off my feet, to change the course of my life.'

'It was the same for me. It is the same for me,' Tawrie confessed and her face softened at the admission. 'It's the same for me. And I've tried very hard over the last month or so to switch it off, to walk away. I've even made plans for my future, but it's not that easy.' She smiled, suggesting this discovery was far from an issue.

The way she repeated herself suggested to Harriet that it was a realisation.

'Can I ask you, Harriet, about this?' She held up the words Bear had transcribed.

'Yes, of course! Let's go sit in the kitchen.' She pulled out a chair for the young woman and sat opposite. 'Gosh, feels like I'm at an interview.' She laughed and Tawrie swallowed.

'That's what Ed said. We sat here and played Uno.'

'I thought you were going to say he'd cooked for you and I would actually have fallen off the chair!'

'He bought crisps, but couldn't find a bowl to put them in.'

Harriet liked the imagining of it and loved the insight into their time together. It sounded unpretentious, honest and the basis of a friendship that she knew from her own experience, as she pictured Charles at home in his apron, was the best foundation on which to build a long-lasting love. Charles . . . for whom she would shuck off this cage around her heart, and for their sons too, who deserved more than a mother and wife who wore the thinnest layer of armour that no matter how tiny, invisible almost, was still a barrier.

'What part of the diary did you want to ask me about?' She gripped the sides of the chair, arms braced as if this might enable her to better withstand anything that was uncomfortable to hear.

'Okay, it feels weird.' Tawrie held her eyeline.

'For both of us, trust me!' She pulled a wide-mouthed face. 'I think it's best we treat it like the removal of a Band-Aid – do it quick!'

Harriet smiled weakly. Her words written in that little green book had been like a Band-Aid: the thing that she reached for to help her feel better, to cover up the wounds, to aid her healing.

Something, she now realised, she had no further use for, as the wound beneath, the cuts once so deep, were now healed.

'Here we go.' Tawrie drew breath. '"*I study other couples, surreptitiously of course. I stare at them through my sunglasses, either as we walk or I sit . . . There's one couple in particular who have caught my attention . . . Always together, engrossed in one another, come rain or shine, as if the whole world exists just for them and whatever is going on around them is merely the backdrop to their love affair. I feel drawn to them, admiring of their apparent devotion and envious of it too. He has thick curly hair, a stocky man, kind eyes, handsome, and she's petite, dark hair too, but straighter. She has big brown eyes and seems coy, smiling gently, as if her happiness is a precious thing, a secret that she carries close to her chest. They fascinate me. Forever arm in arm or hand in hand. If they slow or stop, she places her head on his shoulder. As if only this level of contact will do. They are like one person, split down the middle. Golden.*" It's incredible to me that you're talking about my parents!'

'I was indeed.' She remembered them clearly, even writing the words; it had been like holding up a mirror to her and Hugo and all they had lost.

'I think about them walking, taking the same path that I do each day, walking in my dad's footsteps.'

'I understand.' Harriet thought of her mum, who she missed dearly, and knew that to place her hand on a handle she'd touched, sip from a cup that had felt the curve of her lips or slip a blanket around her shoulders that had brought her mother similar comfort, meant more than she could express.

'Shall I carry on?'

'Yes, please.' Harriet settled back in the chair. It wasn't quite as painful as she'd envisaged; hearing her words brought to life.

'This next bit is hard for me. I've read it over and over a hundred times today, and it's like looking at something that's horrible, scarring and yet compelling, rubbernecking my own parents' misfortune, kind of.'

'Would you like me to read it out loud?'

Tawrie nodded and slid the sheets of paper across the tabletop. Harriet took a beat to scan ahead, familiarise herself with her own jottings, thinking again how lucky the couple were to share what, at the time, had been beyond her reach. 'If you want me to stop at any point just say.'

'I will.'

She read slowly, deliberately. "*The news spread like a lit fuse . . . travelling along its twisted, looping route, gathering gasps and cries as it went along the way. The worst kind of whisper as each fragment of news was added to, as the bigger picture revealed itself.*" They exchanged a lingering look, both understanding what came next and the magnitude of it. "*There's been an accident . . .*" she whispered. "*A man went overboard.*" Oh Tawrie, are you sure you want me to carry on?'

The sight of the young girl's tears falling from her reddened eyes was almost unbearable to witness. The girl nodded and rolled her hand, indicating for Harriet to continue.

"*I found out it was Daniel Gunn . . . Shock doesn't come close. How my heart aches for sweet Annalee, and for Dan too, the handsome man. I feel for his family, his kind mother, and most of all for that little girl, Tawrie, whose daddy is not going to come home.*" She looked up as Tawrie sobbed, covering her face with her hands. "*Tonight, it's as if the whole town weeps . . . but no one will ever weep as hard or as long as Annalee, the woman with the sparkle in her eye, as she walked with her arm linked with that of the man she so loved. I shan't ever forget her happy, happy face, a woman who looked like she had the whole world at her feet and was loving every second of it. How I envied her and how I envy her still, knowing that the strength of feeling she will carry in her heart is something I can only dream of . . .*"

Harriet paused to let the news settle for both her and Tawrie, wanting the girl to know the joy her parents felt in each other's company, a joy that she wished for her and Bear. Also to allow her silent thanks to flow to Charles, who right about that moment was probably fretting over what to make for supper. Her beloved husband, with whom she had the whole world at her feet and loved every second of their life together.

'"*I hope they find Daniel Gunn. I hope they get to lay him to rest and say their goodbyes. I hope his daughter finds peace, safe in the knowledge that her parents adored each other and that she was made in love . . .*"'

'I was made in love.' Tawrie sniffed. 'They loved each other so much!'

'Yes.' Harriet reached across the table and held her arm. 'I only saw her one time after and she looked very different. She'd got old and frail and hollow and broken overnight. And to me that was as desperately sad as the loss of your father.'

She looked towards the wide sash window and took in her reflection, remembering that when she'd sat here among the ruins of her marriage, she too had been frail, hollow, broken. But not any more; she had survived. She had come out the other side stronger.

'It's hard to think that the woman is my . . . my mum.' Tawrie wiped her face on her sleeve. 'She's been . . .' Her mouth moved but the words wouldn't come. '. . . different to that.'

'I think you've probably had two mums. The one before she lost Daniel and the one that came after. I know my kids would probably say the same about me. The old me when my marriage failed and the me now, different.'

Tawrie nodded and sniffed, her words coasting on stuttered breath.

'I've thought for the longest time that, erm, that my dad, might have gone out to deliberately . . . to, erm . . .' Another sheet of

359

distress covered her face. 'That maybe my mum had, because of her behaviour, her issues, driven him to go out on his boat, to stash his watch and wallet and . . .' She couldn't voice it.

Harriet shook her head vigorously. 'God, no! I only met your mother properly once, but I saw them together countless times. They were oblivious to the rest of the world, deeply devoted is how I would have described them and how I heard them described by people who knew them better than me.'

'It's a wonderful thing for me to know, a relief. My nan had told me they were happy, but she sugar-coats everything for me, always has. I thought she was just painting me a picture.'

'We do that when we try to protect our kids. I know when we moved here and I was doing my best to find a way forward with Hugo, I was always beaming at the kids, trying to sell them the idea that everything was going to be grand, as if I could make it so just by saying it enough. But I now know that honesty is everything, truly. And finding something that's yours alone and brings you joy, something you do just for you. For me it's my garden. My little haven where I can escape the noise, the clutter, the kids. I have very boisterous teenage twins.' Just the mention of her boys was enough to fill her with a desperate longing to see them, hold them. She couldn't wait to get home.

'Yes, Ed said.' Tawrie took a deep breath and seemed to settle. 'I swim, that's my thing.'

'Yes, Bear said.' They exchanged a smile. 'Where do you swim?'

'Down at Hele Bay Beach, every morning from March to September and sometimes in the winter too if it's a fine day. It started off as a way to clear my head, get my thoughts straight. I was sick of tootling along in the middle lane – just about coping with life, you know?'

'I do.' It was easy to recall sitting at this very table knowing she was only just keeping her head above water.

'But now it's so much more than that. I love being in the sea. It revitalises me like nothing else. There's something extraordinary about being that close to nature, submerged in it quite literally. I swim with two of my friends and today we saw a school of dolphins leaping out of the water, so close I felt I could have touched them. I won't ever forget it. It's not the first time I've seen them, but all leaping and so close, like they were putting on a show.'

The young woman's eyes sparkled.

'Your family must be so proud of you, Tawrie, and I don't mean that to sound patronising; you're an exceptional girl.'

Tawrie laughed nervously. 'Don't know about that. My cousin might not be talking to me!'

'Why?'

'I'm joking, she will be, but I just quit my job in her café. I need to go find what I really want to do and working for her was preventing me from doing that.'

'It sounds like a smart move.' She smiled. 'Exciting.'

'This last month has been a time of reckoning, made me think about everything. What I do know is that I need to set a path and walk it, and second, my dad probably thought he had all the time in the world, but life's short, isn't it?'

'It is. But don't be hard on yourself, Tawrie. You lost your dad in the most brutal fashion and it tore your family apart, that's hard for anyone to deal with, let alone a little girl. The fact that you're upright and fantastic and functioning is, I think, remarkable.'

'Thank you. Thank you, Harriet.'

It was a day, it seemed, for high emotion, as she too grappled with the desire to sob. What a fool she had been to let her past dictate her present, especially when she really did have it all.

'So, I guess the final question I have, and please don't think I'm interfering, but what happens now for you and Bear?'

Tawrie looked out towards the window, her response considered. 'I told him he was weak and I called him a liar. I was hurt and wanted to hurt him.'

'At least you recognise that. And I can assure you he's neither. Not weak, but rather kind, so kind he'd never do what Hugo did, not intentionally, not maliciously. I think Hugo would still say he was a little hard done by. But Bear knows he messed up. And for the record, I'd vouch for him.'

'With all due respect, Harriet, you're his mum – that's not going to stand up in a court of law!'

'You're probably right.' They both laughed. 'But it's the truth. I'd trust him with my life. I was a little doubtful of the strength of feeling he described, all that love-at-first-sight malarkey.' As she spoke, she thought about her husband, his infinite capacity for kindness, and her heart flexed.

'But now?' Tawrie asked with eyes wide, as if desperate to hear the answer she wanted.

'Now, having met you both, I think you kids need to give it a go. But what do I know? I didn't get it right until I was middle-aged!'

'I should go. I'm supposed to be helping organise the party.' Tawrie stood and made her way to the front door. 'When you see Edgar, Bear, Ed,' she fumbled, 'can you tell him to come to the Gunn Fire and please come too, Harriet. I think it'd be nice, and Mum will be there, probably.'

'I'll tell him, and thank you for the invite. Happy birthday, Tawrie Gunn.'

'Thank you.'

The girl lifted her hand in a wave as she walked swiftly down Fore Street, smiling back over her shoulder. Harriet thought she looked a million miles away from a girl who was tootling in the middle lane of life, just about coping. In fact, she looked like a girl who had her whole future ahead of her and it looked rather golden.

'It's time.' She closed the front door. 'It's time.'

Taking a seat in the old leather chair, she let her hands briefly rest on the arms, before reaching for her phone.

'Harriet! All okay?' There was the unmistakable note of alarm in his question. It was unusual for her to call and she was sure that, like her, the first thing she'd think of if he were calling her was that something might have happened to the kids.

'Yes, all good, Hugo. Kids are fine, just, erm . . .' And then it happened. Harriet Wentworth in that instant turned from the competent scientist, loving wife, and dedicated mother into a woman twenty years younger with the heavy twin yoke of distress and dilemma about her shoulders, weighing her down and down. 'I just wanted to . . .' She tried again from a throat that had narrowed with sadness and recollection.

'You okay, old girl?'

'Yes. Just give me a minute.' Closing her eyes, she tipped her head back and took deep breaths. With the thumb of her left hand she felt the raised bump of the gold band on the underside of her third finger. A gold band she would never have had if she and Hugo had stayed married – and a man like Charles would likely never have come into her life. Both thoughts too terrible to contemplate. Sitting upright, she swallowed. 'I'm in Corner Cottage.'

'Ah.' His acknowledgment, she knew, an understanding of just what a return to the place might mean.

'I . . . I found the diary I used to keep during our— during that . . . that summer.'

'I remember.' He spoke softly.

'It's odd. Even the sight of the little green book was enough to transport me right back to then.'

'I see.' She heard him take a deep breath. 'So come on then, H, let's have it!'

'What?' She'd lost the thread.

'Well, I never hear from you, never directly, not since . . . not since then, really. You never call to chew the fat or make small talk.'

'You want me to call and make small talk?'

'No.' He was as ever direct. 'I mean, I did, once upon a time, shortly after when it was all so . . .'

'Shitty.'

'Yes, when it was all so shitty. So let's just cut to the chase.'

'Hugo, I don't know what you—'

'Well, obviously, you've gone to Ilfracombe, read your diary, had the fires of fury stoked and realised there's a couple of poison-tipped daggers you forgot to stab me with, so get it out of your system. But I can probably guess: "How could I destroy our lives, why did I do it, did I not care about the kids, how has life worked out based on all the very many mistakes and error of judgement I made?"'

'Hugo, just stop!' She was firm.

'Oh, don't worry, you'll get your turn—'

'Hugo,' she interjected again. 'The reason I wanted to call you, and the thing I want to say is—'

'Here we go,' he muttered.

She ignored him. '—is that I forgive you.'

'What?' he asked, calmer now.

'I forgive you and I want nothing for you but happiness and peace.'

'You forgive me?' His voice no more than a scratchy whisper.

'Yes. I forgave you a long time ago, just never said it, never really thought about it, but it occurred to me that maybe we should have this conversation . . . Hugo?'

The sound of his tears was surprising and hard to hear.

'I'm . . . I'm sorry, H.' He sniffed. 'Sorrier than you will ever know.'

It was a shock to her how good it was to hear his remorse so earnestly expressed.

'I've been thinking recently, how long do we have left of life, Hugo? Who knows – five years, ten, twenty? Whatever it is, we need to not let that time in our life when things fell apart be a cloud. That would be crazy, wouldn't it? I mean, we have two amazing kids together; we have an awful lot to be thankful for.'

'We do. We really do. And thank you, H, thank you.' He swallowed his distress. 'Maybe, erm . . .' He coughed. 'Maybe we could all get together: you, me, Charles and Ramona. You could come for dinner, we could invite all the kids! Get the pasta on, garlic bread, whip up a tiramisu, couple of bottles of red . . .'

'That sounds lovely,' she enthused.

'Right then. Bye, H.'

'Goodbye, Hugo.'

She smiled to herself long after the phone call had ended. Charles would rather get a pizza and eat in their little kitchen – anything other than subject himself to an evening like that, and she was inclined to agree . . .

It was an hour or so before she felt composed enough to call her husband.

'Hello, my darling!' His joy at no more than knowing it was her on the end of the line was like a bolt through her chest.

'Charles,' she began, quite unable to get the words out as emotion filled her up.

'Don't rush, Harry, we have all the time in the world, all the time in the world.'

His voice in her ear, linking her across the miles from one house to another, from one time to another, was like a door opening. She sat back in the chair, as she had so many times before, her hair now a little greyer, skin a little more aged, but with a peace in her uncaged heart that was as new as it was exciting, and as she drew breath to speak, it was like a firecracker going off in her chest. She could hear a sound like a note, like music, like . . . She didn't know what. Clarity? As if fog had cleared in her mind. And she knew beyond any shadow of doubt that she'd have gone anywhere with this husband of hers. Anywhere. All she wanted was for him to hold her, talk to her, be with her.

'I just . . . just wanted to say that you are everything and I love you, I love you entirely, for always.'

'And I you, Harry, my love. And I you.'

CHAPTER TWENTY-FIVE

Tawrie Gunn

14 September 2024

Tawrie raced up the steps towards Signal House.

'Here she is! The birthday girl!' Freda shouted from the kitchen where she stood at the countertop, preparing marshmallows on sticks for the Gunn Fire. Connie was at the table, sipping tea.

'Here she is! Off to see the bloody world and leaving her poor cousin in the lurch!' Connie winked over the rim of her mug.

'So I take it Nan knows.' Tawrie narrowed her eyes at the girl she loved and who would make a terrible spy, what with her inability to keep anything secret.

'Nan does indeed.' Freda busied herself at the sink, a surefire clue that she was hiding her emotions and trying to be brave; it tore at her heart.

'I was coming to talk to you now. I forgot that my cousin was the human equivalent of the *North Devon Gazette*. So what do you think, Nan?' she asked quietly.

'I think it's marvellous, little maid! I'm so very proud!' Tawrie and Connie exchanged a long look as Freda dabbed at her eyes with her pinny.

'We all are, Taw, and I'm not at all bitter about the fact that you'll be off figuring out how to deliver all them babies you harp on about, while I'm stuck with Gaynor and Jan, farting around! But it's the right thing, love.'

'I'm always going to be there for you, Con, and you, Nan.' She meant it; the prospect of starting her new career, however, filled her with excitement. With forms filled out and a place on offer, it felt like her adventure was just beginning. 'And I'm not thinking of going that far, only Exeter.'

'I know that, you daft cow!' Connie tutted. 'Mind you, with only one half-decent road, you might as well be in the wilds of Scotland – there ain't no quick in and out of Ilfracombe.'

'True that.' Freda smiled at her weakly, recognising that even if she were only in Exeter – an hour and a half away on a good day – it was very different from having her here at Signal House.

'How's it all going? Anything I need to do?' She realised time was marching on and there were only a few hours until the celebration at Rapparee Cove.

'Nope. Needle and I have built the fire. He's gone off to get the beer. Bar table is all set up, flaming torches are positioned and I've dumped enough cushions and blankets down on the sand that Rapparee looks like an open-air Ikea!'

'Sounds perfect.' She felt the first flicker of joy at the prospect of the party.

'It's gonna be a cracker!' Her nan, it seemed, was similarly looking forward to it.

'Is Mum upstairs?' She pointed overhead. 'I need to talk to her. I need to talk to her urgently.'

'About going away?' Freda asked.

'Yes, but something else too. She . . . she loved my dad, didn't she?'

'She really did, love.' Freda looked out of the window, a little overwhelmed. 'She went out about an hour ago. Try the King Billy maybe?'

'Thanks.'

She had just turned to leave when Connie called out, 'Well, don't keep us guessing, how did it go with the wanker-named blow-in?'

As she tried to think of what to say and how to say it, her face broke into a smile that spoke more than any words. Harriet's biased assessment and their meeting in front of Verity earlier had filled her with something very close to peace. Whatever happened, whether Ed and she shared a future or whether she was able to wave at him in the summer when she was home from college, she knew that either way, it was going to be okay.

'Oh, bloody hell!' Connie slammed her mug on the table in utter disgust. 'I can't deal with that smug, happy face all day; it's enough to make me puke! I've told you before, think miserable thoughts and start frowning a bit.'

Tawrie could feel the love in her cousin's ribbing.

'Leave her alone, Con! It's our birthday!' Her nan shoved a couple of marshmallows into her mouth and danced around the kitchen.

'It is that. Happy birthday, my lovely.' Connie winked.

'I'm going to find Mum.'

'Are you going to be all right?' She saw the concern in Freda's face, which was comical despite her tone as her voice was muffled by marshmallow.

'I am, Nan. I really think I am.'

She took a second to capture the image in her mind: this cosy Gunn collective in the chaotic kitchen, knowing that when she

369

headed off to pastures new, it'd be gatherings like this she would miss the most.

◆　◆　◆

'Looking forward to tonight?' Uncle Sten shouted from the open window of his truck as it crawled past her on Fore Street.

'Yep! Have you got your dancing shoes on, Uncle Sten?'

'Dancing shoes? I don't need no dancing! It's all about the four Ps Taw! The four Ps!' He chuckled and drove on towards the quay.

The King Billy was quiet; Needle was behind the bar.

'All right Taw? Just nipped in to sort the beer for tonight.' He rubbed his hands together. 'We've built one hell of a fire!'

'Oh, we have, have we?' She smiled.

'I reckon I'm winning her round.' He looked like a child at Christmas. 'I spoke to Gary; he's given me a couple of pointers.'

'Needle, I'm not being funny, but if Gary knew what made our Connie tick, they'd not be divorced, now, would they?'

'You've got a point.' He rubbed his chin, as if considering this very thing.

'Have you seen my mum?' A quick glance around the place and it was evident her mother was not in residence.

'No, I've been down at the beach.'

'Well, no worries. I'll try the wine bar.'

'See you later!' he yelled as she sped up and made her way across the street. It was a strange feeling, knowing she could at any point bump into Ed – the thought alone left her a little giddy. Her stomach rolled at the prospect of reunion, but first, she needed to find Annalee.

After she'd visited every pub she could think of, the wine bar and even the beach where Annalee sometimes sat with friends, Tawrie was a little stumped. She called her nan, but her mother had not ventured home. And then it occurred to her: maybe she had made her way down to Rapparee Cove, in preparation for the get-together.

Tawrie walked the coastal path over Hillsborough and sure enough, as she looked down into the secluded cove from the vantage point on the clifftop, she spied the small, dark head of Annalee sitting on a wide cushion just up from the shoreline, staring out to sea. She felt the rise of a lump in her throat, wondering if she'd ever seen such a lonely sight.

Going intentionally slowly, she made her way down the steps, giving Annalee time alone before she disturbed her peace. Under a veil of caution she trod the sand, admiring the huge bonfire that Needle and Connie had constructed, with driftwood and logs piled high in the middle of the cove, as well as the smattering of cushions and blankets that were dotted here and there on the sand. The bar was dressed in a Tiki-themed skirt, and it all boded very well for the evening ahead. Not that the Gunn Fire was paramount in her thoughts. Right now, it was all about talking to her mother. Harriet's diary had allowed her to see her mother from a new angle and it was illuminating. Tawrie felt a little swamped with emotion. All those wasted years . . . but this was no time for maudlin reflection, it was the time for action, for change, the dawn of a new era.

'Mum?' she called softly, not wanting to frighten or surprise her, but equally needing to make her aware of her presence.

Her mother turned sharply and wiped tears from her cheeks. Tawrie's eyes were drawn to the fresh thin silver scar that ran from the top of her eyebrow to her hairline. A grim, permanent reminder of her tumble down the steps.

'I was just . . .' The woman pointed out over the calm sea. The breeze blowing off it was carrying the last of the summer warmth before autumn staked a claim on the landscape and their mood. She made to stand up. 'I'll go.'

This was the point they had arrived at, unable to be in close proximity, properly estranged.

'No. Please stay.' She placed her hand on her bony shoulder. 'I've been looking for you.' Tawrie sat down on the cushion next to her and raised her knees to rest her elbows on them. They hadn't fully conversed since the morning after Annalee's accident when with fatigue at the masthead and frustration bubbling over, they had both spoken plainly. It had been a month of strained relations and Tawrie felt the flare of shame at all the things she'd said. This time, she kept her voice low, calm. 'I really need to talk to you, Mum.'

'What about?' The fear in her mother's eyes was distressing, as was the croak to her voice. There was no mistaking her wariness, a reminder to Tawrie to proceed with caution. If they had spoken more over the years, her question might have been comical – there was so much they needed to talk about!

'I have no . . . no memory of you.'

Annalee laughed out loud. 'No memory of me? I don't get it, I'm right here.' She tapped her fingers over her heart as if she had to make sure she was present. 'I'm right here.'

'No, Mum, you're never right here. You're always planning your escape, hatching a plan to get to the pub, or into some bloke's car or on to a beach, on a jaunt, a jolly, away, away from me.'

Annalee's eyes brimmed. 'No, no, Taw, never away from you.'

'Yes.' Her tone was steady, kind, despite the topic. 'Always, away from me and then always returning drunk, slurred, blurred, gaze askew, clothes twisted, not present, stumbling up the stairs to bed, sometimes alone, often not. And I tell myself that you're a grown woman who can do what she wants with whoever she wants.'

'I don't . . . I don't remember a lot of, erm . . .' Annalee's voice cracked and she fell silent for a beat.

'Do you remember Harriet Stratton, Mum? She stayed in Corner Cottage one summer, the summer when we lost Dad.'

Annalee nodded, her head all of a wobble on her thin neck.

'I had a coffee with her; she had two little ones and then I don't think I saw her again. She left and didn't come back, until yesterday, in fact.'

'Oh.' Her mother looked blank, as if it were very little to do with her.

'It's her son, Ed, that I've been seeing . . . that I saw.' She didn't know how to phrase it.

'The one who broke your heart?' Annalee asked, her eyes wide.

Tawrie nodded. 'I don't think he meant to.'

'Hurts just the same though, right?' Her mum dug her finger in the gritty sand and pushed a hole.

'Yes, it hurts just the same.' She took a breath. 'Harriet kept a diary when she was living in Ilfracombe. She was going through a fairly rough patch: her marriage was ending and she wrote everything down.'

Still her mum dug with her finger, burrowing into the sand, keeping busy, distracted, swallowing frequently, her gaze wide.

'I don't want to upset you on our birthday, and I didn't plan it this way, but it's important we talk.'

'We are talking.'

'I'm going away. Moving to Exeter to study, to become a nurse.'

'Wow!' Annalee looked a little shocked. 'I think . . . I think that's amazing.'

'You do?' Her heart lifted at the reaction.

'Yes, it takes courage to change your life. Courage I can't seem to find.' She gave a false, sharp laugh.

'I think you can find the courage and I also want to talk to you about Dad; the two things seem kind of connected.'

'What do you want to know?' She looked up at her for the first time.

'Everything!' This was the truth; her thirst for the detail that would help build the picture of him could never be sated.

Annalee took a deep breath, as if mentally regrouping. 'It's not been easy for me.'

Tawrie didn't try to fill the silence that followed, giving Annalee time and space to talk.

'I loved him. Loved him so much, still do.' This time her smile was soft. 'He was perfect. Perfect for me. He was all I ever wanted. Good-looking, funny, and he adored us.'

'Did he ever wear nail polish?' It was a question from left field that she'd wanted to ask for the longest time, but had never felt able to because the topic of Dan was almost taboo in the Gunn house. The snippet of memory, those hands lifting her up to see over the harbour wall and feeling so safe, so very safe.

Her mum laughed loudly and unexpectedly, instantly placing her palm over her less than perfect teeth. 'Yes! You liked to paint his nails and he'd let you! His big old hairy hands with purple nail polish on them! His mates used to rib him but he didn't care, said they could hold a pint or throw a punch just the same. That shut them up!'

Purple nail polish with tiny flecks of glitter. She could see it now, smell the acetone . . .

It was with relief and a burst of joy she had the memory confirmed as real. A small part of him that she would carry forever.

'You also used to make him whistle. He had the loudest whistle of anyone on earth and you found it hilarious! It'd send you into giggles!'

Tawrie looked down as her tears gathered.

'Did he drink too?' It was another blunt ask that had been simmering away in her thoughts for some time.

Annalee shot her a look and Tawrie knew the addition of the word too, which had just slipped out, was as telling as it was incendiary.

Her mum shook her head. 'Neither of us were big boozers. I mean, the odd glass, beer gardens in the summer. He liked a pint with Sten and at the Gunn Fire, of course, but not really.'

'So you started drinking, after . . .'

'I don't drink that much. You make me sound like some old wino and I'm not.'

Tawrie stared at her, unsure of where to go in the face of this self-delusion and with little energy for another row, especially today.

'I don't know what to think, Mum. Since he died, it's been chaos. Chaos and sadness for all of us. I'm guessing it must be as exhausting for you as it is for us. I know you like to go out and meet . . . people.'

'People? Men, you mean. I like to meet men, is that what you're driving at?' Annalee scratched at her scalp with her dirty fingernail.

'I guess so. I just think you're worth more, that's all, and it was hard to know how to intervene when I was a kid and, truthfully? I'm just twenty-nine and I still don't really know how to say what I think, or what to do to help you.'

'I don't think anyone or anything can help me.' Her mother pulled a cigarette from a packet and placed it on her bottom lip. Using a disposable lighter to set it alight, she inhaled the noxious smoke like it was fresh air. Tawrie hated the smell.

'I've felt responsible for you for so long, and always hated how I can't fix things. I think me going away will be good for you in some ways. I won't be there to worry and you'll have to take a bit more responsibility and keep an eye on Nan.'

Her mother gave a wry laugh. 'You're not responsible for me and you certainly can't fix things, Tawrie.'

'I wish . . .' She floundered. What did she wish?

'To what, wave a magic wand?' Annalee suggested. 'Turn back time?'

'I guess.' She closed her eyes briefly and let the sea breeze lift her hair.

'The reason' – her mother took a long drag of her cigarette – 'that I pick up men, or rather let them pick me up, is complicated, there are many reasons.'

'How?' she pushed, this felt like progress.

'Take your pick: comfort, company, sex, flattery, a diversion. Any of them will do, but in a haze of booze being wanted by a man, any man, it makes me . . .'

'Makes you what?' she hardly dared ask.

'It makes me forget.' Annalee nodded and toyed with the cigarette between her fingers.

'Forget?'

'Him. Your dad. Dan. My Dan. Just for a minute, I forget how good I had it and how my life felt on track and how one moment of choppy sea, and one moment of distraction and one traffic jam on the A361, which meant Sten was late, and my life changed forever. Forever! And everything, *everything* I thought I knew and everything I had planned toppled into the sea with him. A matter of seconds, Taw. That was all. You'd think, wouldn't you, that for something so life-changing it might be a long, drawn-out thing, giving me time to adjust, to understand what was happening and why; a chance to intervene, change the outcome. But no, just seconds and it was all gone. Just like that.' She clicked her fingers. 'He was gone and I haven't really felt anything since. Nothing.'

Her mother's words were like glass that shredded her heart. It was desperate, it was sorrowful and it was her story too. For the first time in as long as she could recall, she didn't feel disgusted by Annalee's admission, but rather she was full of pity for the shell of the woman who had once had it all.

'In Harriet's diary, she wrote about seeing you and Dad out on your walks around the harbour.'

'We did that every night. I still walk the path, but I do it after dark and I make out he's by my side and I chat to him just the same.'

It was odd to hear how her mother's actions so eerily matched her own.

'I talk to him in the water when I swim, as if he's there with me.' It was a hard confession from a throat constricted with sadness.

'He is there with you. He is.' Annalee stubbed her cigarette into the sand and Tawrie seized the moment and reached for her hand. It trembled in her palm like a frightened bird.

'And sometimes, for the longest time in fact . . .' Tawrie hesitated, knowing that her thoughts were a little odd. '. . . I thought he lived on Lundy and that's why I couldn't go there, in case he wasn't there and I would really lose him then, forever. And that's why I've never wanted to go away to college, Mummy, in case . . . in case he comes back and I'm not here.' Her tears sheeted her face as distress stole her poise. 'In case he's not staying, but only popping in and I miss him. Miss my chance to tell him how much I love him, how much I miss him!'

'Oh, Tawrie!' Annalee looked into her face, her sorrow mirroring her own. 'He isn't coming back. I wish he was!' Her mum's distress was hard to witness, yet strangely unifying too. 'We both lost so much, didn't we?' Annalee asked, as tears ran into her mouth.

'Yes, but we didn't lose each other. And I think he'd want us to do better, wouldn't he?'

'He really would. I . . . I need help, Tawrie! You were right in what you said when we had that row: I need help! I've taken solace in drinking. It helps me to escape, to forget.'

'I don't think it helps anything, not in the long run. We'll get you help, Mum. You're not alone. But it is a mountain only you can decide to climb, no matter how much we will all cheer you on. I want you to succeed, for you! For you and for me and for Nan. You deserve a better life, we all do. I know it's hard but no matter what happens, I will always love you. I'll never stop loving you, Mum.'

Annalee lay her head on her shoulder and Tawrie was shocked by the insubstantial weight of her frail body.

'I'm so lonely!' she sobbed.

'I know, Mum. I know. But this is a huge step, a new beginning. I can feel it.'

'I miss him so much! He took my heart with him, Tawrie, and I can't, even now, twenty years later, I can't figure out how to go on without him. I don't even know if I want to. When I tripped down the steps, as I fell, I kind of hoped that I might not wake up! I miss him!'

Tawrie wrapped her arms around her mother's slight form and held her tight, and there they sat as the beach started to fill with friends, neighbours and family. Dusk pulled light from the day and music started to drift across the cove. Needle lit the flaming torches, and still they sat, side by side, unified in grief and with a greater understanding, which Tawrie knew was the key to becoming closer, to building for their future.

'I need to go and have a word with Needle; I'll be straight back.'

Annalee nodded as Tawrie grabbed the man who had always been there, the man who was practically family, the man who had a boat . . .

◆　◆　◆

The evening grew louder, busier and she and Annalee sat side by side on the shoreline, happy to just be in each other's company.

Nora and Gordy, with their relatives in tow, came over and bent low to kiss her cheek.

'Happy birthday, Gunns!' Gordy shouted and headed off to the bar, pulling Nora with him, his arms around her waist like they were young lovers. It was nice to see. They were greeted by Georgie, the milk delivery guy, and his wife Cleo who was smiley, barefoot and pregnant with their second child. Tawrie felt her mother move a little closer, as if just the sight of couples in love was a little more than she could stand.

'Here we go.' One of Annalee's friends from the pub arrived and handed her a tumbler full of wine. She took it into her shaking hands and sipped it, like medicine, and Tawrie understood that withdrawal from the drug that held her in its grasp was going to be a slow process. The beach was filling up with faces she recognised and some she didn't, but the atmosphere was wonderful. She had planned on going home, showering and changing, but time had caught her out and here she was, grubby jeans, messy hair and a t-shirt she'd worn all day.

A quick glance to her left and she spied Connie and Needle sitting by the newly lit fire, huddled close with a blanket around their shoulders as Sonny raced around the beach with the other kids. This, too, brought her joy. Needle, brilliant Needle who had agreed to help her out; a constant in their lives and that, she understood, was no bad thing.

Freda came alongside and dropped down on to the sand, surprising Tawrie because she hadn't heard her approaching.

'Room for a small one?' she asked, as she nestled next to Tawrie and joined them in looking out over the sea. Her nan kissed her cheek.

'We've just been sitting here talking about Dad.'

Freda nodded. 'He loved this place, Ilfracombe, every inch of it. He loved it in all weathers and he loved nothin' more than to be out at sea looking back at the harbour. The cliffs and the little buildings all perched on the rocks, the big old spire of the church rising up. I've been thinking recently about getting old and dying in a chair in front of the telly.'

'Hey, well this is nice. Happy birthday!' Tawrie cut in and the three of them laughed. It was rare and nice to have Annalee present and joining in, one of the gang.

'No, I'm not getting all maudlin, what I mean is – it's what Dan would have wanted. The way he went. It would have been his perfect end. He was the happiest man I knew, never a day of sadness: he adored you two, he loved his life and he never knew a moment of grief, the lucky thing. It's the rest of us who are swimming in this pool of sorrow. He would never have wanted to leave you, of course not, but how he died? I reckon he'd feel honoured to have been taken by the beautiful briny sea.'

Tawrie recalled the majesty of the dolphins jumping up out of the water, a sight that she knew would stay with her forever, and she more than understood. This love of the sea was a shared thing with her beloved dad.

'I think you're right, Freda.' Annalee spoke up.

Her nan reached across and took her daughter-in-law's hand. 'I never forget, Annalee, that despite all of our troubles, you loved Dan the most and you have stayed. Not like that other flighty thing who married Sten. How could a woman leave her daughter and husband like that?' She shook her head and it was the first time Tawrie had properly considered the fact that Wanda had waltzed off with her Danish skipper, while Annalee, despite her issues, had stayed put, sleeping in the bedroom that used to be hers and Dan's. 'We've got each other, Gunns, we've always got each other.' Freda spoke with strength and Tawrie took comfort from it. 'And I guess you've heard this girl of ours has handed in her notice at the café?' Freda asked her mum.

'I have indeed.' She took a small sip of the wine. 'A nurse, can you believe it?' Annalee's look of pride felt like progress.

'I've always wanted to become a midwife, that's the plan.'

'Just goes to show it's not too late, Tawrie Gunn, it's never too late.' Her mother smiled at her, as if it were as much a reminder to herself as to her daughter.

'I see lover boy is back.' Freda nudged her.

'Yes.' Her heart jumped at the prospect of seeing him.

'Do you love him?' Annalee asked, her tears rallying as if she too could remember what it felt like in those early days.

'I think I do, Mum. I really think I do.'

'Then go get him, Tawrie, and hold him tight and never take a single day for granted.' Annalee's voice cracked at the words.

'I won't.' She stood and dusted the wet sand from her numb bottom. Taking a step away, Tawrie looked down at the two women with whom she shared this special day. 'I love you both. And I'm proud of us all.'

'And we're so proud of you.' Her mother started to cry and Freda moved closer to her.

'Talk of the devil . . .' Freda nodded as Ed made his way down the steps and across the sand.

'Hi.' He shoved his hands in his jeans pocket and stared at Tawrie.

'Hi.' She looked up into the face of this kind man, the man Harriet would trust with her life. She took a step towards him. 'I had a nice chat with Harriet today. I told her to come down tonight.'

'She told me.' He took a step towards her. 'I left her chatting to Charles, her husband. She might pop down later, but I doubt it. Parties aren't really her thing. I think she just wants to get home.'

'I see.' She looked up at him, liking the way his floppy hair fell over his forehead. 'And what's your thing, Edgar Stratton?'

He reached down and took her hand into his. She let her fingers rest there; the touch was electrifying, welcoming and she felt pure delight at the contact. Pulling her towards him, he kissed her firmly on the mouth, sending lightning bolts of joy through her very core.

'You. You're my thing. I love you. I really love you.'

Just to hear those words once again from his lips was enough to fill her with exquisite happiness and she understood perfectly what Annalee had expressed: *He was perfect, perfect for me . . .*

'And I you.' Her voice no more than a whisper.

'This is the life, Tawrie Gunn.' He smiled. 'Someone once reminded me that this is the one life we have, this is it! And so we all need to do more of what makes us happy rather than what we think we should.'

'Like what?'

'Like prioritising our happiness and not doing something because we're expected to or because we happen to find ourselves on that track. We need to jump off! Start over! Because if having to contemplate an existence without you has taught me one thing, it's that life is short. It's too short.'

'I think that "someone" is very wise. That's why I've chucked in my job and I have a place at uni. I'm going to be a midwife. That's the plan.'

'That's brilliant! Just brilliant!' His joy was tangible.

'Oi! Farquhar!' Connie called across the cove from beneath the shelter of her blanket, her face lit by the orange flames that licked the driftwood and crackled as they released fire fairies up into the night sky.

'Who me?' Ed touched his chest.

'Yeah you! Welcome to the family!' She raised her can of cider.

'Thanks!' He pulled Tawrie towards him, no doubt using her as a shield, which made her laugh.

'We'll love you forever, but if you put a foot wrong with our Tawrie Gunn, you'll 'ave me to answer to!'

Needle led the laughter that rippled around the cove, and as the music got louder, the flames danced higher.

'Let's dance!' Tawrie pulled him down the beach. 'Let's dance until we drop!'

'Yes, and then we're going to stay right here on the sand, looking up at the sky and lying here until morning, watching the movement, the light, the shifting darkness.'

'Our checklist,' she breathed.

'Our checklist.' He silenced her with a kiss.

The two were ebullient, giddy, despite not having had much sleep.

'Where are we going?'

He followed, as she skipped along Broad Street with her hand inside Ed's. 'It's so early!' he moaned. 'I want food! I want toast, I need coffee! I need a shower.'

'That's just too bad, I'm in charge!' she sang. 'It's a surprise!'

'It's not your birthday any more, so less of the bossiness. You can't be this demanding – this is just any other day. Besides, don't you have to go for your swim?' He looked back over his shoulder.

'Nope, I spoke to Jago and Maudie, explained that I'd be absent.'

'Actually, I saw them yesterday when I was on my hike around the Torrs.' He pulled a face.

'What did they say?' She was curious, trying to imagine the three of them chatting without her.

'Jago was very frosty and told me that you deserved more than to get lumped with a rotter. Maudie gave me a death stare.' He shivered.

'Ah yes, thought that might be the case. They'll come around.' She squeezed his hand.

'What if they don't?' He sounded horrified.

'Then I'll bin you and let them choose me a young man they approve of!'

'I hope you're joking!' He bent to kiss her.

'I hope we never have to find out!' she countered.

It was as they tripped along the quayside that she spotted Needle out on the water in his boat. She stopped walking and stood rooted to the spot. All bravado whistled along the wind as she faced the reality of her plan. She waved to the man who now stood proudly in his rigid hulled inflatable rib.

'Does your surprise have something to do with Needle and his yacht?'

'It might. Oh God, Ed, I thought I could do it. I want to do it, but I'm not so sure . . .' She pulled back on the pavement, feeling the very real beginnings of panic.

Calmly, he took both of her hands inside his. 'You can do anything. I believe that.' Gone was all humour; his face and tone were serious as he held her gaze. 'Do you trust me?'

'I think so.' The quaver to her voice was hard to disguise as fear lapped at her heels.

'Then we can do this together. We can do anything together. Needle, mate, we're ready for whatever adventure awaits!'

He gripped her hand tightly as, pulse racing, she made her way down the slipway and climbed clumsily into the rib on legs that felt like jelly.

'Welcome aboard!' Needle handed her a life jacket that she placed over her neck and which he fastened for her. 'You're all set. It's a perfect day for it, Taw. No need to fret, my lovely.'

'Where are we going?' Ed sat down next to her on the bench, which she was gripping tightly, holding on for all she was worth, letting her body roll with the swell of the waves in the harbour. The solidity of the man she loved sitting next to her did much to calm her.

'We're going to Lundy.' She blinked. 'I'm taking you to Lundy.' She let the words fall from her mouth.

Lundy. The place that had been a fixation ever since her dad had died, the place where his boat *Ermest* had turned up. The great lump of land visible on the horizon, when the mist and fog allowed, and where, when the mood or melancholy took her, she believed her dad might live, hiding in a cave, or rescued by selkies or mermaids, taken to live in a watery world in its outer edges, trapped.

'I'm scared,' she admitted.

'It's going to be okay, I promise. We are off to Lundy!' Ed sat close to her as Needle expertly manoeuvred the vessel out of the harbour, then turning west towards Hartland Point he picked up speed. The boat bobbed over the crests of the waves and she had to admit that while it wasn't the most comfortable means of transport, it was quite thrilling. Her fear began to dissipate, yet still she held on for dear life.

'Look!' It was twenty minutes into the journey when they were joined by a porpoise swimming alongside. 'That's luck right there!' Needle sat tall with his hands on the wheel and the morning sun lighting the face of a man who knew contentment.

'So, you enjoyed the Gunn Fire then?' she teased.

His grin was infectious. 'Reckon it's the second-best night of my life!' he shouted into the morning light.

'What was the best?' Ed, like her, was curious.

'Well, I haven't had it yet! But it'll be my wedding day, when I can walk down the aisle with Mrs Constance Threader-Smith.'

'Your surname is Threader-Smith! So that's why everyone calls you Needle!' She laughed loudly.

'I thought you knew that!' he shouted over the sound of the spray hitting the hull.

'What's your first name?' Again Ed was on the same page.

'Sebastian,' Needle offered without irony.

'Your name's Sebastian?'

'Yes, why?'

'No reason.' She bit the inside of her lip to stop herself from laughing out loud but knew that she would have great pleasure in telling Connie that she was going to one day be Mrs Sebastian Threader-Smith. Now that was a wanker-name if ever she'd heard one!

As Lundy grew bigger and the boat slowed, Tawrie felt the fold of anxiety in her gut. Her eyes scanned the shallower waters where rocks gathered and the cliffs rose up to the green-covered headland where puffins idled and squawked, chatting no doubt to the seal who swam and sang in the water below. Tawrie was thoughtful, wondering if this was her dad's last sight, this beautiful, beautiful island.

The three were quiet as Needle came alongside the slipway and she and Ed climbed out. It was a moment of trepidation, wondering how she might feel, but this was matched by her delight to have her feet once again on solid ground. He took her hand and with her backpack on his shoulder, the two started to climb the steep path up from the quay.

'What are you going to do, Needle?' she called back, grateful for the ride and worrying a little about abandoning him, while at the same time relishing the thought of time alone with Ed.

'I'm off to the Marisco Tavern. They do a bloody good breakfast!'

His continual optimism, his energy, was, she thought, a good thing for Connie, and for Sonny and Gary too. It was the kind of nature that would make it easier when life threw them a curveball, as she knew it could.

She was aware that sometimes in life an experience or destination is built up in your mind so the reality is never a match for the perfection you have created. Lundy, for her, was the opposite. The island was quiet, without traffic to clutter up the paths or add to the cacophony of life, but it was more than that. With only sporadic internet and phone signal, gone was the underlying hum of connection. There was no chatter of people, only the bleat of goats and the sound of the sheep munching the cud. Waves broke against the bottom of the cliffs and the overwhelming feeling was one of peace. She'd heard the word magical frequently used by visitors to her little town, but this place wrapped her in magic. No wonder she had thought it possible that her dad might be living here among all manner of mythical sea creatures.

After following the coastal path and walking for forty minutes, taking in the breathtaking scenery and letting the gentle wind blow out their cobwebs, they finally came to a stop at Battery Point with a stunning view of the island on both sides.

Ed sat and she plopped down next to him as the sun broke through the cloud.

'This is so beautiful.' She spoke aloud, tipping her head back to feel the warmth on her face. 'I brought breakfast. Open up the backpack.'

Ed did just that and produced a large punnet of glossy red cherries.

'I figured we should make new traditions,' she began.

'I like that thought very much.' He paused, clearly moved. 'One of the things I missed most when my parents divorced was all the little things, the in-jokes, the habits and peculiarities that we as a foursome shared, and it's not about them being exclusive, but that they made me feel like I was part of a gang, part of something that if and when the need arose, might provide a safety net.'

She understood. This fruit was a link to her beloved dad, and now something she'd share with Ed. New traditions; she liked the idea very much.

'But your mum and dad have always been there for you?'

'Yes, yes they have in their own way – they're great, but it's more than that. It's about all the small things that made us special. Playing Uno on Christmas Day after lunch, Dilly mis-saying "car park", so they were "par carks". Until Wendy moved in and insisted on correcting us every time we said it. And that small thing, that little line that connected the tiny dots of our existence was broken. It wasn't Wendy's fault, it must have irritated her, but either way it was broken. These building blocks that constructed all things that we would look back on and recognise as our history. I want that. I want to build a history with you. I want to share moments like this with you and with . . .'

She knew he was going to say 'our kids', and her heart squeezed in anticipation.

'With whatever might come next,' he finished. 'And so I can't tell you how utterly joyful I feel to sit here at Battery Point on Lundy Island eating cherries on the day after your birthday. We'll come again next year, if you like?'

'I do like.' Greedily she took a handful of the shiny fruit and popped one into her mouth. It was sweet and if she closed her eyes she could recall her dad handing her the fruit and how they'd laughed as they gobbed the pips into the flower bed.

'You know I've been here before,' he began.

'Was it with a girl who brought you cherries?'

'No,' he laughed. 'It was with my dad. We had a packed lunch of pasty and crisps and it was the second-best day of my life.'

'Oh yeah?' She smiled. 'And what was the first?'

'Well, I haven't had it yet, but I reckon it'll be when I get to watch Mr Sebastian Threader-Smith and his beloved Constance walk up the aisle!'

She laughed out loud. Then it was quiet, the air suddenly still and she felt clarity and hope in that moment of singular serenity.

'That day, here with my dad . . .' He swallowed the emotion on which his words coasted. 'It was the last day I remember things being perfect. I didn't have to worry about my mum or feel sick about Christmas or where I was going to live, or whether they would they row again. Or even that feeling of being almost split in half and pulled in two different directions. It was as if I knew that things were falling apart and it was paralysing, knowing there was nothing I could do to stop it. Like living beneath a boulder that's teetering and threatening to tumble. And no matter what I was doing, I had one eye on it, waiting for it to come crashing down.'

Tawrie reached out and took his hand; she knew what it felt like to live this way. One eye on Annalee, waiting to catch her when she fell.

'I understand. And I promise never to make you feel that way through my actions – never intentionally.'

'And I you.' He leaned over and kissed her gently.

They were silent for a beat, letting the magic of Lundy wash over them.

'Thank you, Ed, for coming with me, for getting it!' She lifted the cherries in her palm. 'I never wanted to come over here; I thought it was better to look at it from afar.'

'But it's so beautiful!'

'It is, but I guess I figured that if I never came here then it might be true.' She wiped the tears that pooled in her eyes. 'It meant my dad might be living here, happy, missing me, but here, alive. I knew that if I came and saw it for myself, it would confirm that he's gone. Really gone, never coming home, and what then, Ed?'

Reaching out he wiped her tears and pulled her into him. 'Then you properly grieve for him, you finally say goodbye and you let me love you, all of you.'

Tawrie submitted to the deluge of tears that clogged her nose and throat, her body heaving.

Ed held her tightly and it was only when she lifted her head to take a breath that she saw that the sun, now high in the sky, had sent a shaft of light to illuminate the water. It sparkled in an almost straight line, with hues of silver and purple, and if she looked very closely hints of glitter . . . A straight line that led all the way from Lundy to Ilfracombe, an intangible, unbreakable thread that she would, for the rest of her days, wrap around her heart.

Tawrie knew that she had found peace. And on this, the day she found the courage to say goodbye to her father, Daniel Gunn, she felt safe in the knowledge that her parents had adored each other and that she was made in love because what they had shared was truly golden.

'Goodbye, my daddy.'

She whispered into the stillness as the scent of warm cherries filled the air, knowing that she might wander far, but her heart would always live in Ilfracombe, a place that would call to her. Home.

EPILOGUE

Tawrie Stratton

Aged Sixty

It was without a doubt Tawrie's favourite time of the day, when the fire-red sun set over the harbour, and her granddaughter, Minnie, nestled back into her lap, resting her head on her ample bosom. She watched as her daughter Violet's little girl ran her fingers over the crêpey skin on her arm, clearly liking the way it wrinkled and moved under the pressure.

'What's the best place you have ever lived GT?'

This her family nickname, short for Granny Tawrie.

Tawrie stroked the little girl's strawberry-blonde hair and shook with laughter. 'Well, that's easy peasy. This place, Signal House.'

'Because we get to watch the sunset from here on the terrace?' Minnie might have only been seven but was whip-smart and about as sensitive as she was quick.

'Oh, most definitely. But also it's a bit of a trick question!'

'Why is it?' The freckle-faced child turned to face her, the two having enjoyed yet another long summer of beach time and picnics, swimming in the ocean and shell-collecting at Hele Bay Beach. 'Why is it, Gran?' Keen for a response, Minnie pushed impatiently.

'Because apart from my time at university in Exeter, when I got to come home for the odd weekend, it's the only house I've ever properly lived in, little one, and the only place I've ever called home. The Gunns, that was my surname before I became a Stratton, they've lived in Ilfracombe forever, we're part of the landscape.'

'And Nana Freda who died, who we go and visit at St James's, she was a Gunn!'

'Yes, Nana Freda was a fierce Gunn, a marvellous Gunn.' It might have been nearly three decades since her beloved nan had passed away, but sitting here on nights like this it was still possible to feel her presence, to hear her laughter on the summer breeze and feel the warmth of her arms, holding Tawrie fast. 'Yes, part of the landscape. In fact, little one, I reckon if you cut me open I'd leak seawater scooped up from the harbour down there on the quayside.' She pointed the two hundred yards down the hill where the view opened up like a fairy tale: flapping bunting, sparkling festoon lights, the waving masts of boats, chattering loved ones hand in hand, families eating al fresco, kids running in sandals still with sand between their toes, and the call of the gulls circling overhead, relaying messages as they swirled and rose en masse, following the *Barbara B* out into the water and hoping for a fish supper.

'And it's the only place *I've* ever been on holiday!'

'Would you like to go somewhere else, do you think, Minnie-moo?'

Minnie shook her head vigorously, as if entirely unable to imagine her summer anywhere else. This delighted Tawrie more than she could say, as did the fact that Violet longed to be back home here too.

Their daughter had made a first-class job of refurbishing Corner Cottage, and she knew it gave Ed more joy than he could describe when each half-term, summer break and more than the odd week-end, Violet trundled down from London with her husband Duke, Mortimer the Labrador, their new baby Lance, who right now was sleeping inside, and of course Minnie, who had brought more joy to Tawrie's life than she could ever have imagined possible.

On the odd occasion, they were even accompanied by Duke's mother Letitia, who still sighed or huffed before every sentence, made a point of looking out over the harbour as if there were something sour under her schnozzle and pressed the point that they really should try to get over to Biarritz, where the fish was to die for and the sun blissful! Tawrie always nodded that it sounded lovely, before exchanging a long, knowing look with her husband. Biarritz? Was the woman mad? For the love of God, they had Watermouth Cove!

'Yes, but you have many more years ahead of you, little Minnie, who knows where you might end up?'

'I'd like to end up right here.'

'You might say that now, my love, but no one knows what the tide'll bring in. That's the beautiful thing about life. You just never know.'

'Tell me about that day on your birthday when a whole family of dolphins came to say hello!'

It was a story Minnie liked to hear over and over. And one Tawrie was happy to recount.

'Well, I was in the water, when—'

A raucous scream echoed around the garden, a noise that came from out of sight at the bottom of the steep steps that led from Fore Street up to the front garden of their home. She watched her granddaughter sit upright, as if on high alert. The sudden noise and anticipation were jarring and they both stared at the path, waiting. It was almost a relief when two lolling heads appeared at the top of the steps, Ed and Annalee carrying a bag of groceries and meat from Turton's butchers for the planned barbecue.

And cherries, of course, always cherries.

Annalee was a wonder to her. Now in her eighties, she was full of life, her long hair tied into a low ponytail, her eyes bright, skin clear and with a joie de vivre that had been present since she finally reached sobriety just before Tawrie's thirtieth birthday, and months before they welcomed the arrival of Violet. A day when Annalee also turned thirty, of course. Her mother's strength of character in overcoming the foulest of diseases was phenomenal and Tawrie knew she would forever be in awe of her determination to win the hardest of battles. A battle she fought every single day.

Her mother had explained that when living under the cloud of alcoholism, she was quite unable to grieve the loss of the man she had loved, still loved. This was in part why it had felt easier to keep drinking, holding the tsunami of sorrow at bay, which she knew, the moment she was sober enough to face it, might possibly drown her. This fear, this threat on top of the chronic physical aspects of addiction withdrawal, had been too much for the broken-hearted Annalee to cope with.

But when her daughter had left for university, Annalee had figured it was time she stood on her own two feet, and she had done it. Tawrie would forever be thankful. She might not have had her mother holding the safety net for nearly two decades of her life – that job had fallen to Freda, the strongest Gunn – but she had more than made up for it since, standing tall and inviting the world to do its worst, ready to face all and any foe in order to keep her beloved daughter and her family safe. Sobriety had brought with it other gifts: a return of Annalee's wit and patience, a renewed interest in the world that found her reading, walking and sitting in the sunshine, appreciating the stunning part of the world they called home. Her pride in Tawrie was evident. She liked nothing better than to sit on any of the benches around the harbour, engage complete strangers in conversation and tell them how her daughter had delivered 'all the babies in the town'. It wasn't strictly true, but she'd certainly been there at the arrival of a fair few. She was loving her retirement, but there was still the odd day when she missed the noise and bustle of the delivery suite in Barnstaple, knowing how lives were inevitably altered within the walls of that room. Families that changed shape and couples who had to readjust, only children who gained siblings and grandparents who, without fail or guile, declared with absolute certainty that surely this was 'the most beautiful baby ever born!' To which she always replied, 'It really is and I should know, I've seen a fair few.'

She still swam every day when the weather was kind and even some days when it wasn't, but she never swam alone; that was, after all, rule 101 of wild swimming. Ed was a reluctant swimming pal, preferring to paint in the attic room, now a studio, where the light was just so. Violet, when she was home, loved to join her each morning, giving her just enough space at the beginning of her swim so Tawrie could voice her thanks, repeat her mantras and all the other things she had told Violet were conducive to a good start to the day, rather than confess that in those first few minutes of her swim she liked to speak to her dad, her greeting still the same.

Morning, Dad, here I am . . . Well, what news to tell you . . .

Violet also loved hanging out with Rocky, Connie and Needle's son who, born on September the fifteenth, just one day too late to join in the Gunn Fire, was more like a brother, and the two were as thick as thieves. Any misadventure in Violet's formative years and she and Ed could almost guarantee that it was Rocky Threader-Smith who was at the heart of it. He now ran a successful building company, where his grandad Sten liked to idle away the days, giving advice on just about everything! Sten and Gaynor were still, as they reached their end of days, the very best of 'friends' and had shared the same address for decades.

Connie had sold the café some time ago to Georgie and his wife Cleo, who were fine custodians of the little place on the corner. It was bought, apparently, with some inheritance after Cleo's mother had passed away. Cleo's dad had quite unexpectedly moved to Italy where, according to Cleo, he did very little other than eat pasta and drink red wine, prepared by his girlfriend Gianna, a chef. It was still the best place in town for a breakfast, even if the service had gone down a little in Tawrie's estimation. Cleo's niece Domino, a surly girl of sturdy build who was married to a fisherman and had two unruly daughters, lived above the café. Her hobby seemed to be bemoaning her lot in life and treating customers with indifference.

Rocky owned a house on the quay not far from Nora, who had stayed on in the area after her beloved Gordy had died. And with the loss of Amber, Willow, another stunning golden Labrador, had been the glue to help partially fix Nora's heart. She still popped into the Café on the Corner and always ordered carrot cake, with two forks.

Tawrie, of course, didn't know how long she had left of life, but one thing was for sure, with Ed by her side and that big old ocean to walk into every morning, she knew she'd want for nothing else. She might never have managed to swim to Lundy, might not have walked or swam the path she'd intended, but as she sat on the terrace with the fire-red sun slowly sinking behind the wall of night, the air taking on a chill and leaving them once again in soft shadow, she knew that home was the only place she wanted to be.

Harriet and Charles were currently in Boston, the place where they liked to stay with Dilly and Parker and their ever-expanding brood. The twins, Rafe and Louis, now both married and with three boys each, were still rugby mad, as were their sons. Tawrie always felt a little sorry for their wives, who had no choice but to love the sport.

Hugo, her father-in-law, was a less frequent visitor and his contact with Ed was sporadic. The last contact they'd had was a postcard from Goa, where he'd relocated for the winter and was, apparently, in love with a Portuguese yoga teacher who was getting him through his twilight years.

Ed had simply shaken his head and reminded her that his father had always loved love. This was pretty much her husband's approach to much in life: pragmatic, kind and always generous of spirit. It had served him well in all his years as an art teacher.

'Look what I found in the charity shop!' He bounded over and held up a cricket ball, his shirt, she noted, misbuttoned; some things never changed.

'Oh great, that's all we need, more bloody cricket balls!' His collection had almost taken over an attic room. His look of delight at this simple thing made her heart swell.

'Come on GT! Tell me about the dolphins!' Minnie tugged on her sleeve, impatient to hear the tale.

'Ah, yes!' Ed joined in, picking up their conversation. 'The great dolphin day! GT used to belong to a swimming group called the Peacock Swimmers.'

'But peacocks can't swim!'

He and Tawrie exchanged a long, lingering look.

'That's right, clever girl, they can't, but these peacocks did love to bob about in the water, didn't you, my love.'

'We sure did.' She smiled.

She felt a flash of loving nostalgia at the memory of the wonderful Jago and Maudie, who had taken a novice dipper like her and turned her into a wild swimmer – and what a gift that had been. Maudie had passed away only three years after that first meeting – she died peacefully, sitting on her terrace watching the water, and Jago had gone to join his great love only weeks later. She'd never forget Maudie's wisdom:

'Laughing is important. It helps get you through the tough times, the challenges. Taking care of each other isn't only a physical thing, it's about taking care of each other's mental health too. Not easy in this world with all its pressures, but we have always made sure we don't add to the burden; we're kind to each other. We're reliable. We provide a haven.'

Yes, this Tawrie understood. She looked around the terrace of Signal House: a haven.

'But if all you did was bob around, GT, you can't have got very far!' Minnie was as curious as she was funny.

'Don't you believe it, little one. Every time I got into that water and started swimming, I might not have left the bay, but in my mind, I swam for miles and miles and miles.'

'How far did you go?' Her little nose wrinkled.

Ed came to stand behind her and as the sun set, he placed his hands on her shoulders, grounding her, letting love flow right through to her very core. This man who was her anchor in the uncertain sea of life. This man who was driftwood on which she could cling when things got choppy. This man who had helped her heal.

'I swam all the way to Lundy, my darling, all the way to Lundy.'

ABOUT THE AUTHOR

Photo © 2023 Paul Smith @paulsmithpics

Amanda Prowse is an international bestselling author of thirty-one novels, including the chart-topping No.1 titles *What Have I Done?*, *Another Love*, *My Husband's Wife* and *The Girl in the Corner*, which have sold millions of copies around the world.

Other novels by Amanda Prowse include *A Mother's Story*, which won the coveted Sainsbury's eBook of the year Award and *Perfect Daughter*, which was selected as a World Book Night title in 2016. Amanda's seminal first non-fiction work *The Boy Between*, co-authored with her son, was also selected to be a World Book Night title in 2022.

Consistently dominating the bestseller charts, Amanda has been described by the *Daily Mail* as 'the queen of family drama'. Well known for her empathy and positivity, Amanda's second memoir *Women Like Us*, was launched to critical acclaim and received thousands of five-star reviews.

Published by Lake Union, Amanda is the most prolific writer of bestselling contemporary fiction in the UK today; her titles also consistently score the highest online review approval ratings across several genres.

A popular TV and radio personality, Amanda has appeared on numerous daytime ITV programmes. She also makes guest appearances on BBC and independent radio stations, including LBC and Talk FM, where she is known for her insightful observations and infectious humour.

A keen supporter of libraries and library services, Amanda is a proud ambassador for The Reading Agency, where she works tirelessly to promote access to books and adult literacy.

Amanda's ambition is to create stories that keep people from turning the bedside lamp off at night, great characters that ensure you take every step with them, and tales that fill your head so you can't possibly read another book until the memory fades.

Follow the Author on Amazon

If you enjoyed this book, follow Amanda Prowse on Amazon to be notified when the author releases a new book!

To do this, please follow these instructions:

Desktop:

1) Search for the author's name on Amazon or in the Amazon App.
2) Click on the author's name to arrive on their Amazon page.
3) Click the 'Follow' button.

Mobile and Tablet:

1) Search for the author's name on Amazon or in the Amazon App.
2) Click on one of the author's books.
3) Click on the author's name to arrive on their Amazon page.
4) Click the 'Follow' button.

Kindle eReader and Kindle App:

If you enjoyed this book on a Kindle eReader or in the Kindle App, you will find the author 'Follow' button after the last page.